Light

"Beautiful, sexy, and witty, this story had me holding my breath, laughing, and tearing up all at once. An electrifying romance!"

—Ashley Herring Blake, *USA Today* bestselling author of *Iris Kelly Doesn't Date*

"The protagonists are well-developed, with backstories that explain their present actions and reactions. Their Mexican American heritage is a significant part of the story and is woven in skillfully." —*Library Journal* (starred review)

"Gilliland weaves a touching story about loss and letting go with the idea of being worthy of love, even on the bad days."

—*Booklist*

"Lush and beautifully written, *Lightning in Her Hands* is a gorgeous novel full of heart, magic, and family." —*BookPage*

PRAISE FOR

Witch of Wild Things

"In her magical, beautiful adult debut, *Witch of Wild Things*, Raquel Vasquez Gilliland absolutely mesmerizes with a richly woven story encompassing family, friendship, and romantic love. The tenderness between Sage and Tennessee truly captured my heart. Perfect for fans of Lisa Kleypas and yet at the same time gorgeously unique, this earthy and luminous book will leave readers spellbound."

—India Holton, national bestselling author of *The League of Gentlewomen Witches*

"*Witch of Wild Things* is such a beautiful story of family, friendship, and falling in love. I mean, an anonymous AIM chat relationship from high school, with the boy on the other end now all grown up into a tattooed, plant-loving man? Sisters with a thorny, complicated relationship in need of nourishing? A woman who doesn't see herself as the special, rare flower she is . . . until she does? Raquel Vasquez Gilliland's adult debut is everything I love about romance!"

—Alicia Thompson, national bestselling author of *Love in the Time of Serial Killers*

"Raquel Vasquez Gilliland's adult debut is spooky, sexy, and magical. *Witch of Wild Things* is a perfect mix of magical realism and swoony romance, with a fair amount of family drama and love. You'll fall in love with the Flores sisters in this cozy, wonderful novel."

—Elissa Sussman, bestselling author of *Funny You Should Ask*

"*Witch of Wild Things* is a flawless gem. Raquel Vasquez Gilliland's prose is by turns seamless and striking; her storytelling is vulnerable and full of soul. As a Mexican American, reading this novel felt like coming home—it was a song my heart never knew it needed to hear."

—Isabel Cañas, author of *The Hacienda*

"Every page sparkles with magic, family, and the lush beauty of wild things."

—Sangu Mandanna, author of *The Very Secret Society of Irregular Witches*

"You could cut the tension here with a knife, or should we say, a pair of gardening shears."

—*Good Housekeeping*

"A solid, fun novel, full of magic, romance, and characters you can follow along with and root for." —Red Carpet Crash

"Gilliland's adult fiction debut is a beautifully written, entrancing novel that is a must buy for all collections."

—*Library Journal* (starred review)

"Gilliland mixes magical realism, sisterhood, and, of course, love into a sparkling romance that will sweep readers off their feet."

—*Publishers Weekly* (starred review)

BERKLEY TITLES BY RAQUEL VASQUEZ GILLILAND

Witch of Wild Things

Lightning in Her Hands

The Magic of Untamed Hearts

The Magic of Untamed Hearts

Raquel Vasquez Gilliland

BERKLEY ROMANCE
NEW YORK

BERKLEY ROMANCE
Published by Berkley
An imprint of Penguin Random House LLC
1745 Broadway, New York, NY 10019
penguinrandomhouse.com

Book design by Daniel Brount

Library of Congress Cataloging-in-Publication Data

Names: Vasquez Gilliland, Raquel, author.
Title: The magic of untamed hearts / Raquel Vasquez Gilliland.
Description: First edition. | New York: Berkley Romance, 2026.
Identifiers: LCCN 2025018942 (print) | LCCN 2025018943 (ebook) |
ISBN 9780593952481 trade paperback | ISBN 9780593952498 ebook
Subjects: LCGFT: Fiction | Romance fiction | Witch fiction | Novels
Classification: LCC PS3622.A834 M34 2026 (print) | LCC PS3622.A834 (ebook) | DDC 813/.6—dc23/eng/20250604
LC record available at https://lccn.loc.gov/2025018942
LC ebook record available at https://lccn.loc.gov/2025018943

First Edition: January 2026

Printed in the United States of America
1st Printing

The authorized representative in the EU for product safety and compliance is Penguin Random House Ireland, Morrison Chambers, 32 Nassau Street, Dublin D02 YH68, Ireland, https://eu-contact.penguin.ie.

For the women who protected me as I wrote this book (and beyond): Larissa, Kyra, Jessica, Kim, Teri, Jil, Donna, Elizabeth, Emilee, Sierra, Emily, Anna, Laekan, Aida, and Mia

For my ancestors and guides who helped me to survive.

There is no such thing as sin . . .

—THE GOSPEL OF MARY MAGDALENE

It's wondering . . . always wondering
and never understanding:
how can I be so smart and still feel so stupid?

—JENNIFER COOK O'TOOLE, *AUTISM IN HEELS*

The Magic of Untamed Hearts

1

My great-aunt Nadia says that in order to seduce a man successfully, one needs:

1. *The scent of roses (somewhere in the vicinity of the copulation location, I presume);*
2. *Fresh-ground cinnamon in the kitchen molcajete (with a pinch of salt if one feels particularly kinky);*
3. *And lastly, a pitchfork (stuck right into the black garden dirt).*

The Pacifica's Persian Rose perfume (stolen from my sister Sage) I have sprayed on my barely there cleavage should work, I think, for the rose part. *Check.*

I couldn't find any sort of cinnamon besides a jar of already ground cinnamon from Value Vince's Corner Store, so that's what went in the molcajete. And since I'm feeling not just particularly kinky, but more like *insanely* kinky, I went ahead and dumped a tablespoon of salt right on top of it. *Check.*

The pitchfork was the one task that I couldn't complete. I literally spent all morning looking for it. I even asked the pigeons to help me look for one—yes, they can help with that sort of thing, as I am, as my family says, the Witch of Criaturas, or Creatures—but nada. I called my sisters, my tía, but everyone had a different place for me to look, and it wasn't in the garden shed, or leaning next to the side door, or next to Nadia's flower-potting station on the porch. I finally gave up after two hours of relentless searching with a bird on each shoulder, each one cooing little warm pigeon-songs beside my ears.

Long after Grayson Baker—a twentysomething real estate agent who I've gone on exactly four and a half dates with—arrives, long after we've made out on my bed, over my new, fancy comforter printed with watercolor woods, and he's breathless and hard and saying (sort of) sweet things like "Damn, you're hot" and "Damn, this ass" I'm *still* wondering where the hell I'd last seen that damn pitchfork.

It's on the tip of my tongue, the periphery of my memory, and then . . . as Grayson's mouth hovers over my right nipple, it finally hits me.

"Wait, wait," I say, gently pushing him back and jumping up off my bed. I grab my fuzzy pink Juicy Couture robe from one of my bedposts. "Just a sec. I'm so sorry. I need to do something *super* quick."

"Uh." Grayson sits back on the bed, looking me over as I tie the robe across my belly super tight with a double knot. The last thing I need is one of the neighbors to see my tits. They already think I'm a little bit—or a lot, rather—nuts as all hell.

After all, it's not every day that a woman goes into a magical, Rip Van Winkle–esque sleep in the woods for eight whole years.

It's not every day said woman is awakened by her sister and

great-aunt and returns to the Land of the Living—what Nadia calls this realm—telling the town only the truth of where she'd been.

So, naturally, everyone in Cranberry just calls me a liar and wants nothing to do with me except, on occasion, to spy on me so they can spread nasty rumors.

And the last thing I want to hear while I'm shopping at the supermarket this week are whispers about how I kidnapped Grayson and had my way with him, then ran around my yard completely topless while waving a pitchfork around. Hell, by the time *that* gets through town, they'll claim I had Grayson's body dangling on that same pitchfork and then I'll be literally banned from all two grocery stores in Cranberry. Not to mention arrested.

Grayson clears his throat and stares at me without blinking. "What's happening right now?"

"I just have to do this one thing. Fast," I promise.

He tilts his head and furrows his brows. With his pink cheeks and tousled hair from making out, the whole effect makes him look adorable, actually.

I'd spent the last six months on a local dating app, swiping left and left and left, with only the occasional right, chatting with men who, with only a little bit of prodding, were all too enthusiastic about revealing how disgusting and sexist they were. I'd gotten so sick of it that I came to a decision.

Last month I told myself I would go on an actual, real-life date with the first man on the CDS (Cranberry Dating Scene app—terrible, terrible name) who didn't seem like a psychopath.

And I get it. That probably sounds pretty expected and kind of the way these things inherently go. Going on dates is *literally* the point of joining dating apps in the first place.

But honestly? Given the way I'm treated in this town? The prospect of getting dressed up and meeting an actual man in person felt like I was walking off the ledge of a cliff with nothing but long trails of misty, blue-gray clouds beneath me.

Willingly falling off a cliff, this time, I mean.

Almost immediately after I promised myself I would actually go on dates rather than chatting with the occasional sexting, Grayson's profile popped up in my search. Recently divorced, he'd written in his bio. No kids. Looking to have fun as well as deep conversations.

I swiped right and then messaged him with Do you like women who might be considered a bit strange? After only eight minutes, a notification popped up. I love strange women, he'd responded.

His skin was a little bit tan and covered in freckles, his eyes as dark brown as the fur of the sweet deer who like to come to the kitchen windows in the morning to say hello, and his hair was a golden blond and cropped short. He took me to restaurants downtown by the beach, requesting romantic, candlelit tables in the darkest corners, "so we can really get to know each other," he'd explained, winking. Last date, we kissed by his car, parked so near the ocean, I was distracted by the seagulls the entire time. Their calls sounded like warnings, somehow . . . but when I turned my head toward them after, I saw nothing but the sun being swallowed by the blue watercolor of the sea.

The "deep conversations" he'd promised weren't exactly deep at all, unless you counted the depth of his capacity to talk about how much he lifts (Two fifty? Three hundred? Somewhere thereabouts).

But overall, he was . . . nice. He never called me The Girl Who Lies, or Freak, or any other unkind name that's been thrown at me weekly in this town. Grayson was ripped, employed, and, most importantly, not once did he proclaim that he was looking for a tradwife who didn't mind deep-throating at least twice a day. Which was not even close to the worst thing a man had told me via these apps.

While it's true, Grayson doesn't seem super enamored with me . . . it's not like I'm crazy about him, either. And I don't consider that a bad thing, to be honest.

Ever since coming back from a yearslong supernatural sleep, I've felt like a stranger in my own skin. In my own *life*. I don't understand the Land of the Living anymore. I was sixteen when I left it, twenty-four when I returned, and twenty-six now. I've had two whole years to adjust, and yet everything I do is motivated by a very specific desire to stop feeling like the loneliest woman in the world.

Hence, seducing Grayson literally right now.

Maybe if we have sex, we'll *both* become enamored with each other.

And even if not, I'd like to have good sex. I've never experienced it before. If nothing else, orgasms sure would relieve some stress. I just need to ensure those orgasms first. Magically speaking.

"Just give me a second," I tell him, lifting up my pointer finger. "One second."

Grayson huffs just the slightest bit and then shakes his head. "Are you *seriously* leaving?"

His tone is more than a little annoyed, which is bothersome. Annoyed men are not good lovers. I don't know this from experience, but it seems like common sense. Which is why I *really* need to complete the pitchfork part of this ritual before intercourse occurs.

"I will be *right* back. I swear. This is important."

And it is. Rose is for romance. Cinnamon is for heat. And the pitchfork is for orgasms. *The pitchfork pins them on your land and all those orgasms find their way to you.* Nadia'd laughed at me as I took notes. *With the way most men are in bed, mija, you need all the help you can get.*

Romance, I can do without. Heat, whatever the hell that refers to, doesn't seem important. But orgasms are essential to me. I'm not about to have sex for the first time in almost ten years without ensuring my own completion.

For all I know, Grayson will ghost me after this. His annoyance right now certainly isn't making me think he's going to become enamored with me after all. At the very least, the universe—the Land of the Living, let's say—owes me. Preferably in *many* instances of completion.

I run down the stairs, slip on my little outdoor booties at the front door, and race toward the back of the house. It's a sliver of a backyard, if one could even call it that. We live on a cliff that, in the distance, overlooks the Virginian Atlantic shore. If I stare at it too long—the dazzling glitter of sunlight bouncing off the water like fine quartzite on the side of a carved mountain—I can feel the fish and plankton and whales and seagulls that all inhabit that space.

Sometimes, late at night as I'm falling asleep, I can sense what feels like every single creature in this town, Cranberry, from the pink-edged sulphur butterfly babies in their cocoons to the green-wing teal ducks, tiny and shimmering and curled in on themselves, asleep on the edges of the lakes, to the great horned owls, eyes wide as moons and looking for their nighttime breakfast.

This is the life of the Witch of Criaturas.

A few feet to the left of my sister Sage's blue rose, there lies the pitchfork, halfway tucked into some bushes. I grab its wooden handle and find the nearest patch of grass I can and stick it right in there. Luckily it's rained recently, and so the clay beneath the sod is soft enough that the prongs go in with only a little bit of effort. I clap my hands together once when I release the handle and it stays perfectly upright.

"Okay," I announce to the fox who has reached my side. This little guy, I like to call Coffee. His eyes look just like Nadia's Turkish brew that she pours into the dirt for the old gods every morning—one shade between the deepest brown and black. He cocks his head up at me. "It's time for orgasms. Do foxes even have those?" I frown thoughtfully. "I guess I could google it later. But wouldn't that look kind of suspicious in my search history? People don't like me enough as it is . . . and if they thought I was . . ." I shake my head as I get a glimpse of my elderly neighbor, Janie, spying on me from between her curtains. "Go hide," I tell Coffee, and he rushes into the pine trees.

I stare Janie down, but she doesn't slap the curtains shut until I give her a little wave involving only one of my middle fingers.

I rush back in the house, kicking off my slippers at the entrance, and begin to run upstairs. When I hear Grayson's voice, however, I pause. What the hell is he talking for? He's not chatting with Nadia, is he? She's supposed to be at church literally all day. I didn't see her car up front, did I? God, that would be so incredibly awkward.

I tiptoe up, praying I don't hear my great-aunt's voice echoing from my bedroom, where there are no less than three extra-large multipacks of ribbed, super-ribbed, and tropical-flavored condoms piled up in the middle of my dresser. She would have to be incredibly drunk in order to miss that, highly unlikely on a Sunday morning after church.

But as I creep up the stairs—as soundless as Coffee when he

stalks chipmunks and squirrels—another male-sounding voice echoes toward me. It's someone he's talking to on speakerphone. The muffled and electronic tone of the other side of this conversation gives it away.

My first thought is Grayson has answered a call from his dad or tío or something. A distant part of me realizes how badly I'm clinging to the idea that Grayson is a Nice Guy. I even come up with a wholesome scenario in seconds. His family member was worried when Grayson didn't show up to brunch and was just calling to check in. Grayson just answered to reassure them that he was fine, and then he'd hang up and soon I would be having multiple orgasms before kissing him on the cheek goodbye, then getting on with my day.

But then the disembodied voice asks, "So have you bagged the freak yet?"

Grayson laughs. It's a much different laugh than the one he'd used when we'd met up for an early breakfast at a sandwich spot nearby, before he followed me back here, to Nadia's, and I offered him water or tea or coffee before I pulled him into my bedroom, ripped off his shirt, and pushed him onto my mattress.

That laugh was polite and restrained. *This* laugh is cruel. Its edges are as sharp as the thorns of pinecones protecting its tiny seeds from those who would devour them.

Only I don't think Grayson is protecting anything precious. Because his next words are "Not yet. But I'm about to. Then we'll find out if she's got antlers growing out of her pussy."

This time the cruel laugh bursts from his phone's speaker. "Dude. I bet you anything she doesn't shave, either. I bet she's like a bearded collie down there."

Grayson snorts. "I bet she barks when she's getting pounded."

It's strange how the pain of this situation doesn't hit me until the voice adds next, "Well, we'll have to head to Lost Souls tonight, man. I'll get you a beer or two for taking one for the team."

It's not the commentary about antlers . . . or barking . . . or dog hair that makes my heart and stomach feel like they've been split in half with a cleaver. It's "team." It's that the word *team* indicates *more*. More people in on this joke. More people laughing and snorting as they muse about whether there are antlers reaching out of my vagina as though I were perpetually birthing a stag.

I imagine all of Cranberry, all of Virginia even, in on this endless joke that Sky Flores, town freak, is worthy of this level of unkindness. Simply because she's strange.

Which, yes. I disappeared for eight years and no one believes the truth of my story, of where I had been and why.

Yes, I currently spend nearly all my time in the woods, talking to my only friends—the wild turkeys and the coyotes and the wrens.

Yes, I'm also really socially awkward and understand so little about this world that has changed to a nearly unrecognizable state since I've been gone.

But I'm still a human being. A woman who has never hurt anyone.

I don't deserve *this*.

I burst through the open door—as this idiot didn't even have the sense to close it—and catch him giving the man on his phone a virtual tour of my bedroom. The decorative paper I had so carefully pressed into the walls, the furniture I'd scoured thrift stores for, the books from my work piled high on my bedside table. When I was asleep in the woods . . . I had nothing. I could touch nothing. The only person who could hear me, on rare occasion, was my eldest sister Sage.

So I took Sage's old room in the attic and spent ages and lots of money making it mine. Making it sacred. It was another thing I felt I deserved from the universe—a place filled with my most cherished belongings where I could feel truly, sincerely safe.

And now Grayson's in it, desecrating it with a debate about how much my genitalia resembles a dog breed.

"Oh shit," he says, his eyes widening as he slams the end call button on his phone. "I was just—"

I don't let him finish as I stomp toward him. "You said I was *hot*. You said you liked my *ass* as you were grabbing it," I interrupt, breathing hard and throwing my hands to and fro to emphasize every word.

As stupid as it may be, those comments are the only compliments I have heard from someone who is not my relative in a decade. So, okay. They weren't poetry. But they made me feel special when he said them. I felt *wanted*.

Is that why women often sleep with men they know they shouldn't? To feel wanted, even for only two and a half minutes?

I feel like a stranger in my own skin, in my own *life*, all over again. I have to stop myself from pressing my fingers into my arms, into my warm brown skin, to make sure I'm still awake.

Because how could this scenario be anything but a nightmare?

That feeling of being wanted by Grayson has evaporated now, naturally. I feel the exact opposite of wanted—disgusting, undesirable, hated even—and it fills me with an intense sense of magic and rage, one I don't know if I can control. One I don't even care if I *can* control.

I let my voice get even louder. "Why would you insinuate my ass was attractive if you thought I was half-canine? Why would you even get hard for me if you thought you were going to fuck a vaginally antlered woman?" I put my hands on my hips to keep them from shaking with the anger that feels as hot as a thick Virginia summer day in the humid, windless woods. "Why would you take me on four and a half dates and sit through multiple-course meals with me if you thought I was repulsive underneath my clothes?"

Grayson doesn't feel the living magic coursing through me. He doesn't notice the restless crows gathering on the roof next door, within my sight through my bedroom window, each one black and shimmering like an ancient spirit of vengeance. He's gotten his ego back from the shock of my catching him bullying me, and he swaggers across the room and smirks. "Every single guy gets hard over anything vaguely round. Tits, ass. It doesn't matter. It means nothing."

A rustle sounds at the windows, the ones Sage used to grow basil in little pots on, the ones I'd opened well before Grayson arrived in case he turned out to be a disaster and I needed divine, feral help.

Like, for instance, right now.

I close my eyes briefly before I can ask him the next question. "How many people are in on this 'fuck the freak' prank?"

He shrugs and holds out his hand to count with his fingers. He has no shame. I can't believe I'd thought he was *nice*. "Me, and the guy I was just talking to, Jake . . ."

"Jake Cunningworth? That's who was on the phone?" Jake Cunningworth is the man who delivers the mail at my workplace. My *mailman* was just musing about my *pubes*. How am I supposed to look him directly in the eyes ever again?

"Uh-huh. And oh, some buddies from work, and my brother and his buddies from his crew . . ." Really, Grayson is just bragging now. He's not getting laid, so he's attempting to get his own revenge by humiliating me as much as he can.

I shake my head and allow a slight, wry smile to adorn my lips over the Anastasia Beverly Hills matte lipstick in Sugar Plum I'd applied earlier. It was a Christmas gift from my amazing boss, since she knew I was getting into makeup.

It's really too bad for him—and his ego—that I am the Witch of Wild Creatures.

He's still naming people when I murmur toward the window, "All right, babes. Now's a good time as any."

He interrupts himself with a harsh, frightened "What the fuck?" as the first crow flies in, the tips of her wings grazing his head on her way to land on my shoulder.

"Did you just see that?" he asks me, his voice shrill as he stares just to my left, into the black-bead eyes of the bird hanging out next to my face.

Ignoring him, I say the next words slow and firm. "I need you to make me a promise." Another crow swoops in, circling the room, his wingspan so wide and strong that he brings a brush of strong wind with every flap.

"There are fucking birds in here!" Grayson shrieks from where he's now retreated: the corner of the bed, holding a Laura Ashley embroidered throw pillow over his head.

Another crow flies in, its shrieks so loud that Grayson and I both wince. "Geez Louise, Harriet," I murmur, and she lands on my other shoulder, grumbling over my admonishment. "I know, love. You're powerful and can't be contained."

"Are you—" Grayson's pillow is lowered, his eye peeking over its edge in disbelief. "Are you seriously talking to—"

He can't finish his sentence, because the rest of this murder of crows flies in. I stretch out my arm where a couple more land. The others swoop all around his head, their caws muffling his screams. "Make it stop!" he finally begs me.

"You haven't promised me yet." I pout a little and put one of my hands on my hip and stick it out.

"Promised you what? No, fuck it. It doesn't matter. Whatever you want, I promise. Just make these things go away." His voice is choked. "I'll do anything. God."

He's folded so quickly. Boring, really. "Okay, yeah. So, tell your team—the one you're taking one for by planning on sleeping with me, which isn't happening by the way, in case you needed that clarified—that if anyone tries to trick me, or prank me, or fuck with me ever again, these crows will *eat them alive* at my command."

It's not true. I'd never command such a thing, and moreover, that's not how my powers work. No animal is my servant. They are their own creatures, just like I am my own creature. The crows are here not because I called them, but because we are friends, and they sensed my distress. (And also, crows really like fucking things up and freaking humans out. Even, and maybe especially even, me.)

But the truth didn't matter when he and all his little asshole bully friends made their plans to humiliate me. So the truth doesn't matter now.

"I promise!" he yells under the rain of long, ink-black feathers as the crows swirl around and around like a spiral of wraiths.

As soon as his words are out, I nod at my friends, their black eyes as furious as I feel. One by one, they fly out the window, returning to the neighbor's roof in a clatter of claws and caws.

It takes Grayson a good eight seconds to dress and fifteen more to run down the stairs. I sigh when the slam of the front door makes my own bedroom door rattle on its hinge.

When I look out my window, there is a single crow—Leonora,

I've named her—swooping down at his face one last time as he wails and jumps inside his Tesla. The tires squeal as he backs out and races away. The slithering smoke from the rubber burning against the asphalt is now the only sign that he was ever here to start with.

I close my eyes, lie back in bed, and sigh, the iridescent teal and purple feathers now surrounding me as though I'd sewn them across my comforter.

I think again of pinecones and their thorns. In order to protect myself—protect my sensitive and aching heart—I must be sharper. Thornier.

If I'm always going to be the town freak, no matter what?

Well. I better just lean into it.

2

When I was sixteen years old, I fell eighty feet off the side of a cliff while hiking at Cranberry Falls State Park. My sister Teal had jumped up on the wooden rail we'd just been hiking alongside, and dared me to do the same.

I remember how crisp the air was, as though it had sharpened into a blade sometime between morning and afternoon. How dark it had gotten when we'd hiked deeper and deeper into the woods, the canopy overhead coloring us in shades of green and gray shadows like we had stepped into a monochromatic painting. I remember stepping up with my long legs, staring down at the railing under my feet, thinking that it hadn't seemed quite so wobbly when Teal was just on it.

And then there was the slip. The look of panic and horror on Teal's face. Me, opening my mouth to reassure her—we weren't that close to the edge. Or so I'd thought.

I don't remember what happened after that. I can only imagine it, based on the firsthand accounts: that of Teal, obviously. That of my sister Sage, who found me eight years later, in the same woods. And that of my great-aunt Nadia, who keeps the oral records of our ancestral tales—specifically the ones involving the old gods.

The old gods are supposed to be humanoid and immortal, well, *gods*, and they live in the most wild of places—places thick with trees, thick with creatures, thick with spirits. Nadia says our matriarchs moved here, to the Virginia coast, specifically to Cranberry, because they had sensed that this land was still wild enough that it felt like the sort the old gods would inhabit. When I'd asked her if the gods of our ancestors had come to Virginia first, or followed us here after we'd migrated, Nadia just gave me her annoying, warm, *knowing* smile and said simply: "Both."

Anyway, all this to say that, now my own story—my falling—has been added to the family lore of the old gods. Because after I fell, those old gods picked me up—or maybe levitated me, or perhaps pushed me as though I were a rolling pin—to an ancient oak tree, where they cared for me as though I were Sleeping Beauty in a long, *long* slumber.

Believe it or not, that wasn't the worst part of the ordeal.

Losing eight years of full-on life due to a long-ass, supernatural hibernation? Meh.

But during those eight years, I—my consciousness—became a ghost, separated from my body through *espanto*, the name for the phenomenon our precolonial ancestors understood.

When someone experiences a traumatic event that makes them feel enough fear, their spirit splits and begins to wander this realm all on its own. The spirit is essentially untethered and can cause what colonizers have named symptoms of PTSD, or depression, or those of other mental health crises. Our ancestors would call upon a curandera to sing the spirit back to the wounded person. To make them whole again. But that's only if you know you've got espanto to start with—if you know that you are actually still *alive*. Which I did not.

As far as I knew, I had died when I fell. None of us were aware, not even me, that my very-much-living body was tucked into an old tree, being tended to by ancestral deities. My ghost was bound to my eldest sister Sage through her tears. When she cried, my form got stronger, and she could see me. She said it was as though I were really right in front of her, made all the more horrifying when she tried to touch me and her hand would simply slip right through my body.

When Sage didn't cry—and believe me, that woman is really good at suppressing tears—I became fuzzy, like how the fog comes over the sea sometimes, slithering and shadowy and opaque, and nothing felt real.

It was horrible. Like living in the grayest of dreams, in which edges went in and out of focus, in which everything became as dull as the inside of my grandmother Sonya's colorless mini-mansion. Even sound became dull echoes, as though someone were calling for me but they were too far for me to sense, over and over again.

I thought if I could get Sage to make up with Teal, who she had a falling out with over my "death," then I could move on to some afterlife that was better than the cloudy blob I'd been experiencing. But something else happened instead.

Sage found me—my body—asleep in the woods, inside the hollow of an ancient oak tree. Light sparkled over me from between the leaves above. And below me were leaves, arranged as though someone had woven together a cottagecore bed. *Step in*, Nadia had told me, the ghost. And I did. I stepped in, and I returned to this world, the World of the Living, rather than the World of What Is In Between.

It was startling. Correction: It *still* startles me, being back to this realm. Colors are so bright, I sometimes spend whole days marveling at the way the sky is a living watercolor painting, turning from indigo to gray to blue, violet and hot pink and clementine, and sometimes all these colors at once. Dotted with clouds that shapeshift like Nadia says some of our most magical ancestors used to: from a rabbit with spotted ears to running cats to two humans, kissing and kissing like they would die if they stopped. All to dissipate and become formless once more. Once as I watched the sky like this, I swear I felt an old god nearby. I might've even heard him say: *This is just like creation.* But when I turned my head, there was no one there but late-afternoon shadows spilled across Nadia's garden.

In a way, things have been amazing ever since returning. I can *eat* again. Nadia's flan, and her enchiladas, oozing with all kinds of cheese. Big slices of pizza the size of my head from downtown pizzerias, their crusts just the slightest bit charred, dipped in garlic butter. Fresh papaya, orange as sunset, sliced up with lime squeezed all over it, eaten with my bare hands while surrounded by lavender bubbles in the bath.

But some things really suck, too. I made the mistake of telling the police, the first responders who had shown up the day I returned, that I'd simply lost my memory. That one moment I fell, and the next, I woke up still in the woods—just eight years had passed.

I felt comfortable with that version of events because . . . well. It's true. One moment I fell, the next I awoke in the woods. These are all literal facts, and that doesn't change just because I left out eight years of living as a ghost in a fathomless, foggy void.

But I guess the facts were simply not enough, because ever

since, the entire town, save like two people, treat me like I'm a lying freak.

It doesn't help that I basically live in the woods, and the only time I see people other than my family, it's because I've startled them while they were hiking. Maybe or maybe not while holding several baby foxes in my arms.

One of the people who treats me like I'm human would be my neighbor, William. Whose front door I am currently standing in front of, with a heavy covered ceramic dish balanced in my hands.

I use my elbow to tap the doorbell, but there's no answer. I then use the tip of my leather shoe to "knock."

Finally, the door rattles, and there William is, in all his grumpy, bedhead, cardigan glory. "About time," he grumbles, opening the door wide to let me in.

"Excuse me, but I've been here for five whole minutes." I shut the door behind me with my hip, a little difficult to do in my narrow tweed pencil skirt. I have the evening shift at the library tonight, so I'm dressed for work. Black Mary Janes, small fishnet stockings, the aforementioned pencil skirt, and a cream, button-down silk top. Teal helped me with fine-tuning this style, the one she calls "sexy librarian." I have to admit, I do feel sexy when I get dressed up for work. It's too bad there is no one else to appreciate it besides my sisters and my boss.

Not even William gives me a second glance, instead opting to point at the dish in my hands. "Lasagna?"

"Yes, sir. Should only take a few minutes to preheat in the microwave. And you can have the leftovers if you want, as usual."

He makes an old-man-grump sound in response, but I can tell he's pleased. He isn't the sort of guy who will go all out and make a homemade lasagna just for himself.

Back during my ghost days, I snooped on my neighbors a *lot*. Ethical? Maybe not. Okay, definitely not. But I had *literally* nothing else going on. I'd spend my time frolicking from house to house, cutting through backyards filled with overgrown switchgrass and dandelions, or paved brick pathways, hopping over firepits and barking dogs (who sensed I was there but I don't think could ever actually see me). I could slide into anyone's home through the doors, walls, windows, and once, I walked right through an upright washer and dryer unit. Eventually, I kinda found myself zoning in on William, who we used to call Old Man Noemi back when we were little kids.

Here's the thing I've learned about people from my time as a ghost. People often, if not always, say things they don't mean. They will dance around their words till I'm damn dizzy from trying to follow conversations. They will compliment how "confident" you are, but the second you turn your head, they will give knowing smirks to their friends, implying that you should be ashamed. They will say they're "fine" but look as upset as a baby bird who tried to fly just a touch too early and swooped to the forest floor with a plop.

You know what doesn't lie, though? Objects. The myriad of things people surround themselves with and use and collect.

Down the street, Mr. and Mrs. Garcia seemed like the perfect couple—she would smile wide-eyed smiles as he told everyone about his promotion and new car and how they were saving up for a bigger house by the beach.

When I entered their home, though, the objects told the truth. The surplus of first-aid supplies she kept for when he lost his temper and took it out on her. The divorce attorney's number, scrawled on a tiny piece of paper, hidden in the pages of an old family Bible. Eventually, and thankfully, their lives revealed the truths inherent in these objects—Mr. Garcia lives alone in that big, dusty house, and he yells at the television each evening instead of Mrs. Garcia. And now *she* rents a little bungalow near downtown, enamored with her newest companions: two fuzzy gray and white kittens named Possum and Squirrel.

With William's house, I walked in as my ghostly form and saw that he'd been living on Hungry-Man frozen dinners, their packages piled in neat little rows in the recycling bin in the garage. There was a tiny wooden container of handwritten recipes in the kitchen, shoved behind the toaster. I knew his late wife, Emmie, must've written them, because there were little notes on a few of the cards—things like *William's favorite* and *William's birthday dinner.*

William would never tell anyone that he hadn't had a home-cooked meal in years, but the objects in his home told the truth better than he ever could. So after I adjusted to the Land of the Living . . . I began bringing him food, once a week.

"I'm not a damn charity case!" he'd grumped that first time I'd shown up with a pot filled with picadillo and rice.

"Of course you're not," I'd responded. "But we have too much food. Are you really the kind of person to let it go to waste?"

He narrowed his eyes at the pot and opened the door wide before disappearing into the kitchen without a word. I could barely hide my smile when I walked in and he was setting the table with paper plates and plastic cutlery.

And so began our tradition. Friday nights for Sky Flores were not for partying, or going with groups of friends to the movies, or climbing trees to take naps with black bears. They were for William, who I've come to think of as a grandfather of sorts.

"You caught me about to fill up the bird feeder," he tells me, lifting a bag of black oil sunflower seeds leaning by the back door. "I'll be two minutes."

"Okay. I'll get everything set up."

He nods and disappears into the backyard. I pull the dollar store paper plates from the cupboard, stacking two on top of one another for each of us, since these things are thinner than paper, and Nadia's lasagna is no match for dollar store anything. I'm pouring iced tea from the fridge into two identical blue melamine cups when I'm startled by the gruff voice of a man behind me.

"Who the hell are you?"

It's not William, who I can see through the window is currently cursing out the bird feeder's lid that won't pop back on without a fight.

And William has only one person who could be visiting. One person who has ever visited since I could remember.

When I turn, I narrow my eyes when I see I am correct.

Standing in front of me is a tall, gorgeous man. Thirty-five years of age. Former journalist for *The New York Times*. Wearing a green flannel button-down with the sleeves rolled up and a pair of light-wash gray jeans. Barefoot and looking angry as all hell to see me in his grandfather's kitchen.

Adam Noemi. William's grandson.

The once-love-of-my-life turned to just-another-town-bully.

3

I HAVE TO ADMIT SOMETHING.

Snooping around William Noemi's place when I was a ghost wasn't one hundred percent altruistic. It wasn't a high percentage of boredom, either.

A couple of years ago, when my body hadn't yet been discovered, Sage was staying at Nadia's, and crying a lot. A lot—a lot. Poor thing was going through it, between her fighting with Teal and Nadia and the high emotional roller coaster of falling in love with her now-husband, Tenn, all at the same time. Because of all that weeping, I was called to her, by her side through the connection between us with her tears, sometimes multiple times a day. She still hasn't the faintest idea why tears drew me to her like bees to early spring dandelions . . . only that it was just some mysterious side effect of being a Flores bruja. I know better, though.

Anyway, one night, I stayed with her after she'd cried herself to sleep. Once I made sure her breath was deep and sound, I took a walk.

IF THERE WAS ANYTHING TO LIKE ABOUT BEING A GHOST, IT was that the laws of physics didn't apply to me. I could walk through stone garden walls and somersault through the wide trunks of old trees. I could punch someone right in the eye and my fist would go through them as though they were nothing more than a figment of someone's imagination.

What I loved best, though, was jumping.

From the balcony of the attic floor of Nadia's home that night . . . I jumped. Without hesitation. It didn't seem like I was any *lighter* when jumping—my ghost-body hit the ground with as much force as any regular, still-very-alive body. Maybe that's why I loved it so much. It made me feel alive.

Or maybe it made me feel like I was about to die all over again, and perhaps that time, everything would end for real.

It didn't end for real that night, obviously. So I walked around Catalina Street, stepping in and out of yards, gardens, homes. I walked past Jackie Piper, the single mom who had fallen asleep on the sofa between her two children, a huge, almost empty popcorn bowl in her lap, a Disney movie finishing up on the television. I stepped next into the huge, three-story Victorian-style home that Carter Velasquez, my sister Teal's husband, used to live in with his whole family when we were growing up, multigenerational style. It had been purchased by a man who was trying to flip it, but it was turning out to be more of a hassle than he'd anticipated. I stepped over piles of pipes and torn-out cupboards, trying to run my hand over the huge quartz countertop piece leaning against the kitchen wall, to no avail—my hand simply went through the smooth crystal, as brilliant as a slice of moon under the streetlights glaring in through the windows.

The actual moon was full that night as I wandered into William's yard. I stopped short when I realized there was a vehicle in the driveway I hadn't seen before—a brand-new Jeep, even shinier than the quartz countertop under the blue moonlight. And then I heard the sound of giggling.

It was a man and a woman. I watched in awe as they stepped into the porchlight, him tall and slim, and her short and thick. "Let me just check on him and we'll go back to my place," he promised her with a voice as slow and deep as hot honey drizzled over some impossibly sexy dessert.

I followed him inside and watched as he picked up an umbrella that had fallen to the floor by the front door, as he made his way into the hallway and flipped on the light switch, and as he opened the door of his grandfather's bedroom.

"Gramps?"

"Go away."

Adam let out a deep chuckle that made my stomach drop. I hadn't even seen him yet—he was still covered in shadows—but something about him even all the way back then . . . even with me, as literally just a ghost, listening to him laugh with his voice as rich as tiramisu . . . I knew Adam Noemi was . . . God, the word *special* doesn't convey him properly. *Extraordinary* sounds like too much. But there was something intense and strange and wonderful about him that made me *want* to know him, even though this was an impossible, impossible want.

He walked deeper into the room. "Guess you're okay if you can begin with your classic rudeness."

William was sitting up in bed, wearing pajamas with blue and green stripes. "Don't you have a date with your girlfriend or something?"

"You know I don't do relationships."

William snorted. "When I was your age, you know what I was doing? Not cavorting around like a teenager, I'll tell you that much."

Adam sat on the edge of the bed and said, "I know. You'd already met her. Love at first sight."

"And I was married with two kids! Not jerking women around!"

"I'm not jerking her around. She knows it's casual." Adam sighed and turned toward the television. In even the ugly gray glare of the screen, I could tell he was beautiful. His eyes were blue like the sea. His skin was freckled, his hair kind of pink gold in the dark bedroom. He looked a bit like an angel, and I suppressed a giggle. The grumpy old man, the angel, and the ghost. I don't know why it was so funny to me, but I snorted a bit.

The strangest thing happened then. His eyes tilted left and landed on me. He blinked. Then he blinked again. He stood, and that was when William said, "What the hell is the matter with you?"

Adam shook his head, still staring in my direction. "Nothing. Nothing. Have you taken that cough medicine I got you?"

"Oh, go to hell."

Adam made sure William wasn't running a fever (while William bitched the whole while, somehow even with a thermometer in his mouth) and then he was back out the front door. His beautiful not-girlfriend was leaning against his Jeep, her hair dark like my sister Teal's, and just as resplendent as the vehicle. She put her phone down as he approached, his boots crunching the gravel.

"I thought you'd forgotten about me." She smiled. She was just as curvy as Sage, all hips and breasts with a round belly, and when she smiled, I could tell that she was just a little bit, or maybe a lot, in love with him. *She knows it's casual*, Adam had said, but just from the sparkling in her eyes, I knew she was hoping she could change his mind.

"Never," he said, and he picked her up as she squealed, and kissed her.

He put her down slowly, their lips never parting, and he curled his hands around her waist.

I knew I needed to turn around and go back home. Or maybe snoop through some other neighbors' houses, or even other neighborhoods. What Adam and his not-girlfriend were doing—it was personal and private.

But I stepped closer. I felt like a ghostly anthropologist, observing how contemporary humans kissed. Was it different from when I last kissed a guy, seven years before?

I thought I could maybe make out their tongues. Her arms were thrown around his neck. His hand lifted to cup her breast, and she moaned a little too loudly, I guess, because he looked up at his grandfather's house, maybe to make sure William wasn't on his way to curse them out—but once again, his eyes landed on me. He looked at me. Up and down, like he could see me.

"We should get out of here," he said, still staring at me.

I was a ghost and I *still* got goose bumps in that moment—they flowed over my body as though I'd stepped under a freezing waterfall.

It was like he was saying those words to *me*. It was like I was *alive*.

We should get out of here.

Although he only stared at me for all of two seconds, I felt like I somehow had an opportunity to respond. To interact with someone, anyone else. To feel like I wasn't the most lonely and forgotten ghost in all the worlds.

But before I knew it, before I could even try to respond, his lady friend said, "Yes." She hopped in as he opened the door for her, and soon, they were driving away, the headlights cutting right through my body like machetes made of light as he swerved toward the road.

And then I was left alone. Just as I always was in the end.

ADAM NEVER LOOKED DIRECTLY AT ME AGAIN, BUT THAT DIDN'T stop me from trying to get him to. I snooped on him and William every chance possible that summer. I danced in his face. I yelled in his ears. I did everything I could to make him *see* me once more. I was desperate, absolutely desperate, for someone else to see me other than my weeping sister Sage.

But something happened that summer that I wasn't anticipating. And it was me accidentally developing a massive crush on that son of a bitch.

It came from the tender way Adam made breakfast for William every morning when he visited—two over-easy eggs, whole wheat toast, sliced tomatoes with salt and pepper, and, to William's dismay, two slices of turkey bacon. And how he'd make sure William finished his plate. How he'd try and refill the bird feeder before it was even half-empty, so William wouldn't have to balance on his unstable-looking wooden ladder. How he'd help his pregnant neighbor carry in groceries and, when the baby arrived, mow her lawn after taking care of William's.

Adam seemed generous and thoughtful with a high emotional intelligence. I had thought he was the perfect man.

And then he had to completely ruin it one year later.

4

SEEING ADAM HERE AND NOW, WHEN I HAD BEEN ASSURED by the Cranberry rumor network that he was firmly living downtown and only came to see William on the weekends, well. It catches me off guard. But I remember my promise to myself. *Be sharper. Don't let them see how much they've hurt you.*

So I fold up my arms and say, "Excuse me? Who the hell are *you*?"

He doesn't seem to expect this, but his widening eyes quickly narrow. "Ahh. Sky Flores." The way he says my name is exactly like everyone else in town does—not hiding at all his deep suspicion that my presence means instant bad news. "So nice of you to bring dinner to Gramps every week. What's next? You're going to sweet-talk him into giving you his credit card number, and next thing you know, you'll be in . . . I don't know, Canada? And he'll be losing the house."

I scowl and tilt my head at the same time. I certainly wasn't expecting that kind of accusation. "Are you unwell? Seriously. What you just said is pure nonsense." The last time Adam had said anything about me that I know of, it was when he was chatting with Teal at a wedding last year. He'd told her I'd been *helping* his grandfather . . . not trying to take advantage of him. I glance at his eyes, searching for some sign that maybe he was having an aneurysm. Maybe he'd been possessed, even.

"Adam! What the hell are you doing, being so rude to my guest?"

William had apparently finally won his battle with the bird feeder lid. Adam and I were so loud, I guess neither of us heard the back door slide open. William points a finger at Adam. "If your mother could see you now . . ."

Adam's shoulders drop as he runs a hand over his five-o'clock shadow. "Gramps, I told you. You can't just let people you barely know—"

"Barely know?" I yelp. "Your grandfather and I have been friends for a year!"

Adam hardly registers my protests. "You can't let her in and walk away. You need to be more diligent. While you were changing the bird feeder, she could've gotten your wallet, your social—"

"Do I look like the kind of dumbass who can be preyed on?" William demands to know, but he doesn't let Adam answer. "Son, I know you're not in a good place in your life right now, but that doesn't give you the right—"

As William keeps shouting, I take tiny steps backward toward the front door. To hell with being sharp as a pinecone. I do not like the idea of spending my pre-work meal between two yelling men. I would rather hang out with the bears in the woods, thank you very much.

"And you!" William points at me. "Where the hell is that lasagna?"

"It's in the dish I brought in. You can eat it all if you want. I'm going to—"

"You're going to sit down and eat it with me. Like we always do." William glares at Adam. "And my grandson will join us."

William leaves no room for objection or interpretation. So I slink into the kitchen and prepare three pieces of Nadia's lasagna. Nadia didn't make it—I did—but I used her recipe. Her "secret" is to use spices dried from the herbs she grows in her garden. She melts a little bit of butter and tosses them in, letting them cook for a couple of minutes to release all their flavor. Then she adds it to the béchamel sauce. As a result, this lasagna isn't just good, it's downright addictive.

I serve William first, then Adam, who sits like a sullen teenager, his posture slack, elbows on the table. This version of him is new to me. From my ghost-spying days, I remember Adam as always confident, even in the most casual of scenarios. He was kind and polite and thoughtful. Thinking about the last time I spied on him, though . . . maybe this immature, paranoid person is the *real* him.

Adam Noemi has been a sort of intellectual hero of Cranberry for a good long while—ever since he got a free ride to Yale and immediately began working full time at *The New York Times* after graduating. For a small town like ours, that was huge. Adam basically became our local celebrity. Every time he would visit town again, it was the same old story. Everyone wanted to buy him a drink at Lost Souls, the only legitimate bar in town. And every woman wanted to be his fling for the summer, or holiday break, or for whatever amount of time he happened to find himself back in Cranberry for the moment.

The last I heard, Adam had left the *Times* and taken up a

major editorial position at the local paper in town. When my Amá Sonya told me that, I totally freaked out. I asked about a thousand questions in the group chat on the whole situation, which my sisters assumed were because I had a crush on the guy.

But the truth was . . . being around Adam just makes me feel shame now. I was hoping he'd gone back to the city and would stay there.

As he digs into his lasagna, I feel angry and indignant all over again. "You know I've been bringing William meals for a while. Why are you now convinced I'm gonna run off to Canada with all his money?"

William gives Adam a glare with one bushy white eyebrow raised way up. "It's a good question," he barks.

Adam sighs and runs a hand over his face. "Look. I've been researching scams specifically targeting the elderl—" He pauses when William's glare turns into a death stare. "—older folks for a piece I'm working on. Some of these scammers play a long game." Adam looks right at me as he says it, then glances at his meal before pointing his fork at William. "And since, you know, our last trip to the doctor's, they warned me—"

William clears his throat so loud and suddenly, I swallow my bite wrong, standing to cough toward a corner of the room. I want to refute Adam's baseless and, to be honest, hurtful accusations—because frankly, this is just ridiculous at this point—but I can't even form words in my brain amid the choking.

"Dammit, woman," William says. "Don't drop dead in my kitchen."

"I'm fine," I sputter between coughs, grabbing my water. "Food went down the wrong way, is all."

"Does that woman at your work still have you climbing ladders taller than the damn basement?" William barks at me as I'm frantically sipping water. He's definitely agitated. Normally he and I have a calm chat with our shared meal—as calm as can be, with William's disposition—but Adam has obviously ruffled some feathers. William clearly doesn't want to talk about whatever doctor's visit Adam is referring to, but he also doesn't appreciate being forced to initiate the conversation.

"Where do you work?" Adam asks. It's nearly too sharp of a tone to be a question.

"She's got a gig at the library. They have her in the basement, crawling all in the damn dust, and she's climbing ladders in shoes that look like they're devices made for prisoners of war!"

I sit down, finally confident I can speak without hacking. "They're kitten heels, William." My voice is hoarse.

"Kitten heels," he mutters. "Damn lion heels, made with damn lion teeth!"

I smother a giggle and stare at my still nearly full plate of lasagna. For maybe the hundredth time in the last month, I regret telling William about my amazing *Beauty and the Beast*–style library ladders. He's convinced I'm going to fall and break every part of my body. Just because I fell off a cliff ten years ago doesn't mean I'm going to fall off of literally everything else, but William *and* my sisters don't seem to understand that.

William begins to yell about the weather, and I know he's still pretty upset that our dinner isn't going like it normally does. Which really isn't my fault—the man could've told me his rude grandson would be here. Then we could have rescheduled.

The *second* everyone's finished, I stand and begin gathering their plates. "As usual, William, keep the lasagna, okay?"

He grumbles the same thing he always does when I leave the man some food. "I'm not a damn charity case."

"And you also don't like to waste food, and neither do I."

I pack up the lasagna and place it in the fridge, and as I begin to load the dishwasher, Adam appears and grabs the cups out of my hand. "I'll do that."

I raise my hands in surrender and turn to William. "Same time next week, then."

"See ya."

As I reach to open the door, Adam, once again, pulls an object—this time, the doorknob—out of my hand. The way he positions his body around me, it's like he's security, making sure I haven't stolen anything. If he tries to pat me down, looking for William's wallet or something, I'm going to knee him so hard, he'll be the one choking this time, only on his own balls.

"I'll walk you out." His voice is friendly but very false. One thing about being the Witch of Criaturas is I can almost always tell when people are lying. I may not be able to immediately and intimately connect with them the way I can with animals, but the thing is? We humans are also animals. Our bodies do not lie to each other, even as our words do.

I march up to my vehicle—a cute little blue car that my sister Teal purchased for me as a kind of way to say *Sorry for daring you to climb on a railing and how it suspended your life for eight years.* When I turn around, I catch Adam's eyes on my ass. He glances up at my face too slow for me to miss it. I remember Grayson's words: *Every single guy gets hard over anything vaguely round. Tits, ass. It doesn't matter. It means nothing.*

"What do you want to know?" I ask. "I've got three minutes so make it snappy."

He closes his eyes briefly, as though I'm the one who followed him to his car, accusing him of trying to scam my grandparent. He glances around, for what reason I don't know, and when his blue eyes land on mine, I break the contact immediately by focusing on his Adam's apple as he swallows. "Why did you first start bringing Gramps food? Why do you keep doing it, huh? What—what's in it for you?" Now he looks concerned, and I can see that under his hardened exterior, beneath the frown, the crossed arms, the tense jaw, there is a protectiveness. He wants to protect his grandfather. And I get that. I do.

But it doesn't make up for the last time he and I spoke. In the parking lot of Teal's ex's wedding that we all attended last summer.

I DON'T DO CROWDS OR LOUD MUSIC. THEY BOTH MAKE ME feel like my skin is going to vibrate right off into a pile on the floor, and after about thirty minutes of this sensation, I feel raw, like I need to hide under my comforters, or in the darkest part of the forest, for several days until I feel like myself again.

So I had escaped from the reception to the courtyard, where I found friends—chipmunks, tiny and soft, little white stripes on their bodies so delicate it was like they were painted on. Pigeons were there, too, cooing and chatting. As I held one of each in the crooks of my arms, Adam walked out, saw me, and blinked. It was so similar to the time it appeared like he saw me as a ghost, it took my breath away, so much so that I couldn't speak.

And then he furrowed his brow and said, "Is that a *pigeon*?"

He spent the next ten minutes scolding me for handling wild animals. He went over diseases and ticks and infections, referencing work trips he had made to jungles in Brazil and Bolivia and the old gods know where else . . . not noticing once that I was shrinking into my skin, feeling smaller and smaller as he treated me as though I were an especially stupid twelve-year-old who should know better.

That wasn't the worst part, though.

I was feeling too defeated to return to the reception. So I wandered around the beach instead, wanting to allow the seagulls to land on my arms and shoulders but feeling ridiculous for it, thanks to Adam's condescending rant. I sat on a bench facing the parking lot, and that was when I heard him again.

"I just saw the fucking craziest thing . . . Yes, a *chipmunk*. Who does that?" Adam's voice came in and out, and then I heard a woman laughing in response.

"Oh my God, you didn't know about the Freak of Cranberry? Literally everyone says she lives in the woods like a dirty old hag and talks to animals. It's insane. You should do a story on her."

Adam had laughed uproariously. "There's no way. My career would be ruined."

"Oh, shh, shh," the woman said between giggles. Her hair shone copper red in the sunlight, and she was just as toned and lean as my sister Teal. "There she is. Don't say anything or she'll, like, growl at us or something."

They walked by me briskly, neither one even glancing my way. By the time they got to the woman's car, they were laughing about something else, and then they hopped in and she drove them away.

To say I was devastated was an understatement. I couldn't have kept my tears in even if I'd tried. A seagull landed by my hand, pecking very lightly at my fingernails, in the same way a cat might nip at their owner, asking something like *What's up? Why are you so sad?* Or, you know, knowing seagulls, it also might've been *Hey, can you sneak me a big grilled steak from the party?*

My sister Teal came out of the reception hall right then. "Teal!" I called, hoping I could bum a ride with her, since the last thing I wanted was to spend another second thinking about how the man I'd idealized for the last year had just *laughed* when someone called me a freak.

But she didn't hear me. She was quickly followed by Carter, her soon-to-be husband, though I certainly didn't know it at the time. They yelled at each other over his car for about a minute, and then *they* got in and sped away, too.

So I sat there for a while, as the sweet seagull hung out, leaning against my forearm. I realized that this crush I'd been nurturing on Adam for so long was, well, pure delusion. This was a painful truth to acknowledge. I swallowed many times to keep from bubbling tears again.

ADAM WASN'T INTO ME, LIKE, AT *ALL*. AND THE THING IS, IT'S fine for someone to not be sexually attracted to someone else. I get it. Adam didn't owe me interest or flirtation or anything like that. But it was still a hard, hard blow to the ego, considering that up until then, I'm still embarrassed to admit, before I fell asleep at night, I'd imagine the way his face would look when he fell in love with me. I'd think about our first kiss, how he would be so into it, he would make some kind of awkward-yet-hot sound when our tongues touched. I'd fantasize in vivid detail about when he realized that the ghost he saw that one night at his grandfather's wasn't a ghost at all, but a real woman with real desires and real powers.

I truly thought the old gods had connected us in some cosmic, world-defining way, because there was no way a man could make eye contact with my lonely, wandering spirit twice in a row and it wouldn't mean something.

But it really didn't mean anything at all. He dismissed me like I was nothing.

I hate being dismissed like I'm nothing. I hate being reminded of the feeling of being as inconsequential as a ghost who only appears when her eldest sister decides to cry.

Adam's still waiting for a response. I shrug. "What's in it for me? Well, obviously I've spent the last year meticulously searching for his birth certificate so I can steal his identity."

Adam runs his hand over the stubble of his chin. "This isn't a joking matter."

I scoff. "You made it into a joke by accusing me of hurtful things with no evidence whatsoever." I dig in my purse for my keys. This conversation needs to be over, like, yesterday. "Why don't you ask me if I've exposed him to squirrel germs or chipmunk ticks while you're at it? That's what you were so *concerned* about last time we spoke."

His eyebrows furrow, etching a deep line between them. "Pardon me?" He shakes his head. "Squirrels? What the hell does any of what you just said mean?"

I narrow my eyes as I process all of this information. "You don't remember me at all, do you?"

He blinks. "I—uh. Remember you? Like, we—" He kind of gestures his hands around and my stomach sinks when I realize he's asking if he and I had ever had sex. His smile fades away when he sees the disgusted look on my face. He blinks, then snaps his fingers. "Right. Nate Bowen's wedding. You had the animals." He chuckles to himself and then glances at me up and down quickly. "You look . . ." He clears his throat. "Different."

I don't even understand what we're talking about anymore. He's just wasting my time on a whole new level now. I sigh and say, "You want to know what's in it for me, Adam?" I lift my hand and gesture toward William's home. "I know what it's like to be lonely and forgotten, and your grandfather knows what that's like, too. When I bring him dinner—" I can't help it. My eyes well over and tears, probably stained with eyeliner and mascara, make their way down my face. A jaw-dropped Adam trails their movement. "What I 'get out of it' is I am a little less lonely and forgotten, too. Okay? I'm not trying to steal William's savings or get him to be my sugar daddy or whatever the hell else you're thinking, because, ew, but it's not entirely altruistic, either. Are you happy now?"

Adam says nothing. He opens his mouth, then closes it, then opens it again. I honestly think I have rendered him speechless. I do not have time for speechless, so I nod and say, "I have a shift at work now. I already reminded William. You're not invited, by the way." Trying to hold my poise, despite the makeup certainly smearing my face, I get in the vehicle and only stop *just* short of squealing my tires on the way out.

The sky is settling into a glorious sunset as I make my way to the library, with the clouds shaped like roses and tulips and dinosaurs, each one dipped in yellow ocher and tangerine and rose gold. Early summer in Cranberry is my favorite. Always has been. But the beauty of the sky meeting the distant lines of evergreens and tulip trees can only do so much to improve my mood.

I can't believe I cried in front of Adam Noemi. Of all the things I wouldn't want to do in front of that man, weeping may well be at the top of the list.

I was supposed to be like a goddamn pinecone! Not stand there and basically unzip my skin and let him see every single feeling coursing through me. A second wave of embarrassment hits me as I pull into the library parking lot, and when I stop the car, I bury my face in my hands and let out a long, painful groan.

Oh well. At least he'll for sure leave me alone now.

5

BEHIND THE FANCY, RED-BRICKED, NEW TOWN LIBRARY, there is a building that is now rendered the *former* Cranberry Public Library. It's nestled between woods made up of oaks and pines and waxy-leaf tulip trees, with the occasional wild cranberry bush tucked in, full of ripening fruit this time of year like an adornment of rubies and amethysts. The building itself is ancient, the gray stained sidewalk leading up to the glass doors cracked, the doors themselves so heavy and swollen, they get stuck about a dozen times a day and I have to put a foot on the doorframe to get the momentum to swing one open.

After all that, I enter the main floor, where my boss, Anise, greets me. She wears a violet pantsuit that looks stunning on her curvy figure and dark brown complexion. She's matched her lipstick to the suit and she gives me a wide smile, her eyes crinkling up like she's genuinely happy to see me. I know she's forty-eight years old because we celebrated her birthday with cupcakes only a month ago, though she doesn't look a day over thirty-six. Anise is one of the few people in town who is consistently nice to me, but even then, I sometimes get scared that her kindness isn't real.

"How you doing this evening, Sky?"

I'm thankful I cleaned up my makeup in the car, so I can more easily lie. "Great! Had some lasagna for dinner."

Anise raises an eyebrow. "Nadia made lasagna and you didn't bring me any? What the hell?"

"Don't worry, don't worry, there's two whole pans. I left one with William, so I'll bring you some of the other one tomorrow, okay?"

"You better."

I make my way to the elevators, which are for sure as old as this whole building. They take an age to open, and when I step inside, they creak in a way that reminds me of what it must sound like inside a great blue whale experiencing extraordinary indigestion.

After incremental drops down to the basement, the doors open so reluctantly, I get the feeling they're experiencing pain in their old age. After patting them a little bit as they groan getting the final inches widened, I tell them, "Great job," and step into the basement.

Crooked cherrywood bookshelves are arranged in a bit of a labyrinth, the books within faded, with paper so brittle, I have to put on white gloves when handling them. To my left and right, the walls are filled from top to bottom with even more books, and each of these has its own swinging library ladder, just like what Belle had in *Beauty and the Beast*. Those are what William acts like are going to kill me ever since I had to open my big mouth about them. To be fair, they creak about as much as the elevators, and Anise did warn me to use them slowly, which I may or may not have neglected to do . . . but still. I've fallen from much, *much* higher up and turned out . . . sort of okay.

There are little slits of windows along each wall, letting in wide, short rays of the glowing terra-cotta sunset. Every time I step in here, I feel like I've entered into a just-unearthed dwelling that's one thousand years old, and it's filled with equally old relics and words and the smell of leather, paper, and cherrywood.

It's dark. It's dusty. And I fucking *love* it in here.

The carpet is faded blue-gray and leaves a lot to be desired, but I walk briskly across it to my desk. I found this desk when I first started here, in a storage room on the second floor, covered in piles of unused fax paper. I decided to ask for forgiveness rather than permission with regard to my claim to it. I donated the paper to the children's library, as scrap for children to draw on, and then I pushed the desk onto the elevator, not certain if it would break the surely already unraveling cables that hold it up.

So far no one has noticed or cared about the missing storage desk, so as far as I can surmise, it's officially mine now. My desk looks a bit messy to anyone else but me, were anyone around to actually see it besides me, that is. But I know where everything is. My notes are categorized on Post-its in a shape on my desktop as labyrinthian as the shelves on this floor. A book is opened to its center, where I'd left my work from last night, the pages as thin as rice paper, the words so faded, some spots are unfortunately illegible.

Technically, my job title is library technician, the same job I'd had briefly at St. Theresa's. I kind of pretend it's a bit fancier in my head—and it certainly is fancier than what I was doing at St. Theresa's, which was basically working as a glorified receptionist. So now I call myself a library historian, or a preserver of history. Specifically, I was hired for the Cranberry Codex Restoration Project. Basically, when the big move happened from this building to the new and shiny library out there, they left behind the oldest books, many of which were donations from local wealthy families. This means that a good percentage of the books have local historical significance.

I spend my days slowly going through the hundreds, maybe thousands of books left behind. And I have a checklist that assists me in discerning if the book has the kind of significance the city is hoping for. If it does, I catalog the book in the library system and organize it on one of the few shelves I emptied my first week here. Anise will then take a look and let me know if the book needs to be documented—scanned—or not, and I do that work as well. Scanning old books is my least favorite part of my job, because that means I need to leave my sacred space—the dusty, dark, old basement—and go to the well-lit, floor-to-ceiling-windows-surrounded new library building up front. With *people*.

I hate people.

I didn't start out hating people. Once upon a time, Sky Flores was the quirky, tall girl who the other girls in school would invite to get smoothies and French fries on the weekends. My junior year, three boys had crushes on me, and so from them, I got to pick my first boyfriend ever. His name was Ramón and he had the longest, curliest lashes I'd ever seen, and whenever we kissed, they would flutter like a storybook princess's. I had sex for the first time in the back of his old blue pickup truck when we were both sixteen. "That was amazing," he'd said. "Really?" I'd responded. He didn't get mad at my tone or anything like that. He laughed and said we'd find out what I liked together.

Eight weeks later, I fell.

I recently saw Ramón at Piggly Wiggly. He had his toddler daughter sitting in the front of the cart, making baby noises at him. He saw me watching them from the poultry section and immediately froze, those eyelashes going up and down over my frame, whatever for, I don't know. Could he not believe I was there? Was he remembering that summer and how close we'd been? I would even say high school sweethearts. The old gods know there's been no one else, for me at least.

I can't say, because he then pushed his cart past me and pretended like I was never there at all.

My sisters said he'd cried at the memorial they'd thrown for me, since everyone assumed I was dead and all. So I don't understand why he just acted like I stopped existing. Even an "Oh, hi, Sky" would've been better than . . . *that*. And it's not like I expected to pick up where we'd left off. I knew he was married. I knew he'd made that beautiful baby with his wife. But we were friends once. Like, *best* friends, even.

That's why I no longer like people. Falling didn't just take away too many years from my life. It also kind of ruined my life. Because Ramón pretending he didn't know me is actually an example of the kindest thing strangers do to me whenever I leave my home or my workplace basement. The alternative is far worse.

For some reason, Adam's face opens up in my brain, the image as clear as if I'd taken a photograph. What was it William had said to him? Something like *I know you're going through a rough time right now* . . . What on earth could Adam's rough time entail? What could the golden child of Cranberry have had go wrong for him? He could have any journalist job he wants, it seems, and any woman, too. The whole town *worships* him. He's tall, and beautiful, and his voice so gravelly and intense, it *almost* distracted me from the bizarre and dumb words coming out of his mouth this evening.

I close my eyes and decide to abandon the book I'm analyzing at the moment for the restoration project. I really need my sisters right now.

GROUP CHAT: HERMANAS DE FLORES

Me: What are y'all up to right now? Want to get lunch this weekend?

It only takes a few minutes for the typing bubbles to begin, and I smile and allow myself to relax just a little bit.

Teal: I need to finish up the wallet inventory this weekend!!! How about . . . let me check my planner . . . not next week, but the following Wednesday?

Me: um. Let me check my planner now . . . okay, Wednesday lunch. Two weeks from this Wednesday.

Teal: Oh, on Wednesday I can only do dinner. Does that work?

Sage: Tenn's auntie is in town to help with Oak that week. So I will have a babysitter.

Me: I work on Wednesday night, right through dinner time. What about breakfast?

Sage: I'll be sleeping in that week. I need it.

Teal: You'll probably be sleeping all damn day. Be honest with yourself. That baby literally won't sleep more than ten minutes at once. I timed it the last time I watched him.

Me: You got to watch Oak? When?

Sage: Oh, just when I needed a quick shower last week. I gotta run, chicas. Tenn's about to be home and I am depositing the baby in his arms and heading straight to bed.

Teal: Let me get back to you later tonight, Sky. I have to finish up this belt.

I stare at the conversation, trying to put all of these weird pieces together in a way that makes sense. Like how many times I've offered to watch Oak, my baby nephew who is an adorable chunk at almost four months old, and Sage has always turned me down. *I* could let her nap, but busy-bee Teal watched the baby instead? How does that make sense? And I know Teal's getting ready to debut her leather accessory collection at an artisan co-op downtown, which means she has a zillion deadlines, and I get that but . . . surely she has to eat sometime? Right?

I think about the last time I saw Sage, three or maybe four weeks ago, when she came over to Nadia's with Oak and I made her a half dozen corn flour quesadillas filled with grilled onions and peppers and mushrooms.

"You know, maybe you should stay away from the woods," she'd said, her tone kind of weird, like it was something she'd been rehearsing. "Go out with friends instead. Let people see you differently. Once they see you differently, they'll treat you differently."

Go out with friends instead? *What friends?* I had wanted to demand. But instead I just hummed a sound of agreement and changed the subject to Oak.

Her suggestions still don't sit right with my spirit, even weeks later. It's like she was keeping something from me, though I don't know what.

I close my eyes and lean back in my old wooden chair. Even

without that weird conversation with Sage, I keep getting the feeling like I'm drifting away from my sisters, and I have no idea how I'm supposed to stop us from becoming virtual strangers. When I first came back to the Land of the Living, we all hung out a lot. We would grab meals and drink moonshine at Nadia's and go swimming at the beach. It was awesome, like the old days, before I fell.

But then Sage got engaged and pregnant, and Teal got married and is starting her own business . . . and ever since, I keep getting overwhelmed with the sensation that my sisters, my best friends, my *only* friends, are leaving me in the dust.

I guess it's to be expected. Their lives weren't interrupted like mine was. They're not ostracized wherever they go in Cranberry. So now they are . . . you know, *living*. Meanwhile I feel like I'm only half living, and really struggling with just that amount.

I grab my key ring from my work tote and pull up my desk key, the one that opens the top secret drawer on the lower right side of my desk. I have officially gone from mildly pissed off to full-blown grumpy, which means I need my emergency stash of distractions.

Sliding the drawer open, it contains one Halloween-sized bag of various dark chocolates, a few romance novels "borrowed" from Nadia (she doesn't know I'm borrowing them, is all), and finally, one banged-up sketchbook in the color of mint green. The sketchbook is what I pull out. First, I mean. I definitely grab a handful of chocolates right after.

I flip open the book to a random page, and it lands on a cutout of an old newspaper article, one I'd found in this very room. I copied it and pasted it here not one month ago.

INEBRIATED WOMEN ARRESTED DOWNTOWN, it reads. *Thirteen elderly women were arrested for public intoxication behind Gerald's, the general store*. I flip to another page, where another pasted headline announces: *NUDE WOMEN FOUND DANCING IN CRANBERRY FALLS STATE PARK. Officers report that the women dispersed with a quickness and none could be caught for questioning. It is estimated that there were at least ten, and no more than fifteen*. Finally, I land on the last page, the one I'd updated a couple of days ago: *WITCHCRAFT ACCUSATIONS DISMISSED BY CITY COURTS*. This one is much more vague: *Judge Stateson has dismissed the accusations against several Cranberry City residents, stating that the evidence is purely circumstantial.*

Since I started this position, I've noticed a pattern while going through some of the old records in here. Stories of groups of women gathering, often in the wilderness. Locals complaining about "strange sightings" near St. Theresa's. Things like that.

To make a long story short, the city of Cranberry had some kind of weird matriarchal cult back in the day. And I kinda think it's still happening.

What I'm going to do with this information . . . I haven't a clue. But having my own little harmless mystery to solve is *way* more fun than dealing with people. [Shudders.]

And also . . . maybe figuring out the origins of this cult can somehow help me feel like I belong in this town, you know? If somewhere along the way, a Flores woman was involved in these shenanigans. Even if I'm never accepted, I can stand strong knowing that I have deep ancestral connections. Magical ones, even.

So instead of reading the boring old terrain map book on my desk, I go over the articles again and again, taking notes of the similarities between them. After all that, I go back to the pile of old newspapers, using my gloved hands to smooth them out to see if I can find another to add to my sketchbook scrapbook.

My alarm goes off to let me know I only have five minutes till my shift ends. I began setting alarms because without them, I've accidentally stayed here up to an hour later, so absorbed in my research and reading and chocolate-popping. I sigh at the pile of gold foil candy wrappers at my desk and begin to clean up.

I lock the front doors, since Anise's shift ended about four hours ago, and marvel at how strange it feels, being alone in a parking lot in the dark with absolutely no fear. I could call security to escort me to my car, but I'm not in danger, thanks to all the animals who are always near.

Even now, I can sense the hum of their bodies surrounding me: the slate gray and dried-leaf brown coyotes in the woods behind the old building; the sleeping, sweet wrens in the pine trees to my right; the distant bear mama and her two babies, asleep under the porch of an abandoned home in the neighborhood behind the building. I am always with family. That's what animals are to me. It's a privilege I will never take for granted: the fact that I know if any man tried to hurt me, he would find himself mangled without my having to lift a single finger.

It's only after I've gotten home, showered, and braided my hair that I realize Teal never wrote me back like she said she would. My stomach feels as though it is filled with rocks when I check the group chat, refreshing it a few times as though somehow a message from her will magically appear.

I know she didn't intend to forget about me . . . but she did.

And the old gods know I *hate* being forgotten like I'm just a ghost.

6

ON THE WEEKENDS THE LIBRARY CLOSES AT EIGHT IN THE evening rather than at ten at night, and so the sun is just beginning its deep orange descent into the dark silhouette of the landscape as Anise and I exit the building when she asks me, "What are you doing tonight? Want to get a drink and something to eat at Lost Souls?"

I am so startled, I nearly fall onto the parking lot asphalt. "Whoa," she laughs. "It's just a question."

"Right. Of course." I shake my head and pretend it's totally normal for someone who is not a blood relative to ask me to hang out. "Um." I honestly don't know what to say.

Anise leans on her hip and points her car keys at me. Her outfit is gorgeous as usual, with a white pinstripe blazer and a navy silk blouse over dark-wash jeans. Thanks to Teal forcing me to get my whole "sexy librarian" wardrobe last year, I think Anise and I are the best dressed of the whole library, which makes it ironic that almost no one will ever know it, considering we work in virtual isolation. "Look. That lasagna was the best thing I've eaten in a month. And you always bring extra food, and you don't have to. Let me treat you now, as a thank-you."

I shift my weight on my feet, barely having the courage to make eye contact with her. "And . . . Dennis doesn't mind?"

She snorts. "Tonight's poker night. He won't even notice if I get home late. He'll be having too much fun."

I shrug and nod and say, "Um. Yeah. Okay."

We agree to meet there, and on the way, it hits me, what I've gotten myself into.

I've just agreed to have a drink in *public*. At the very place where I *know* a group of people were going to laugh at my being sexually pranked. I have to pull over into the Burger King parking lot and take a few long deep breaths to get the feeling like my skin is crawling and detaching to stop.

This morning I went to the store to pick up eggs, milk, and cheese, and you know what happened while I was waiting in line to check out? An old white woman behind me said, "You know, I really hate liars," to literally no one while staring at me in the face. Because the whole town thinks I actually ran away for eight years and came back and just *said* I woke up in the woods.

I remembered my promise to myself to be sharper. Be the pinecone.

So I turned around and hissed at her, like a cat. It was a good hiss, too. I rolled my eyes in my head, scrunched my eyebrows as deeply as I could, and bared every single tooth in the process.

It was *so* satisfying to see her eyes widen as she jumped back.

But then it kind of backfired. Because she threw her hands all around and screamed, "This woman is possessed! I just looked into the eyes of the devil! Jesus protect me!"

In the end, she looked way more foolish than me, because the small crowd that gathered found a woman screaming about demons to be the only commotion.

I couldn't help the feeling of despondence that came over me like the deep gray clouds Teal pulls into town when she's sad. My grand idea to be just as mean back to these rude bullies, to be the pinecone and all that . . . all it ended up doing was drawing more attention to *me*. More attention to the fact that I am the town's number one outcast. Maybe they were looking at her this morning. But all day today, I am the one who is going to be gossiped about by inadvertently adding to my own rumor mill. Not everyone will think I'm possessed when they hear what happened, but they *will* think to themselves, *What is that lying freak going to do next?*

I open my phone to text my sisters but stop when I see that Teal still hasn't gotten back to me. I can't double-text my sister, can I? That is literally the one person you shouldn't have to double-text. I probably wouldn't have hesitated to write her again even a year ago, but now the fear comes over me that Teal will see my name in her notifications and roll her eyes. I toss my phone back in my purse.

I take one last long, deep breath. I can do this. I can. Who cares if people at the bar think there's a demon residing in my body? Maybe they'll leave me alone for once. And on that thought, I should probably just roll with the rumor. Dress in all black. Put on vampire fangs with a hooked tail attached to my ass under a long, velvet cape. Get some contacts in the color of hellfire. If they're scared I'm going to devour their souls, they'll stop being mean to me, right?

I turn the car back on and check the time. That freak-out only took four minutes, so I'm not too behind Anise. I'll just tell her I caught all the red lights if she asks, that way I won't have to explain anything about this morning or why people are going to start crossing themselves and tossing holy water my way once they encounter me now.

When I step into Lost Souls, for about seven seconds, no one notices. I can take a moment to take in the décor—the realistic skeletons pinned on the walls, grinning at me. The tealights lighting the skull candleholders in the middle of every table, the way the flickering flames wink in the eye sockets. I can pretend, for one moment, what it would be like to be seen as a normal, boring woman who just stepped into an establishment oddly obsessed with bones. Who I might've become if I hadn't fallen eight years ago. At the time, I wanted to become a radiologist at the local hospital. I wanted to do ultrasounds on pregnant people and see their happy faces when I told them the baby's sex, or how wiggly and cute their baby looked that day.

I had planned on marrying Ramón and having a family of my own. I imagined getting together with my sisters and watching the little cousins all play while we sipped margaritas or some equally fancy-sounding alcoholic beverage to my teen mind. Teal was the only one of us who didn't want kids. Sage and I have always wanted them.

I smile, thinking of little Oak and all the rolls on his chubby little legs. I need to see him and Sage this weekend. Maybe I'll surprise her and bring something good to eat, and maybe the buffer of food will stop more weird suggestions from Sage, too.

By the time I'm done with these internal musings, I realize that everyone is either directly staring at me with scowls on their faces, or they are trying and failing to pretend not to notice me. I close my eyes briefly and scan the room once more. Anise waves her hand at me from the way, way back. Good. Maybe in the shadows, people will forget I'm here.

First, I order a blueberry-flavored beer at the bar, which makes the men next to me laugh and laugh about "girly drinks." The bartender, a gorgeous woman with *Swati* on her name tag and intricate tattoos going up and down her arms, yells, "Shut up, assholes," at them as she hands me my frosty glass.

I keep my eyes down as I make my way toward Anise, who is drinking a martini with extra olives. She hands me a menu. "Want to share the loaded chips?"

I glance down the long list of appetizers. It doesn't hit me how hungry I am until I realize that literally everything looks good, from the garlic Parmesan tater tots to the deep-fried mac and cheese balls. "I didn't realize they updated the menu so much."

"Oh yeah, they expanded it months ago. They got a new chef and everything." Anise laughs. "It even made the news. Where have you been?"

I try hard to make my laugh as lighthearted-sounding as hers. Where have I been? One of two places: the dusty basement of our work building, and my bedroom—the upstairs attic room Sage occupied until she moved in with Tenn. That's it. That's where I have been. Either below the ground, surrounded by old creaking bones and the old creaking earth, or way above, looking down at the cliff jutting right up toward the back of Nadia's two-story home like a sea-sharpened claw. And that's how I like it.

"Let's get the chips," I say instead of answering the question.

Luckily Anise doesn't seem to notice, or if she does, she pretends otherwise. We begin with awkward small talk about work. Well, it's awkward on my end. Anise is warm and friendly as usual, updating me about the ongoing feud she has with the

FedEx guy (the man keeps leaving packages in the muddy grass, and Anise has been printing progressively more passive-aggressive signs to direct him to the nearest dry concrete spot by the door). She never seems to question each word and sentence before saying it, like I do. Because of that, small talk is exhausting for me, and so when the chips arrive, I focus mostly on eating and listening.

And eventually, I realize . . . this whole outing is . . . actually *fine*. I didn't need to have a panic attack on the way here after all. I genuinely laugh a few times with her, rare for me since I'm so hypervigilant in public, and I'm *smiling* as we make our way toward the front door after we finish our meal and pay.

I wonder if this kind of connection would be possible not just with Anise, but the whole town. Or at least, like, half the town would be amazing. Maybe a whole bunch of people will forget they hate me, eventually. Maybe—

"Hey! Hey, Bird Girl!" a ruddy-faced, sloppily dressed man calls to me as I pass his table. "You gonna call your little birdy friends to scare me away?"

"What the hell?" Anise mutters. She places her hand at my forearm and we increase our speed toward the front door.

"Well, guess what? It's not going to work." The man lowers his voice, both in volume and tone. "I will strangle each and every one."

My hackles rise even more than normal when a stranger heckles me. Threatening the animals . . . it's as though he's told me he is going to strangle *me* in the middle of this crowded bar. I turn my head toward him slowly. "What did you just say?"

He gives me a drunken grin. I don't recognize the woman he's with, but she looks mildly embarrassed. "I *said*, I'm going to *strangle*—"

"Sky."

I jump back as another male voice appears, this time behind me. When I turn around, I breathe a sigh of relief, because it's just Adam Noemi. Although I don't trust Adam as far as I can throw him, he definitely isn't the sort to be on the same level of the "I will strangle your birds" dude. Even though, on second glance, Adam does kind of look enraged . . . but he glances behind me at the drunk guy, and I realize it's not me he's mad at. Not at all.

Adam squeezes around me to get between me and the yelling man. Anise then angles her way next to me to get between me and Adam. "You good?" she asks.

I begin to nod, but then decide to just shrug . . . because honestly, who the hell knows? I can't remember the last time *good* could describe anything I was feeling, except maybe when I held baby Oak for the first time, his little fist wrapped around my finger as he slept. And that feels like absolute *ages* ago.

"Peter. What the hell are you doing?" Adam's face is red. His jaw is clenched. When he points to the yelly guy, his hand is actually shaking. "What the fuck are you yelling about strangling to Sky for? Jesus Christ, man."

Peter's body language transforms so quickly, and so fluidly, I can hardly believe what I am witnessing. He had just been laughing, flexing his arms, puffing his chest as he tried to bring me down. But now? He shrinks into himself. His smile becomes an expression of concern, his eyebrows furrowing. "Adam. Uh. I didn't realize she was . . ." He stumbles on his words as Adam continues to give him a remarkable death stare. "I didn't know you—that you and her—that she . . ." He's trying to say, *I didn't know* you *gave a shit about the Town Freak* but he's either too dumb or inebriated or maybe even both to say it without being insulting. Finally he gives up and raises his arms in surrender. "I'm sorry, man."

Adam shakes his head. "Why are you apologizing to *me*?"

The entire bar is so silent, the only sounds I can make out are the distant kitchen pots and pans behind the bar. Peter makes eye contact with me, then glances down and says, "Sorry."

"Sorry for what?" Adam barks, doing his absolute best impression of William.

"Adam, that's good," I say, lightly touching his arm. He glances down at my hand, and when he looks at me, something weird happens in my belly. Because as sharp as his face was, staring at Peter, it is completely softened now, taking me in. It's the complete opposite of how he looked at me a week or so ago, hurling baseless accusations, and I'm so unnerved by it, I feel like I'm gonna trip while just standing here.

"Nothing about this is good," he tells me.

I nod. It's the truth, after all. "I know. But he apologized. I'm going to leave with my friend now."

Anise gives me a concerned glance as we make our way to the front. The second the doors close behind us, she asks, "Are you okay, Sky?"

I put on a smile—the one I always perform when my sisters ask the same question. Or at least the question they used to ask me until they got all busy adulting and having their own families and stuff. "Yup."

The way Anise looks at me, I suspect I'm not convincing her as well as I did with my sisters. "Well, can I give you a hug? That angry white man in there was scary as hell."

I almost break into tears when her arms wrap around me. I should've known Anise gives good hugs like this—tight and warm. "Thank you."

Anise doesn't leave until she sees me in my car, keys in my hand. I wave at her as she pulls away and then let out a deep, shaky sigh. I need to get home as fast as possible so I can hide under all my elaborate, expensive covers, listen to Chappell Roan, and cry my heart out.

But before I can slide my key into the ignition, there's a knock on the window that makes my heart feel like it's jumped into my throat.

I roll down my window when I see it's Adam. "Hey." The line of the streetlamps lights up his hair as though it were spun from coppery gold. He says nothing else, but he examines my face closely, as though he's searching for some sign of injury. I don't get it. It's not like Peter punched me in the nose or something.

I should probably thank him. That's what a normal person would do, right? But when I open my mouth, instead I ask, "Can I help you?"

He nods. "Yeah. Let me buy you a drink."

I frown. "Buy me a drink? What for? If anything, I owe you one for what you did . . . in there. Thanks for that. By the way."

Adam chuckles and shakes his head. "Actually, I owe you an apology. I can do that with a drink. You like the blueberry beer here, was it? I can get you another." He points toward the Lost Souls sign, neon blue and red and orange in the night. Each *O* is a skull and crossbones.

"Maybe another time. I don't want to go back in there." After the spectacle that just occurred, there's no way I am on track to the town forgetting all about me and my "lies."

Adam nods as he lets out a breath. "What about at Gramps's?"

I blink. "Um." I shrug. "Okay." It's not like I have anything better to do. And if Adam wants to apologize for being a suspicious jerk to me the other week, I'll welcome it. After no one apologizing for their bad behavior in this town for over a year, two in a day is definitely going to set the record for a long, long time. May as well bask in the glory.

I follow his car all the way back to Catalina Street, the sky full of misty clouds that obscure the blinking stars. Sometimes I wonder if my gifts can reach far into the universe somehow. Chances are, Earth isn't the only planet that contains life, right? What if there are animals out there somewhere, orbiting a star we don't even know exists yet? I wonder if they can sense my grief and loneliness in the faraway places of space, and on days when I feel happy or sad or strange for no reason, it's because I'm sensing them right back. This is something I want to ask my sisters, too, about their *gifts*. Can Teal, who controls the weather, affect the perpetual red hurricane on Jupiter? Can Sage, who communes with plants, make extraterrestrial flowers bloom?

Since Nadia's is only across the street from William's, I leave my vehicle in her driveway and walk over. Adam leans against his Jeep, eyes on me in a way that makes me feel a bit strange. I was expecting him to be inside already, preparing drinks, but nope. He's watching me with that same warm, soft expression, like I mean something to him, which makes exactly no sense. It's unnerving in more ways than one—it also reminds me of that one night, when I was still a ghost, and he was with that curvy girl. How he'd looked right at me and said, *We should get out of here.*

He leans his head toward the front door, and when I walk up, he beats me there and holds it open for me. "Do you like whiskey?" he asks. "I'm afraid that's all Gramps keeps around here."

"No blueberry beer for William, huh?"

"Nope." He smiles. "And his bedroom light's out, so he won't be joining us. Which is too bad, because Gramps is hilarious when he's tipsy."

"I need to see that sometime for sure," I say. "About the whiskey . . . I'd rather have some water or tea, if that's okay by you."

He nods. "I don't even drink, so that's more than fine."

"You don't?" Maybe it's rude to inquire more, but I can't help it. "So you were at Lost Souls for the loaded chips?"

"Something like that." I sit at the dining table, which has a full view of the open kitchen—the eucalyptus green walls, the scuffed yellow linoleum floor, the rusty appliances that all look like they're one big family feast away from collapsing. Adam bends down to find the kettle in the cupboard, then fills it with water and places it on the stovetop. I begrudgingly admit to myself that I admire the way he moves his body—even just the basic task of boiling water for tea is imbued with intent. He fully inhabits his form in the way animals do. Which isn't an insult in my book. Far from it, in fact.

William's stove apparently has a deceptive exterior—it actually works really fast. By the time Adam's got the tea bags in the mugs, the kettle is already whistling. He pours the tea and brings them over, the steam fluttering around him, reminding me of that night again—when I'd thought he'd looked like an angel.

"I'm sorry I accused you of trying to take advantage of Gramps," he begins, his deep voice flowing around me just like the tea steam. "It's no excuse, but I've been going through a lot lately. And I've also been really scared for him." Adam sighs. "His doc thinks he has some early signs of dementia."

I about drop my tea mug to clutch at my heart. "Adam. *No.*"

Adam nods, his eyes dropping to my hand briefly before falling to his own mug. "He asked me to keep an extra eye on him, and make sure he was even more protected than usual from things like scams." He glances at me. "I know Gramps wouldn't want you to know this, but I'm telling you so you can keep an eye on him as well." Adam blinks rapidly while taking a deep breath. He's trying not to cry.

I place my hand over his on the table. "It's okay. I won't tell him I know. And I'll watch him. I can see your house from my bedroom. Whenever I can, I'll make sure he isn't—" I rack my brain for things that people with dementia might do. "Wandering around or anything like that. I can check on him throughout the week, too, if you want. Bring him more meals and stuff like that."

Adam lets out a deep sigh. "Thanks for understanding. And I don't think we're at that level yet, but I appreciate the offer."

I lift my hand, only then realizing how warm his had been. The tea is too hot to sip, but I wish I could, because I need a second . . . or, like, a million seconds . . . to process this. To cry. William is up there in years, but he's so stubborn and sturdy, I assumed he'd be around for a couple more decades, at least. I say a prayer to the old gods that whatever the symptoms his doctor's worried about are, it's just regular old-age stuff.

"Well, let me know anytime if there's anything you need with William. I . . . I really do care about him, Adam. He's been one of my only—" I pause, taking a moment to swallow. "He's a good friend."

Adam nods and sips his tea, grimacing.

I frown. "What's the matter?"

He laughs and shakes his head. "Nothing. I just really fucking hate tea."

This gets a chuckle out of me. "Why did you make some for yourself, then?"

He runs a hand over the stubble of his chin. "I have no idea, Sky."

I take a sip of my own tea. It's a blend of mint and maybe

echinacea root. Very herbal and green. I'm sure if Sage were here, she could give it a single glance and tell me every ingredient.

I swallow and glance at Adam once more. "I'm glad you explained your behavior to me. About the accusations and all that. I understand it, especially given—" I wave my hand toward William's bedroom. "But . . ."

"But . . ." he says, giving me a soft half smile.

I set my mug down again. "But you owe me two apologies, actually. I'm still waiting for the other one."

Adam raises his eyebrows. "Uhh—"

"At Nate Bowen's wedding to Fern?"

His eyebrows drop. "Oh?"

I roll my eyes. "You were incredibly condescending toward me when I was just chilling with some pigeons and chipmunks."

"Well—"

I continue on before he can give me another annoying lecture about various pathogens living on feathers. "And then I heard you laughing about it—about *me*—in the parking lot afterward. When you left with that woman. Remember that?"

Adam buries his face in his hands. "Fuuuck."

I tap my fingers against the hard wood of the table. "That's not an apology."

Adam keeps his hands over his face and I think he might be nodding under them. "Fuck," he repeats.

I shake my head. "Still not an apology."

He lets his hands fall to the table and stares right at me. The eye contact is a little intense, so I force my own gaze to the swallowing motion of his Adam's apple. "I'm sorry for being condescending to you that day. The day of the wedding. And I'm sorry for laughing at you later. It's not an excuse but . . . I'd been drinking. I am . . . I didn't know it at the time, but I am my worst self when I've had a few too many."

"It's why you stopped?" I ask. "Drinking, I mean?"

Adam nods. "Luckily I stopped before it became more serious of a problem."

"Well. Yeah. That's a good thing." I look down.

"I don't mean to make you uncomfortable. Sorry. I was just being as honest as I can. I was an asshole to you back then. And I was an asshole to you last week. I know you heard Gramps . . . I'm not in a good place. I'm unemployed—"

"You lost your job? But I thought you were working for the . . ." I let my voice trail off, realizing that these details are probably none of my business. But last I had heard, Adam moved back into town to work for the *Cranberry Chronicle*. I guess that's why I'm so surprised.

Adam sighs. "Yes, after only about six months, they let me go. They said I wasn't pulling in readers like they had hoped I would, and the *Chronicle*'s tiny budget got hit with more cuts, so . . ." He shrugs. "I've been living off savings. I am moving back in with my grandfather while in my thirties. It's just been one thing after another, you know?"

"You moved in?" I ask, suddenly more than unnerved by this information. "I thought you were living downtown and only visited William on the weekends."

Adam laughs. "Kinda hard to keep a place with no income. I'm almost finished packing and should be all settled here within a few days." He clears his throat. "As I was saying, though. No matter what I'm going through, I shouldn't have taken that out on you. Again, I'm sorry."

I take a tiny sip of tea to try and figure out what to say next.

I'm still frazzled by the idea of Adam living here, so close to Nadia's place. It reminds me of when I was a ghost. When he'd stay at William's for long vacations and I would jump out an attic window to watch him read and write and go in the backyard, put his hands in his pockets and glance up at the twinkling stars, maybe the same stars whose planets have animals that I might be, in some distant, cosmic way, magically connected to.

The words feel as though they come from my heart. "I'm sorry you're going through it."

He nods. "Well. Yeah. I've been laid off twice in the last two years because of the ongoing decline of journalism. I really need to get my name back there in some huge way, I think. It would be great if, like, an incredibly compelling story just, like, fell into my lap." He laughs as though he's said some impossible thing. "Especially considering how Gramps's medications and doctor visits are adding up. His health insurance keeps dropping the ball. But, yeah. That's what I really need to get back to newspaper journalism. A big break."

I swallow. I can scarcely believe what I am about to say next, but . . . I think of how becoming sharp like a pinecone didn't work *at all.* I then remember the immediate regret on Peter's face, after he'd been heckling me with absolutely no sign of remorse. All because of Adam shutting it down.

Even if Adam's in the middle of what sounds like a serious rough patch . . . this whole town still respects him. Peter at the bar wouldn't have given a crap about Adam's opinion of his behavior otherwise. Which means . . . maybe through him, I can get *them* to respect *me*.

Not *like* me. I'm not delusional. But just . . . treat me like a real human, even if they give me a wide berth most of the time? The idea of going to the store or even taking a walk downtown to watch the sunset along the coast without intense anxiety and panic is too good to pass up.

So I nod. Decision made. I make my voice low and mysterious. "What about the true story of a girl who fell eighty feet in a state park? Whose body was never discovered? But then she was found in the same park, eight years later, with no memory of where she'd been?"

Adam swallows his sip of tea. I can tell that he is sort of intrigued, but then he shakes his head. "No . . . I mean, that's a little too . . ."

I interrupt him by putting my hand over his. He glances down quickly and up again, swallowing, this time without any tea. "But what if she actually does remember where she'd been? And you would be the first person who's not family to know the true story?"

I try so hard to frame it like a true crime podcast intro. I know those are addicting to a lot of people, Anise included. She always has some episode on when she's doing mindless work, like organizing books or sweeping. Sometimes I will hang out to listen for a few minutes, even delaying my eventual nesting in my favorite place in the whole world, my desk in the basement. It's the language they use, and the music, honestly. I need some dramatic theme music attached to my offer right now.

Instead, Adam scratches the red gold of his hair and brings his hand to cup his mug once more. "But what would be in it for you?"

Respect. Dignity. I open my mouth to pick one of these, or a synonym, but then what actually comes out is this:

"A . . . friend?"

7

Adam stares at me for a long moment, one of his thick brown eyebrows raised. "A . . . friend." He forms the word as though he's never heard it before, as though it's in an entirely different language even.

I nod. "Yes. Like, you could pretend to be my friend. And, you know, vice versa. 'Cause that's the way these things go, right?" I cross my legs in the chair, but my legs are so damn long that my knees jab into the edges of the tabletop, and so I uncross them and settle for resting my feet on the seat across from me.

Adam sits back in his chair during my adjustments. "Look, I'm not trying to be snarky or anything like that, but I don't understand how us pretending to be friends would be payment for the exclusive story of where you were for, what was it? Nine years."

"Eight years," I correct, and then shrug. "Look. Everyone in town is completely obsessed with you. You are universally beloved in Cranberry." I expect him to gloat or even just smile, but instead a hint of a frown appears at the corner of his lips. "Maybe if folks see us being friends, they won't be so mean to me, you know?"

Adam's still frowning. "I think you're overestimating my influence in this town."

I roll my eyes. "Adam, you literally saw how Peter treated me at the bar tonight. Do you think that's an isolated incident? Spoiler: It's not. Not at all. But for the first time ever, he *apologized*. Someone finally fucking apologized for treating me like garbage, and it's because of you. Forgive me for saying it, but it sounds like you're *underestimating* your influence in this town."

Adam runs his hands over his face again, chuckling like he can't believe he's having this conversation, his voice deep enough that I feel it in my ribs, my hips, and, as much as I hate to admit it, a bit more south than that. I begin to tap at my knees under the table to distract myself from those unwanted sensations.

"People respect you. They like you. And if Cranberry saw you *choosing* to be my friend?" I gesture to the window, where nothing but the pitch black of night can be seen right now. Not even the closest plants or patio furniture are visible, but this doesn't stop me from sensing the raccoon cutting through the backyard, two bruised, sweet apple cores in her mouth. "If people saw you making that choice, they wouldn't bully me so bad. In theory, at least."

Adam leans back in his chair. "Okay. So . . . why pretend, then? Couldn't we become friends for real?"

"Maybe?" I shrug and stare at my hands. I'm still tapping my thighs with my fingertips, trying to keep my stress levels down with the repetitive motion. "You don't really know me yet. I'm really weird."

He stares at me for a moment, starting with my hair, and lowering down to my cheeks, my chin, my belly, down to my tapping fingers. He seems to realize that it very much looks like he's checking me out, when he and I both know that's not the case, and so he clears this throat and firmly drops his gaze onto his now-empty tea mug. "You're not . . . Sky. You're not off-putting, or repulsive, or whatever you seem to be thinking about yourself. At all. Trust me."

"*Trust* you?" I barely stop myself from rolling my eyes and stand instead, taking our mugs to the sink. "*You* haven't been called *freak* or *liar* or *the devil* for the last two years. *You* didn't have greasy French fries dumped on your head the last time you decided to try having a meal by yourself. Frankly, you telling me that I seem to think these things about myself is incredibly invalidating."

I'm standing in the entryway to the kitchen, my hands on my hips. He's swiveled around in the chair to face me, his blue eyes almost black in the dim lighting. "Someone dumped food on your head?" he finally asks, like he can't wrap his mind around it.

I close my eyes and sigh. I won't dignify that with a response. "The friendship thing . . . that's an experiment. It's possible that what happened to me . . . what I went through . . . is too much for them to get over." I realize that the mugs are still in my hands, and I turn to rinse them and place them carefully in the dishwasher. William really needs to replace this piece of garbage. Some of the prongs are broken, meaning they don't hold up dinnerware like they should. I learned this the hard way by shattering an old diner-style coffee mug months ago.

I turn to face Adam, who's now stood up and is at the entrance to the kitchen. I'm tall—five-eleven—but Adam is taller still. I wonder briefly what it'd be like if he hugged me, his big frame feeling so warm and so safe. I shake my head free of the thought.

"So . . . I mean, like I was just saying. I don't even know if fake friendship would even work. But—" I swallow, horrified that I think I might cry in front of Adam Noemi again, and so I use every iota of willpower to stop any tears from forming. "If it did, it would be worth it. One hundred percent. To give you the exclusive to my story. And let's be honest. Given the emails and calls and randoms appearing on my doorstep the last two years, wanting to interview me? There is a large potential readership. It could definitely be the big break you're used to, even if the friendship part of it turns out to be a waste of my time."

"Being friends would be a waste of your time? Even if we became friends for real?" He sounds tough, but that toughness is covering a vague wound. The old gods know why. This man has countless friends.

"There's no guarantee with regard to a real friendship." I know I sound a bit snide with the word *real*, but I can't help it. I do not believe Adam and I are compatible as friends. The evidence for the argument that we could be simply doesn't exist. "You could decide you want nothing to do with me after writing your piece on me. Just like everyone else." I lift my hand to gesture around. "I mean, I get that that makes me sound like I have trust issues, but they're not there for no reason. I can guarantee you a story, and you can only guarantee me the *illusion* of friendship. Not a genuine friendship. So it's the illusion that has to be the basis of our agreement." I sigh and walk around him—my shoulder sliding against his in such a way that I wonder if shoulders can be uncommon erogenous zones, a thought I immediately suppress for its stupidity—and grab my purse from the table. "Thanks for what you did tonight. I guess this means that you can stay for the next dinner I bring William next week. If you want."

I walk to the front door, but once again, so quickly that I get déjà vu, Adam beats me to the doorknob to open it for me. "Oh, th—"

"Okay," he says. "Deal."

"Deal?" My voice comes out unsure and squeaky. "To . . . public, illusory friendship in return for my story?"

"In exchange for your exclusive story about what happened that day, and in the eight years after," Adam clarifies.

I nod. "Okay! Okay. This is good." Another thought occurs to me, this one making my stomach sink a little bit. "And you'll—I mean. I know you need to be objective in your writing."

Adam raises an eyebrow. "Yes?"

I close my eyes briefly before settling on his. They're sparkling and so blue, I think of a list of dumb things—Picasso's blue period. *Untitled (Blue Divided by Blue)* by Mark Rothko. The blue whales I can sense when I'm in bed trying to fall asleep, gliding across the blue, blue water with their families, each one singing sacred whale songs. I shake my head. "In the piece, I need you to extend me some grace, but you don't have to act like you believe every word I say." Because the old gods know, there are going to be words he's going to find difficult to take in. "Just don't make me sound crazy. Don't make me sound like a liar. Otherwise, it will ruin all the work of our potentially real friendship."

"I won't." He says it so calmly and confidently that I'm surprised that I really, really want to believe him. "Of course I won't."

He holds out his hand and I place mine in his. After a brief, super awkward shake, wherein I certainly do not notice how big his hand is, I pull mine back and point to the still half-open door. "Okay. Thanks. Good night, then."

"Good night, Sky." He gives me a half smile and steps outside.

I think he might walk me to Nadia's, like this is the end of a date or something, but he stops at William's ancient, threadbare welcome mat, arms crossed. I walk across the street and when I make it inside, I press my eyes to the door screen, where I can see Adam, still watching, from the still-open door of William's house, the front light all warm and ambery, making him appear a bit like an angel . . . or a ghost.

I SPEND MY SUNDAY OFF IN NADIA'S SUNFLOWER-YELLOW kitchen, melting honey and butter together, kneading sweet dough, and frying up the eggplant I brought home from the farmer's market last week. All this for Sage, and, indirectly, baby Oak. Sage says breastfeeding hunger is *unreal*. Which I can believe, based on the last time Teal and I have gotten her away for a meal since she's had him. We watched this woman inhale two burgers and three slices of pepperoni and roasted red pepper pizza, and ten minutes later ask about dessert. She said Tenn can barely keep her fed even with frequent trips to get fast-food sandwiches and burritos and fries. So I decided to surprise her today with a mountain of good, home-cooked deliciousness.

"Hello!" As soon as she answers the door to her apartment, I hold up a basket filled with honey butter rolls, all still ooey and gooey and warm from the oven.

"Hey!" Sage is dressed in a soft-looking pink pajama set, with what probably is a milk stain on her chest. She leans in for a half hug around the basket. "What's all that?"

"Carbs."

"Mmm. My favorite."

"There's more where this came from. Give me a second."

I rush toward the car and grab two more pans, one filled with eggplant parmigiana, the mozzarella a fancy buffalo sort I'd picked up from a cheese shop just outside of town, and the other, cinnamon bread pudding, another one of Nadia's famous recipes. Her secret to that one is using both vanilla and almond extract in equal parts, as well as adding nutmeg to the cinnamon topping. The result is fairly intoxicating, perfect for a nursing mama needing calories. Sage lets me in much more quickly this time, and I place all the dishes on the countertop next to the rolls. She's got one in each hand, moaning as she eats. "Good?" I ask.

"*So* good. Oh my God."

I glance around, noting the stacks of dirty cups in the sink, the little piles of unwashed laundry all over, wondering if she would be mad if I offered to clean up later. "Is Oak asleep?"

"Yeah, thank God." Sage's mouth is so full, I can barely understand her. "He nursed for literally one hour straight. My nipples are so numb, I wouldn't even notice if they fell off."

I snort. "Noo! That sounds awful, Sage."

"Meh. It's better than when he tries to bite them off." She shudders as she grabs another roll from the basket.

"Can I go see him?" I ask.

Sage nods and says, "Sure—" But then she grabs my arm. "Jesus Christ, Sky, is that a *snake* on your arm?"

"What? Oh." I lift up my left forearm, where a black garden snake named Geri has wrapped herself around me. Made things pretty difficult while I was trying to cook all morning, but she's stubborn and wouldn't let go even when I offered her an egg for a yummy snack. "This is just—she wanted to come for the ride."

Sage sighs and puts her hand on her head. "I don't want snakes around my baby, Sky."

I shake my head. "I mean, Geri . . . she won't—"

Sage moves her fingers to my arm—the one without any

snakes curled around it. She makes her voice gentle and sweet-sounding, but I can feel the frustration beneath her tone. "Sky. I know that what you want, more than anything, is for people to treat you normally. To take you seriously. But that means you need to stop—" She lifts her hand once more and points to Geri. "You have to stop doing things like wandering around with animals wrapped around your body." She furrows her brow and frowns. "Especially to see a *baby*?"

I shake my head. "I mean, I don't get groceries with snakes wrapped around my arms." Though, come to think of it, if I did, I bet people would actually treat me better than they currently do, considering how ubiquitous snake phobias are. "And I know she wouldn't hurt Oak. You know how it is with our gifts. We *know* these things. We can *feel* them."

"It's not just that. I heard about the birds you sicced on Grayson Baker." Sage folds the cloth napkin over the rolls, covering them once more. "This isn't how you're going to win over the town. Besides the fact that *no one is supposed to know* about our gifts like that." She hisses this last part and it's so weird how she morphs into a person I don't recognize at all. Sage has always been the soft one, so soft that she struggles with nonconfrontation and people-pleasing.

I kinda wish she were struggling with nonconfrontation and people-pleasing right now, to be honest. It's hard to pinpoint my emotions, but it kinda feels like she just drop-kicked me in the stomach.

My mouth opens and closes. I have no idea what to say, but somehow, with effort, I form words. "You heard that Grayson Baker took a bet from his friends to fuck me to see if I had antlers coming from my vagina and you think . . . I *shouldn't* have called the crows to scare him shitless?"

Sage's eyes widen. "Wait, what? No! I didn't hear that version. Jesus. He did that to you?"

I am somehow feeling even more small than usual. I begin to pick up the pieces that I was left with from my last text messages with Sage and Teal. How consistently Sage has blown me off, even though I have far more free time than Teal does for helping her. "You haven't wanted me to see the baby, have you? That's why you never accept my offers for me to watch him."

Sage sighs, but she doesn't deny it. "Look, you spend all your days in the woods with animals that are covered in ticks, and I get that this is our *gift*, I understand more than anyone, Sky, but I'm also a mother now. I don't want the baby to get sick. And I didn't want to tell you all that because I knew you'd give me that kicked-puppy-dog face you're giving me right now, and I can't. I can't take care of you and my child at the same time."

All her words turn into arrows and slice right through my chest into my heart. "Oh."

In the distance, Oak begins to cry.

Sage sighs. "Hold on. Just a second."

But I don't wait for a second, or even half a second. I turn and walk out the door, making sure it's locked behind me. And then I run to my car and slide in. I squeal my tires leaving her apartment complex's parking lot, Geri's smooth, cool scales against my arm the whole while.

8

OUR MOTHER LEFT US WHEN I WAS A BABY. TEAL WAS FIVE, and Sage was seven. I don't even remember her, not even the suggestion of a memory. No hint of a fragrance note. No distant lullabies. Nada. But her abandoning us, it hit Teal and Sage hard. Especially Sage.

We were left with Nadia, who, for some ungodly reason, decided Sage was old enough to raise me and Teal. At *seven* years old.

Sage potty-trained me and introduced me to solid foods. My first taste of something not puréed was Nadia's famous caramel flan. Sage laughs when she tells the story. Me, sitting in a scuffed-up high chair in Nadia's yellow-walled kitchen, my eyes fluttering as I tasted heaven in flan form. And my next move was to grab the rest of the piece of flan in my little fist and shove it in, and all over, my face.

Until I was sixteen, Sage was, for all intents and purposes, the only mother figure I knew. Me and Teal, we got to be the kids.

Sage's childhood was stolen from her, first by our good-for-nothing mother, and second by Nadia's neglect.

Sage always said she never understood why she and I were connected when I was a ghost. Why when she cried, I appeared to her, looking as though I had never been anything but alive, solid with matter.

But I always knew why. When a child becomes frightened, that child always longs for her mother. And though it wasn't either of our choices, Sage raised me. Me and Teal both. That's how we were connected. If our biological mother had loved us properly, and if I had still fallen, I'm certain I would've come to her via her tears. But that's not what happened.

As I fell, I screamed for Sage. Not our mother. Sage.

I probably shouldn't have run out of Sage's apartment like that. But I've worked really hard on not burdening Sage anymore, not after everything she has gone through for me, including having to deal with me when I was a ghost for all those years.

I made her old room my safe place. I got a real, grown-up job. Every time she and Teal ask me if I'm okay, I give them a big-toothed smile and say *Yes* with as much feeling as I can muster.

But finding out that despite that, Sage still feels like I need to be parented. Emotionally coddled. *I can't take care of you and my child at the same time.* Shame runs over me, warm and clammy, like a sudden fog descending on an unbearably hot beach day.

I make it back to Nadia's, and when I check the time on the dashboard, I gasp when I see it's taken me fifteen minutes less than usual. I wonder how many traffic laws I'd accidentally broken as I drove home in this somewhat hysterical state.

Since it's Sunday, Nadia will be at church all day and probably till late in the night, too. So that means that after placing Geri back in the garden, I can stomp and sob as loudly as I want, up the stairs and into my bedroom.

When this was Sage's room, it was decorated with a botanical, rustic, cottagecore style. The walls were white and chipped, the windows always had plants in front of them, and there were paintings of leaves and flowers over the bed. It was understated, allowing the view of the distant ocean through the balcony French doors to be the main feature of the whole room.

When I moved in, the first thing I did was take a few days off work to apply wallpaper over the too-much-white of the walls. (I told Anise I was going on vacation. I hated lying to her, but also the truth seemed a bit pathetic. Luckily I had and have plenty of PTO.)

The wallpaper pattern I had chosen was of a forest. It wasn't a landscape—no, you didn't get the feeling like the forest was somewhere *out there*. Instead, my bed felt like it was placed right in the middle of the gently swaying, birdsong-filled woods. Trees grew out of the ground all around me in curvy, stylized linework, their green, soft-looking leaves highlighted in flecks of gold, the canopy filled with a pale blue, magical fog. Animals watched from secret places—the big eyes of an owl behind the leaves of an oak. A fox curled up in a thicket of ferns, taking a nap with one ear turned toward the viewer. A serpent, spotted with yellow and red, curved on a branch, its black eyes glittering with copper flecks.

The whole thing was a bitch to put up all by myself. But I did it, and it was *so* worth it.

I placed a huge green rug embroidered with gold flower designs at the foot of my bed, which was the same one Sage had used—a brass wire bedframe that I had polished until it gleamed exactly like yellow gold. I put a lacquer over it so it wouldn't patina and would stay shiny.

I didn't want to put up bookshelves that would cover the wallpaper, so instead I found some tall, polished maple bookshelf nightstands for either side of the bed. It only took me two weeks to fill them so thoroughly that books were basically pouring out of the shelves now. Over the bed I hung a photograph of Ana Mendieta's *The Vivification of the Flesh*—labyrinth-esque lines she drew, or maybe painted, on warm brown paper that resemble . . . well. They kind of resemble the old gods to me, if only I could remember what they looked like.

When I wasn't a ghost, walking the earth, either vividly and in color after Sage's tears, or distantly and in a thick cloud, I was . . . elsewhere. Back in my body inside the cavern of the ancient oak tree in Cranberry Falls State Park. I remember dappled light from above, pouring over me in a broken sheet of gold, and the wind through the leaves of the trees, coupled with birdsong and the occasional owl's hoot. Sometimes I remember someone holding my hand . . . maybe. Or brushing my hair. Maybe. Nadia says these were the old gods, taking care of me, to answer her prayers for my protection. After all, none of my family knew where my body had ended up. Nadia definitely neglected us, but she did pray relentlessly for my safekeeping. From this, I have learned that prayers to the old gods are powerful.

I remember my supernatural hibernation, all eight years of memory fragments from the woods, in the way we remember dreams. The more I try, the more I forget.

I suppose it doesn't really matter now. I look around my room and remember something else I wish I could forget, something that makes my heart pinch. Teal and Sage still haven't come by to see my bedroom since I've done it up. It's been . . . what? I count on my fingers. Almost a year since I moved in here . . . and four months since I redid the whole attic.

I pick up my phone and find messages and texts from both of my sisters. Sage has left many apologies. I'm so sleep-deprived. I'm sorry, Sky. Thank you for the food. Teal has added in, Look, Sage told me what happened. We're both just worried about you. Maybe you and I can meet up like we said we would, and just chat about some things?

I roll my eyes at the "like we said we would." *We* didn't say anything. *She* left me on read.

And the "we're both just worried about you" is a rough read. It means they've been talking about me, while being too busy for me at the same time.

I stare at my phone for a few minutes and finally realize what my subconscious has been dancing around for a good long while now. My sisters have many priorities, and I am simply no longer one of them. The acceptance hurts, but it also comes with relief. The pieces of the puzzle in my hands have finally come together. I have answers now, and with the answers, I can make decisions on where to go from here.

I'm not going to fight them on this any longer. I'm not interested in bending over backward and doing somersaults to get my own family to remember I exist. Or to get them to just be up front with me and say, "Please leave the snakes at home." I would've done it. I wish Sage or Teal had just *told* me.

For the last weeks, even for the better part of the last few months, Teal and Sage have been living their lives and leaving me out of it. They've done nothing that would make me believe anything is going to change in the future. So. I just need to do the same.

I text Teal back, Sounds great! Get back to me with a date

when you can and we'll set something up. These words are Teal's kryptonite because she never gets back about dates, ever.

Next I write Sage, Don't worry about it. I know you're exhausted and busy. This, I really mean. Whenever you have some free time, hit me up and we can get pizza, yum!

The message is as childish as Sage implied I am. But I don't know what else to say. I don't want her to contact me, and if she thinks I've forgiven her, she won't. It'll be just like before.

They each "heart" my messages—neither of them responds with words—and I bite back a bitter laugh.

I sit back on my bed and let my mind wander for a few minutes. It doesn't take much time at all to come to a significant conclusion: In order for me to do what I just said—live my life, leave my sisters out of it—I need to . . . well, get a life to live, right?

I close the text messages and open up a new app, one whose icon is a city skyline in the shape of a heart. *Sign up for today!* the screen announces cheerfully. *And conquer loneliness for tomorrow!*

A few months ago, someone launched this dating app, Matchmakr, for all the largest cities in the Northeast—New York, Philadelphia, D.C., and more. Even though the name kind of makes my skin crawl, I downloaded it the second I heard of it . . . but something a bit like the threat of humiliation kept me from making a profile. Making a profile on a locally used dating app felt a great deal safer. Stupid, really, considering that I will never escape my reputation.

No one from Cranberry would ever want the girl who lied, the antler vagina girl, et cetera ad infinitum. If I'd had my doubts about this before, they all were shattered by Grayson Baker and his cruel, stupid friends.

But no one knows Sky Flores in Baltimore or New York City.

Hell, in those places, even if they did know me, it probably wouldn't faze men from bigger cities. They probably walk by women with far more bizarre backstories than me literally every day. The street musician with her banjo, the living statue painted in white bronze from head to toe—I could be considered in an eccentric category alongside them, you know? I snort as I imagine it: me, standing on the corner of a busy downtown, a sign hanging around my neck: ASK ME ABOUT THE OLD GODS!

I look around and sigh. My room is magnificent, and whenever I spend time in here, I feel so peaceful. I did this. All by myself. And I'm so proud of it.

I'm gainfully employed. My job is fascinating. I love my boss. And I love my daily walks in the woods to be with the crows, the deer, the voles.

But I want something more.

I want someone to prioritize me so deeply, to remember me so consistently, that I never feel like a stranger in my own skin when I'm around them. I snort when I remember there's only been one person who I've fantasized about having that with since ghosthood—and he's just agreed to be my fake friend in exchange for the story of my trauma, basically. My snort quickly becomes a sigh.

The truth is, I want what my sisters each have. A family of my own.

With my heart pounding, I hit the cityscape heart on the app button and tap *Create an Account*.

9

MATCHMAKR: YOUR PROFILE

@salt&seagirl's short biography:

I like to sit on the roof and think.

I think people are far too focused on the past, especially when we are committed to starting over.

I like to chat for a while before meeting.

Get to know @salt&seagirl with Three Random Questions:

Favorite time of day: *dusk*

Favorite dessert: *crepes*

How close are you with your family?

~~*I'm really close with my sisters—*~~

~~*I live with my great aunt—*~~

Not very. I don't have much of a family.

! You have four new messages.

I'M SETTLED AT WORK, IN THE MIDDLE OF READING THROUGH an incredibly boring old text written by some old white dude who has a hard-on for increasing tithes for the poor (literally that's the only thing this book is about. Why the poor need to "absolve" their sins by paying more to the church. Which will . . . keep them even poorer? I swear, men, especially white men, have been the same for all of time: thinking their boring, stupid ideas will automatically captivate willing audiences). When I can't take it anymore, I shelve Sir Thomas Buchanan's hopefully *only* masterpiece in "potential recycling," because Anise told me I can't label books as "literary dumpster fires" in case her boss, or her boss's boss, ever dropped by to check on me and my pile of chocolate wrappers piled high on my technically stolen desk here in the basement. Not that they ever would. But I do it for Anise's peace of mind.

I grab my phone to think about ordering lunch—I'd been too upset to meal prep yesterday, which is what I usually do Sunday nights—when notifications from Matchmakr pop up all over my screen like confetti. "Oh," I say, putting one hand on my stomach. All of a sudden I feel too nervous to be hungry.

I open the app, tap the messages button with the red, vibrating notifications, and deflate.

Hey sexy. Show me that ass, says the first one.

lol what the fuck is a crepe, asks the next.

Chat for a while befor meeting? Typical female. All u do is lead us men on and USE us for FREE. DINNeR.

Block.

When I'd first heard various young women around town talking about how online dating was a shit show nowadays, I . . . somehow thought they were referring to when they actually got to the *dating* part. That the men they'd decided to go out with didn't tip the server or asked them what kind of underwear they had on even before ordering drinks or otherwise displayed some enormous red flag immediately.

I didn't realize until I first tried out a dating app that they meant it was a shit show before *chatting virtually* had even *begun*.

I don't know why I thought a regional app would be any different. I guess, you know, I had imagined that men in big cities would be more patient and sophisticated compared to a high percentage of the men in Cranberry. When I was fourteen, my high school band took a trip to Baltimore to perform at a little amphitheater downtown. I remember almost nothing about the performance itself, but what's seared in my mind is just after it, the moment we stepped out into the city street right as the sun was folded into the sky, the lights in the tall buildings and coffee shops and bakeries all glowing spun gold. The sidewalks were full of people in business-casual wear making their way home for the day. I always thought, surrounded by that many perspectives, each human their own whole universe, it would make someone a great deal more contemplative than say, your average Grayson Baker. But, I was wrong. Everywhere it seems, men are . . . ugh, *men*.

I'm about to clear my inbox when my gaze settles on the fourth message.

So, what do you think about on the roof?

It's from a profile with the name @tryingsomethingnew, which I find instantly intriguing. After all, I'm literally doing the same thing. Trying something new. And scary. And . . . kind of exciting, now that I have one (1) single message that doesn't appear to be remotely creepy or weirdly angry.

A quick look at his profile shows that he's a man who enjoys kayaking and hate-watching reality television (especially house-flipping shows), and he loves potatoes in all forms. Sounds like Not a Murderer so far, unlike literally all the others.

I write back: It's kind of different every time. Sometimes I think about the whales in the ocean . . . because I can see the distant waves from my rooftop. Right? And whales sing in different languages. Or dialects, maybe.

I hit send and then immediately wish I could undo the message. This is already too much of an info dump straight from my brain. I'm supposed to be flirty and sexy, not . . . discussing whale dialects. I'm supposed to be the *opposite* of Weird Girl Who Hangs Out with Wolves in the Forest.

I begin composing an apology when his reply comes through. Have you ever heard about the loneliest whale in the world? He sends an article about "52 Blue," a whale who sings at 52 hertz. Fifty-two hertz is too high a frequency for 52 Blue to be able to connect with any other whales . . . which is lonely indeed. Whales, like humans, are a social species.

Before I can respond, @tryingsomethingnew sends another link. This one is to a recording of 52 Blue's call. I turn up the volume on my cell phone. When I hit play, I can't help myself. My eyes fill with tears.

The Flores women, as far as we can remember, have been born with *gifts*. Supernatural gifts. Magic gifts. Nadia has always said that our gifts come from some Flores woman long ago offending the old gods—a sure way to attract some kind of generational curse. But I don't know how she can know that for sure. It's never made sense to me. How can my connection with those who are more than human be a punishment of some kind? We call them *gifts* because they *feel* like gifts because they *are* gifts.

Nadia says that we must keep our gifts a secret because way back in the day, missionaries called them demonic and tried to beat them out of our ancestors. Which, valid. I can see her reasoning on that.

From what I've been reading, though, our Indigenous ancestors interacted with this world in ways that colonizers would call evil, or uncivilized, or superstitious, or any combination of these. Seems to me, colonizers have *long*, long ago closed themselves off to magic. They insist that everything in the Land of the Living can be explained by some kind of dogmatism, rooted in religion or science, whatever dogma they're into at the moment. And so they refuse to see the world as it is, full of old, *wild* magic.

And when they hear us talking about old, wild magic? It's just misguided superstition! When they happen to get a glimpse of that old, wild magic? It's the work of demons!

What an insanely sad way to live, you know? Where you have to reject the most beautiful things about this life for no reason other than an inherited, cultural fear of What Cannot Be Fully Known.

Because of the violence of colonization, I no longer know our ancestral tribes. I do not know who we were, before the lands of our people became Mexico and then Texas.

But what I do know for certain? The magic of my ancestors still exists, inside all of our bodies.

It's not a punishment from the old gods. It's an act of resistance against the new gods.

Sage's gift is plants. Teal's is the weather. Nadia's gift is psychic abilities, and my grandmother, Amá Sonya, can see ghosts.

But animals are my gift, and that's why I can sense so deeply the emotion of this beautiful, sweet whale . . . the loneliness of swimming, and calling, and calling, with no one answering. No one coming around to see you. To be unseen, even though you are right there, screaming at the top of your strong whale lungs.

This song is the song of ghosts. I would know. I would know.

Instead of typing up that dissertation, I keep my response short. Beautiful and haunting.

Yes is all he writes back.

I try to think of something fascinating to share with him. To move him the way he's already moved me. But instead, my phone chirps and a text pops up from Anise. A strapping young man is here to see you. She adds the eyes emoji, which I know now, after studying an online emoji dictionary after returning to the Land of the Living, indicates her intrigue.

I stare at the message with an extraordinarily confused expression on my face. Who the hell would ever come to see *me*? Especially here at work?

I immediately think of Grayson Baker and everyone who was in on the Antlered Vagina Prank. Would they really try something just as horrific here, at my job? In front of Anise? I rack my brain, feeling like my thoughts have become a jumble just as disorderly as the labyrinth of shelves and books in the basement—but I can't think of anyone else who'd come to see me, unless they were delivering food. Which I hadn't even ordered yet, thanks to @tryingsomethingnew and his distractions.

I take the stairs instead of the elevator, darting around the shelves to spy on whoever he is before he spots me. I blink when he finally comes into view. It's Adam.

He's got on gray jeans paired with a navy Henley, the sleeves rolled up to reveal his veined, thick forearms. A simple leather rucksack the color of toasted pistachios is slung over one shoulder. Black Vans adorn his feet.

The outfit is simple. I would even say a bit uninspired. But he's a beautiful man, so it doesn't matter what he's wearing. His angled, wide face breaks into a stunning smile at something Anise says, and even from here I can see how his blue eyes twinkle like an artist used the same shade to paint a cloudless desert sky or something. He's fresh-shaved and I think he's even had a trim since I've last seen him, the golden red hair on the top of his head just a bit longer than the sides and back.

He glances around and spots me, instantly double-taking. He's kind enough to not ask why I'm hidden behind a shelf, peeking at him like a creeper. "There you are."

I walk over from my spying spot, as casual as I can pretend to be. "Hi. What are . . . you . . . doing here?" I don't mean to make it sound like I've never put words together to form a question before, but my brain has shut down sometime between me being afraid I'm about to be horrifically pranked at work and realizing it's Adam who's here to see me.

He shrugs and gives me a slow smile. "It's lunchtime. Anise was just telling me you haven't taken your break yet."

"Oh." It's all I can think of to say. Is he . . . asking me to lunch? Anise raises her eyebrows at me, like *Are you seriously going to hesitate on going out with him?* I can't help but hesitate, though. He didn't ask me out, is the thing, he just made a few factual statements. How can I infer lunch date intentions if he doesn't actually say those words? Also, although I understand he and I did make an agreement to become illusory friends, this feels a bit sudden. I figured at some point, he and I would sit down with a planner and schedule some Cranberry appearances. Not . . . this.

I ignore her expression. "Well, I'm working, so—"

I'm not really sure how I was planning on ending that sentence, but luckily Anise doesn't let me finish. "Why don't you let this fine young man feed you, Sky? I'll steer the ship while you're away."

I swallow. "But—the ship doesn't really need to be steered, does it? What if you, you know, joined . . ."

She shakes her head and raises her eyebrows, stopping my question without saying a single word. I suspect I'm missing a joke here, but I am much too socially awkward to figure it out with the time frame I'm dealing with. In an ideal world, I'd get at least ten minutes after every conversation to go over everything everyone said a few times, making sure I didn't miss something integral. Like jokes. But unfortunately, no one seems to have time for the introspection I require. Regardless, Anise isn't going to let up on this. I can tell by the exasperated look on her face. So I say to Adam, "Well, okay, but I only have an hour."

"Hour and a half," Anise amends. When I give her a look of complete confusion, she says, "I'm the boss and that's the rule. Some days you get lunch and a half. So go, shoo. Be cute together, somewhere else."

And just like that, my boss forces me to go out on my first friendship outing with Adam Noemi.

10

I AM CURRENTLY SITTING ON THE PASSENGER SIDE OF ADAM'S black Jeep, watching the town whip by in lines of green-gold, cerulean blue, and the bright white of clouds as he pretty much small-talks his face off.

Since I've gotten in here, he's talked about the weather. The traffic. The tune-up his car is scheduled for later this week. And now he's back to the weather. "Did you see, we're getting a late cool front on Thursday, provided the sea doesn't push it east . . ." And then he goes on to explain the history of Earth's air currents.

Why is he telling me all this information? I don't know if I'm so puzzled because I don't understand basic things like small talk, or . . . if this is something else. It's almost like he's *nervous*. At first I refuse to entertain the idea. He's *Adam Noemi*. The talented, successful journalist who's had a thousand adventures all over the world but came back to Cranberry to become a caretaker for William. Beloved by everyone who catches the barest glimpse of him. He would never, not in one million years, behave nervously around *me* because he doesn't have a single reason to.

But what if he is? my mind hisses as he launches into describing what a sand storm is to me in exquisite detail.

Finally, he is in the middle of taking a breath when I ask the first thing that comes to mind, which of course is "Have you ever wondered if foxes have orgasms?"

I guess it's lucky he inhaled, because he spends the next minute in the middle of choking. His face turns pink and I offer him my water bottle because I don't know what else to do. He shakes his head and, after a moment, his breath returns, and then he . . . well, he laughs. He laughs *really* hard, and I can't stop staring at him, because *wow.* If I thought he looked lovely before . . . now he's . . . I can't even explain it. The way his eyes almost shut because they crinkle up so much. The dimples deep in his cheeks.

He's as stunning as a shattered topaz daybreak over the salt-skinned sea.

"You've gotta stop doing that." These are his first words after the laughter dies down.

I glance at him, nervous now. His laugh unnerved me in a way I'm not sure how to process. "Doing what?"

He glances at me, then back to the road. "Knocking the wind out of me." He chuckles lightly. "That was the . . . fourth time. No. Fifth."

I think back to all our interactions and I can only think of three times he could claim I'd knocked the wind out of him. One: when we first met and I was holding wild animals. Two: when I asked him to write a piece on my eight-year-long disappearance. Three: just now, apparently.

Before I can open my mouth to ask about the remaining two, Adam pulls into Gilded Cranberry Golf Club. As far as I know, it's the only country club in town, and I'm certain I'd never be welcome inside. "What the hell are we here for?" I can't hide the dismay, and to be honest, even fear in my voice.

Adam turns and gives me a grin that I assume is intended to be reassuring but is anything but. "You want people to see us together." He clears his throat. "As friends. This is the spot. Trust me."

"But—" I look at the white, colonial-style buildings. They gleam like they don't share this planet with dirt and dust and pollen, the ornate pillars sharp as bayonets. The only kind of landscaping as far as I can see is nonnative grass trimmed to 1.5 inches and two boxwood hedges flanking the entrance that I'm pretty sure are made of plastic. I know Amá Sonya has a membership here, but all that does is confirm that the Gilded Cranberry is exactly the kind of "spot" where I don't belong. "That doesn't look like a fun place."

Adam gives me a smile. "Depends on your idea of fun, sure. But the food is surprisingly really, really good." He parks the car and turns toward me. When he sees my face he says, "Are you okay?"

I shake my head, my eyes wide. I can't speak, or else I'm pretty sure a panic attack is going to come out instead of words. Adam surveys me, then asks another question. "I know this is going to sound kind of weird, but . . . is it okay if I hold your hand?"

It definitely is a very weird thing to say, but the weirdness is distracting me from my panic in a good way. I lift my hand and wave it a little bit, in an effort to say *Go for it* without speaking the words, because I'm still not sure if I can enunciate anything properly right now.

He reaches across the center console, and gently, the way someone might approach a bird with an injured wing, he slowly takes my hand in his. He's so warm. I'm shocked at how much it instantly grounds me. "Sky." He says my name in an especially gravelly voice. "No one's going to be mean to you. I'll make sure of it. I promise."

I have to look away from his face when I nod. "Okay."

"Okay?"

I take a shaky breath. "If anyone can stop folks from being mean to me, it's you."

He smiles then, his eyes lighting up. "You really trust me?"

I furrow my brow. "What? No."

At my response, Adam throws his head back and laughs. I take the opportunity to wriggle my hand from his, feeling a bit stupid that I miss touching his warm palm. "Do you always say what's on your mind?" he asks.

I've always been a direct communicator, but sometimes I wonder if my time between the Land of the Dead and the Land of the Living during my supernatural sleep made me less inclined to dance around the meanings of what I want to say. Instead of explaining all this, I shrug. "What's the alternative?"

"Touché." We both look at the colonial monster-face building and he adds, "We can go somewhere else. Get some hot dogs by the beach where no one can see us. That would be just fine, I promise. We can do a big public outing another day."

"No. Let's get this over with." I'm surprised at how sure I sound. "I really hate hot dogs, anyway."

Gilded Cranberry Country Club has four enormous wooden doors up front, between the immaculate white columns that look pre-offended at the idea of moths, or beetles, or any other sort of bugs crawling upon them. "This looks like my grandmother's house," I say as we walk up.

"Yeah? Is she the president or something?"

"She thinks she is. That's for sure."

I don't have a huge family in town. It's me and my sisters, Nadia, and Amá Sonya. Even though I live with Nadia, I just . . . don't see her much. She's supposed to retire this year and for some reason that means she's picking up more shifts than ever at the Cranberry Wood State Park Welcome Center, especially now that the center is open for longer hours while tourist season is underway. When she's not at work, she's at St. Theresa's Catholic Church for Wanderers and Pilgrims.

Some of my memories pre-fall are fuzzy, but Sage says that Nadia's always been this way. Distant, off in her own life, not really paying any attention to any of us. I can't remember it. Probably because my needs were being met by Sage, and I just didn't even think about where she was getting her needs met.

And then there's Amá Sonya, my maternal grandmother. I feel kind of pathetic admitting this, but . . . Amá Sonya leaves me on read *a lot*. She has no problem bantering with—well, more like insulting, her love language—my sisters, but with me? She runs out of steam fast. I say the wrong things to her, I know it. But I don't know what the right things to say to my grandmother are anymore. So I think she ignores me mostly because I am too awkward for her to deal with. That, and to Amá Sonya, the most important thing is her reputation. She doesn't like to be seen with me because then the town is reminded that I, the Local Feral Girl, am *her* granddaughter. And think of the pearl-clutching that would ensue!

But you know what? That's fine. Because it means I am making my *own* life now, and I don't have to try and get in touch with my grandmother anymore, hoping for her to show a crumb of interest in me. I'm trying something new, just like my new chat friend, @tryingsomethingnew.

I take a deep breath as Adam holds one of the doors open for me and I'm greeted with freezing cold air-conditioning.

Adam tells the check-in desk that I'm his guest. One of them, a woman about his age, does a double take when she sees me, but to her credit, all she does is smile and nod politely. "Ready?" Adam asks as he holds out his arm to escort me to the dining room.

We have to walk down this crazy long hallway first, with windows cut out on one side, pouring long rectangles of butter-yellow light on the other, making it seem like we're in a horror film. "I feel like I could be hunted for sport here," I whisper to him, and when he bursts out laughing, I can't help but smile as I catalog the crinkles on the outer edges of his eyes and the crescent shapes of his dimples. Guy's got a hell of a laugh, I'll give him that. No wonder women line up to be his flavor of the month.

The dining room is also well-lit with a domed ceiling, cream-colored walls, and tables covered in cloths with a subtle floral print in mint. It's about half-full, I'd say, which maybe makes sense since we are here for a rather late lunch. A few people peek at us from behind menus and wineglasses, but I guess folks here are too polite to say things like *Hey! There's that Weird Lying Bird Girl!* loud enough for me to hear.

After taking the seat Adam pulls out for me, I hold up the menu, printed in a spiral, cursive font, and murmur, "Everyone is looking at us," in a bit of a singsong tone.

"They're wondering how lucky I am to be here with such a beautiful woman."

I give him my most impressive glare. "You're not here *with* me. We're supposed to be friends, remember?" I glance around again. "Oh, for the old gods' sake, you're right. They are thinking you're *with* me, aren't they?"

Adam winces. "Yeah. I didn't consider that, actually."

I shake my head. "You definitely did not."

Adam glances at his own menu. "Would it help if I stood and announced that we're just friends?"

I consider it for a few seconds, then shake my head. "I imagine it would seem like we are protesting too much. Better to just—" I gesture to the menu. "Eat something and then run out before we end up in all the local Facebook groups."

Adam chuckles softly to himself.

"What is it?" I ask.

He shakes his head. "Nothing. Just, you saying what's on your mind, as usual. It's . . ." He takes a sip of the ice water from his goblet. "It's refreshing."

I stare at him for a long moment, wondering if he's being sarcastic. Usually people really don't like me saying what's on my mind, as he puts it. This trait isn't new. I didn't wake up in the woods with a random penchant for sucking at socializing. I've always sucked at it. Seems to me that everyone else got a handbook called *How to Correctly Interact with Other Humans* at birth, but I lost my copy *real* early on. By the time I was in high school, I had a group of friends who seemed to appreciate my "quirkiness," as they called it, but they all refuse to speak to me now, so I can't let myself hold on to that momentary acceptance of my personality as proof that I'm actually likable as a person. Taking all this into account, I assume that Adam is just being nice to me with his comment. "What a kind thing to say," I respond robotically, and then promptly call the nearest server over, because I'm so hungry, I'm certain my stomach is about to eat itself.

Adam orders brisket with corn bread and macaroni and cheese. I get the blackened mahi mahi with coleslaw and hush puppies.

As soon as the server rushes away, an older white woman in a peach suit and pearl earrings approaches. "Adam! Why, I haven't seen you around here in ages. How are you doing, kid?"

Adam stands to greet her and shake her husband's hand. He introduces me (emphasizing the word *friend*), and they are both kind enough to pretend like they hadn't heard of Sky Flores the Town Liar before. They seem to be really obsessed with him, but given he's the closest thing Cranberry has to a celebrity, I guess this is probably normal. They don't even leave when the server brings our food. Adam redirects their attention to the clock, announces that he and I don't have much time and have to get to eating, and then once they leave, he sits back down and it's as though they'd never arrived.

Adam and I eat in blissful, quiet peace for a little while, and then he puts down his fork and claps his hands together while staring intently at me. "So how do you want to do this?"

"Do . . . this," I repeat. It's not specific enough, and my mind wanders and settles on a conclusion as to what he's referencing that sounds unlikely, but I say it anyway, lowering my voice to a whisper. "You wanna dine and dash?"

Adam snorts so loud, I'm pretty sure an elderly woman behind him clutches her pearls. He covers his mouth to hide his laugh and I take a sip of my water, smiling, trying to look like I intended the joke.

"Me interviewing you," he clarifies finally.

"Right." I lower my voice. This lunch has been going so well, so far. I don't want to ruin it by announcing I'm the weird animal girl. Even if no one hears, it feels like it would be in the air. Like it would surround us and somehow people would see the invisible words and remember they're supposed to hate me. "I've never been interviewed before. So why don't you tell me what you're thinking?"

"Well, I was thinking it would be good to set up maybe three to four appointments. For the first one, I'll just ask you about your background, and your family. Nothing invasive, just light conversation— What is it? What's the matter?"

I must be making a face of disgust at the idea of a whole *appointment* made up of what sounds just like *small talk*. "What? Nothing." I smile. "That sounds great."

"Right." He eyes me, clearly disbelieving. But when I don't respond, he narrows his eyes.

"It's getting kinda late, isn't it?" I ask, pretending like I don't understand his nonverbal communication to explain why I seem so uncomfortable with this appointment.

Adam checks his watch. "Shit, you're right. I should probably drive you back to work soon. Are you working tomorrow? Why don't you stop by Gramps's afterward?"

I blink. That doesn't feel like enough time to prepare, but could someone like me really prepare for anything related to acute socializing? "Oh sure. Tomorrow. After work. That sounds perfect."

We talk a bit more as we finish up our plates and wait for the check, with Adam driving the conversation like in the car. Which I appreciate this time. It's not that I don't want to talk with him anymore . . . it's that I'm . . . well, completely overwhelmed.

I went out in public. To the damn *country club*. Two days ago, if anyone had asked me, "What's the one place The Girl Who Lied mustn't ever go, ever," I honestly would have said Gilded Cranberry, maybe tied with accompanying Amá Sonya to one of her HOA meetings. Country clubs—and HOAs, for that matter—think they're some kind of hallmarks of civilization. I am a wild witch who speaks with crows. I always imagined I would get the most verbal abuse in a place like that, even if it were disguised in polite, Southern hospitality, which is often worse than anything direct, because I never know that people are being mean to me until well after the fact.

But nothing like that happened at all. Because of Adam.

I stare at him hard as he chuckles with the server, noting that the freckles on his left cheek look a little bit like they're in the shape of a crescent moon.

What must it be like, to be so admired and likable that people even obey your unannounced rule of *Don't be mean to this weird woman I'm with*? Can I speak with Carolina wrens? Yes. Can I even begin to imagine the kind of power Adam wields? Not in a universe's lifetime.

After lunch, when we reach my work, I can't help myself. I turn toward him, put a hand on his forearm, and say, "Thank you for being nice to me today."

He slides his hand down my arm, over my wrist, until he's cupping my palm, my fingers resting gently against his skin. The sensation is alarming in a way I find intriguing. I decide that's probably a good sign to let go. He's watching me so closely, his eyes as sharp and glittery as seaside rocks, and I don't know what else to say, so I end with this fine farewell: "Um. Bye."

He doesn't leave until I'm safely in the building, and it's sincerely disgusting how much I like it.

11

@tryingsomethingnew: Hey salt girl. You still up?

@salt&seagirl: Yeah? What's up? You want to send me some more whale songs so that I can cry or something?

@tryingsomethingnew: Did the whale's song really make you cry?

@salt&seagirl: Yeah. I was at work so I couldn't bawl or anything.

@tryingsomethingnew: Ngl, it made me tear up too.

@salt&seagirl: So you're not one of those tough guys, then?

@tryingsomethingnew: I'm not tough at all. I'm very soft and gooey, in fact.

@salt&seagirl: like a half-baked cinnamon roll?

@tryingsomethingnew: With extra icing, even.

@tryingsomethingnew: If you were a dessert, what would you be?

@salt&seagirl: Hmm. Hmm. Let me think. . . . A tomato pie!

@tryingsomethingnew: Tomato pie is definitely not dessert haha.

@salt&seagirl: Exactly. People kind of find me surprising, or weird, and no one chooses me for dessert ☹

@tryingsomethingnew: I've kind of had the opposite problem, to be honest. Too many folks trying to choose me.

@salt&seagirl: Too many hands taking the poor cinnamon rolls.

@tryingsomethingnew: Exactly. And now I feel kind of empty. Like I need to whip up some new dough and make myself all over again.

@salt&seagirl: So now you're . . . drumroll . . . trying something new?

@tryingsomethingnew: Now I'm trying something new 😊

THE NEXT MORNING, I AWAKEN TO BIRDSONG. I KEEP MY EYES closed as I identify the sources: Carolina wrens. Cardinals. A distant American bluebird, chirping to nothing more than the joyful return of light. It's strange to think about sometimes, how we humans, and most other animals, must sleep regularly. We become vulnerable by necessity. We visit the World of Dreams, which Nadia says is a gateway to all the other worlds that exist.

The World of Dreams feels an awful lot like being a ghost to me, so sometimes I awaken frightened that I can't touch anything. That no one but Sage can hear me. I hate it when that happens. Right now, I place my hand upon my chest, where my heart drums slowly, rhythmically. I once read that the first sound we know is of the heartbeat of our mother. This is true for any creature with a heart, I think. I could not feel my own heart when I was a ghost, and so the pulse of it beneath my palm is a small comfort. I am still firmly a part of the Land of the Living.

I'm sure someone would say my occasional need to touch things, to go through objects or feel the warmth of my own skin in a panic, is some kind of trauma response. But I just don't foresee a mental health professional truly understanding that I really was a ghost—and that it wasn't some elaborate delusion or hallucination. So for now, I've got to just deal with the fact that sometimes I freak out and need to determine that I'm actually alive.

After washing my face, I pick up my phone and see texts from my sisters. Hey, how are you doing? Wanna get lunch sometime next week? Teal asks. I was wondering if you'd like to see Oak . . . maybe we could go to a park? writes Sage.

I roll my eyes. It's obvious they had some kind of "Let's Make Ourselves Feel Better by Discussing Sky" meeting. There's no other reason they'd both text me at once, when I've been trying to get them to write me regularly, at least *something* more than the brief hi, what's up, let's do something, oh okay, let me know when you're free every three weeks.

I think about @tryingsomethingnew. We'd chatted till well past midnight last night, and I'm already starting to get warm fuzzies just from *thinking* about him. Which, I know, I know. I'm not stupid. It's only been one day, and he may well be a ninety-year-old man typing from the shared desktop in his assisted living community. But it's just been *so long* since someone has wanted to get to know me. Without all this Eight Years of Sleep in an Oak Tree baggage in the way.

Even when I readjusted to the World of the Living and got closer with my sisters two years ago, everything that came from them was through an obvious veil of concern. They used what they thought were sneaky questions to make sure I was doing things like eating and going to bed at a normal hour and not spending too much time in the woods. They also kept checking in on my mental health, knowing how the town always treated me.

Which I appreciate. I do. And I understand completely that they have good intentions. But the problem is, their well-meant concern kept getting in the way of genuine connection between us. And that's how I became a burden to them, rather than their third sister they could just hang out with. If you can't be with someone without trying to figure out if they are on the verge of a crisis of some kind, then it's stressful to be around them. That's how someone becomes a burden. That's how *I* became a burden.

I can't take care of you and my child at the same time.

Even just reading these texts alone, I can tell they don't want to actually hang out with me. These are just obligatory check-ins. Guilty offers to hang out. If I took either of them up on it, I would feel awkward the whole time, wondering if they were counting the minutes till they could get to the more important stuff in their lives—their work. Their families. I would rather take a nap in the woods with Coffee the fox.

Instead of telling them no, which will just cause more upheaval than I currently have the energy to deal with, I decide to casually text with them back and forth, acting like I'm settling on a date for each of their propositions.

When Sage suggests next Thursday, I write, "Oh no, I'm supposed to be getting lunch with Teal that day."

When Teal suggests next Sunday, I write, "Oh, I'm going to the park with Sage and Oak that day."

And then I tell them both that I have to get ready for work, and I will text them back later, to finalize the plans.

I light a candle on my dresser, one I made myself from Teal's old candle-making supplies she gave me. It's nothing special. I melted the golden beeswax and poured it in a mason jar after fixing a wick inside it.

But with the flame undulating with my breath, I ask its smoke to take my prayer to the old gods. I apologize for lying to my sisters but explain that I need time without people limiting me with their ideas on who I am and what I should be doing. I ask the old gods to keep my sisters confused for just a little while. I know I need to tell them, eventually, all the ways they've been hurting me, but I'm not ready yet. This is another way I feel unlike everyone else—I need *so much time* to process things, it feels like the events are ancient history by the time I figure out how I even feel about them in the first place!

I allow the candle to burn as long as possible, blowing it out only just before I leave for work. I watch the smoke form into what appears to be a woman with the head of a bird before dissipating into the morning light coming through the little windows like poured honey.

@tryingsomethingnew: What are you doing, Salt Sea Girl? Are you in the ocean right now?

@salt&seagirl: I sure am. Swimming with the whales as we speak. What's up?

@tryingsomethingnew: Just wondering where you are in the Northeast. Not that you have to tell me, of course. I'm just curious how far away you are.

@salt&seagirl: Oh, this little seaside town in Virginia. *really* little, haha.

@tryingsomethingnew: Oh wow. Same, actually

@salt&seagirl: You live in a small seaside town in Virginia?

@tryingsomethingnew: Yeah, I do. I'm sure you haven't heard of it. Well, maybe you have, considering your proximity. But it's a little town called Cranberry.

@salt&seagirl: ARE YOU FREAKING KIDDING ME

@salt&seagirl: I LIVE IN CRANBERRY!

@tryingsomethingnew: You're kidding

@salt&seagirl: I'm totally, totally not. I swear over the ancestors I'm not.

@tryingsomethingnew: That's . . . wow. Quite the coincidence.

@tryingsomethingnew: I guess that makes us meeting sometime easier. Whenever you're ready for that, if ever.

@salt&seagirl: Well, I'm not ready now, but who knows? You know?

@tryingsomethingnew: I know 😊

Finding out that @tryingsomethingnew also lives in Cranberry was a bit exciting at first, but after taking some time to process the information, I realize it's not such a great development after all. The chances of him knowing Sky Flores, and thinking she's a freak, have officially skyrocketed. This all means he definitely cannot know who I am now.

Between that and the whole annoying texting shenanigans that went down with my sisters, my mood is impossibly sour for the rest of the day. As a treat, I allow myself one hour to investigate the potential creepy Cranberry witch cult, even though it means going into the new library building and navigating stares and whispers so I can get my hands on various history books about the town.

I can only relax once I'm alone in my dungeon, the newly checked-out book pile in front of me on my beloved stolen desk. I breathe out a sigh of relief as I sit, open my secret drawer, pull out my journal and a handful of chocolates, and begin to read.

After about thirty minutes, it's becoming clear to me that there's something weird about the church. St. Theresa's Catholic Church for Wanderers and Pilgrims, to be specific.

It's the place I, Teal, and Sage were basically raised in. Half my childhood memories are connected with that spot, from attending Mass multiple times a week, to being forced to attend Bible studies and confirmation classes. We baked for the bake sales and put together Thanksgiving dinners for the unhoused and sang in the choir.

According to one rather large and unwieldy tome, there used to be rumors that St. Theresa's was haunted. Maybe those rumors still exist, but I'm assuming they're not as prevalent, because for all the time I've spent there, I'd never heard about it, not once. But right here, in *Cranberry: A Brief History through the Ages*, it begins by talking about the voices people can hear through the church walls, and random thumping and banging underfoot, as though someone, or many someones, were trapped below.

It also says that the church's construction was delayed for nearly a decade, with contracts being canceled as well as project managers just up and quitting for seemingly no good reason. In 1902, the town's mayor had even canceled the construction, only for it to resume the following year. I don't know if any of this is relevant to my investigation, but these facts are interesting enough to note in my little research scrapbook. They might make sense later, or they may never contribute to my side project. Either way, I'm absorbed just enough that my heart doesn't hurt as bad when I think about my sisters. Even if none of this comes to fruition, the effort is worth it for the distraction alone.

We need to talk.

I receive this cryptic message from Amá Sonya on my way home from work. It definitely makes me pause, considering I haven't heard from my grandmother in about five weeks, after I'd given up on asking her to brunch. I know for a fact she brunches with Teal once or twice a month, and has been for the last decade or so, but naturally the embarrassing granddaughter gets left on read for such a suggestion.

I'd been thinking I should change into something better for my meeting with Adam when I get home—my top is currently wrinkled to hell after a day bending over to grab stacks of books from the way-bottom shelves—but now I'm wondering if my prayer to the old gods backfired and instead of leaving me alone for a bit, the whole family is currently intent on tracking my whereabouts.

"Fuck." The curse comes from under my breath when I see that Amá is already parked in my normal spot at Nadia's. She's at the door, and thankfully Nadia is home, because Amá is already inside by the time I've driven by the front of the house.

I drive around the block once more, wondering what the hell I should do. Normal people, under normal circumstances, would just say *I'm sorry, Amá, but I already have plans. Let's meet up on the weekend instead.* But normal people do not have intrusive, entitled bitches for grandmothers.

If I went inside that house right now, Amá Sonya would sit me down and force me to have whatever kind of talk she thinks I owe her, and if I were in a hurry, she'd make it last longer. An hour. Hours, even. It's too damn stressful for me to deal with right now when I'm already stupidly nervous about seeing Adam again so soon.

I decide to leave my car parked on Basque Street, the one right next to Catalina. Then, dressed in a black tweed pencil skirt, black leather kitten heels, and a very wrinkled pale turquoise button-down top, I cut through people's side yards to get to William's backyard.

Coffee, the fox, follows me, darting all around me like the cutest one-man security team. "Hey, you. Where have you been? Visiting your cliffside girlfriend?" He does this growl-mew in response. Kind of a *none of your business*, but also *yes* at the same time. I cover my mouth as I laugh, and he's got the biggest dog-like grin on his face. Why can't talking with humans be this easygoing?

I'm now in William's side yard, and I hide behind what I'm pretty sure are some elderberry bushes, trying to spy on Nadia and Sonya across the street. Another text chimes in. Where are you, nieta? You can't be too far . . . It's like I'm being taunted by a damn serial killer.

She texts again, and this time, it's a blurry photo of me and Adam having lunch at the country club. I roll my eyes. *That's* what she wants to talk about. She wants to interrogate me to see if I'm dating Adam, or to ask when the wedding is, probably. Adam's very high on the social currency in Cranberry. My imaginary betrothal to him would make Amá Sonya basically froth at the mouth. She *loves* social currency.

"Sky?"

I turn and see Adam leaning over from the side of the house, a puzzled expression on his face. He looks kind of adorable when confused—his blue eyes narrowed, his beautiful head tilted—but the problem is, he's in full view of Nadia's house. "Shh," I hiss. "Come here. Or else she'll see you and take you away to her gingerbread house."

Adam's brows furrow even more deeply.

"Come quick! Or she'll put you in her oven and eat you for dinner!"

"Okay. Okay. I'm coming." He jogs over and squeezes in next to me behind the elderberries. "So there's a crazy lady loose on the street, is what you're saying."

"Exactly. My grandmother." I narrow my eyes at Nadia's. "You got any binoculars?"

"Not on my person."

I sigh. "That's okay."

We sit in silence for a few minutes, just listening to a distant propeller plane, the sound of our own breaths, the crickets beginning to chirp in a humming symphony. Finally Adam turns to me and says, "Care to explain what's going on?"

I roll my eyes. "My grandmother found out you and I went to the country club yesterday. So now she's probably planning our wedding. If we run into her right now, we'll be walking away with a huge-ass diamond ring on my finger and our engagement set to be announced for tomorrow's paper."

Adam chuckles. "Okay. Good call on the . . . ah. Hiding?"

"Yeah. We're hiding."

Adam turns to me. "Is your family always like this?"

I shake my head. "Planning someone else's whole life for them, you mean? Only her, really, and only when she feels like it's going to make her look better, you know?"

Adam nods and frowns. "Yeah. I know all about that, actually."

I turn to him and for some reason, it only just now hits me how close we are. How there are flecks of warm silver in the blue of his eyes that I'd never noticed before. The caramel-colored freckles on his nose are almost in the shape of a seven-pointed star, to thematically match the crescent of freckles on his cheek. I blink when I realize he's watching me, too. But his focus is on my lips.

He clears his throat and tears his gaze away. "When is it safe to go inside?"

"I'd give it a few more minutes, honestly." The old bat is nothing if not persistent.

"Okay. Well. Why don't we start, then, since I had planned on asking you a few questions while we were out this evening." He pulls out his phone and pulls up a recorder app. "You don't mind?"

I shake my head. This whole thing with Amá Sonya has distracted me enough that I barely feel any of the nerves that were bothering me so badly earlier. Plus, there's something easier about being outside, curled up against elderberry bushes, instead of sitting at the kitchen table, Adam asking questions like I'm at a job interview or something.

"Why don't we start at the beginning?" Adam suggests.

I nod. "Okay." I take a deep breath. The beginning. I can do this. "In the beginning, there were nothing but gods. Gods and this earth."

Adam blinks. "Okay. I was thinking more like . . . when were you born, what was your childhood like . . ."

I frown. "You didn't specify, though. How was I supposed to know what beginning you meant if you didn't specify?" I shake my head. "Let me finish this beginning first."

Adam holds up a hand to indicate surrender. "Okay. I'm listening."

All around us, the earth settles into some kind of deep, almost-twilight golden peace. The sun is setting, lighting us up in goldenrod and marigold and native multibloom sunflowers. The pollinators feasting on elderberry blooms buzz all around us, making me feel like I'm about to shiver or something. I take another deep breath. "In the beginning, there were nothing but gods. Gods and this earth. This is the oldest world, by the way. The World of the Gods. Then the gods decided—I'm not sure why, maybe they were bored just hanging out by themselves, being mighty and powerful all the time—but the gods decided to make all kinds of worlds. Each of these worlds required a counterpart. So they made the World of the Living—our world—and then they also had to make the World of the Dead. They made the World of Spirits, so they had to make a world of ghosts. A world of shadows required a world of light.

"A long time ago, one of our ancestors—I mean *my* ancestors, not the universal 'our'—made a deal with a god. She wanted to travel the worlds freely, but in return, she had to give an offering to the gods. The offering was a tiny sliver of community."

"A sliver of community. So what did that look like?" Adam asks. He is riveted, and to be honest, so am I. I've never heard this tale like this before. Yes, I *have* heard it in bits and pieces from Nadia my whole life, save eight years. But I am certain the ancestors are telling it through me now, with the fullness and details coming upon me as though they were being uploaded into my brain *The Matrix*–style.

I shrug. "I'm not sure. Because we only know about the offering through its counterpart—what she got in return."

"And what was that?"

I turned to Adam. "She was given a gift. We don't know what the first gift of this Flores woman looked like, but each female descendant has a gift." I swallow. "I haven't gotten permission to share anyone's gifts with you. But my gift is animals. Which you have already seen." I turn away from the intensity of his gaze. It's also making me want to shiver, as though his attention has become one thousand bumblebees, giving me goose bumps without touching me at all. "In exchange for our gifts, we give up community. Because we cannot tell anyone about the gifts. This is the rule elders have imposed on Flores women for generations. For us, it was Nadia who hammered that into us. We can't tell. I realize I am breaking that agreement now, but . . ."

"I appreciate you sharing this with me," Adam says. It's a formal response but there is awe in his voice. I have a feeling like we are both surrounded by ancestors now, like maybe his have arrived to listen to mine. It's making the words I'm saying weave a kind of magic around us, through us, as though each letter has become an iridescent spider, weaving connections neither of us can see but both of us can *feel.*

"My great-aunt Nadia says that white people always want to do bad things to brown girls with gifts, thus them needing to be hidden away. But because our gifts are an innate part of us, we also have to hide this essential part of who we are from everyone else. And so we can only truly trust each other to be our true selves." I shake my head, looking at the distant sunset. The clouds are now a strange mix of red and gray, feeling almost foreboding. "And if we can't trust each other, then we have no one."

Adam lays his hand out, palm up. It's an offering. Though I cannot understand why I would want to, I take it. His calluses are rough against my soft skin, his hand warm and big and enveloping mine completely.

"What made you decide to tell me about the gifts, Sky?" he asks, staring at our hands.

I turn toward him, looking at his star-freckled nose. I am as honest as I can be. "I don't know."

I don't tell him this, but if I had to take a guess, it would be that I'm so fucking tired of being lonely all the time.

12

WHEN I FINALLY GET HOME FROM ADAM'S, AMÁ SONYA is long gone. She left one last text, You can't hide forever, once again giving me the feeling that my grandmother is a creepy criminal rather than a snobby, luxe designer–wearing busybody.

I feel a mix between energized and unsettled after spending the entire evening with Adam. We'd gone inside and kept more of a distance from one another as we chatted more about the specific beginning he'd first wanted of me—when I was born, what my childhood was like, how it was growing up with Nadia, Sage, and Teal in Cranberry. But I feel like a part of me is still somehow hiding with him under the curved, white-blooming elderberry bushes—too close to him and yet not close enough. It's the "not close enough" that's bothering me. Why would I want to be closer to him than that—a step away from basically being pressed against his long, lean body? And yet the idea of it makes *my* body hum as though Teal decided to toss a lightning bolt right into my spine.

What I do know is that these thoughts are dangerous. They

are the strange-shaped, glittery footprints in the woods that seem intriguing but lead nowhere good. I need to cut it out and distract myself, fast.

I pull up Matchmakr and frown when I see there are no new messages from @tryingsomethingnew. I've gotten some new messages, in general—more of the usual perverted bullshit, but none from him.

"Well," I tell myself. "He can't start all the conversations, can he?"

I sit back on my bed and try to think of an opener that's both philosophical and mind-blowing. But none of the questions that come to me are either of these things. The most "mind-blowing" one is *Have you ever eaten ass before?* Which I am legitimately curious about! But I don't think either of us is ready for that kind of a conversation. Or at least I'm not. I jumped the gun with sexting with Grayson Baker on the local dating app, and look where that got me.

Finally, I type Have you ever been in love?

As soon as I hit the send button, I regret it immediately. When I ask questions, it's because I want to know the answers. But I've discovered that many people think questions have all kinds of hidden meanings and agendas. My mind goes through every possibility I can think of, as far as his interpreting this question. The worst suggestion that arrives is that I sound like a lovestruck teenager, hoping he'll confess that he's realized he's in love with *me*.

I'm so horrified, I wonder frantically if I can unsend it and ask him about eating ass instead.

I toss my phone on the bed, stand, and rush to the bathroom. I brush my teeth. I smooth sunshine-colored serums and grape-scented moisturizer on my face. I slip on a ruby-red satin nightgown

Teal left behind when she moved in with her husband, Carter. It's the softest article of clothing I own, which means it's quite high in value with regard to my whole wardrobe. Sure, I own a Chanel suit, and a vintage Hermès pencil skirt, but *softness* is currency for me, as far as materials that must be held against my skin. I'm constantly removing hanging tags, and sometimes have smooth liners put in dresses by a tailor Amá Sonya frequents, all so they can be wearable. It's a treasure when a piece of clothing is perfectly silky as is, no adjustments needed.

I get in bed, brace myself, and pick up the phone again. Dammit, there's a new notification from @tryingsomethingnew.

I wince, tapping the app open. But his response isn't at all what I had feared.

@tryingsomethingnew: I really want you to like me, so I want to say yes. But I'm afraid not. I've had a lot of flings, to be honest, nothing serious or long enough to develop those kinds of feelings.

@salt&seagirl: Oh. Well, I'd rather you be honest with me than tell me what you think I want to hear, anyway. I've never been in love, either. Um . . . do you ever want to be in love? You think?

@tryingsomethingnew: Hmm. I used to think not, based on my parents' really fucked-up relationship. But after spending a lot of time with my grandparents, I think that if I could have what they had . . . yeah, falling in love sounds like it could be really amazing. You?

I sink into the bed even deeper, wondering if I should be honest with him. I don't want to scare him off. But it would be hypocritical of me to say I appreciate his truthfulness and then refrain from it myself. I take a deep breath and begin typing.

@salt&seagirl: My sisters have recently met and married the loves of their lives, and I've been wanting the same for myself. Their partners like . . . support them. Laugh at their jokes. They really *see* them for who they are, you know? I would love that.

@tryingsomethingnew: Yeah, seeing a relationship work in the way it's meant to. It definitely makes you long for something that's always felt out of reach for one reason or another.

@salt&seagirl: Yes!! That is the perfect way to describe it! It feels out of reach, especially considering—I swallow and make another commitment to the truth—you know, that my life has been really strange, and that's ultimately made *me* really strange, and all of that mixed with my imperfections and faults . . . imagining someone not just accepting all of that but also *loving* it, because it's a part of me? *faints* lol

@tryingsomethingnew: That is definitely the important part. Being loved fully, even the strangest parts, the pieces of you that no one else seems to understand. Too often relationships begin with an idealized version of the other, not the truth of who they are, you know?

@salt&seagirl: What makes you strange? If you don't mind my asking?

@tryingsomethingnew: Oh . . . let's see. Hmm. Sometimes I watch people and participate in poor man's prophecy. I don't know if you've heard of that before, but I listen for whatever snippets of conversation I can hear, then I try and interpret them as fortune-telling. I don't know anyone else who does that, tbh. What about you, what makes you strange?

@salt&seagirl: I DO THAT TOO OMG

@salt&seagirl: I read about it in an old book at my work! Ancient Greeks used to practice this form of fortune-telling! I knew my sister was pregnant because a lady at the store was clutching a bunch of herbs (that share my sister's name) and joking about them all having babies (because they were harvested with a bunch of sprouts!)

@tryingsomethingnew: That's amazing. I've never heard anything quite that accurate and specific before.

@tryingsomethingnew: Still, this is quite the coincidence. Seems like we're strange peas in a pod then, you and me.

@salt&seagirl: 🙂

A FEW DAYS LATER, AFTER GOING THROUGH WHAT FELT LIKE AN endless pile of books for categorizing for the Codex Restoration Project at work, I decide, as a little treat, to get some Oreos and a too-sweet hazelnut coffee from the vending machines in the main building, and then settle back into my dungeon, opening my super secret desk drawer filled with evidence that Cranberry has hosted and may still very well host some type of cult.

I pull out my scrapbook and look over the materials with a pen in hand. I spent so long gathering them that I really haven't allowed myself to figure out what I'm looking at, exactly. So now I begin making a list of patterns:

POTENTIAL EVIDENCE OF CRANBERRY WITCH(?) CULT

1. *Woman-centered*
2. *The number thirteen (as far as women in cult)*
3. *Meeting in woods and other natural spots*
4. *Nudity (?)*
5. *Some type of connection to St. Theresa's*

I tap my pen and read more, trying to pull out something, anything else, from my collection of scattered newspaper clippings, but nothing pops through for me, even after going over the articles multiple times. Only two newspaper pieces mention that there were *thirteen* women discovered doing some type of witchy shenanigans. A couple say that they were in the woods, but about three more reference the church. One bystander in one article claims the women were "nude," which, maybe, but probably it was wishful thinking on his part is my guess.

I pull out my phone and open the Matchmakr app. @tryingsomethingnew and I have chatted literally every day, and dare I say, he's beginning to actually feel like a friend now. I haven't had a sincere, nonrelated friend since before I fell, to be honest.

I thought my sisters and I were friends again . . . and if we were, I'd be texting them about my new love interest to see what they thought of him. Hell, I'd be texting them to get their ideas on what this cult business is all about. But they're busy with their super grown-up lives and probably wouldn't want to hear about it, anyway.

So instead I type to this anonymous man, who I still know could actually be someone's great-grandfather, chatting me up between bingo games. You ever heard of a cult being discovered, or even, like, referred to here in town?

He responds almost immediately. Umm . . . not that I can recall. Why? What's up, you just got recruited or something?

I laugh and then type out a short summary of what I've been looking at.

Hmm. I know the church has a kind of weird history. I remember doing some research on it, back in the day, for a project related to an old job.

Oh, I hope this is as promising as it sounds. I feel giddy as I type back. Yeah? What kind of history?

I'm trying to remember. It's been like a decade, lol . . .

I wait very impatiently as he collects his thoughts, tapping my pointy boot against the corner of my desk leg. So the weirdest thing I remember is something about its architecture that doesn't add up. Stairs that go nowhere . . . a couple of doors in weird spots that won't open. I contacted the diocese at one point, and they pretty much attributed it to confused builders from when it was built. It was kind of a dead end.

Holy crap, this is seriously amazing! Your dead end could be my new lead. Thanks for telling me that.

You're welcome, my friend 😊

Even though I was just literally so excited to think of this guy as my friend . . . him calling me "friend" feels a bit like lead's been plopped right into my belly. Does that make sense or what? I'm glad he's my friend, but I don't want him to think of me as *just* a friend, either. *He's an elderly man, possibly*, I remind myself. *He's probably married with, like, twelve great-grandchildren*. I swallow and wonder way too hard on what to write back—I'm glad we're friends. Are you a great-granddaddy, perchance?—when my phone pings with a text. It's Adam.

I frown when my stomach fills with a thousand pale blue-winged moths. "Stop it," I hiss to my midsection. The way my body responds to Adam keeps troubling me. Butterflies should be for @tryingsomethingnew, not the man who thought I was trying to scam his grandfather out of house and home. Sure, he's apologized, and he has been lovely since, but he hasn't once acted particularly interested in me. *Except when he stared at your lips the other day*, my mind helpfully supplies, *as though he wanted to kiss you*. I throw my head back, suppress a shriek of frustration, close my eyes, count to ten, and look down to open up Adam's text.

What are you doing tomorrow?

What does he mean, what am I doing tomorrow? It's Friday. I'm bringing food to your place for William. You can have some if you want.

Let's hang out before then. I'll pick you up?

Oh no. My stomach betrays me immediately. The little blue moths have multiplied by about one hundred billion now, making me feel like they are able to lift me in flight from in there.

I pull up my group chat with my sisters. They would know what to tell me. I'm sure Sage, ever the romantic, would encourage me to flirt with Adam and tell him about the effect he's having on me in some noncreepy manner. Teal would have the best advice, though, which would guide me on how to immediately drop all these sensations that indicate I might (still) have a crush on him.

But they haven't written in a good long while, which I should be happy about. It's what I wanted. I did a whole spell and everything! And yet seeing the lack of updates makes me want to suppress yet another shriek of frustration.

I close out the group chat and pull up Adam's text again. Sure. What time should I be ready?

13

NADIA IS HOME BY THE TIME ADAM ARRIVES THE NEXT morning. "Who's this?" she asks, pointing him out through the kitchen window. A lean form is walking up the driveway, his big hands in his pockets. He's wearing a green Henley paired with dark-wash jeans and leather boots. That same rucksack, which I think must be part of his signature look, is slung over his left shoulder.

"That's Adam," I say. I'm filling up my reusable water bottle. "Adam Noemi? William's grandson?"

"Oh, he's the one you have a crush on." Nadia's pulling on her black blazer, the same one she's worn to work for, like, the last two decades, with a cup of espresso in hand. Every morning, for as long as any of us sisters can remember, Nadia makes two cups of espresso—one for her, and one for the old gods, which she pours right into the dirt. I always imagined that the black liquid worked itself into tiny veins in the earth, like a cardiovascular system made up of caffeine, popping up on the other side of town to an old god like a fountain, and he would lower his little cup to fill it and throw it right back.

When Nadia looks up at me, she's got a gleam in her eyes that I can't say I appreciate. "Ahh, yes. And he's got a crush on you now, too."

"Don't say that," I hiss just as Adam knocks on the door.

She laughs. "Mija, you *know* that I know these things."

I do know she knows stuff. That's literally her superpower. Her *gift*. But I can't hear things like that right now. The moths in my belly, which of course made a reappearance as soon as our meetup time appeared, now feel like they've made their way right to my throat. Plus he's literally on the other side of the door! What if he heard her making claims to *know* things like that?

Nadia must be feeling fresh today, because she beats me to the door so fast, no one would ever guess she was an septuagenarian with two synthetic knees. "Adam!" she says, as though I didn't just have to explain who he was to her. "What a pleasant surprise! Why don't you come in. Do you need some coffee or water or tea?"

"No, ma'am," Adam says, smiling with both his dimples out. "Sky and I were just about to hang out for a little while."

"Is that right." Nadia smirks at me.

Adam must sense her tone, because he quickly adds, "Sky's a really great friend. You must be so proud of her."

Friend. There that word is again.

As much as I have gotten on my knees and begged the old gods for real friends in the last year or two, I kind of hate that word right about now.

But I put my hand on my belly as the little moths dwindle and dwindle until it feels like only a handful. And then, only one. Oh, thank the old gods. Adam calling me a friend cured me of my nerves and hopefully any and all attraction to him. I can like the word after all.

"We gotta run," I tell Nadia, giving her a kiss on the cheek. "Will you be home for dinner?"

I know she won't, but I always ask. I've invited her to join me and William just about every week since I first started bringing him food. She's never come. Not once. In fact, I can't remember the last time Nadia and I sat down and had any kind of meal together. Oh sure, in the beginning of my Great Return from the Land of the Old Gods, as she still refers to it from time to time, she would make sure I had food. She'd cook for me and bring it to my room, or meal plan like a wild woman and fill the fridge with nutritionally balanced portions in mismatched Tupperware. Which of course I appreciated.

But the second I began to cook my own shit, she stopped. And I know. I'm twenty-six years old. I don't need my elderly auntie to feed me like I'm a baby or something. But it's weird, living with someone and never seeing them except in passing. Someone could spy on her big, almost always empty house, and think we were roommates, not family.

Just like people would see me, Teal, and Sage and think we were friends—there that word is again—who drifted apart, not sisters.

So it doesn't surprise me the least bit when Nadia turns down the dinner invite. Again.

"Oh, amor, I can't tonight. You know I work late on Fridays. I'll be stopping by the church on the way home because Mother Michelle's giving me extra keys to the sanctuary this weekend, for the big summer festival, in case someone gets locked out." Nadia looks between me and Adam. "You know what?"

"Um," I say, because I suspect Nadia's about to suggest something embarrassing.

And I'm right. She smiles big and continues with "You two should definitely go to that! What a *great* idea. The summer festival St. Theresa's puts on every year?"

"Nadia—" I say. "We really need to be—"

"No, no, please. Just one second." She is digging through a handbag the size of a Smart car as she holds her other hand up, pointing her red acrylic nail right at my heart.

Even though she may very well stab me with those bloodred claws, I rush to the front door, flinging it open. "Sorry, Nadia!" I call. "We're just in a hurry, maybe you can—"

And as I'm trying to drag Adam out the door, Nadia shoves tickets to the festival into our hands. "Here's some ride and food coins, too! But don't tell no one I gave this to you, you hear?"

"Thank you, Tía. Have a good day," I say as robotically as possible as I shut the door behind me.

Adam's grinning by the time we get in the car. "She always like that?"

"Matchmaking, you mean?"

He laughs in response and my cheeks heat up so quickly, I must look like a tomato pie. Damn Nadia and her busybody *knowing*. I could've done without hearing Adam think about how hilarious I am as a romantic prospect. Or maybe it's not so bad. I'm pretty sure every moth has evaporated now.

"Sometimes she is. Latine elders, especially the women. It's how they are. They're always trying to get in their kids' business, whether we like it or not."

Adam chuckles. "Sometimes Gramps gets like that with me. It's annoying as fuck."

I think of when I was a ghost, watching William yell at Adam about "jerking women around." I wonder if Adam has ever been in love. "It really is."

When we get in the car, I shove all the festival shit Nadia gave me into my purse and turn to him. "So. Where are we going?"

Adam turns his head to look at me. "It's completely up to you. But I was thinking . . . Cranberry Falls."

I nod. "You want to go to the scene of the crime, so to speak."

"Only if you're comfortable with it. Otherwise, I was thinking I could ask you some questions someplace less emotionally resonant for you. Maybe the beach."

I shake my head. "We can go to Cranberry Falls. I've gone back, like, a hundred times already. It's no big deal."

Adam turns on some oldies radio station, one that plays the likes of Creedence Clearwater, Jimi Hendrix, and Fleetwood Mac, and we spend most of the drive in silence, just listening.

Cranberry has two state parks, one called Cranberry Wood, and the other Cranberry Falls. Cranberry Wood is on the west side of town, and it's mainly made up of biking trails, a few hiking trails, and some pickleball courts near the main parking lot. Cranberry Falls is much more popular. It has a few hiking trails—obviously, since Teal and I were on one of those when I fell—but the big appeal is Crescent Beach, a hidden, seemingly secret little stretch of white shore. Though it is the main appeal of Cranberry Falls, Crescent Beach isn't ever near as busy and crowded as the beach downtown. It doesn't have the downtown shops, and you can't buy food here, you have to pack it, but for many people, it's worth the effort.

When Adam and I get out of the car, it's clear that's where most of the people in the parking lot are headed. They have little red wagons full of snacks and kids, and they take the trailhead marked *Crescent Beach* with a crescent moon painted in white on the sign, over the top of the wood-etched words.

Adam and I take the one called *Falls* instead, marked with

three long, vertically painted curvy lines—leading to the waterfalls the park is named for.

"Do you think it's weird that I fell in a place called Falls?" I ask as we begin, the tall pine trees already shading us from the late-morning sunshine.

Adam gives me a side smile. "I think . . . a lot of things seem to be more coincidental, or poetic, than they should be sometimes."

I hum in agreement and follow him as we ascend. He holds his arm out for me at the narrow spots, which is thoughtful but unnecessary. I wasn't lying before. I've come back here a million times since my return. I know this terrain by now the same way I know the secret places in the neighborhood and what the neighbors keep in their junk drawers, from my Ghost Times.

Whenever I visit Cranberry Falls, it's always to do the same damn thing. I go to where I fell, right next to where the city has now placed a huge new metal and wood railing, and try to . . . well. I'm not sure, exactly. Remember? Or maybe get something back that I'd lost? I don't know. It's similar to when I climb onto the roof a couple evenings a week and watch the distant sea, just barely making out the distant lines of bright seafoam. Being high up feels natural now. Maybe I've grown into my namesake. And maybe that's why I took the attic room a few months after Sage moved out of it, too. I feel strangely at home when there is a great deal of space between me and the black earth.

"So tell me more about your gift, Sky." Adam offers his arm again, and I gently place my hand upon it. He's so warm, I can feel it through his windbreaker.

"Um . . . okay. You want to know anything specific?"

Adam shakes his head. "Just whatever you want to say about it. I'll ask questions if they arise."

I glance around as the trail leads us through a bit of flat land. The trees are old and thick here, reminding me of where I'd spent eight long years. That's one place I haven't gone back to yet, that ancient, hollowed oak where Sage and Nadia found me. Again, I don't know why. But I have a feeling it's got something to do with ghosts.

"Nadia says all human lineages can be traced to something not quite human. Plant, animal, mineral." I sidestep some Spanish moss, long and rough as an old man's beard. "Cloud. Lightning. Stone. This explains . . . well, do you know the feeling of doing something or being near something and it feels like you lose yourself in a sense of belonging?"

Adam's quiet for a few minutes, and then he laughs. "Yeah. Knitting."

I'm so surprised by his response that I stop short before continuing on. "Knitting?"

"I took it up after I stopped drinking. I'm fucking terrible at it, Sky."

He laughs again, the strands of sunlight coming through the canopy making it look like his eyes have stars in them. I lower my eyes to his dimples and imagine very briefly how it would feel to kiss them. I shake my head and look away.

"But while I'm knitting, I lose myself and find myself at the same time. It's hard to explain, but I feel as though I become more and less than human when I'm clicking my grandmother's old knitting needles."

I smile. "That explains it really well, actually. That's kind of what our gifts feel like. Or at least mine does. I feel like I belong to the World of Criaturas, and that belonging somehow makes me more and less human at the same time."

"So I belong to knitting, then. The world of knitting." He scoffs like he's making a light joke.

I smile. "The worlds were made from weaving and knitting, Adam. How many creation stories include the fiber arts? Including spiderwebs?"

Adam stops as I speak, and so I stop, too. He swallows, his eyelashes lowering, and I'm alarmed to note that he is watching my lips again. Like before, he seems to notice it after I do. He clears his throat, coughs, and looks away. "So . . . you could, like, make an animal come to you if you want? Like you could . . . show me how your gift works?"

I frown and turn ahead, walking away from him. I don't respond as we both climb over some rocks jutting out into the path. I'm not sure how. Finally, after we've made it past the boulders, I dust my hands against the front of my clothes and say, "You've already seen how my gift works, though. Remember? The pigeons and the chipmunks?"

"Right. I was just wondering if you could do it again." Adam flashes me a smile that is too wide and friendly. It's his fake journalist smile, is my guess.

I don't smile in return. I keep my head down and catch my breath. "Like, what were you thinking?"

Adam shrugs. "I don't know. A hawk . . . ?"

It doesn't feel right. Proving to him by using the animals—my friends—as though they were puppets. I don't doubt they would come to me if I asked. But they would only do that because I've proven that I don't ask without good reason. "I don't want to."

He turns away, shielding his face from the sunshine with his hand as he glances up. "Uh-huh. Not a problem."

His tone makes my hackles rise. He doesn't think I can do it, when it's not about "can" or "can't" at all. I roll my eyes. Freaking colonizer mindset, always wanting proof of things, always thinking a thing must be seen in order to be known.

We reach the cliff quickly after that, and he says, placing his hands on the wooden part of the new rail, "How do you feel?"

I shake my head. I don't want to say the truth—that I'm annoyed specifically with him. "Uh. You know. This feels completely normal, I guess."

He quirks his head at me. "You told the police that you woke up in the woods. But you then implied with me, at Gramps's, that there was more to the story."

I nod and shrug. I kind of don't want to tell him this precious truth right now. But he and I made a deal. I inhale slowly. "Remember the old gods I told you about? According to Nadia, they were who took my body into an oak tree that way." I point down, deep in the woods. "And they took care of me. During that time, I didn't know I was in the woods, of course. I thought I was dead. A ghost."

"A ghost," Adam repeats slowly.

"Yes. I wandered around Cranberry. As a ghost. After eight years, my sister and grandmother took me to my body and I returned to it with their help."

"A . . . ghost." If he repeats the phrase one more time, he might fall off the cliff this time.

I don't mean it. I don't want to actually hurt Adam. But I'm so frustrated, I want to at least kick some really big rocks down the ledge. This conversation has nothing of the other night's magic and connection. When it felt like he was sincerely *listening* to me. Instead, I feel like all he's doing is considering that I might seriously be crazy, after I begged for him not to at the beginning of this arrangement.

"If the old gods are powerful enough to take your body and care for it while your, ah, spirit is elsewhere . . . why didn't they just save you whole? Spirit and all?"

I sigh. "Very few things the old gods do make sense in the Land of the Living."

Adam pauses. "I see." It's that tone again. Disbelieving along with . . . a trace of arrogance. Isn't it a part of his profession to make his interviewees *not* feel like liars?

"Don't do that," I snap.

He looks at me quickly, needing to turn around to do so. It's only now that I realize I'm against the wall of dirt lining the trail, as far away from the edge of the cliff as possible. Rocks are piercing my back painfully but I don't want to move. I don't feel safe.

"Do what, Sky?" he asks, his voice warm.

"You know what, Adam. You're acting like I'm delusional or something. I'm telling you the truth. I and the truth deserve to be treated with respect."

Adam shakes his head. "You've just unloaded a lot of . . . controversial information. It's just—"

"Oh, that's what we're calling the things that Western science is too up its own ass to understand? 'Controversial information'?" I shake my head. "Whatever, man." I turn around and begin to go back to where we'd come from, Adam fast on my heels.

"Sky. There's been . . . a misunderstanding—"

"Has there?" I turn around fast and he almost trips. I grab his arms and hold him steady. "Seems to me that I've understood this perfectly. You're completely closed off to my story. To my *life*. Shouldn't the person who hears it first actually try to believe what happened to me?"

Adam blinks. "That's not how journalism works, Sky."

That tells me all I need to know. I breathe out a big sigh. "Got it." I look down briefly and say, "I just wanna go home now."

He nods. "Okay. Let's head back."

Adam tries to talk to me on the hike back, about simple things like the weather and the birds. I don't respond. What is there to say?

Just before we reach the parking lot, I'm startled when something sharp hits my shoulder. "Oh gods," I shriek, but then freeze when I see it's . . . well. It's a hawk. A gorgeous, red-tailed hawk with eyes so black, they look like they contain two entirely new universes.

Adam jumps back when he sees. "Jesus Christ."

I don't know why a hawk landed on me in front of Adam. It's almost like a sign, to keep doing what I'm doing with him. Keep telling him the truth. But right now, I just want to be as far away from this man as possible. I stroke the hawk's beautiful burnt sienna feathers lightly. They somehow feel soft and sharp at the same time. "Why hello. Go on and have a good day, would you?"

And then he flies away, his big wide wings as graceful as blown glass made alive.

Adam's eyes are wide as well. I anticipate him going into an intense conversation about the "coincidence" of that hawk "randomly" landing on me. But instead, he doesn't say a word. We drive home in silence. The only thing he tells me is to have a good evening when I turn toward Nadia's. I say nothing in response.

The only thing I can think when I'm inside is *What a waste of a perfectly good hike.*

14

ADAM IS NOWHERE TO BE FOUND WHEN I BRING DINNER over for William later, which relieves and annoys me at once. On one hand, I don't think I could take the awkwardness of being extra unsure of what to say around him. On the other, it pisses me off that he thinks he can treat me like I am insane and disappear without a trace. I didn't take him for the sort to run away after being a piece of crap to someone, but then again, it seems like I didn't really know Adam after all. Even with all the spying on him as a ghost a couple of years back.

Luckily, William doesn't seem to either notice or mind my emotional distress. "What are these things?" he asks, grabbing his now third helping of dinner.

"They're enchiladas," I say, picking at my own plate. Not even Nadia's world-famous extra-cheesy enchiladas can help my mood.

I listen to William wax on for a while about how too many damn people are moving into town, when he shocks me with this question: "So what the hell are your intentions with Adam, anyway?"

I blink. "Come again?"

William ignores my question. "Just go easy on him, will ya? The kid hasn't had a lot of good luck lately. After his mother died, and then him having to stop drinking, and then losing all those jobs—"

"Jesus Christ, William. Don't tell me any more of his business like that. Adam and I aren't dating."

He looks at me and raises one white, fuzzy eyebrow. "You sure about that?"

I nod. "Oh yes. I'm sure."

"Then why did he come in here earlier, after seeing you, stomping around and looking like someone punched him in the face?"

I shrug. "He was an idiot to me earlier and I called him out on it."

William scoffs. "Damn kid. He's got no sense when it comes to a good woman, does he?"

I don't know what to say to that. I'm oddly touched that William thinks I'm a good woman. Good enough to be romantically entangled with his grandson, even. But after everything that's happened with him, *I* don't think Adam's good enough to be entangled with *me*.

Specifically after today, I'm having a difficult time remembering what it was like to crush on Adam, anyway. I shake my head when I realize William's waiting for a response still. "I don't know about that. He's doing a reporting piece on me, and we had a disagreement." I shrug. "It's not a big deal."

"Not a big deal. He's looking like someone told him his mother's dead again, and you're looking like someone told you that the damn animals in the forest all dropped dead—"

I gasp. "William! Enough with all the dead talk, man!"

"You two better have made up by next week!" William points his finger at me. "I don't want to deal with you two moping around again, you hear?"

Well, I guess I can see where Adam got some of his lack of tact from. I refrain from sighing too loudly as I stand. "Sure thing, William. Let me pack up the leftovers for you before I go, okay?"

Nadia's car still isn't back when I walk home, for some strange reason, and that makes me extra annoyed as I imagine where Adam could be, because his vehicle is nowhere to be seen, either. Because, honestly, the first thing that comes to mind is him, looking charming and attractive as usual, sitting next to a beautiful woman at some swanky restaurant downtown or even in the next town over. I imagine his big hand on the small of her back, and how warm and safe it would feel for her there. How he'd whisper in her ear the things he was planning on doing to her later. How she'd giggle and blush.

How she'd be *normal*. How she wouldn't be a woman who lost eight years in a way he would never believe. How because of that, he'd think *she* was worthy of his respect.

I try and distract myself from my bad mood first with food. I couldn't finish my plate at William's, so I open all the cupboards in the kitchen, trying to brainstorm and find something that would hit the spot. I settle for s'mores—made up with value-brand cinnamon graham crackers, a few pieces of mint dark chocolate, and big, honking marshmallows that I roast over the flames of the gas range. I eat them in the living room while watching *Gilmore Girls*, the Thanksgiving episode where Lorelai and Rory get invited to so many Thanksgivings that they have to micro-schedule their whole day and appetites, around, like, ten different meals.

As the credits roll, it hits me that Thanksgiving is about five months away and . . . what if I don't hear from my sisters before then? What if Nadia and I are still strangers who happen to live in the same dwelling? I'll have the literal opposite problem that Lorelai and Rory had. Everyone will be doing their own thing for the holiday. And they'll all have forgotten me.

I know this thinking is a bit dramatic, but right now, it not only feels possible, it feels probable.

I take a breath and stand, brushing the s'mores crumbs off my clothes. And then I put on my garden shoes and step outside.

The sky is brilliant, with the clouds lined up from one side to the other, appearing white and a thousand shades of blue in the shadows against the setting sun. There's the ever-so-slightest chill in the air, and I wrap my arms around my middle as I make my way to the backyard.

I sit in the middle of the moss-and-grass mixture, between the roses climbing over the half-rotted wooden fences and the cedar trellises holding vines of cucumbers and tomatoes. Nadia's growing a lot of unusual heirlooms this year—yellow cucumbers that look more like lemons than any cucumber I've seen. Tomatoes that aren't rounded but instead are the shape of icicles, the colors of fire—iron oxide, orange sunset, solar flare yellow, even little dots of the blue of flames—all on a single fruit. "Anyone there?" I call.

There's a loud rustle of leaves from beyond the cliff, and then, climbing over, is a black bear.

I know this bear. She used to come and play with me when she was a baby during last year's spring, while her mother ate the soft lettuce shoots and not-quite-ripe raspberries in Nadia's garden.

"Lily," I say, the name I gave her because after smelling a daylily, she sneezed the most perfect baby bear sneeze. She smiles in the way only bears can and meanders my way.

Our gifts always come with a *knowing* that is hard to describe in words. I *know* which animals care for me and which ones don't. Although my gift allows me to tune in to all the animals in my area—even the ones inside the skin of the ocean miles away from me right now, enveloped in wild, cerulean waves—not all animals want a connection with me. This must be respected. A relationship that is one-sided isn't a relationship at all.

The ones who do come to me, or allow me to come to them, it's because consent in having a friendship has been established by nonverbal communication. It's almost like a piece of my soul runs out and says to the animal's soul: *Is it okay to play?* And then my soul returns with the answer, which honestly comes through as a simple knowledge in my belly.

Lily has always wanted to be friends. When she reaches me, she plops over, belly up, doing a silly bear growl until I scratch her. Her fur is coarse, with a couple of dried leaves stuck to her. "How have you been, lovely?" I ask.

And before I know it . . . I'm crying. The tears drip off my face and onto her fur. They catch the last remaining light in the sky, reflecting the halo of deep gold and orange around me. It looks like she's wearing jewels. Citrine and yellow diamond tears.

I take a shuddering breath and ask her a question. It's a dangerous one, but it's one that's been in the back of my mind for a long while. For two years, even, ever since I returned to myself and awoke inside the hollowed-out cavern of an ancient oak tree.

"Why doesn't anyone want me?"

It comes out in a whisper. It comes out alongside two, three, four more tears. Four more jewels beading upon her fur, which is as deep brown as roasted coffee beans, or the darkest percentage of chocolate you can find in a bar.

It's not just the fact that no one wants me romantically. It's also friendship. It's also *family*.

How can I have spent eight years alone in the woods, only to return to the World of the Living and feel more lonely than I ever have in my life?

In a good portion of Nadia's books, protagonists who are like me, who are alone and forgotten by those closest to them, end up *finding* family. Found family is maybe my most favorite trope of all time. It provides more hope than any other, in my opinion. It means that I can create family, somehow, even if I'm starting with little to nothing.

But what happens when no one outside of my little-to-nothing situation will even give me a chance?

After I fell, Sage couldn't bear the pain so much that she moved away.

Maybe that's what I need to do. Save up money and find a new home. And there, finally find my true family.

What are you up to, Salt Sea Girl?

I lay in bed for a long time after crying all over poor Lily's fur. She licked up the tears and nuzzled the crook of my elbow, letting me lean on her until I relaxed enough to come back inside.

And now I'm still in bed, staring at the message from @tryingsomethingnew. Wondering what, or even if, I should write back, considering the mood I'm currently in.

Exhausted. Wrung out. Heart still aching a bit too much for my liking.

Hey, I finally type back. I'm simply too starved for human communication, I reckon, to just ignore the closest thing I have to a real friend right now. I just had the absolute shittiest day. Hope yours is better than mine.

I'm sorry to hear that. Damn. No, mine was rather shitty, too, actually. Do you want to talk about it? Your day, I mean?

I close my eyes, trying to find the words. It's so much easier to talk to the nonhuman animals most of the time. Someone was cruel to me. I don't want to get into details. What made your day shitty?

There's a long pause. And finally, he writes, I got into a fight with a friend. Totally my fault. Now I'm just in bed, eating my feelings with this ridiculous chocolate pudding I picked up from the store.

A photo comes in of the pudding—chocolate, in a plastic container. Topped with crumbled cookies and a couple of rainbow-colored gummy worms.

Oh my God! Dirt in a cup! I haven't had one of those since I was, like, ten.

You calling me immature? 😉

Him sending the winking face emoji perks my nervous system right up. I guess it's what some type of neurological professional would call a dopamine hit. Whatever it is, I love it.

Of course not, I write back. Clearly your tastes are refined af. Dirt in a cup is delicious.

It's gone now. I basically inhaled it.

I swallow as an idea comes to me.

What if I . . . seduced this man?

Seriously. What have I got to lose?

I don't mean that the end result of this experiment I'm considering is that we'd meet up and fuck. I'm very much done with those kinds of adventures, thanks to stupid Grayson Baker. But sexting is still a thing, right? Not a thing I really tried before. Talking "sexy" with Grayson meant reading about his preferences and turn-ons in a long list, and him literally never asking to know mine in return. So . . . why not "try something new" with @tryingsomethingnew?

The worst that could happen is he wouldn't want to chat anymore.

And the thing is? As soon as he finds out who I really am, that's going to happen anyway. Learning he's from Cranberry—that's a given. It kind of makes me sad to admit it to myself, since I like him so much, but there's no way he would ever want me once he learns my name.

I take a deep breath. The dopamine and whatever other feel-good hormones are rushing through me now as I jump to my dresser and change into the most casually skimpy outfit I can find.

He's written me: So what are you up to now? Besides being jealous of my awesome dessert?

I lie in bed and respond with I am taking selfies. Want to see one?

Sure.

Is it okay if it's NSFW?

There's a bit of a pause, but then he writes again: Sure.

Oh gods, why do I always promise selfies before I've even taken them? *Learn, Sky, learn*, I scold myself, and then I snap a short series of myself as I lie back on the bed, my honey-brown hair fanned around me in beach waves, my eyes looking as dark as midnight in the low light. I'm wearing a sheer, even tight, little white tank top without a bra.

I blur my face with the photo editing app and send the first photo. It shows me pulling down my top just a little bit, so that a good amount of cleavage is on display.

You're gorgeous, he writes back.

I can't help my grin. I'm just not used to this kind of romantic attention, considering most of the eligible bachelors in town would rather run away from me than shower me with compliments. Or even one single compliment.

Your turn, I type.

I laugh when his photo loads. It's him, lying in bed, the empty pudding cup balanced between his pectoral muscles. Another picture comes quickly—he's lifted his shirt some in this one, revealing the line of his happy trail and one of the cuts of the V at his hips.

I send another photo in response; this time, a peek of my areola is exposed through another lowering of my top. He sends one of his shirt rolled up almost all the way to his collarbone. It's like we're playing some kind of virtual striptease. It's tame, as far as sexy games go, but I find it thrilling. Intoxicating, even.

For my final photo, my top is all the way off, showing both breasts, tight brown nipples and all.

Jesus Christ. Look at you. is the first thing he types back. After a few seconds, more words appear. damn you look so damn good, and I guess he means it, because he doesn't even include the proper punctuation he usually does.

I swallow and then do my next super brave thing of the night. Can I see you? Face covered, I mean?

His next photo is of him, in almost the same position as me, except one of his hands is back under his head. His whole head is scribbled over in navy blue, but I can tell I like the way he looks by the hint of his chin. His shirt is completely off now, like me. I take note of how strong his shoulders look. He has chestnut brown chest hair, and in the dim lighting, I think I can see some freckles.

You're beautiful, I write immediately.

I'm blushing is his response.

I bite back a smile. Are you . . . ?

Am I . . . ?

You know. Turned on, or whatever?

My duck feels like a fucking steel pipe right now.

Duck?!

Damn it! Autocorrect. Dick. It's dick.

I'm laughing aloud now. Your poor duck sounds uncomfortable 😊

That's one word for it hahaha.

I pause for a few seconds, and my hands shake as I type once more. What if I wanted you to touch yourself right now? Would you do it?

Jesus Christ, Salt Sea Girl. You're killing me.

I blink when I don't see a specific response to the question come through. Oh, I'm sorry. I didn't mean to overstep.

No, no. I mean, yes. I would. Is that what you want? For me to touch myself?

My next inhale is shaky. I do. If you want to. And if you want me to . . . I want to touch myself too.

Fuck. Fuck. Okay, hold on a second. I wait what feels like forever, but in actuality is only, like, thirty seconds. Jesus. I'm so hard already. I'm not going to last.

You don't have to last, I type.

Tell me how wet you are.

I slip my hand under my panties and begin typing with my other hand. Dripping. I'm dripping.

Jesus. Jesus. Tell me more. How do you like to touch yourself?

I laugh and change my phone to voice to text. I can't do this with one hand anymore.

I like to spread my legs wide, as wide as I can. I'm really flexible. And . . . I get my fingers all wet and slide them over my clit.

Fuck. That's so hot. Fuck.

I like to put one or two fingers inside myself and wiggle them. I pretend it's someone's tongue.

I'm going to come. Can I come? Christ I'm so close.

Come for me, I say to the voice to text.

I then imagine what he'd sound like. How gruff his voice might get once he goes over the edge. How hard he'd get, how long he'd go for. How the muscles of his whole body would get so tense, he'd shake as he lost control. Before I know it, my own fingers are moving lightning-fast and I'm right there, too, moaning, shivering, contracting.

Are you still there? I whisper to the voice to text.

Just a sec.

I take the opportunity to clean myself up. After drying my hands in my bathroom, I check and see what he's written.

I don't think I've come that hard in my life.

I laugh. You needed that, huh?

He responds with, Did you get to?

I did. Just after you, I think.

How was it?

I lie back and smile. I almost type that I fantasized about him coming, and that's what made me lose control. But I'm afraid he'll think that's too personal or something.

So I write back instead, It was really, really good. I'm still trembling a little.

We chat a little more about this and that—the busy days we

had, how we hope both of our tomorrows will be better. And then he says he feels like he's about to pass out, so we both say good night.

I squeal to myself after I turn out the lights for bed. Lame, I know. But . . . *wow*. Even if just virtual . . . that felt like a *real* connection with someone. Someone who really found me to be worthy of desire.

I swear, as cliché as it sounds, I fall asleep with a smile on my face.

15

I KNOW IT'S SILLY, BUT I AM IN THE ABSOLUTE BEST MOOD THE following morning. I choose my favorite outfit for work—a well-tailored, knee-length pastel blue dress with cap sleeves and a sweetheart neckline, paired with black leather Mary Janes and the fancy black handbag Teal and Amá Sonya forced me to get last year. Teal called it a "carryall" and insisted I needed something like that for my new job.

While Teal has, like, fifty handbags, I'm pretty sure Sage only has one—an old, stained leather belt bag from the dirty work she does at her job. I guess that would make me somewhere in the middle of the two, with five handbags. The carryall is the nicest, but I have a decent little collection of Coach, Louis Vuitton, and Anthropologie.

Before getting in my car, I send @tryingsomethingnew a message—just a simple, standard Good morning 😉. I then blast Olivia Rodrigo on the way to work. Not even thinking about my sisters can bring me down right now. Sex endorphins—even without actually having had sex—are powerful as hell, I'm beginning to realize. People don't need family, all they need is lots of awesome sex. I'm sure that's a very unhealthy conclusion, but it's what I'm telling myself right now, simply because it makes me hopeful for my future.

I pull into work and immediately say, "Oh fuck."

Turns out, there is, in fact, something in my life strong enough to render any bonding hormones useless, and that would be the sight of my grandmother, dressed like she's just returned from a service at the Vatican, leaning against her Bentley in enormous Chanel sunglasses, looking for all the world like she would rather be anywhere else in said world.

So why *isn't* she anywhere else? Why does she have to bother me here, at my place of employment?

I force a pleasant expression on my face after I park my car, grab my bag, and approach her. "Amá." I lean and air-kiss each cheek. She barely makes the effort to do the same to me. "I wasn't expecting you this morning."

She makes a sour face. "And why would you? You refuse to respond to my texts. My calls. I may as well not even exist for all the respect you pay me."

I nod. "Well, yes, but also, I've been busy—"

"Busy nada." And then she snarls and begins to, I assume, curse me out in Spanish.

Sage knows the most Spanish of all of us. Teal makes out okay if people speak slowly. But me? I really missed out when I disappeared for eight years. I felt like speaking English again was an adjustment, and I sadly lost all the basics for Spanish in that time frame. And honestly, right now, I'm not unthankful for the lack of skill. Amá Sonya certainly isn't singing my praises, from the snarl on her face and the way she keeps fisting her hands like she's five seconds away from punching me out.

When she finally stops to take a breath, I ask, "Would you like to come inside? My planner is in there. We can make an arrangement like you've been requesting."

She puts her hands on her hips and says nothing. I'm afraid she's going to tell me off again, so I quickly add, "My boss is in there. She might be wondering why we are so emotional out here."

This straightens Amá out like nothing else I could have said. Amá Sonya hates the idea of appearing anything but the epitome of perfection. She's convinced that everyone is watching her all the time, just waiting for her to show all her flaws (flaws she claims don't exist), so the whole town can gossip about her behind her back.

It strikes me again that this is why Amá Sonya has shown virtually no interest in me since my return, except to make sure my wardrobe is reflecting well on her. And now, obviously, when she suspects I may be entangled with the most beloved man in town. In general, she's embarrassed to be seen with me. I've long suspected it, but it may as well be a foregone conclusion now. *I'm* embarrassed I didn't conclude it sooner, is all.

What if that's another element to why my family happily ignores my existence? Are they all embarrassed of me, too?

"Let's see your planner, then," Amá Sonya says as she straightens her back and gestures for me to lead the way.

Inside, Amá Sonya is the essence of sweet Southern charm as I introduce her to Anise, all smiles that don't quite reach her eyes, all compliments on Anise's outfit, which, to be fair, is glorious today—a brown tweed A-line skirt paired with a white silk blouse and pumpkin orange blazer. But as soon as we get in the elevator, Amá's mask drops, and her regular expression—the one that screams unimpressed with *everything*—returns. "What is this?"

she asks, gesturing to the elevator. "They can't provide you with something that isn't about to implode? One day you're going to get stuck in this abomination and no one will know for weeks!"

"Careful, Amá Sonya," I respond as the doors squeak open. "You almost sound like you care about my well-being, there."

"Of course I care," she snaps back. "What kind of abuela would I be if I didn't care about my youngest granddaughter?"

The elevator doors creak and shake open, and her nose scrunches as she takes in my floor. I know that she sees nothing but dark, germ-covered books collecting dust every which way. She's probably thinking to herself how bad it would look for her if I really did get stuck down here and no one noticed. So I try and distract her from making any more commentary about my workspace by leaping to my desk and grabbing my planner. "So. How does next . . . Friday morning work for you? Shall we get breakfast to catch up?" I grab a pen on my desk and hold it up, acting like I am just so eager to set up an appointment with her. When probably she knows just as well as I do that I'm actually eager to get her out of here so I can get to work in peace.

Instead of answering my question, she asks, "How long has Adam Noemi been courting you?"

And there it is. I don't hold back my sigh. "He's not courting me, Amá."

"Good."

I blink. "Good?"

She glares at me. "Did I stutter?"

I shake my head. "But . . . I thought you'd want someone like him to be seen with . . ." *Someone like me* is what I don't say.

Amá aggressively shakes her head. "That man hasn't been able to keep a job in the last two years—"

"It's not his fault his industry is failing under the enormous pressures of—"

She holds up a hand just as I realize that defending Adam isn't going to help her believe he's not courting me. She continues on as though I haven't spoken: "I admit that, perhaps three years ago, he would have been a good match—"

"When I was still unconscious in the woods?" I ask, but she ignores me.

"But now? No. He's still charmed the town but that won't last long, not once he's unemployed for much longer." She raises an eyebrow. "The most important thing when it comes to men, Sky, is—"

"Love?" I ask. "Respect?" She rolls her eyes. She knows that I know exactly what she means.

"Money. Money is the only thing that makes men worth the headache. And that man has very little money."

I shake my head. "It doesn't matter how much money he does or doesn't have. He's not interested in me. That's been made very clear." If he were, he wouldn't have treated me like I was off my rocker when I trusted him with the truth—exactly where I was and who I was with in my eight years' disappearance. That information is *precious*. It's inextricably connected to significant and personal family lore for us Flores women, as well as historical and cosmic lore, regarding our ancestors in the past and the timeless old gods. And he just . . . acted like I'd made it all up on the spot.

No genuinely interested man behaves like *that*. At the very least, he'd pretend to think I was sane.

Now Amá Sonya blinks. "And why wouldn't he be interested in you? Does he have any better prospects? What's wrong with him?"

I am oddly flattered at her being so outraged that Adam doesn't want me, until she adds, "We all know how you're seen around here. He may try and seduce you because he knows he may well be on your level soon. Don't let him. Your destiny is to rise above."

Well, the reminder of *my level* is exactly the last thing I needed to hear about right now. I close my planner and toss the pen on it. "Are we done?"

She raises her eyebrow at me. "Next Friday. Breakfast. I'll pick you up."

I shake my head. "No, you won't."

"Excuse me?"

"If I'm not good enough for you to answer any of my texts regarding meeting for brunch for the last three months? Then I'm not good enough for breakfast on Friday. Why don't you keep doing what you've been doing, Amá, and stick to dining with people on *your level*"—I raise my hand high—"and not mine." I drop my arm and she follows the movement with a scowl on her face.

She opens her mouth to argue, but something in my face stops her. I'm not a little kid she can boss around anymore, and I think that information might finally be dawning on her. Instead, she stomps away in the prissiest way possible and presses the button to the elevator. "You *will* see me, Sky, because the fantasmas"—she whispers this—"have told me that you have tricked your sisters into not seeing you."

"Ghosts?" I ask. Because that is her gift. Amá Sonya can see, and communicate with, ghosts. Once, she saw me when I was a ghost, when Sage brought me to her so we could figure out what the hell was happening to me back then.

"Shh." She looks around, as though we may be surrounded by

fantasmas any second. "I was informed that you have Teal thinking that you're seeing Sage, and Sage thinking that you're seeing Teal."

I shrug. I guess there's no point in denying it.

She steps into the elevator and points at me. "Breakfast. Friday. Or they will find out about your deception."

I roll my eyes so far back I can see my brain. When I blink my gaze back to normal, the shuttering elevator doors have closed over my lovely grandmother.

NADIA ISN'T AROUND WHEN I GET HOME AFTER WORK, TO ABsolutely no one's surprise. But I *am* pretty startled when I spot Adam sitting on the porch.

He stands when I approach, his hands in his pockets. His eyes are serious, and deep, deep blue. I almost stop walking when we make eye contact, but with sheer power of will, and remembering the hurt he caused me, I hold my head high and say, "May I help you with something?"

"I'm sorry." He shakes his head. "Sky . . . I'm sorry. I said things that were hurtful, because I was trying so hard to be neutral. I shouldn't have."

It's not quite enough for me, this apology. I look at his eyes again before settling my focus between his eyebrows instead. Most of the time, direct eye contact is a bit much for me, but emotional situations like these? It makes me feel like an alarm is going off in my body. "What do you mean, you 'shouldn't have'? You shouldn't have said hurtful things or you shouldn't have tried to be neutral?"

"Both," he responds simply. "It was disrespectful to expect you to show me your gift like it was a magic trick. But also . . ."

He glances down and back at me. "I try to approach my stories with, as cliché as this sounds, an open heart. I aim to trust that what someone is telling me is their truth. I admit, some of the things you said startled me, and so I—"

"Got a nasty, arrogant tone," I supply.

"That. Yes. But." He reaches into his pocket and pulls out a slip of paper. "When I got home last night, I wrote out a list." He swallows.

I switch my weight to my other hip. "Okay . . ."

He sits back down on the porch step and makes a gesture for me to join him. I have to admit, he's piqued my interest, so I sit next to him, keeping as much space between us as possible.

I glance at his paper and read the title. "'A List of Impossible Ghostly Things.'"

He chuckles. "Yes." He clears his throat and he begins to read. "Number one. The night my mother died, I felt her kiss me on the forehead. I smelled her perfume. The next day, I found out she'd already been gone when I felt these.

"Number two. Sometimes I see my grandmother's shadow in Gramps's home. Kind of like when you round the corner and you see that someone is there but you don't see them yet? Like that. I'll see the shadow, I swear I can almost hear her humming in the kitchen, but when I walk inside, no one is there."

As he speaks, I can almost see what he's remembered in my own mind. His mother's perfume, violets and roses. William's wife, singing a little tune as she cooks in her apron. It's almost as though these memories become Alive Things and walk through me.

"And lastly. Um. This is possibly the weirdest one."

I fold my arms. "Go on."

"A couple of times . . . two years or so ago, at Gramps's, when I stayed with him to help him recover from the flu?"

I clear my throat now. That was the time when I'd been spying on him the most. I'm still not exactly proud of the fact. "Yeah?"

"I saw eyes."

I swallow. "Eyes."

"Yeah. Like in midair. I'd see a pair of eyes watching me. Brown ones, I think, but they were kind of faded. I thought I was losing my mind, but then they stopped."

My heart is beating a little faster. Could it seriously be true? Those times when it seemed like Adam was looking right at me? He sensed me?

"I'm telling you this, Sky, because I want you to know that I understand there are things about this world that don't seem to make sense. That, you know, 'Western civilization'"—he makes air quotes—"denies can exist. People experience shit all the time that is downright miraculous and magical—I would know, I've interviewed plenty of them—and we go on with our lives as though magic doesn't exist." He glances at me and I feel a pang in my heart when I realize that he's tearing up. His eyes are glassy. "I don't wanna live that way anymore. Convincing myself that magic . . . that things that cannot be explained . . . can't exist. You know?"

I nod. Although I can't relate to living as though magic doesn't exist, I can understand wanting something more than what seems possible. Wanting meaning. Belonging. Because this is what my gift, what my magic brings to me.

"Anyway. I just want you to know that I'm going to trust that, you know. What you're telling me—it's the truth." He laughs. "The weird thing is . . ." He then shakes his head, as though deciding against telling me what's on his mind.

"Say it." My voice is gentle and firm.

He nods. "The weird thing is, ever since you started telling me . . . about the creation of this world. Of all the worlds. And about your experience, being taken and cared for by old gods. It all *felt* true. And I think that's what bothered me the most. How can something feel true in my body but still not make sense in my brain?"

"It's another 'Western civilization' thing." I put my hand over his, where it lies on his knee. "The idea that consciousness is in the brain. My family knows that the whole body is conscious. Just like the whole earth is, and everything on this earth."

Adam laughs and covers his face with his other hand. "See. What you just said. That feels true, too." He shakes his head and drops his hand. "I'm sorry, Sky. I hope you can forgive me."

He opened his whole heart to me just now, in a really vulnerable way. I think he's sincerely humbled over what transpired between us at Cranberry Falls. Adam is flawed, but he's also trying. I can accept that. "I forgive you."

"Yeah?" He says it like he wasn't expecting it at all, his face bursting into that wide smile that makes my knees feel like they're gonna give out, even though I'm literally still sitting.

"Yeah." I reach behind me for my bag and pull out two tickets to the summer festival Nadia forced upon us only a few days prior. "Wanna hit up the festival tonight?"

"Sure." He smiles as he stands and offers his arm. I take it to help myself up, and for some reason, I wrongly estimate my ascent. As soon as my legs have straightened, I realize I'm close to him. Too close. I can smell the salt and nutmeg of his skin. I can see his freckles more clearly than ever before, how they're all as perfectly round as planets. Finally, I allow myself a glance at his lips. Peachy-pink. A freckle hovering on the right edge of his top lip. The bottom just a touch fuller.

Adam clears his throat and I toss my gaze right down to my

handbag, where I'd left it in a plop on the step. Before I can grab it, Adam says, "Sky." His voice is husky in a way that makes the blue moths, all one hundred billion of them, return to my stomach instantly. I glance at him, and his breath is slightly heavy, as though he's nervous, or . . . aroused? "Sometimes, the way you look at me . . ." He trails off and shakes his head.

"Yes?" I ask.

"Never mind. It's nothing." He angles his head toward his car across the street. "I'll drive?"

Inside his car, he taps his fingers on the steering wheel at red lights, seemingly lost in thought. I want to ask him what he means, about the way I "sometimes" look at him. I'm well aware I was staring at his mouth too long. Does he think I want to kiss him? If so, I've caught him looking at *my* mouth with even more frequency. Does that mean he wants to kiss me?

In a stunning turn of events, I realize I am much too shy to ask for clarification. Normally, I don't care about hurdling over codes of social decency if it means I'll understand what the hell is happening. But not today, Satan. Not today.

We get out of his car—Adam rushes over to open my door wide for me—and take in the scene. The main parking lot of the church has been turned into, for all intents and purposes, a carnival. There are rides, including bumper cars and a small Ferris wheel, and loads of vendors selling treats like fresh caramel popcorn, candy apples, churros, and elephant ears, both of the latter covered in mountains of powdered sugar like snow. The smell of fried food surrounds us like a cloud of deliciousness.

"Where do you want to start?" he asks.

I smile. "Well. I *am* starving, if I didn't mention that earlier."

"Food it is."

Adam insists on buying me my dinner of choice—nachos,

covered in radioactive, glow-in-the-dark spicy cheese dip. He gets a turkey leg for himself, and we sit on a bench right in front of the Ferris wheel, watching the blue, purple, and green lights of it twinkle like dancing UFOs in the oncoming night.

"So, is anything new with you?" He raises an eyebrow at me. "Besides dancing in the woods with pelicans and dolphins—"

I laugh. "Okay, neither of those live in the woods. But . . ." Now I'm the one clearing my throat. "I think I met someone."

Adam immediately drops the pile of napkins in his fist. "Shit."

I jump up to help him collect them. I pull out the hand sanitizer, and after we are germ-free, we return to our food. "So you met someone," he says, and then he attacks his turkey leg with what can only be described as violence.

I furrow my brow at him. "I mean, maybe. He seems interested in me. And . . . he's definitely sexually attracted to me."

Adam frowns. "What do you mean, definitely? He told you that this early on, but you don't even know if he's a romantic prospect yet?"

I shrug. "Sometimes you can just tell if someone wants you or not. You know?"

He doesn't respond, instead opting to tear another slab of meat from the poor turkey leg.

"Anyway, I was just thinking. If he and I . . . ever . . . you know." I raise my eyebrow as Adam frowns at me again, even deeper this time. "I was wondering, since you're a man. And I'm interested in a man's perspective and experience. What's the best way to give a man a really great orgasm?"

Adam's mouth is super full, so it takes a minute before he can speak. "Uh. Are you sure you're okay talking about something like this with me?"

I shrug. "I guess, I thought we were supposed to be friends.

Don't friends give each other advice on stuff like this?" I blink. "Unless—oh, I'm so sorry. I didn't think that you'd be uncomfortable with—okay. Subject change. Ummm." I force my brain to come up with something else to talk about, quickly, but all that comes out is a jangle of words. "Duck confetti. Tree mothers. Knitting! Knitting. You like knitting, right?"

Adam smiles. "All that. Everything you just said. Especially the duck confetti. All ways to give a man an orgasm he'll never forget."

I stare blankly for a moment, and then I snort-laugh. I laugh so hard, I have to bend over a little bit. Just imagining seducing a man with . . . duck confetti? Whatever the hell that even is? I double over entirely, imagining shiny little duck papers flying down from the ceiling of my bedroom in front of some bewildered man. I'm wiping my face by the time I am able to get myself upright again.

"Jesus." He looks at my face all over, as though he's seeing me for the first time. "I feel like I would do anything to get you to laugh like that."

Before he can say another word, a man and a woman walk up. "Adam!"

Adam stands, doing a strange half hug with the man, and then a real hug for the woman. "Hey, Doug. Fatima. How are you guys doing?"

After a moment of small talk, he turns and introduces me. "You all know Sky." It's not a question, given the smallness of our town and the largeness of my reputation. I'm glad Adam says it with warmth, even smiling at me as he says my name.

Fatima also offers me a big smile, but Doug blinks at me, as though he isn't sure what to say. "Huh." He turns back to Adam and keeps talking as though I'm not there.

I sort of expect Adam to redirect me into the conversation relatively soon, but maybe it gets a bit too difficult, because all of a sudden, a big group of people find their way to us, everyone weaving in and out to greet Adam, loudly and drunkenly.

I don't mind being on the outside looking in at times like these. Most of these people seem . . . I don't know. Superficial, I guess. They don't seem to know Adam. They don't know that Adam is the most gentlemanly man in the whole town, someone who will grab your groceries or open the door even if it's clear you don't need help. They don't know that when he laughs, his eyes sparkle, like they're made of sapphires caught in riverbeds in Montana or something. They don't know that he always checks in on his grandfather, even if William is feeling just fine.

They don't know Adam. And judging by the way Adam's smile doesn't reach his eyes—thus not one Montana sapphire sparkle in sight—I think he feels that, too.

But Adam makes no effort to extricate himself. And that's when I spot another small group of men walking up, including . . . oh gods. Including Grayson Baker.

My heart begins to beat so fast, I can feel it wanting to jump out of my chest and splatter all over the floor.

The last time I saw Grayson, I was half naked in my bedroom, allowing my crow brethren to attack him. I repeat the memory of him shrieking in my mind like an incantation. *I'm* the powerful one here. *He's* the one who should be afraid.

But maybe time has made him return to his arrogant ways, because when he sees me, he smirks. And then he looks at me down and up, and up and down, and winks.

I'm hyperventilating by the time that wink happens.

And Adam has been pulled into the massive group of people. It's so *loud*. Even if I'd shouted his name, he wouldn't hear me.

The sounds of people shouting and shrieking press in on my chest and I feel like I can't breathe even more. *I've got to get out of here.* That's what my body keeps screaming to me.

So I do the only thing I can think to do.

I turn and run.

16

I HONESTLY DON'T KNOW WHERE I'M GOING, BUT MY FEET seem to. They carry me right into the sanctuary of the church.

I haven't been to the actual church building in so long, I'd almost forgotten what it looks like. The sanctuary itself is tall, with pointed arches, everything made of white brick and pale gray cement. The doors are open tonight, and I push them, letting the freezing cold air within surround me, carrying with it the faint smell of lemon cleaners and spicy incense.

The windows are also tall and skinny like the interior, with black boards framing the stained glass. On one side of the church, the stained glass depicts key scenes from the Old Testament; on the other, it's all the key scenes from Jesus's life.

It hits me, what @tryingsomethingnew had told me about the church. The weird doors. The weird architecture. I want to kick myself for spending so much time with *people* that I lost sight of my little investigation into the possible Cranberry witches' cult.

There are a couple of women praying right in front of the altar. The church always has its doors open between Masses for that purpose—to allow people to come and talk to Jesus. They're so immersed in their divine conversations that no one looks at me as I walk around the perimeter of the sanctuary, looking for anything unusual.

I walk around to the bathrooms and examine both the men's and women's. The church store is closed, but when I stop to examine it, peeking in though the door windows, I notice something a little bit strange. Almost all the relics are not of Jesus, Mary, or random angels. They're of Mary Magdalene. There are prints of old paintings, little saint cards depicting her being carried by angels, her hair dark and flowing, her gaze tilted toward the heavens. For some reason, I don't remember the focus on Mary Magdalene when I was a kid. Has the church store always been this way? Or did this change happen when I was in a coma in an oak tree?

My phone beeps. It's Adam.

Hey, where are you? Is everything okay?

I don't know what to say to him. I'm not mad at him, exactly, but I don't feel great about how easily he'd forgotten me when his adoring fans appeared. Just two hours ago, he was pouring his heart out to me about his List of Impossible Ghostly Things. Just forty-five minutes ago, he was telling me he'd do anything to see me smile. And now he's only *just* noticed I ran away—I check the time—twenty minutes after I'd left him.

I'm fine, I tell him. Thanks for checking in.

Where are you?

I swallow. I don't want him to know how hurt I feel right now. Oh, around. I have a ride home so you don't have to—

"There you are." Before I finish the response, Adam's voice, Adam's words, are behind me, surrounding me just as the church air had earlier when I first stepped inside.

I open my mouth to say something, I'm not sure what, when he wraps his arms around me in a big hug.

"Oh," I say, and after a moment, I put one arm around his shoulders and the other around his waist.

His lips touch my neck. Not in a kiss, exactly, but in relief. "I was so worried about you. Why did you turn your phone off?"

"I didn't?" I say into this shoulder. His voice is reverberating into my skin. It's making goose bumps trail down my body. It's making my nipples hard.

"I called you, like, a dozen times. It went straight to voice mail." He pulls back and looks around. "I'm pretty sure most of this building is shit service. You been here this whole time?"

I nod.

He swallows. "Why—why did you leave me?"

In response, I can't help it: I burst into tears.

"Sky. Sky," he murmurs, pulling me back into his arms. It feels so good to be wrapped up by him, by his large, warm body. I hold him tight and my shoulders shake as I try to get words out.

"It's Grayson Baker," I sob.

"Baker? The one who was just out there with Fatima and them?"

"Yeah. He tricked me. He . . . we were going to hook up but he humiliated me instead. I was half-naked . . . he had his friend on the phone . . ."

I don't even get to finish the sentence when Adam pulls back. I'm startled into silence. I've never seen *this* Adam before. His jaw is clenched so tightly, I can see the muscles ticcing in it. His eyes are . . . not sparkling, that's for damn sure. They're sharp. Violently so.

"He humiliated you? He tricked you?" His voice is nearly a growl. I wonder if he realizes it.

I close my eyes. More tears trail down my cheeks, and then Adam's warm fingers are there, brushing them away. "I would have been fine if he had pretended like I wasn't there just now. But he looked at me and smirked and, and then he *winked*. I just had to run, you know?"

Adam nods. "I know." His jaw is still firm. His eyes still as bright as a blazing fire. "You ready to go?"

I nod, and he wraps an arm around me. We walk quickly, past the Wild Whirly Whirl ride, past the popcorn and candy apple vendors, slowing once we are near the Ferris wheel. "One second," he tells me, releasing my shoulder. I miss the warmth of his arm. Stupid, I know.

He walks over to the crowd still by the benches he and I had dinner at. "Baker," he shouts.

Grayson stands up, a big smile on his face, his arms wide. "What's up, Noemi?"

"This." And then Adam punches Grayson right across the face.

Grayson collapses instantly. Three seconds later, someone shouts, "He's out cold!"

Adam walks away from the scene without once looking back. He comes back to me and grabs my hand. "You ready?"

I nod without speaking, because the words just won't come to me right now. What can I possibly say to that? To what just happened? I'm still trying to process it.

Did Adam Noemi really punch Grayson Baker in the face?

All because he'd hurt me?

I want to shiver. I want to high-five Adam. I want to cry all over again.

But I don't do any of these, instead opting for the continuation of my stunned silence. We get in his car once more; this time the night around us is thick as ink. Adam starts the car, and we drive home in silence. He's seething, I think. I can feel the tension and frustration emanating from him in hot, sharp waves. One punch wasn't enough for him.

He pulls into Nadia's driveway and turns the car off. He turns to me. "Are you okay?"

"Are *you* okay?" I ask him, gesturing to his hand. "That looked—you know. That was kind of a hard punch, it looked like."

"Yeah, well." Adam rubs his knuckles. "He deserved worse." He shakes his head. "I'll be fine. Are you okay, Sky?"

I nod. "Yeah. I'm good."

"Good." He sighs and lets his head fall back on his seat. He covers his face with his hand and chuckles. "I haven't gotten into a brawl since I was a teenager."

"To be fair, I don't think knocking a man out with one punch counts as a brawl."

Adam lowers his hands and looks at me, no longer laughing. He's serious, what about, I don't know. The streetlamps around us paint him in sheets of amber. He looks like he did that one night, when I was still a ghost—angelic. "Sky," he says, and his voice is husky once more, just like before, when he caught me staring right at his lips way too hard.

A knock on the window has both of us jumping, with me shrieking as though the whole car had shattered. But it's just Nadia.

Of course. Nadia is literally never here when I'm craving company. But when I have company? Here she is, smiling like she *knows* something I don't, waving at us from outside the vehicle, gesturing for Adam to roll the window down.

Once he does, she says, "Adam! What a nice surprise! Want to come in for some flan?"

Adam smiles. His eyes stay a bit weary. "Thank you so much for the offer, Ms. Flores. But I need to check on my grandfather."

Nadia, of course, has to push it, by offering to wrap up flan for him and William, but Adam is firm in declining. It's clear he wants to be alone. "Nadia," I say, getting out of the car. "I'll bring them your flan tomorrow, okay?"

"Well. Okay." She gives me the stink eye, as though *I* were the one having trouble understanding Adam's clear boundaries, and then waves at Adam. "Good night, young man!"

He nods and waves, turning the car back on and slowly driving across the street to William's. Meanwhile, I turn to Nadia and raise my eyebrows.

"Adam already knows you're trying to play matchmaker. So you can cut it out now."

"Cut out what?" she asks in a fake innocent voice. But then she adds, "Is it matchmaking if I already *know* what's coming? Eh?" I roll my eyes as we both climb the three steps to the porch side by side. Since she's in her seventies and putting off another knee replacement her doctor has recommended for a decade, she goes a great deal slower than I normally do. I offer my arm, but Nadia hisses and lightly smacks it, as though I had gravely offended her as well as all the ancestors instead of just offering help.

"Amá Sonya came into my work and told me Adam wasn't a good match because he has no money."

"Ah." Now Nadia looks sincerely offended. She and her sister, Sonya, act like they hate each other's guts about ninety-eight percent of the time. In the other two percent, they merely tolerate one another. "So you want to take her advice? End up in a marriage like hers?"

I frown. "She is mostly alone. He's always away. That's what makes her happy, right?"

Nadia raises her eyebrow. "If you think your grandmother is happy, I have some seaside property in Oklahoma to sell you, amor."

I roll my eyes. "Whatever." I open up the fridge to pull out some cold water.

"He punched that man for you, no? That's love."

I abruptly place the pitcher back on the shelf. "You know that? From your *knowing*? Already?"

Nadia lifts her phone. "My knowing is fast. But sometimes the Cranberry grapevine is faster. There's a video in the WhatsApp chat I'm in with the nuns."

"Let me see."

"Ah-ah-ah," she says, pulling her phone back. "Why do you need to see, if that man isn't your true love? Huh?"

I roll my eyes. "Whatever. I'm sure it will be in the Cranberry Facebook group soon enough."

"Sí. Then *everyone* will see his love for you!" she calls as I stomp upstairs.

AFTER SHOWERING, AND WASHING MY FACE, AND APPLYING moisturizer, I don't open up any social media groups. Instead, I pull up Matchmakr, frowning when there are no new messages from @tryingsomethingnew. My little Good morning 😉 looks lonely and a bit pathetic now.

It takes me a long time to decide to just let it be. The last time he and I communicated, we got all spicy and both allegedly had orgasms thanks to turning each other on. What if he's the kind of guy who abandons a woman after fooling around with her? I may have spent basically all my adult years in a supernatural hibernation in the forest, but I still know how some men can be. And if that describes him, well, maybe I don't want to know him like that anymore.

I want to text my sisters so bad right now. Tears sting at my eyes. I need someone to really listen to me and everything I'm going through. Between Adam and this anonymous man, between Nadia and Amá Sonya trying to get in my head, I feel so confused. My thoughts are pulling me this way and that, leaving me feeling groundless and numb.

It's like I have a pile of yarn in front of me, all wound up and tangled. Sage and Teal would be able to help me sort it.

But what good is their help if they forget I'm their sister? If they forget I need them?

This is how I end up crying myself to sleep.

17

WHEN I AWAKEN, I FEEL PRETTY PATHETIC FOR HOW sorry I'd felt for myself the night before. If I want to repair my relationship with my sisters, I need to stop being so passive. I need to figure out where I really stand with them, and stop making assumptions. I know, more than anyone, that people perceive us as feeling and thinking one way, when it's often the total opposite of what they decided.

And honestly, I have Adam to thank for this development. Him defending me at the summer festival . . . it made me realize that I deserve to do that for myself.

I don't have to go into work until the late afternoon. So, after dropping off the flan in William's arms, as I promised to Nadia I would, I go into my room and pull out a glass beeswax candle. I wrap a piece of string around it, imagining it as the string that connects me to my sisters. I want to strengthen this string. I want to cancel the spell I had performed before, that made them each think the other was taking care of me so they didn't have to.

I light the candle and ask the old gods to do all of this with their far-reaching, cosmic, old-god magic. I light the candle and watch it sway with my breath, back and forth, imagining the intention reaching my sisters in curls of flame-like golden tendrils.

Last year I told Teal that I had found a book of old family spells at my work. We used one of the spells to find our mother, who was in town to arrogantly use a part of Teal's gift she had stolen to make art and profit from this theft. The problem was, our mother's gift is staying unseen. She can disappear right in front of your eyes. I watched her try to do it. It's as though she can open up a new universe to slip into, and if she doesn't want to see you again, you'll never see her again. End of story.

But I came out of my deep sleep in the woods with a kind of *knowing* about how magic works, some of the time. And I know that we can create spells with the old gods and they would be just as effective as something ancient from some unearthed book.

Teal would've never believed in a spell we just made up. But when I said it was from this powerful old book? She created a line of supernatural light. We followed this line to our mother. And Teal got her stolen magic back.

Maybe I should feel bad for lying to my sisters, but I don't. Teal is more whole, and healed, for it. Sage got to confront our mother and hopefully find some kind of closure, which she desperately needed.

But because of that whole event, because of the knowledge I had been given by possibly the old gods themselves, I know that the most powerful magic is one that I—or anyone—can imagine into being. Old books are awesome, but it is the intent of the practitioner that provides the energy behind a spell—like plugging into a primal source of world-making electricity. Which means old books are never necessary, except for sometimes making us a little more confident in our own abilities.

My phone pings when the candle is three-quarters of the way burnt. It's Sage. Hey, how have you been? I feel like we haven't spoken in forever. 😊

Just as the flame burns out, leaving nothing but a trail of spiraling smoke, a text comes through from Teal. What's up? Carter says he saw you at the festival last night with Adam? 👀

I open our group text and address them both at once. Not to be dramatic or anything, but my entire life feels like it's falling apart, and I need my sisters. Please come to Nadia's for lunch. I made enchiladas we can heat up. Plus there's plenty of coconut flan.

I wince when they respond back, mostly expecting them to blow me off once again. But instead, what happens is this:

Sage: I'm on my way.

Teal: Me too.

I immediately make my way to the kitchen to thank the old gods Nadia's way. With a fresh cup of espresso, poured directly into the earth, the caffeine making its way to their old-god cups just like veins and fountains.

IT'S TEAL WHO ARRIVES FIRST. SHE'S GOT ON A SPANDEX BLACK tank top and some loose joggers and Nike shoes, like she's either just completed a run or is planning on one right after this. When she walks into the kitchen, I point to the white pan on the stove. "Everything is hot. I'm just getting out the top—" But before I can finish, she has run up to me and has wrapped her arms around me.

"What's happening?" I cry out, trying to hold back the tears stinging my eyes. "It's just enchiladas."

"You're bananas if you think I'm here for enchiladas." When she pulls back, her own eyes are glazed over as well. "Well, just for them, anyhow."

Then Sage is pushing through the door, the baby carrier in her hands.

"Oh! You brought Oak!" I reach for him but pull back when I remember what happened the last time I wanted to hold him. "Sorry. I forgot."

And Sage instantly bursts into tears. "Oh God. I'm the worst sister in the whole world."

"Will everyone stop crying?" Teal says through her own tears.

"I'm so sorry, Sky." Sage places the carrier on the floor by the pantry and throws her arms around me. "I'm sorry. I wasn't myself. I really wasn't. Tenn made me go to the doctor." She pulls back, wiping her face. "It's postpartum depression."

"Oh . . ." I nod, thinking about how weird she's been. "That actually makes sense."

"Postpartum depression? Are you on an SSRI now?" Teal asks. Maybe I shouldn't be, but I'm a little bit relieved that she doesn't know, either. That this, too, wasn't a secret they both decided I was too naïve to know.

Sage nods. "Yeah. The doctor doesn't think I'll need to be on it long." She swallows. "I think it's already helping, to be honest. Even though she said it could take a while for me to notice an improvement." She turns to me. "I unloaded on you the worst, Sky. I'm sorry. I know you don't have bird flu or whatever. I just got so damn paranoid because of the depression, you know? I wouldn't even let Tenn hold him . . . I didn't realize it until Tenn sat me down and told me I was wrecking myself by pushing everyone I loved away."

"That's why you stopped responding to my messages," Teal says.

Sage nods. "That's why."

"Let's go in the living room," I suggest. "Get everyone comfy. And fed."

Teal and I serve Sage's plate and bring her a tray so she can eat while nursing Oak. Then we get our own food, and as we're settling on the sofas, I say to Teal, "So why haven't *you* answered my last several hundred texts?"

Teal sighs. "I'm a bastard. No, seriously. I became a freaking workaholic. I was sewing bags and wallets till two in the morning, and then I wouldn't even let myself sleep in. Carter told me I was using my work as a way to escape . . . which, you know. Is kind of a thing people with bipolar can be prone to do. Anyway, I'm sorry for blowing you off. When Carter told me about seeing you and Adam—"

"Sky!" shrieks Sage. "You and Adam?"

Teal rolls her eyes playfully at the interruption. "As I was *saying*. When Carter told me about seeing the two of you, it made me realize I didn't know anything about what you were going through. Either of you. I'm so sorry about that, you guys." She gives me and Sage additional hugs.

"Thanks." I'm not sure what else to say. I'm glad for this reconciliation, but what if everything just goes back to how it was once they both leave? My heart doesn't want to open to the idea that my sisters are back. I want to curl in on myself and protect it instead.

Sage senses this and says, "Don't worry. I will work for getting your trust back." She unlatches Oak, who is now peacefully asleep, milk-drunk as can be. And then she stands and places him in my arms.

"Oh," I breathe, watching the rise and fall of his belly, full of milk. His mouth is still pursed as though he is breastfeeding, and he even sucks a little bit at nothing. His eyelashes are so long, they lie neatly against his cheeks like pine needles. I know he gets those from Tenn. Boys always get the good eyelashes. "What a beautiful baby," I coo at him.

"Okay," Sage says, waving me off. "What is going on with you and Adam?"

"Let me get some flan first!" Teal says, jumping up.

She returns with enormous pieces of coconut flan balanced on three plates, one for each of us. "Gracias," Sage says, and I echo her thanks when Teal serves me. Though Sage offers to put Oak back in the carrier, I instead put the plate on the tray she was using, holding the fork with my free hand.

"That poor kid is covered with crumbs by the end of the day," Sage says, laughing when I almost drop flan on him. "It's his own fault, though. He's a freaking milk beast. I have to constantly eat or else I wanna faint."

"Yeah, yeah, the baby likes milk," Teal says, turning to me. "So, you're dating Adam now? How did that come about?"

I shake my head. "We're not dating. But there is someone who I might be sorta . . . involved with? Maybe? Maybe not anymore, though?"

"What does *that* mean?" Sage asks through a mouthful of flan.

I take a big breath and try my best to explain everything that's happened within the last couple of weeks, between Adam and our agreement, as well as how the chats were going with @tryingsomethingnew. I leave out the erotic details of our last . . . ah, encounter. But they get the gist of it.

"Anyway. Yeah. That's basically it."

"It's not basically it," Teal says. "Why did you conveniently leave out the part where he punched that asshole Grayson Baker last night? Tell him thanks for that, by the way, because it saves me the trouble of having to beat his ass for what he did to you." She frowns thoughtfully. "But I might do it anyway."

Teal really could kick anyone's ass. She spends at least seventy-five percent of her time working out and lifting weights the size of me. "You shouldn't waste your time and energy."

"But Adam put a lot of time and energy into punching that guy out," Sage said. "In front of half the damn town, too! Don't tell me that man doesn't have feelings for you."

I look down. "He doesn't. I mean, he's said some sweet things to me, but I think he really only sees me as a friend." Yes, he's given me some smoldering glances lately, but I can't rely on facial expressions alone to figure out how someone feels about me. I'd rather just hear it direct right from their mouth.

"Well, there's one way to find out," Teal says. "You gotta test him."

Sage wrinkles her nose. "Test him how? Because playing games is usually immature crap."

Teal shrugs. "Why don't you tell him that Amá Sonya's setting you up on a blind date this Friday? It's not a lie."

"Amá Sonya's *what?*" I ask. "She told me she's picking me up for breakfast!"

"Of course she did, the nasty old bat," Teal says, rolling her eyes. "When I had brunch with her on Sunday, she was going on about how she'd found you a 'nice, young, loaded man,' emphasis on the *loaded*, to take you out to breakfast on Friday."

It feels like someone's hit a bunch of pool balls into my stomach, scattering them every which way. "But . . . why? What if I don't want to have a meal with a man I've never met?"

"You don't have to go," Sage says gently.

"But if you did, you could let it slip to Adam that you're going on a date. If he wants you like the way I think . . . he's not going to be happy about it. Not one little bit." Teal smiles triumphantly, like she knows she's already right.

"I mean . . ." I ponder this. "I could just tell him, because we're friends. Or at least, I'm pretty sure we're friends by now." Surely punching Grayson Baker puts him firmly in some kind of *friends* category. "If it comes up, I mean."

"But are you okay with going on this date?" Sage asks. "Because we can put a stop to it right now. I will literally call up Amá Sonya and tell her it's not happening."

I shrug. "I mean . . . sure. I can always leave him if he gets creepy, or rude, or something."

"Or you could call Adam to come get you if any of that happens," Teal says.

I glare at her. "Have you been colluding with Nadia? Since when have you been a matchmaker?"

Sage perks up at this. "Oh? Has Nadia mentioned *knowing* something between you and Adam?"

"Just like she *knew* about me and Carter," Teal says in a singsong voice.

I decide now's as good a time as any to change the subject. Talking about whatever Nadia claims to know just confuses me further. "So, what about the online guy?"

Teal shrugs. "What about him?"

"I mean. It felt like we had a real connection there . . ."

"Until he ghosted you after getting off," Teal finishes.

"Oh, I don't know," Sage says. "I mean. You guys know that's how Tenn and I first connected."

"But you knew who he was," Teal says. "This internet random could literally be anyone."

Sage suggests, "Keep chatting with him. But be very careful. Stay anon for a really long time, till you know he's not—"

"Another version of that Baker asshole," Teal supplies.

"Good point," I say sullenly, looking down at Oak, who is stretching and looking for some milk that I definitely do not have.

"He might be a good one, too," Sage says, softly lifting Oak to her chest. "Just give it time. If he's hiding red flags, they will show themselves sooner or later. They always do."

Since I have to get to work within the hour, Teal cleans the kitchen while Sage finishes up giving Oak his snack. As I say goodbye to my sisters, a thought occurs to me. "Hey, did you guys notice that the church store only sells Mary Magdalene stuff now? That's kind of weird, right?"

"Oh," Sage says. "That's always been that way. You never heard the rumors there's a cult connected to her at the church?"

Goose bumps prick over my arms and I wrap them around myself. "No. Really? A *cult*?"

"Uh-huh. I always tried to ask Nadia about it but all she would do is smile and act like I was asking why is the moon made of cheese."

"Wait, Nadia's in a cult?" Teal asks.

"It would make a lot of sense, no?" Sage replies. "That woman lives at the church. Always has."

"What about . . ." I think about what @tryingsomethingnew told me. "You know. Secret doors and rooms and stuff. Do you know of any in the church? Does the cult have those spots?"

Sage raises an eyebrow at me, like she's curious about why I'm asking, but decides to just humor me without questioning it. "The only weird room I know is in the director of education's office. And that was, like, fifteen years ago. It might be a different office now. But back then at least, there was a weird, short door between the bookshelves. When I tried to open it up, it was locked. I only tried once, though. Honestly, it was probably filled with just a bunch of extra Bibles." Sage kisses my cheek. "I gotta run. I'm starving, and I need to nap with this dude once he and I have both eaten again."

Teal gives me a hug. "I'll be in touch," she says. "I promise." And true to her word, even before she's left Nadia's in her car, she texts me. Two weeks from now. My little shop's grand opening. Bring Adam 😉

18

I GO ANOTHER WHOLE DAY WITHOUT SPEAKING TO @TRYING somethingnew. When I scroll back on our last exchange, I feel a little embarrassed, at first, at how unapologetically horny we were. How unapologetically horny *I* was. But then I shake my head, holding my shame at bay. What we did was fun and consensual. Even if I never speak to him again, I refuse to regret it.

I don't see or hear from Adam for another several days, until the incredibly inconvenient time of me walking outside the house on Friday morning, gearing myself up for the blind date Amá has set me up on without even telling me.

Dress well, she'd texted the night before. Dress like the wife you want to be.

I'm so glad Teal spilled the beans on the date, because it would've been so weird to get that text from my grandmother without any context. Because of course, Amá Sonya hasn't told me anything about the date herself.

I'd decided on a peach-pink dress, very body-conforming, but it looks a little less slutty with the delicate lace layer of embroidery over the satinlike material. I'd left my hair down, in beach waves, clipping the front back with sparkling butterfly hair clips, leaving a couple of long curls by my crown. I'd slipped on strappy sandals the color of almonds and applied light pink makeup over my cheeks and lips.

I had intended to be ready much earlier, but by the time I walk outside, I only have two minutes until either Amá or this random guy is supposed to arrive to pick me up. Because of course, that information wasn't conveyed to me, either.

And then, all of a sudden, there is Adam, for some reason, leaning against my car, tapping on his phone.

I furrow my brow. Adam wouldn't be my blind date, would he? No. Amá Sonya made her feelings about him very clear. My brain just can't seem to wrap around why he's randomly in the driveway this early in the morning.

"Adam?" I call, approaching him.

"Oh hey, I was just about to—" When Adam looks up, his phone slips from his hand, falling to the driveway so hard, it bounces twice my way. I lean down to pick it up, but apparently he's got the same idea, and the top of his head rams right into my shoulder, but before I can fall on my ass, he grabs me to bring me toward him to keep me upright, I assume. The problem is, he wasn't exactly in a stable position, having just leaned over to get the phone, too. So when he pulls me in, I land on him just as he unceremoniously falls flat on his ass.

I am sitting in Adam Noemi's lap. I am *sitting* in Adam Noemi's *lap* as the morning sun turns his warm honey hair into spun gold. I feel frozen in place as he asks, "Shit. I'm so sorry. Are you okay?"

Instead of responding straightaway, I realize many things at once. His big hand on my waist. How solid his thighs are beneath my bottom. How good he smells—like he's just been hiking in the woods. Pine, cranberry, leather.

I shake my head when I realize he's still waiting for a response. What was the question again? Right. "I'm fine. I'm sorry about that, too." I make to get up. He keeps his hand on my waist as he rises alongside me, in case I accidentally fall again, I'm guessing.

Once we're both standing, he looks at me up and down and up again. He doesn't even try to hide his appreciation. He even whistles! Which does nothing to help the blush forming on my cheeks. "I told you, Sky, you gotta stop taking my breath away. Jesus. Look at you."

His words remind me of @tryingsomethingnew, when I first sent him that spicy selfie. *Look at you*. This only makes me blush even harder.

"I was going to see if you wanted to go to the beach, but . . ." He puts a hand on his head as he surveys me again. "What do you have going on? A hot date or something?"

I open my mouth, and close it. "Well . . ."

His eyes widen and he begins to nod rapidly. "Oh. Right. That guy you said you were . . ."

I shake my head. "Oh, it's not him. It's just . . ."

He laughs. "Oh, another guy. Wow, you're . . . I mean, I can't say I blame them. Blame anyone for . . . Christ. I'm babbling."

It's at this moment that a Lincoln I've never seen before pulls into the driveway. Inside is a man I've never seen before, either. He gets out, wearing a sharp gray suit, one that matches the salt-and-pepper of his hair.

"Oh God," I say under my breath. "He's old enough to be my dad."

Adam whips his gaze to me. "You don't know him?"

I shake my head. "My grandmother set me up. She didn't even ask."

"Sky?" the man smiles at me warmly. "Sky Flores. I'm Jacob Clearwoods. Attorney. Your grandmother is great friends with my mom. They're always getting up to no good at those fundraisers the ladies at the Gilded Cranberry are throwing."

His mother is probably the same age as my grandmother. Doing the math, this guy was probably in law school when I was born.

I don't mind the idea of older men. I mean, look at Adam. He's nine or so years older than me. But at least he was still a little kid when I came into this world. What on earth would I even say to a guy like Jacob? What could we possibly talk about? His children, who are probably more age-appropriate for me to date?

"Oh wow. I'm so sorry, Jacob, but there's been a mistake," Adam says quickly, noticing my hyperventilating and probably crazed eyes. "Sky didn't know about this date, and she wouldn't have said yes to it because . . . ah. Well, she and I are together."

I glance at him so fast, I want to fall over again. "We—"

"Yes, babe." Adam puts an arm around me and pulls me close. He places a warm kiss on my forehead and whispers, "Go with it," before turning back to a befuddled Jacob. "Coming up on, what? Three months next week."

"Oh wow," Jacob says. "And Sonya really had no—"

I shake my head. "You know how elders are. She's so forgetful. Just the other day, she forgot how doors worked. We had to pull her out of the window because she literally got stuck trying to get in her own home!" I only just barely suppress my giggle. Take that, Amá Sonya. Now the whole country club will be chatting about your deteriorating brain capacity.

"Oh, I'm so sorry to hear that," Jacob says. "So . . ." He looks between me and Adam again, and then pauses.

"I'm Adam Noemi, by the way," Adam says, cutting off Jacob's next words.

Jacob beams in response and points to Adam as they shake hands. "Say, aren't you that famous news reporter that moved to New York City from high school?"

And just like that, Jacob completely forgets that I exist. All of a sudden, he and Adam are chortling like they're in the middle of a yearslong bromance. By the time Jacob leaves, they've exchanged numbers to play a round of golf later in the month.

I slow-blink. "Damn. Your peopling skills are unreal."

Adam looks at me and sighs. It's not a sad sigh, but it's also . . . not exactly happy. Like he's just accepted something he's been fighting for a really long time. "How about the beach?" he asks. "Do you wanna go with me?" He fusses at his phone with one hand, his other in his hair, and he's jiggling one of his legs. If I didn't know any better, I'd say that Adam seems . . . *nervous*.

My stomach interrupts my thoughts with a growl, and we both laugh. "I need food," I say, putting a hand on my belly.

"Noted. Let's get food and head to the beach."

I grab a beach bag and throw a swimsuit, a towel, and some SPF in it. I'm too hungry to change now—I can do that later. I run down, and Adam's got his Jeep in the driveway, waiting for me.

"How do you feel about breakfast burritos?" he asks as he opens the door for me.

"Yes. All of them. Now, please."

He laughs, his eyes doing that sparkling thing again. "Where do you think Mr. Jacob was about to take you?"

"Probably someplace nice, to be honest. But he was going to ruin it by showing me photos of his great-grandchildren."

Adam bursts into laughter again. "I wasn't going to say anything, but . . . yeah. He was up there in years, wasn't he?"

I shake my head. "I don't know what my grandmother was thinking."

"Does she appreciate money? 'Cause he and his whole family are old money."

I nod. "She appreciates little else, to be honest."

Adam cuts me a glance with the corner of his eye. "And what about you? Do you appreciate money?"

I pause. "I like having food in my cupboards and gas in my tank."

"Right. But your grandma wasn't setting you up with Jacob Clearwoods for food security. She was trying to hook you up with Hamptons parties and wine tastings in Napa . . ."

"Yeah, I know. I know." I close my eyes for a moment. "I've never cared about that." I shake my head. "I just want someone who's . . . you know."

He grins. "Sexy? Smart? Charming?"

I shake my head again, smiling as I consider the answer to his question. "Someone nice."

"Nice."

We're pulling into the breakfast place, getting in line at the drive-through. "Nice is boring, though, Sky."

"Nice is not boring!" I wave my hands. "What's the opposite of nice? Huh? It's mean. I don't want someone mean, I want someone nice."

"But that goes without saying, doesn't it?"

I frown and look away. "You'd think. But no. It doesn't go without saying."

Thankfully, he doesn't say anything to this. Or, at least, I don't think he will, as he takes my order and insists on paying for my egg-and-chorizo burrito with extra avocado and cheese, alongside a veggie burrito with scrambled tofu for himself. But it happens fast—as I'm inhaling my burrito in the most unladylike manner possible—he says, while driving back toward the main road, staring straight ahead, "You deserve so much better than what this fucking town has given you, Sky."

"Hmm," I say through a full mouth. When I swallow, I add, "Thanks?"

He's kind of lost in thought, I think, running a hand over the dark red scruff at his chin. "If it were up to me . . ."

But he doesn't finish the sentence. He instead grins and says, "You like swimming?"

I want to ask him, *What? If it were up to you, what?* Maybe he'd go around punching everyone in the face, like he did to Grayson. Or maybe . . . I don't know. I can't think of anything else. Him pretending to be my friend is the only alternative, and we're already doing that literally right now. That's why he asked me to the beach, right? So folks could see us being friends, per our agreement.

"Um. I like swimming. Especially when the water is warm." I close my eyes and smile. "I hate it when it's weird and barely warm, with extra-cold pockets you swim through like there's a collection of subterranean air conditioners working in there." I glance his way. "What about you? You like swimming?"

He nods. "It's how I exercise, since high school. I used to be on the swim team. But now I just go to the Y and do laps a few days a week." We turn down the skinny, pine-tree-lined road, heading back toward Cranberry Falls. I guess he wants to do the more private Crescent Beach today, rather than the one downtown. Which is fine, of course. Just a surprising choice, given that we're supposed to be seen as friends. "So what's up with that other guy you were seeing, or whatever?" he asks out of nowhere.

"What guy?"

He laughs. "The one you mentioned the other night, at the festival? You were talking to him, and—"

"Oh right." He means @tryingsomethingnew. "I think he ghosted me, actually."

"Jesus. Why?"

I blink at him. "Why not? People ghost each other all the time, don't they?"

"I know, I know." He pulls into a parking space and sighs with a kind of hopeless-sounding chuckle coming out at the same time. "It's just . . . it's so weird someone would ghost *you*, though."

I snort so loud. "Cut it out, man."

He grabs the food back from my lap and pulls out his burrito. "I'm serious, Sky."

I don't know what to say to that. I think of Teal, wanting me to be matched with this man. Of Nadia, with her *knowing*, or whatever.

The truth is, at this point . . . even I can admit to myself that Adam's behavior might be that of a man who may have a tiny crush on me. Big deal, though. What Amá Sonya said to me . . . that he wants me because he knows that soon he'll be on my "level"—it cuts to the core of my fear with him, and any other man, to be honest.

Adam's going to figure out I'm too weird for him. Spending too much time in the woods, too caught up in my own pastime of solving harmless mysteries. Too strange a background, having spent eight years basically comatose inside an ancient, hollowed oak tree. Adam, who is funny and kind, intelligent and beautiful—as soon as he gets his footing back with his work, he's going to want someone better. That's what I've got to keep in mind.

"I'm going to change really quick. Is that okay?"

He tilts his head. "Uh, sure, but do you want me to—"

I slide my hands under the skirt of my dress and pull my underwear down.

"What the—" Adam says as I shimmy the nude seamless G-string under my feet.

"Don't freak out. I'm just putting on my swimsuit."

"Here? In the car?" His voice has gotten squeaky. When I turn to him, I smile when I see that his face is all pink. He's staring at my legs, like knowing I'm wearing nothing under this dress is doing something to him.

"Nothing's going to show. Come on. I'm just going to slide it on under my dress, and then pull my dress—"

"Okay, okay. Okay. I'm going to—you know. Give you some privacy. Okay? Okay."

"You've said 'okay' like two hundred times in the last thirty seconds."

"Okay." He winks at me, still pink-cheeked, and grabs his food and is out the door. He eats with his back toward me, his shoulders looking a bit tense.

I pull on my suit—a one-piece the color of rubies, with a built-in shelf bra that makes my chest look like I'm actually capable of cleavage—and then pull my dress over my head. I undo my bra next, pulling the straps under my arms and getting the whole thing free, rolled up in the dress, and in the beach bag. I get out of the car wearing my suit and sandals, my bag on my shoulder. "Ready!"

"You're decent?" he asks without turning around.

"No. I'm completely naked." He chokes a bit and I can't stop my big smile. Why is he so easy to tease? He's the kind of guy who's always hooking up with beautiful women. Me getting dressed next to him while showing nothing but my legs and arms shouldn't affect him like this.

"Sky." His head drops back. "You're killing me. You're killing me over here."

"It's a joke. I'm dressed."

He turns slowly, like he can't be sure I'm not actually completely nude in the middle of this extremely public parking lot. "Relax. It's not even a bikini."

"I don't know how to relax around you. You're always—"

"Taking your breath away?" I ask, walking over to him.

He takes one deep breath, like he has to remind himself to do it. To breathe. He looks me over in a way that gives me goose bumps on the back of my head and down my spine. His eyes on my hips, my legs, my breasts. He looks like he wants to do wicked things to me, right now, in this very public parking lot.

Are you seriously that into me? I want to ask. It feels impossible.

But maybe it's one of those *Men will get hard over any round object* things. That's what I'm going to tell myself, anyway.

And it's a good thing, too, because he realizes what he's doing and shakes his head and swallows, forcing his eyes to meet my gaze. "Shall we?"

We walk with a couple of feet between us on the trail, in silence for a few minutes, when he says, "I was wondering if you could give me contact information for your sisters. So I can interview them for the piece."

I'm not sure how I feel about this. I mean, I should've known it was coming. Any kind of article like this always has interviews with the subject's inner circle. But I wince when I imagine Teal turning it around on him, to find out his intentions with me or whatever. I'll have to talk to her beforehand and make sure she knows that would be overstepping. "Sure. Let me let them know first, and then I can give you their info." I glance at him. "You . . . haven't asked me anything about . . . you know. My experience. Since we were last here . . ."

"And I was an enormous ass to you. I remember." He nods. "Whenever you're comfortable. I can ask a few more questions. I promise I'll be . . ." He takes in a brief but shuddering breath. "I'll be nice."

"Thank you," I say as I duck under a low evergreen branch.

Adam shakes his head. "Thanking me for being nice." He chuckles. "Like I said, Sky. You deserve so much better."

19

WE DON'T SAY ANYTHING AS THE PATH TURNS FROM packed dirt and fallen leaves to sand the color of sparkling champagne, and then we enter the threshold to Crescent Beach. It's an unbearably glorious day. The blue of the sky is as vivid as Adam's eyes, and it's filled with whipped-cream clouds that lazily drift by over us. "No one is here?" I ask, looking around.

"They're all probably grabbing lunch first to bring in their picnic baskets," Adam says, taking my hand and pulling me toward the shore. At a nice, smooth spot of sand, he sets down a big old quilt. I have a seat on it and begin to put sunscreen on my arms, my legs, my chest. Adam watches intently until . . . he doesn't. He whips his gaze away from me and forces it onto the skyline, the muscles in his neck tense.

Round objects, I tell myself.

"I'm going to do some laps," he tells me, pulling his shirt over his head.

And . . . oh.

Now I'm the one trying to force my gaze away.

Only it's not happening.

His body is smooth. His shoulders wide. He has a hint of a belly between the cuts in his hips. His body is lean and soft at once, with dark auburn hair on his chest and trailing down to . . . ahem. Lower. His arms look strong, and I want to feel his bare chest over mine. The thought comes so fast and true that it echoes almost painfully in my mind. The image of me, in bed, and Adam's chest hair sliding against my breasts.

Thankfully Adam is kicking off his shoes, so he doesn't see me with my jaw dropped open like I'm seeing another human for the first time in my existence. "Want to join?"

I shake my head wordlessly, then clear my throat when I see him tilt his head at me. Am I blushing? Oh gods. I think I'm blushing again. "I'm going to sunbathe for a little while first."

"Sounds good." He walks up to the water, the freckles on his back visible in the light, wading in the water for a bit before diving in. I watch as his arms appear and slice into the skin of sea, over and over.

I sit and come to a number of stressful conclusions about what just occurred. One, my reaction to seeing Adam without his shirt on provoked a great deal of erotic thoughts. Acknowledging these thoughts means I have to accept that I have a crush on him again. I lay a hand on my belly, where the blue-winged moths have once again descended, making me feel like if there were only a handful more of them, they'd lift me right off the sand.

I look up at the clouds—puffy, white, the texture of whipped marshmallow carefully laid over hot cocoa. I wonder how long I've had my feelings for Adam rekindled. This happens to me a lot—I don't often understand my emotions until the reality of what I'm feeling punches me right in the heart, like what happened just now. My instinct is to get up and pace the beach, analyzing my situation. Make a pros and cons list of whether it's wise to have feelings for Adam at all. Instead, I keep my gaze on the clouds as they march by, soft and satiny-looking. *I'm at the beach*, I remind myself. *I can just enjoy myself now, and analyze as much as I'd like later.*

Once I feel calm enough, I push up onto my feet and approach the water. I sigh when the foamy wave rushes up, over my feet. It's warm today, thank the old gods. I walk in, deeper and deeper, until the water is at my shoulders, and I feel as weightless as though I were a ghost, suspended in midair.

I'm not sure where Adam is—somewhere farther out, to my right, I think—so I just close my eyes and let myself feel this ocean. Feel it with my gift, meaning I tap into whatever magic in our lineage connects us with these powers. The whole ocean is *alive*. This great, alive water-being is full of creatures who do not see themselves as separate from the water, and just a handful who do. There is a sea turtle in the distance, her shell wide enough for a human to curl up on. There are schools of fish all around me, murmuring like starlings in the sky. And maybe twenty feet away is a sand tiger shark, the water slinking over her smooth skin like wind.

The sound of water sloshing has me opening my eyes to Adam, appearing in front of me, salt water sliding down his body in a way that makes me think about licking him, and then feeling vaguely horrified by the impulse. "Hey," he says, smiling and wiping his eyes.

I clear my throat. I'm a little nervous because of what happened the last time I told him about my gift . . . but I'm so tired of hiding myself. With him, with everyone . . . I even hide *myself* from *myself* sometimes. I wonder if that's why I still have a hard time feeling like I belong in my own skin. Either way, I'm tired of it. I'm tired of keeping everything I am hidden away all the time.

"Do you want to pet a shark?" I ask him.

His eyes widen and he looks around. "There's a fucking shark here?"

"She's not that close."

He slides through the water and puts an arm around my waist, pulling me toward the shore. "Adam!" I laugh, pulling his arm off me. "She's a sand tiger shark. They don't attack humans."

"But I'm guessing they still have rows of sharp teeth in their mouths that they could use to bite a limb or two off." He grabs my hand now.

"Adam. If *you* want to leave, fine. But I'm going to pet her." I can *feel* that she's friendly. That her nervous system would like it if I gently touched her. She's just waiting for me to say *okay*.

Adam's gaze is serious. "I'm not leaving you. But I also really don't like sharks, Sky."

I look at him. "Do you wanna pet one or not?"

He laughs and looks around. "Jesus. I feel insane right now." My heart drops when I think about what he might be implying. That he feels insane because he thinks *I'm* insane. And maybe my insanity is leaking over to him like spilled ink across a pristine pond. But then he adds softly, "Hell yes. Let's pet a damn shark." He pauses. "It's not that big, is it?"

I shake my head. "No." And I close my eyes again and say to her (I feel distinctly the shark is a female), "Okay. If you want to come, you can come."

She moves quickly, her nose butting up against my knee within only a couple of seconds. Adam doesn't see her at first, but when he does, he says, "Holy *shit*. Sky. You said it wasn't big!"

"She's not. She's small for a sand tiger shark."

I bend down and dip my hand into the water, and she swims around me, bumping up so that my fingers glide along the top of her head, and down her body. She is smooth, with the slightest hint of soft ridges, the way the most gentle of sandpaper feels when it's touched as gently as possible. She's absolutely gorgeous. The color of the warm sand under our feet. Almost six feet long. "Wow, you're so beautiful," I coo.

"Sky. What the hell is even happening?" Adam whispers. He's closer to me now, an arm out, but I don't think to pet her. He's ready to grab me and take me away.

I make my voice calm, to show how unbothered I am. Maybe it will calm him, too. "It's okay. I told you. She wants to be petted."

Adam shakes his head. "Okay. Okay." He bends and drops his hand into the water, and she immediately approaches, slowly, as though she knows how afraid he is. He leans just a bit and slides his fingers over her head. She darts back my way, and I do the same with my hand, gliding my whole hand over her slippery skin.

"Fuck. You're right. She's like a puppy." He exhales a laugh.

The shark darts around us once more, grabbing one last, short petting session with the both of us, and then she slips away to deeper water. "She got bored," I say with a smile, turning toward the skyline. It's gotten cloudier, but more of the pale, bright meringue pie topping sort. In the distance, sun rays fall in sheets of yellow gold, lighting the water in swaths of glitter.

Before I can process it, Adam presses his wet, warm body to my back. He wraps his arm around my belly and pulls me closer to him, so we are flush—my shoulders at his chest, his hips at my lower back. "Sky," he says, placing his chin to the back of my head. I feel his breath at my scalp. "My heart is still racing. I can't believe I just petted a shark. My hands . . ." He tightens the one that's now at my hip. "They're still shaking." He chuckles breathlessly.

"Do you need me to distract you?" I don't dare move. He feels so good this close. I want to pretend that it's not from a fear response. I want to pretend he's touching me because he's mine.

"Please. Distract me," he responds.

I want to think of something sexy to say. Something enticing and hot, something that will make him want me in the ways I'm beginning to want him. But the thing is, I'm still scared by my response to Adam. I'm still leaning against him, feeling the hairs of his chest against my shoulders, feeling his warm, solid form, and the only conclusion that keeps blaring through my brain is *Not close enough! Not close enough!*

By the sheer power of my will, I don't blurt out anything slutty, or even flirty. Instead, I say, "I haven't been back to the tree." I take a step forward and Adam releases the hand he'd had on me. When I turn around, he's pink-faced and breathless. He glances at my lips and then away so quickly, I wonder if I imagined it. "The tree?" he finally asks. Then he shakes his head quickly. "Right. The tree. Where you were for those eight years . . ."

I nod. "It's right over there." I point to the patch of woods where we'd come from. "What if we went there? For your story? You can accompany me for my first time back."

Adam takes one big, shuddering breath and nods. "We could do that. Sure. Of course."

I didn't exactly dress for hiking, but luckily, the big oak tree is on flat ground, and it's not too far off trail. I remember how frustrated Sage was after she found me . . . how *close* I'd been that whole time. And none of us ever knew, not even me.

When we reach the oak, it's about midday. Sunlight falls straight into the forest through the openings in the canopy, like someone holding out their hand for poured honey milk. The tree itself is ancient, the kind of tree that makes you feel like you're in the presence of something wild and holy, like it could have been here before creation somehow.

Its branches open like a hug from all directions, some of them so large and heavy that they rest on the forest floor. The bits of its leaves that catch the honey-milk light are edged in gold. Adam whistles when he follows my pointer finger to it. "Whoa," he says, his voice soft with reverence, and we both just stare at the tree for a little while, the same way you'd stop and marvel at an unexpected clear night full of stars spread across the black sky like crushed quartz on a chalkboard.

I walk forward, to the trunk that might be as wide as a car and a half or so. It had to be this large for me to be able to lie down inside its hidden chamber for years and years.

I have to bend down to the trunk opening to get inside, but once I'm in, I can stand. Adam follows me, his eyes wide. He looks around and frowns. "It's kind of weird that there's yellow leaves in here." He sticks his head back out to glance at the forest floor, then comes all the way back inside again. "And only in here."

It's true. And it is weird, but weird in an expected way, if you understand the inexplicable happenings of the old gods. It's as though they unrolled a little carpet in here, made entirely of leaves in the color of marigolds and sunflowers and expansive Cranberry sunrises from the viewpoint of Nadia's roof.

"Sage and Nadia found me here. I was with them, as a ghost. And my body was . . ." I point to the ground, where several leaves flutter, though there is no discernible wind. "Completely fine. Completely asleep."

"How did you get back in?" His voice is soft and his eyes . . . he's believing me this time. He's opened his heart, just like he said he would. He's trying.

"Nadia said, just step in. I don't know how it happened, to be honest, but I do know that—" I close my eyes and take a breath. I don't want to cry right now. When I open them, Adam's closer, like he's ready to hug me, or grab my hand, whatever I need. "I do know that I wanted to live. I wanted to eat cherries, I wanted to swim in the ocean, I wanted to pet Coffee—"

"Coffee?" he murmurs.

"My favorite fox."

This makes him smile, that megawatt one that makes his eyes glitter and crinkle up and his dimples deepen all the way in.

"I wanted to kiss someone again." I say it without thinking, my eyes firmly on his smile, which drops slowly as his face turns serious again, the same kind of serious as it always gets when he's looking at *my* lips. At that moment, I realize that he and I have been wanting to kiss each other for a while now. It makes me bold enough to voice it. "Can we finally kiss yet, Adam?"

He steps forward and places his hands on my face, cupping my cheeks. I close my eyes at how good it feels, his warm, calloused hands so gentle against my skin, and when I open them, he's leaned in so far that he's a breath away. "You sure?" he asks.

"Yes," I whisper firmly, and then his lips are on mine.

We start softly, kind of like a dozen little pop kisses, until I can't take it anymore and I reach my hand around the back of his neck and pull him in deeper. He sucks my lower lip in his mouth, and I clutch at his biceps with my other hand—it just feels so good. When our tongues meet, I moan, which makes him give a low groan, and one of his hands lowers to the small of my back, pushing me closer and closer, until my breasts press against his chest, our legs intertwined. It's still not close enough.

He laughs, pressing his forehead to mine. "I knew . . . God, I knew it would be like this with you."

"Like what?"

He pulls back, making eye contact, and for once, it doesn't feel like too much. "Like everything."

I think I know exactly what he means by this. I suspect that I knew it would be *like everything* with Adam even when I was a ghost, my body still asleep inside this ancient, powerful tree.

"Is it okay if we kiss again?" he asks, and this time, I'm the one who laughs.

"Of course," I say, and when he leans in, I swear, a handful of sun-yellow leaves lift up off the floor of the tree trunk, fluttering and surrounding us like ecstatic blue moths.

WE WALK BACK FROM THE OAK TREE IN SILENCE, BOTH OF OUR mouths a bit swollen from all that making out in the woods and whatnot, and then Adam says, "You bringing food over again for Gramps?"

I freeze. "Shit. Today's Friday." I mean, I knew it was Friday, but it's also somehow hitting me again that it's *Friday*. "I can't believe I forgot to cook something."

Adam gently nudges my shoulder with his. "Hey. No worries. I can order pizza."

I shake my head. "No. He needs something wholesome and homemade. Otherwise he lives on nothing but super processed food."

Adam's eyes warm completely as he gazes all over my face.

My eyes, eyebrows, down to my lips—again with the lips, even though we just kissed!—before he blinks away. "I'll cook, then."

I raise my brows. "You can cook?"

He tilts his head with a grin. "I'm going to pretend you didn't ask me that."

"Hey. You're forgetting that I've been trying to date for the first time this year. Tons of men refuse to learn how to cook. When I've asked stuff like *What's a specialty meal you make?*, they respond with something like *Why should I learn how to cook when my wife's going to handle all that anyway?*"

Adam shakes his head. "Shameful. Men who probably think they're natural leaders or some shit and they're too dependent and unintelligent to even feed themselves properly."

We begin walking again, returning to the beach path but going the way to the parking lot. The ground has fully shifted on this trail from sand to the soft, dark forest floor. I love the textures of this earth. Sometimes I take off my shoes in the woods to feel the mud between my toes. It feels so good. Primordial, maybe. Many creation myths begin with the gods forming humans and more-than-humans out of dirt.

"Eggplant parmigiana, by the way," he says.

I tilt my head up at him. "Hmm?"

"My specialty meal I like to make."

"Oh." I furrow my brow. "Yum?"

"I'll make it tonight. Come by at your normal time and I'll try and have it ready by the time you get there."

I stop again. I can't help the smile on my face. "Really? You'll cook for William?"

"Yes. I'll cook for Gramps. And for you, Sky." His eyes are so serious. They seem far too serious for the conversation we're having.

"You can ask me questions tomorrow at dinner, if you want. And I'll have my sisters' permission to give you their information by then."

He blinks and nods. I can see the reminder sweeping over him—I am his subject. Maybe a friend. But there have to be boundaries between us. Otherwise, my heart's going to get broken. I don't know what the consequences for Adam might be—maybe he couldn't ethically publish his piece or something—but I'm not keen on nursing any more broken hearts.

"Sure. Sounds like a plan," he says as we reach the parking lot. And I think it's just my inner pessimist thinking it, maybe, but the tone of his voice sounds a bit sad as he says it.

20

I GET A PHONE CALL FROM TEAL JUST AS I'M CHOOSING WHAT to wear for dinner at William's. "Well?" she asks.

"Well what?" I put the phone on speaker so I can keep going through the armoire.

"Hold on. Sage wants me to three-way her in the call."

I hear a number of beeps and then a ring tone. Sage picks up in the middle of the first one. "Did Adam get mad about your date? Also, how was the date?"

My first thought is my sisters somehow learned that Adam and I grabbed burritos and then went to the beach. Even excluding the part where we visited the wild, wide oak in the woods and proceeded to make out inside it, the whole thing sounds very date-ish. I pause on perusing through my dresses.

Was that a date? It sure felt like one. It's not like Crescent Beach is ever busy, unlike the downtown beach, so it doesn't make sense for Adam to bring me there to do a pretend-friendship outing. And the only reason we discussed the topic for his piece was that I brought it up. I took us to the tree. If it weren't for that, would he have asked me questions about what happened to me at all?

Did Adam and I literally just go on our first date, and I didn't even know it?

"Sky?" Teal asks. "Did we lose you when I got Sage on?"

I shake my head even though they can't see me. "No, no. Sorry, I just got really confused by the three hundred questions that were just asked."

Sage laughs. "Okay. Touché. Let's start with: Did you go on the date?"

I pull out a lemon yellow sundress and place it on my comforter. "I did not."

"Oh. So you told Amá Sonya you changed your mind?"

"Nope. The guy arrived and he was old enough to be my grandparent."

"He was not," Teal gasps.

"Okay. Maybe a young grandparent, but still. There was a thirty-year age gap or so. Which . . . that's fine for someone else, but not for me."

"So what did you do?" Teal asks. "Cancel on him by telling him you're sorry you don't know the signs of a heart attack?"

I laugh. "No. Adam told him that he and I were dating. And that was why I couldn't go to breakfast."

Now they both gasp. "What the hell?" Sage says. "You didn't mention Adam being there!"

They make me back up the story to tell them every single detail. Which I do. Sort of. For some reason, I just don't want to tell them about the beach. About the burritos. My revelation that it might have been a not-date date is a little overwhelming now.

Especially since, of course, my sisters are already making baseless claims about Adam's motivations.

"See. I told you," Teal says. "That man wants you."

"It really does sound like he couldn't stand to see you with someone else," Sage agrees.

I tilt my head and make a hmm-ing noise. "I mean. Maybe he's got a crush."

"Maybe?" Teal practically shouts. "He literally chased off your date. Who was *in the driveway* to pick you up!"

"You guys!" I sit on the bed and bury my face in my hands. "Maybe—yes, maybe he's got a crush. But he's probably trying to be ethical, because of the article and stuff. I need to respect that." I use the opportunity to change the subject. "By the way, he wants to interview the two of you for it. If you're okay with that, I mean. And Teal? No interrogating him about his feelings for me."

"Aw, man!"

We playfully bicker for a few more minutes, before asking Sage about how she's doing (much better, the SSRIs are finally kicking in), how the baby is doing (still obsessed with milk), and how Teal's leather launch is doing (she's still working hard to meet the deadlines, but Carter is forcing her to take the necessary breaks). When we end the call, I realize that my eyes are stinging. I lie back on the bed and let the tears fall down the sides of my cheeks.

It's only just now hit me, for some reason. But my sisters are back. They remembered me. They care about me.

They love me.

Maybe there really isn't a reason to try and move away the first second I can. Because having my sisters by my side . . . it makes me feel like I can accomplish anything. Even surviving in this town. Maybe even, one day, *thriving* in this town.

I DECIDE ON A CROPPED TURQUOISE TANK TOP AND HIGH-waisted, frayed short-shorts. Nadia isn't home when I leave. If I left a note, I wonder how long it would take her to read it. Days? A week? Who am I kidding—she would never even notice it.

I sigh and grab my bag, slipping on my shoes before going out the front door.

Before I can knock on William's door, Adam throws it open, his face sweet and happy. "Hey! You made it!"

"Yes?" I give him a confused smile in return. "Aren't I, like, ten minutes early, even?"

"Are you?" He glances at the silvery wall clock. "Oh yeah. Huh. Well, I've got the eggplant all fried up. But I need to build the thing and roast it in the oven for a few minutes."

"I can help."

Adam doesn't want my help, I guess, because he shakes his head rather aggressively. "Go sit," he says.

I blink. I'm just not used to anyone taking care of my food, and it feels awkward to not get in the kitchen and get my hands dirty. "Are you—"

"Sky. Sit." Adam points at the sofa on his way back to the kitchen, and damned if I didn't enjoy the hint of sharp in his demanding tone.

William's in his chair in the living room, looking like he's about to fall asleep. "William?" I ask. "You tired?"

"I'm eighty-four years old," he responds without opening his eyes. "I'm always damned tired as all hell."

"And grumpy as all hell, too," I add.

William grunts in response, and then asks me a question I was not prepared for, especially from him. "You believe in ghosts?"

I blink, all of a sudden nervous that he might know the truth about me. About how I'd spent eight years wandering the World of the Living as, for all intents and purposes, a ghost, a ghost who specifically spent an inordinate amount of time in this very house. "Um." Best to just be honest, I guess. "Yeah. I do."

William grunts and reclines his chair even farther, so his gaze is on the ceiling. "Last night I saw my wife."

"Oh?" I turn toward him. "What . . . I mean, did she say anything?"

"Not a thing. I walked in the bedroom, and she was there, sitting on the edge of the bed. Wearing that one purple nightgown . . . She smiled at me, I blinked, she was gone. Been trying to figure out if my mind is gone since."

Ah. He wants reassurance, I imagine, especially since his doctor thinks he has some signs of dementia. The reminder of this feels like a little pang right into my gut. "I believe in ghosts, William. She was probably making sure you're okay. Maybe double-checking that you weren't living on Hungry-Man frozen dinners."

William chuckles. "She did get on my case about all the salt in crap like that." He takes a breath. "Well, you're making sure I get something to eat that isn't made of garbage. She'd like that."

My heart feels a sharp sting, but not one of pain. I think this is William's way of saying thank you. I didn't bring him food for gratitude. But all the same, it's touching to hear it. Enough to make my eyes get the slightest bit teary.

"All right," Adam says, plates balanced on his arms. "It's time. Hope you guys are hungry. I kind of made a lot."

William and I approach as Adam sets the table and grabs us water bottles from the fridge. As I approach the table, Adam pulls out my chair for me, a big smile on his face. "Oh. Thanks," I say, settling in.

When I look up, William is glancing between the both of us, his eyebrow raised. But luckily, I guess he's too hungry to say anything about "us kids" again, because about a half second later, his mouth is entirely full.

"This looks so beautiful," I tell Adam, because it really does. There are four breaded and fried eggplant slices overlapping around my plate. The sauce drizzles onto the plate, under the most perfectly crispy and gooey cheese. He even placed a garnish of fresh basil in the middle.

I can feel Adam's eyes on me as I take the first bite, which makes me a little nervous. It's a lot of pressure, trying a meal in front of the person who made it. What if I don't pass the test on what a proper reaction is supposed to look like for them? But the food is so good, I don't stop and consider what reaction to perform for Adam. Instead, I close my eyes and moan a little bit. "Wow. This really is your specialty," I say after swallowing.

"Specialty," William snorts. "If this is your specialty, why haven't you ever made it for me before?"

"Uh, maybe because you told me you weren't going to eat any of my, and I quote, 'vegetarian shit'?"

William grunts in response, which confirms he's definitely told Adam that before.

"Are you transitioning to vegetarianism?" I ask Adam, because I've seen him eat meat a time or two in the last two weeks.

Adam shakes his head. "When I first moved to the city, I was broke. I couldn't afford meat. So I had to get creative. And ever since, I've always incorporated vegetarian meals. I guess they're kind of comforting now."

"Plus your mother didn't eat meat," William says.

Adam winces. Only a fraction of a second before he catches himself, but it's there all the same. I remember that William said

Adam lost his mother recently . . . and that Adam hasn't once mentioned it to me. I wish it wouldn't be weird of me to grab his hand right now. I really want to comfort him somehow, like all the ways he has done the same for me.

"Right," Adam says, his voice pretty monotone. "She didn't."

I'm afraid William is going to volunteer more information Adam doesn't want out there, so I say quickly, "My aunt is famous for her cheese enchiladas. They're completely vegetarian. I can make them again next Friday."

Adam smiles at me. "I'd love to try them." He clears his throat and lowers his gaze to his almost empty plate. "And I can come over and help you cook beforehand. I'd like to learn some more. You're really good at it."

I blink and then smile. "You think so?"

Adam laughs. "Hasn't anyone told you how good a cook you are?"

William pushes his chair back with a loud squeak. "Well, I'm going to lie down. Can't take listening to you kids flirt like this anymore."

"Flirt?" I ask, before I can stop myself.

"Yeah," William says, walking away toward his bedroom. "Flirting like damn lovebirds!" He shuts the door behind him.

I frown at Adam, who just shakes his head good-naturedly. "Don't mind him. He had a bad night. He's probably going to sleep for, like, fourteen hours now. He needs it, though." He glances at my plate. "You good? There's more if—"

"Yes." I hold up my plate with a smile. "More."

Adam winks at me as he takes my plate and gives me a generous second helping. He sits across from me, where William was, and pushes his grandfather's empty dishes away from between us.

"So, ah. I have a few more questions to ask you. If you're up for it now rather than later."

I nod. "Sure. Go ahead."

Adam pulls out a little Moleskine notebook from his back pocket, and a black Bic pen from his front pocket. "Petting the shark this morning. That shark . . . you were communicating with her, right? When you closed your eyes . . . and she came. It was like she heard your voice. And understood what you're saying."

I swallow my bite and take a sip of water. "Yeah. With my gift . . . it's like . . . well. You know how you just sense things without questioning them? That information is taken into your brain without your permission. For instance, the feel of the wood under you as you sit, or—" I glance over him. "How your shirt, that fabric, is soft against your skin. We are in this room, right, and the air-conditioning is going on and off, and the draft is just behind you. So in the same way you and I, too, for that matter, take in these sensory interactions, I feel more. I feel that there is a squirrel on the roof right now, trying to decide if he wants to shimmy down the drainpipe or make the leap onto the juniper right there—" I point through the window into the backyard, and as though on cue, the squirrel makes it onto the tree branch, everything green-gold in the setting sunlight. "I know the bears, their babies, the birds. I know the creatures underground, too. The groundhogs, the moles . . . sometimes, oftentimes, or even all the time, really, I can sense that nothing exists without a community of life holding it together."

Adam is furiously taking notes. After a minute, he stops and says, "Kinda makes you think, doesn't it? Everything really does need a community to hold it together. In ecosystems . . . and humans, too. That's what the leaders in my AA meetings say. That alcohol is often a way to stave off loneliness, and so one way we can stifle cravings is to make sure we are in community."

"You have that at least," I offer. "The whole town loves you."

Adam frowns at his notes, then looks up at me. His eyes are almost glowing blue against the pumpkin orange of the sky through the window behind him. "They're not my community, Sky. They think they know me, but they don't. Community necessitates knowing one another."

I furrow my brow. "Oh. But . . ." I shake my head. "But you're beloved. They love you because of your work, and don't people get to know you through your work?"

He shrugs. "A small part of me, okay. But they like, more than anything, the idea of me. They think that I can mirror their success with my own. That their being acquainted with me makes them successful by osmosis. Most of them . . . they want to get to know themselves by the reflections in my eyes."

"That's—" I search for the right word. "That's poetic. And sad."

"It is sad. You know how many people I had to call for help when I found myself unemployed with nowhere to stay?"

I shake my head.

Adam points to William's bedroom. "One. And yeah, I know more people would have offered. But only Gramps would've accepted me and my fuckups and allowed me the space to figure out how to fix my life. Most people aren't there for anything deep or uncomfortable. They want to rub shoulders. They want to network. They want a quick fuck. But they don't want the whole human."

I take a deep breath and push my now empty plate away. "I see that. I guess that's why everyone is so mean to me. All they can see is my wholeness when they look at me. They can't pretend they don't know about my weird layers."

Adam nods slowly. "I'm going to write that down. You're absolutely right."

I wonder if maybe my being seen around town with Adam isn't all he's doing to help me. It kind of sounds like this piece might vindicate me. I don't want to get my hopes up. But what if it's published and it makes people realize I'm not insane? That I'm likable? That I'm valuable as a human being, just as I am, no matter what has happened to me in my past?

Adam closes his book and slides it into his pocket. The pen is next to be returned to its storage space.

I blink. "You're done with the questions."

He smiles at me. "I'm done with the questions."

"But . . ." Why am I panicking? Maybe because of the idea that once he's done with this piece . . . he'll be done with me. Sure, he offered to cook dinner with me in a week. But what then? What about kissing in the woods? My brain feels like it's malfunctioning, words flying by at hyperspeed, devoid of all meaning. I swallow.

"But . . ." he says warmly. Right. I never finished my sentence.

"But what about coming over? You've never been inside Nadia's before. I could show you more stuff that might be helpful for your piece." I rack my brain. "Old photos and things like that."

"Ah." Adam stands and stretches. I try very hard not to gaze at the sliver of his underbelly becoming exposed in the process. I fail. "That does sound helpful, actually. Why don't we plan on something for . . . I don't know. Sunday?"

"Sunday?"

"Sure. Why don't I come over and bring you food. Since you're always bringing Gramps food."

"Oh." I look down, thinking. "Well. Sure."

We settle on a time, and after that, I help him load the dishwasher. When I finish washing my hands, the night has fully arrived outside, the streetlamps having lit up orange in the darkness. "I better get going," I say.

"Yeah. I have to get up early myself." Adam smiles at me. "I actually got a temporary job helping that guy fix up his house right there." He points just behind me. "He bought it to flip it, but it needs a lot more work than he anticipated."

I remember that neighbor, from when I was a ghost, wandering all the neighborhood homes, looking for secrets and other signs of life . . . "He's been trying to get that house ready for flipping for a while." I smile at him. "I'm happy for you. Congratulations on your new job."

"New temporary job," Adam clarifies.

"Right. The temporary job." His emphasis on *temporary* makes me wonder if his time in Cranberry, too, is temporary. Will I wake up one day, and he's back in New York City? Living the big-city life, having adventures with a big-city woman?

Probably, to be honest. He lived there for almost all of his adult life, since the second he graduated high school. He obviously couldn't wait to get out of here. It's something I need to remember. No matter how much we end up . . . doing things . . . like kissing inside an ancient oak tree. I have to remember to protect my heart.

I walk toward the door and smile at him. "Have a good—"

"Wait a second." He puts his hand on mine, reaching for the knob. "What just happened to you? What are you thinking about?"

I tilt my head. "Come again?"

"You were doing that smile of yours. The real smile. And then it turned into . . . I don't know. Not *Sky's* smile. A pretend smile."

"Oh. That." I close my eyes briefly. "I was just thinking about how you're going to move away soon." Oh God. Why did I say the truth? Now he's going to think I'm a too-attached creeper.

"Wait, who said that?" He furrows his brows.

"I . . . no one. I just assumed—"

"I don't have any plans to move. I'm staying with Gramps and taking care of him. I mean, yeah, I moved in because my life imploded. But after being here for a bit, it's clear to me that he needs care. He's been lying to me about his independence and abilities." Adam runs a hand over his hair and his face. "And I get it. He's proud as hell. But he needs help."

"Oh. Sorry." I glance down at my shoes. "I didn't mean to assume. I just thought you wanted to write my article as fast as possible so you could get your *Times* job back, or another big-time job—"

"Sky." He takes one step closer, his gaze lowering to my lips for about half a second before he tears it toward my own. "I can do that kind of work virtually."

"Virtually," I repeat, because his proximity and the scent of him—the sea, the forest, the sky—are scrambling my brain.

"Yeah." He reaches behind me, his arm grazing my hip as he opens the door. His shoulder is to my shoulder, his head just behind me, and he shifts so his voice is at my ear as he says in a lower, firm voice, "I'm not going anywhere."

I nod. I manage, somehow, to mumble good night and bid him farewell, and stumble out into the night. He watches me until I'm safe inside Nadia's. I know this because I watched him through the window when I got inside.

I walk upstairs and get through my whole bedtime ritual—the shower, the skincare, the braiding of my hair. I grab my phone and there are two messages.

The first is from Amá Sonya: Sky Temple Flores. You told me you were not being courted by that man. She adds: We will be having lunch early next week to discuss how you can gracefully remove yourself from your current mistakes.

I roll my eyes and delete the messages without responding. If she's mad about my "dating" Adam, then she hasn't heard about the rumors over her own declining memory. I guess that's the silver lining. If Amá knew that I had spread a lie that made her look bad? She'd be speeding on the highway to get here and berate me in person and probably throw some of her Chanel stilettos at me, too.

The next message notification is through the dating app. I'm almost shocked to see that it's from @tryingsomethingnew. Yeah, we messaged each other last only a few days ago, but so much has happened since then that it feels like it's been weeks, or even months somehow.

I click it open. Wow. I'd been expecting a line like *Hey, how's it been?* But there's a whole paragraph instead:

> In the last day, I realized I have feelings for someone in my life. I've probably been in denial about it for a while now, but something happened that knocked sense into my head. I wanted to let you know because it wouldn't be right for you and me to continue amorous exchanges while I feel this way about someone else. I am open to staying friends and cheering you on as you date others on this app, if that's something you'd be okay with.

I sit with these words for a moment, reading them once more to take them in. I search myself, my body, to find any place with the sting of pain or betrayal. But it's not there.

The truth is . . . if @tryingsomethingnew hadn't written this message, I would have had to write him something similar. Because these feelings for Adam aren't going away. After today . . . and tonight . . . the old gods know what I feel isn't going *anywhere*. Just like Adam. *I'm not going anywhere*.

Please, no worries. I hope it works out for you and this person. Sincerely. And it would be so cool to stay friends. Truthfully, you're my only friend.

That seems like the right response, so I leave it at that. Maybe we'll be friends or maybe he'll get swept away into his romance. Either way, I wish him well. Not too many men would be honest and decent with a situation like that.

That evening, I glance over the pile of books on my side tables and pull out a few with titles like *The Female Orgasm* and *Mutual Ecstasy*, each complete with covers featuring hot couples embracing in little to no clothing, their heads rolled back and their mouths open like they're in the middle of multiples.

The fact is, I'm not exactly experienced when it comes to sex. That's gotta be no surprise to anyone. It's not like I had ample opportunity to get my back blown out while hibernating in the woods for eight years. But I'm still a little embarrassed, and so I devote a few hours to some intensive research. If Adam and I continue on like we have been, then chances are we will have sex at some point. I don't want to make a fool of myself when that time comes.

When I lie down to sleep that night, Adam is all I can think about. I think it's safe to admit to myself that I want him so bad, it scares me. But I don't want to think about my heart anymore, and how I've got to protect it. I don't want to think about the fact that we haven't even talked about the kiss or what it means. I don't want to think about anything except for this afternoon, when it was just him and me, possibly the first and only humans to ever kiss inside that specific oak tree. The tree that cradled me as I traveled in the World of Not Quite Living and Not Quite Dead. The way his tongue slipped into my mouth. How hard he'd been, right on my hip.

I'm still so turned on, I'm realizing. I'm not sure I've actually had a chance to recover from what happened yet. Reading about sex the last few hours certainly didn't help with matters. So I slip my hand into my underwear, imagining my fingers are Adam's fingers. I gasp when I touch my clit—I'm so ready to come, it only takes seconds, especially when I think about Adam, hovering over me, his forearm working as he fingers me hard and fast. When it happens, I basically levitate off the bed, and my first thought when it's over is wondering how it would be with Adam for real.

21

THE NEXT DAY I FIND MYSELF APPROACHING MY WORK building early, the light around me as bright as butter. I'd tried not to be too much of a creep, scanning for Adam as I made my way to my car in the driveway this morning, but he wasn't around, to my disappointment. I don't know why I thought he would be. I mean, sure, he appeared yesterday morning, but what was I expecting? That he'd greet me just as the sun rises from now on with flowers and a kiss?

At work, I open the front door with the three keys that keep it dead-bolted, and as I do so, I freeze. A few thoughts pop into my mind.

One: Sage said there was at least one mysterious door at St. Theresa's. In the director of education's office, or at least what used to be the director of education's office when we were little kids.

Two: Nadia mentioned that she would have copies of the church keys for the festival. Chances are, she's already given them back to whoever put them in her care but . . . I could double-check, just in case.

I begin strategizing at work, trying not to get too excited since I know all I could be getting worked up about is a thread of nothing but dead ends in my investigation.

In the basement, I go through about fifteen books, categorizing them before lunch. "You want a pizza?" Anise had asked. "I'm feeling pizza." So she and I share a medium super garlic pizza (garlic butter sauce, topped with garlic cheese and roasted garlic cloves—safe to say this place is protected from vampires today) from a hole-in-the-wall down the street as we chat about our lives. She tells me about her partner's new recipes he's been trying (the savory French toast especially sounds amazing), and because I can sense she's going to ask about him, I tell her that Adam is writing a story on me. She raises her eyebrows and gives me a look that is identical to Nadia's *knowing* expressions, but unlike Nadia, Anise respects that I'm not ready to talk about what else might be happening between me and Adam.

"Oh, Sky, this reference book from downtown came in for you," she tells me as I'm dusting off my hands and getting ready to return to my lair. "It's a chunk." She groans as she lifts it from her desk to hand to me.

Cranberry Architecture: 1799–Present. I had put in a request for this interlibrary loan when @tryingsomethingnew first told me about his research on St. Theresa's being not exactly what it seems. I'm kind of shocked the downtown branch came through—the reference librarian there is kinda mean and known for turning down loan requests more often than not. This is miraculous, and on the day I'm trying to come up with an in-field investigative adventure, too? The old gods are coming through for me. That's what it feels like, anyhow.

I help clean up quickly, then basically dart back to the dungeon, book in my arms. I begin flipping through it in the slow-ass, old-ass elevator, so engrossed in trying to find what I want that I almost miss getting through the doors before they close.

When I make it to my desk, I only barely restrain myself from pushing all its contents to the floor in order to make room for the ten-pound, literary monstrosity. Instead, I hastily put everything in little piles here and there, then have a seat. After about twenty minutes of intense perusing, I gasp and pull out my phone to send a photo of the book's cover to @tryingsomethingnew.

He writes back immediately. Jealous. I didn't get that one myself. The librarian at the downtown branch refused to let me even look at it, much less borrow it!

I chuckle to myself and almost write that she's pretty well-known for her greedy ways, but then decide that maybe that gives away too much of me. He might figure out I work in a library or something, from that info. It's unlikely that he would even care, but best to be safe. I still really don't have a clue who he is. Images of a catfishing elderly man surrounded by children pop into my head to solidify this fact.

Got lucky I guess, I write back. Did you want to hear what I found? I ask.

On the edge of my seat here.

I grin as I type back. Nothing.

. . . Was that supposed to be the big reveal you seemed to be setting up for?

I giggle. I'm having way too much fun here. Not yet . . . Listen to this. Chapter Eleven is on St. Theresa's. There's a pretty boring introduction paragraph on the whole thing on page 111.

Like: Blah, blah, with a heavy Catholic population from recent Irish immigrants, Cranberry found herself in need of a church of the Catholic persuasion.

Please tell me that was a direct quote.

I laugh and ignore him. But! Guess what.

Come on, sea salt girl. You're killing me over here.

I blink, because I heard that phrase only the other day. *You're killing me over here*. From Adam, when I was teasing him in the beach parking lot. I shake my head at the way my belly resounds as though this is something worth looking into, like it's a clue to some mystery I haven't even noticed yet. Weird.

It's a common phrase. Kind of a strange coincidence, given the timing. But still, a coincidence all the same.

I type quickly. He's waited long enough. Someone took out the rest of the chapter.

. . . took out?

Yeah. They had a razor, or some similar sharp object, and cut the pages so close to the book spine that I have to damn near break it to see the edges of what's left of them.

Jesus. Wow. That's . . . I don't even know what to say. What the hell is going on with that church?

I know!!! Right!! Anyway, my—I almost type *sister* but decide on *cousin*—cousin told me there may be a secret passageway in one of the education offices. I'm going to check it out sometime in the coming week.

Are you going to tell them the truth of what you're up to?

Hell no! So they can kill me for knowing their secrets?

I thought religious people were supposed to not agree with things like murder.

Have you ever studied any religion? Murder is, like, their favorite thing. Especially if their secrets—power—are threatened.

Touche.

We joke a little more at what the heck St. Theresa's could be hiding—What if it's a den of bears? I ask, and he responds with Wouldn't a den of lions be more biblical?, which has me cackling—and then it's close enough to the time for me to clock out that I say goodbye so I can tidy up. As I gather books and reorganize my pens, I think to myself that although I really don't know @tryingsomethingnew, he seems like a good person. I seriously wish him well with the lucky girl he has feelings for.

THE NEXT DAY, I SPEND WHAT FEELS LIKE HOURS GETTING ready for Adam. He said he would bring food for dinner, and that just means I start trying to figure out what to wear just after lunch—which is just a slice of toast with butter and jam, because my stomach is too nervous for something more.

I decide on a pink slip dress. It's a little bit coppery, so a lot like rose gold, reminding me of how the whole atmosphere turns a strange sort of pink if a thunderstorm comes just before sunset. For my makeup, I go along with a tutorial I found on YouTube on "glow girl skin." It involves a lot of shimmer eye shadow and overlapping layers of highlighter, but after putting on a bright pink lip gloss, I look like I'm an ethereal elf visiting from some distant fairy planet.

I go downstairs to make sure the kitchen table is clear before he arrives and stop short when I find Nadia sitting down with a cup of espresso. "Hey," I say, walking in. "I didn't know you were home."

"Oh, just decided to stay in for the early evening. In about two hours, I have to be at church for a baptism. I'll bring you some cake."

"Thanks," I say, holding back a wince. Good gods. Nadia is literally never home, but she decides to spend the evening here the first time I have plans with a man? What in the hell are the chances?

Nadia looks up from her little blue cup and it's like she's seeing me for the first time. She gestures to my dress. "What's this? You got a hot date?"

My cheeks heat immediately. Between that and her *knowing*, there is no use lying to her about my feelings for Adam. But it's so annoying that she can ignore me about ninety-five percent of the time and decide she is entitled to the details of my life in the totally random and never-planned remaining five percent of interaction.

"No," I say, because that is the truth. "Adam said he would bring food as a thank-you for all the times I brought Friday meals to William."

"Ah, I see. You have a young, single, attractive man coming over to bring you, a young, single, and attractive woman, food on behalf of his grandfather?" She gives me a look that clearly says *Give me a break, Sky.*

I hold back a huff because this is already exhausting and difficult to navigate, and it really shouldn't be. I shouldn't have to sit here and explain my personal life to someone who hasn't earned the right to know. So I add, completely without thinking, "Also, he's taking photos of me and the house for his article, remember the article? That's why I dressed up."

I really don't like lying, especially to Nadia, but I feel like she's given me no choice. Is her gift telling her I'm totally making shit up right now?

It doesn't seem so, because she jumps up immediately and says, "Why didn't you say something? Sky Temple, I haven't done a deep clean in two weeks!" Next thing I know, she's got on her yellow rubber gloves with a super-sized bottle of Fabuloso in her hands, and she's hissing at me to put away the dishes on the drying rack.

This situation is irritating, but not as irritating as her prying into the deep, dark secrets in my head and in my life. I'm congratulating myself on thoroughly distracting her when Adam, I presume, knocks on the door.

"Stall him!" Nadia shouts from the downstairs bathroom. "I need four more minutes!"

"Nadia, it's not—"

"Sky!"

It's her warning tone, the one that's stating she's about thirty seconds away from throwing her slippers at me. So I shut up and go to the door. When I open it, it's all I can do to not let my jaw topple to the ground.

Adam is . . . wow. He's wearing a phthalo green dress shirt with the sleeves unbuttoned and rolled up, revealing his veined and hairy forearms. His dress pants are dark gray, nearly indigo, with black shiny boots. In his hand is a huge bag of something that smells incredible.

"You look beautiful," I tell him. His neck instantly turns red.

"Look who's talking," he says in return. I step out and shut the door behind me.

"Oh," he says. "I thought we would eat . . . you know. In there." He frowns. "That's what we had agreed, right?"

"Yes. I'm sorry, but—" I lower my voice to a whisper. "Nadia's home. I lied and told her you were here for a house tour? And to take photos of me?"

Adam blinks and tilts his head. "Is that . . . a normal occurrence for you guys?"

I smack his arm lightly. "For the article, silly."

"Ah." He nods. "Right. Well, I mean. That actually could be helpful. I don't typically do the photos of my domestic pieces, but sure." He pauses. "So why are we still outside?"

I roll my eyes. "She's freaking out and cleaning. Because of the photos of her home."

"Ah." He stands on tiptoe for a moment, then lowers back down. "Should we . . . help her?"

"Uhh—" Nadia would probably rather eat a plate of bird bones and shards of glass for dinner. But luckily, she saves me from responding by throwing the door open behind me so quickly, I nearly fall onto Adam. He holds my waist to keep me upright, and of course, it's the first thing Nadia's eyes spot.

She raises an eyebrow at me and turns to Adam with a big smile on her face. "Welcome to our humble abode." She then shoos us inside.

Adam looks around, his eyes searching all the details of the kitchen, which is the first room after the dark porch filled with nothing more interesting than drying herbs and lines of shoes. I can see the way he shifts and takes in information, his brain bumping from one thing to the next: from the yellow ocher of the walls, to the green, shiny, and now-smelling-of-Fabuloso floors, to the stained glass of red butterflies and yellow poppies framing the windows. When Sage, Teal, and I were little, we used to trace the way they'd cross the floor and furniture in the sunlight, and in particular, we'd "feed" the light-bugs popcorn that Nadia's old cat then used to eat. "What a great place," Adam tells us. "It has so much character."

Nadia beams. This is the exact right thing to say to her. She prides herself on a home that has a personality; one that cannot be easily replicated. I think this is in some part a response to the way Amá Sonya measures what makes an honorable home—by how much it resembles something found in a colonial-style house magazine, or maybe a bougie prison of some sort. "I bought it over thirty years ago. The cabinets are original, and so are the hardwood floors here in the living room and, oh, the staircase is original, too . . ."

"Uh, should we eat before the food gets cold?" Adam's still holding the huge bag, so I grab it to place it on the table.

"Why don't you set the table?" Nadia tells me. It's not a question, it is an order. I learned this the hard way in early childhood, which even then maybe took longer than it should, but I'll never understand why people ask questions when they mean to command. "I will show Adam the first two floors in the meantime."

"Why only—" I begin to ask, but she takes Adam's arm and begins to educate him on the Tiffany lamp collection in the next room. I was going to ask *Why only the first two floors?* Technically the third floor is the attic. And since the whole third floor and attic is now my room, I might assume that Nadia was trying to respect my privacy or something. But Latine elders seldom understand the concept. Again, I found this out the hard way years ago. Latine elders are *always* in their kids' business, whether we want it or not. Amá Sonya is the same. A few months ago when I joined Teal at brunch with Sonya, she hiss-whispered a lecture to me because she could see my panty lines under my skirt. The next time I saw her, she gifted me seamless underwear along with several silk slips that probably cost the equivalent of several of my paychecks.

So I know better than to argue with Nadia, even though part of me wants to rush up and make sure that she's not telling him embarrassing stories about my childhood. I just let her boss Adam around as I grab the plates she literally just had me put away in the cabinets. I make three place settings, because even if Adam didn't bring enough food, it would be rude to just eat in front of Nadia.

I fill everyone's glass with ice water, and since they're taking one zillion years at this point, I open the bag of food. Inside are five big, lidded containers. I can't read the notes on the plastic lids, but it's definitely Indian food. He must've gone over to the nearest town for it, since Cranberry doesn't have an Indian restaurant, which is sad and bananas at the same time.

There are many types of curry and rice, with feta and garlic naan wrapped up in tinfoil, alongside onion bhajia, spinach bhajia, and thick-sliced fried potatoes. There's enough food for me to put everything in serving dishes, and I'm just about finished with that when Nadia and Adam finally return. He's holding up his iPhone with what I assume is a photography attachment on it. The man is ready for anything, even spur-of-the-moment lies. I'll give him that.

"Oh, you set a place for me?" Nadia asks. "I don't need—"

"You need to eat, no? Unless—" I look to Adam. "You don't mind, do you?"

"Not at all. Please, join us, Nadia," he says with his charming smile.

Nadia shakes her head. "You kids should enjoy yourselves."

"There's so much food. I didn't know what Sky liked, so I basically got one of everything." Adam smiles again. "And when's the last time you had Indian, anyway?"

That convinces Nadia. She also knows it's a travesty that we don't have accessible Indian food in this town. And honestly, it smells too good to pass up. So we all sit and eat, trying a little bit of this and that, and we also chat about this and that. Adam, with what a good journalist he is and all, asks Nadia engaging questions about growing up in Cranberry in the forties and fifties. It's pretty wild to think about the changes Nadia, Sonya, and the rest of that generation have seen in their lifetimes. "Almost no one in town had indoor plumbing back then," Nadia confides. "There were outhouses in everyone's backyard, with the moons on the top, as far as the eye could see."

I want to ask her questions, too. Like, did she ever hear of a weird cult connected to the church, and oh right, does she happen to be a current member of that cult? Did they meet up underground to cavort with bears and lions? But I keep my mouth shut. Because if what Sage says is true, and I have no reason to doubt her—if Nadia always changed the subject when she asked about it, that means no one will get anywhere with her on the topic. That's how Nadia is. Amá Sonya, too, for that matter. Pretty hypocritical behavior from ladies who insist they've got some right to know what we've all got going on in our lives.

Teal questioned Amá Sonya a *lot* last year to figure out if she knew if our mother was in town, and instead of answering like a normal human, all Sonya did was act like Teal slapped her across the face.

And you know what? Amá Sonya *did* know something about our mother being in town. And if I assume these sisters are more alike than they think . . . Nadia's gotta know something about this cult, or whatever it really is. If she's not running the whole damn thing herself.

"This was delicious," Nadia says as she stands. "Let me get the dishes."

"We can do that, Nadia." I reach for the plate she's picked up, but she pulls back before I can touch it. "Don't you have to get to the baptism?"

"Not for another thirty minutes. Let your tía take care of you."

I want to roll my eyes, but I don't. That statement, though—what an unbelievable implication, that I don't "let" Nadia "take care" of me. Okay, I roll my eyes when she turns away. I simply cannot hold back.

Adam catches it and tilts his head at me in question. I shake my own in response.

"Why don't you show Adam your room?" Nadia asks. "I completely forgot the attic in the tour." Her voice is high and awkward. The vieja is lying through her teeth. She didn't forget. She made it so that when she left, Adam and I would be alone. In my room. In close proximity to my bed. I close my eyes and laugh.

"What's so funny?" Nadia asks. She won't make eye contact with me. "He didn't even get one picture of you so far. Get one on the balcony, maybe. Adam, you should see the view from up there." Nadia pretends to gasp. "Or, on your bed, mija. You have that pretty duvet on it, don't you. Would look great alongside your dress."

I glance at Adam so we can share another secret exchange about how silly this is. It's clear my elderly auntie is trying to get us to bang. That's nuts.

But when my gaze lands on him . . . I'm taken aback. He's staring at my hips, and he drags his eyes all the way up, stopping at my eyes. He takes a breath in sharply, like somehow he forgot to breathe in the last two minutes.

I'm taken aback and all of a sudden, I am besieged with images of kissing a pink-cheeked Adam in my room, surrounded by my fairy-tale forest wallpaper. On the balcony, after I point out the distant, glimmering skin of the sea. In my bed, on my, yes, very pretty duvet cover.

Dammit, I think I've forgotten to take a breath in the last couple of minutes, too.

Nadia turns around, thankfully after I snap my jaw shut and hopefully don't look like I'm thinking about what she seems to be planning way too hard. "Go, go!" She waves the both of us toward the stairs. "I'll be home very, very late. Don't wait up!" she calls as we walk up.

22

"WELL, THIS IS IT." MY DOOR IS AJAR, REVEALING MY enormous bedroom. I walk in and open my arms in an unspoken welcome to Adam.

"Wow." He looks around, doing the same thing he did in the kitchen. Noting every detail, from the deeply detailed wallpaper to the patinaed silver handles of the armoire. The slat windows are letting in beams of light in the color of copper, and the whole room looks like dusk decided to make this place its home.

"This looks like the room of some dark woodland fairy princess." Adam pulls out his phone contraption combo and begins taking photos. My bed, the windows, the light, the view over the balcony. I watch him as he works, his body moving fluidly as he enters some kind of zone that gives me a glimpse of how powerful a storyteller he is. Because that's what journalists do, right? They tell stories.

"Has this always been your room?" he asks.

I shake my head. "It was my older sister's room."

"Sage, right?"

I nod, smiling. "Yeah. I moved in a little while after she moved out."

"I don't blame you. What a space."

He takes a few more pictures, then approaches the bed with his camera out. I think he might take a detail of my comforter, but he freezes when he notices . . . something.

"What is it?" I ask, wondering if some strange bug is crawling on the bed. My windows aren't exactly airtight. As old as this house is, and as little as Nadia has had it renovated, *nothing* is exactly airtight.

"Uhh." He looks at me, then back at the bed. "Can you do me a quick favor?"

"Sure . . ."

He gestures for me to sit on the bed, which I do.

"Lie back. I promise this isn't weird. Or, not creepy, I mean. It's plenty weird. But could you lie back?"

I kick my shoes off and lie back on the bed. Adam studies me, and his breath catches and he throws his head back and laughs and then exhales a big sigh.

I smile up at him with a furrowed brow. "What's happening? This isn't going to be my portrait for the piece, is it? Because I gotta say, this isn't my best angle."

"No. No. Okay, this is probably going to be even more weird, and maybe even seem creepy, and I promise that it's not. But . . ." He glances up at me, a hand on his head, ruffling his hair in a variety of directions. "Right. You work at the library. You literally work at the library."

I push up into a sitting position. "You're wrong. This actually seems very creepy, in addition to weird. Can you tell me what's happening in your brain right now? I'm beginning to fear it's an aneurysm or something."

He sits on the bed next to me, drawing one leg up so he can face me. He places his phone on the nightstand and says, "Ahh—so by any chance, are you trying to figure out if there is a secret lair under St. Theresa's?"

I tilt my head at him. "Well . . . yes. But how—" I look around, as though the answers I'm looking for are scattered in midair like emerald-winged hummingbirds. I told Sage I was curious about the architecture at St. Theresa's, but she has no idea I'm actually planning an investigative trip there in the near future. The only one who knows that is . . .

"Oh!" I turn toward him and lean forward. I don't know why I am being so intense but . . . I guess, this is an incredibly intense conversation. Maybe one of the most intense of my life. "Holy shit. You're—"

"Username @tryingsomethingnew?" he finishes with a sheepish smile. "That what you were going to say?"

I can't bring myself to smile back. I need a direct response so I can begin to thoroughly process this ridiculously wild turn of events. "Adam, answer the question: Are you seriously the guy I've been chatting with on Matchmakr?"

He sighs through his smile. "I'm the guy you've been chatting with on Matchmakr." He shakes his head. "What are the chances, right? That not only were we both from Cranberry . . . but that it was also . . ."

"Us," I finish. I look around with wide eyes. These chances are actually astronomical, which always indicates to me the old gods must've had some hand in it. I file the thought away to be investigated later. "And. You figured it out. By . . . seeing me on my bed . . ."

"The photos you sent me. The way your hair was against your shoulders. Near your . . ." He gestures to my chest, then turns bright red so fast, I wonder if someone could faint from blushing so furiously. He definitely shouldn't stand up anytime soon. "I mean. You know."

I snort. "Yeah, I know."

"And the comforter. The sticks, the berries. I looked at that photo . . ." Somehow he's gotten even redder. "For a while. You're . . . uh . . . you're very compelling."

It hits me that he also sent me a photo. Him lying back on the bed, his broad shoulders relaxed on the bed, his chest hair, ready for my hands to run through it . . .

I blink when I remember something. Something incredibly important. "But—you met someone. You . . ." My heart sinks and my voice rises in pitch just a little bit. "There's someone else you want."

Adam shakes his head slowly and smiles at me. "There's no one else I want, Sky."

That kind of sounds like he means me. I can't help my gasp when what he says clicks. He does mean me . . . doesn't he? God, indirect language is difficult, especially during highly emotional conversations like these. "You mean . . ."

He nods. "You're the woman I was talking about."

I am processing this whole exchange so slowly. But I can't help it. I'm overstimulated—my heart is beating fast. My breath is a little bit too shallow. If I lifted my hands, I bet they'd tremble from my nerves right now. "But . . . Adam. *I'm* me." It's not articulate, but it's the shortest way I can convey the barrage of thoughts slamming around in my brain like ongoing collisions of high-speed trains.

He tilts his head and frowns. "What does that mean?"

I shake my head again. "It means . . . why would someone like you want me? Besides, you know. Pure physical attraction from close proximity in the last couple of weeks."

Adam blinks and his jaw clenches. "Is that what you think has been happening between us? Pure physical attraction? Is that . . . what this is for you?"

I shake my head emphatically. "Of course it isn't. I . . . what I feel for you is a lot more and a lot deeper than just what's physical between us. But you. And me. Does that make sense to you? I mean, be for real, Adam. You are so accomplished and educated and worldly. And I'm the girl no one wants to even be seen with." My arms and hands are flying around for emphasis, but I think all these gestures are just making me look like a drunk octopus, so I try and sit on my hands instead. "Because of what happened to me, I have almost no experience with literally anything. I've only had one job. I've never left Cranberry before. And . . . I've only had sex three times before, when I was a teenager. So I'm *massively* behind you in that department, too." I swallow and look away. If he's giving me a look of pity, I'm not going to be able to take it without bursting into tears. And I really, *really* don't want to burst into tears right now. "I'm the crazy woman who speaks with animals. Who spent eight years in a strange, inexplicable coma. Who you're writing a piece on. That's . . . that's who I am to you, ultimately."

"Is that what you think?" Adam's voice is a little bit hoarse, as though what I've said has made him a bit emotional, too. When I dare to glance at him, he's staring at me so intensely, his eyes look like the blue of the hottest part of candle flames. "Jesus. If that's what you think . . . I've been doing this all wrong."

"Doing what all wrong?" I ask.

He swallows. "Trying to get you to understand what I'm feeling . . . without actually saying it directly, I guess."

I shake my head. "I don't do well with indirect."

He nods. "I'm figuring that out now."

"Sorry," I supply, because I know that most people find directness to not be exactly the most desirable quality in a person, much less someone to have feelings for.

"Please don't be. Please. I'm trying to figure out the words for you. Just give me a few seconds, okay? I need the words to be perfect." He closes his eyes and takes a big shuddering breath. When he opens them, he looks at me up and down slowly, a little bit lusty, sure, but also like I'm something kind of . . . precious to him. Which feels strange and new. *Very* strange and new.

"Sky. I can't believe that you think that I think you are in anyway deficient. And I'm not saying this to shame you because you came to that conclusion. That's on me, actually. I'm so sorry I have behaved in a way that supported that conclusion." I open my mouth to speak, to tell him there is no need to apologize, but he's already on his next sentence. "When I look at you, I see a woman who is kind and caring and brave. So fucking brave. What this town has put you through . . . the fact that you aren't constantly bitter and resentful is a testament to your strength and decency."

I don't even realize I have my hand on my heart until I realize I can feel how hard it's beating against my palm. "Oh. Thank you."

He shakes his head. "I'm not finished."

I lean back and take a deep breath, hoping to calm my nervous system the tiniest bit so I remember every second of this conversation for the rest of my life. "Okay. Well, I'm not going to stop you from giving a speech about how awesome you think I am."

He shakes his head again, a smile curving upon his face, the beginnings of his dimples showing as though I'd lightly pressed my thumbs there. "It's not how awesome I *think* you are. It's literally how awesome you *are*." He laughs a little bit. "And it's not just your character. I'm sure you've figured out by now how attractive I find you."

I smile. "I mean. I kinda figured you might've had a little crush on me. But I'm open to hearing the details."

He lifts his hands and gestures to me. "You. Look at you." I widen my smile to a grin now because he had said the same to me as @tryingsomethingnew. And it's beginning to dawn on me how lovely that is, that the man I was sexting and joking with on- and offline is one and the same. It's Adam. It was Adam the whole time, and considering the moments I first developed feelings for Adam—years ago, when I was still a ghost? It's always been Adam.

He swallows as he looks at me up and down and down and up, so slowly that I have to suppress a shiver. "You . . . I've told you this before. But Sky . . . the first time I saw you at Gramps's . . . you literally took my breath away."

"When you accused me of elder abuse?" I asked.

He buries his face in his hands. "Sometimes when I am flustered . . . and I was worried about him . . ."

I gently touch his knee. "I'm teasing. I know."

He glances at my hand, still over his leg. His muscle jumps under my palm. "All you've done since is take my breath away. Over and over again. It's a wonder I get enough oxygen around you." He softly places his hand over mine and looks up at me, right into my eyes. "Every time you're near me, it's never near enough. Your hair . . . it smells like blueberries. And I just want to smell it more. Your skin is so soft. At night, before I go to bed, I think about that day at the beach, after, when we kissed and when I got to touch you and I . . ." He laughs and the pink returns to his neck. "I do some things I probably shouldn't say."

I inhale a bit sharply when I realize what he's probably referring to. Without my explicit permission, I glance down at his lap and feel entirely too warm when it's clear that he's hard. We're not even talking in detail about salacious things . . . he's only remembering our spicy little kiss moment . . . and he's already hard. And he actually likes me, too! It's not just about round objects.

I try not to sound like I'm begging, but I don't think I succeed. "Tell me. I want to hear about it." I gesture to his lap. "About what you do when you think about kissing me in the woods."

23

He chokes out a laugh, and his cheeks pinken to almost how red his neck was earlier. "I . . . well. I'm sure you've guessed it by now. I touch myself."

"How?" I ask. "I mean, I know you mean that you masturbate. But tell me. I want to know . . . what you're thinking about. And how you grip your cock. Things like that. I'd like to enjoy the finer details, if it's good with you, of course."

His back is ramrod straight and he laughs again. "See. This is what I'm saying. I feel like I can't breathe around you. You're so direct. No, please don't apologize." I snap my mouth shut. "It's a good thing. I like it. I fucking love it." He takes a deep breath and leans back, reaching behind himself to rest on his left hand. Then he lowers himself on the bed so that he is lying back, his torso adjacent to me, his feet still on the ground. "Well. Okay. I'm going to close my eyes now, because I'm probably about to embarrass myself. But I imagine . . . well. The sound of your voice as you moaned when I kissed you. I wonder about how you touch yourself. How you tease yourself. I imagine that, too. And then I think about how you wrapped your leg around me. How hot you felt. I bet you were so wet. Were you?" He goes against his own rules and looks up at me. "You were wet, weren't you?"

I nod. "I was so wet. I could feel it between my legs when I walked all the way until I showered after I got home."

He drops his head back and says in a sharp exhale, "Fuck. Sky. Fuck." He takes another deep breath. "Did you touch yourself after?"

I nod. "Yes. But tell me how you touch *yourself.* You forgot that part."

"Right. Damn. My brain feels like mush right now, thanks to how intensely turned on I am." He chuckles and closes his eyes once more. "Uh. I . . . Well, I try to make it last."

"You edge yourself?"

"Sort of. Yeah, actually, I guess you could call it that. I think about how you would sound. The way you'd moan . . . the way you'd squirm when my mouth was on you. I imagine making you come on my mouth, my hands pulling and pinching your nipples, and then turning you over and eating your ass, fingering you till you came again."

I don't know why, but those are all the words that push me from mostly horny to unimaginably, almost painfully horny. The space between my legs goes from wet to a waterfall by just listening to the last two sentences from his lips. "Oh my God," I say, and it definitely comes out as a moan, and I definitely am too turned on to care.

"And imagining you like that is what makes me come. I have thought about fucking you. Of course I have. But imagining your face against your pillow, your ass up in the air, you coming so hard that your pussy is like a vise around my fingers inside you . . . that's when I usually go right over the edge, whether I want to or not."

I swallow and squeeze my thighs together. I try not to look at the wet spot growing on his trousers and fail. "How do you do it? Do you like to jerk off fast or slow or—"

"Both. Yes. Everything. I have to slow down to last. It's been so long since I've been with anyone. It's been almost two years. I didn't think I'd even want anyone again until you were in Gramps's earlier this summer, wearing that sexy fucking little pencil skirt and looking at me like you wanted to kiss me and kill me at the same time."

I smile at him then. "I looked like I wanted to kiss you?"

He huffs. "That must make me sound incredibly arrogant, right? But when I first walked in. When you first saw me. Your eyes lit up like you were happy to see me. As though you'd forgotten how I had treated you the last time I saw you . . . and then you remembered, and you went from the kissing to the killing just like that." He snaps his fingers together.

"Well, it's not like you didn't earn it."

He holds up his hands in surrender. "I earned it. I earned it. I admit that."

I swallow and tell myself that I am brave enough to ask what I want to ask him next. "Can I touch you, Adam? Don't worry if you don't want me to," I add quickly, just in case I'm having a fever dream and have completely misinterpreted everything about this whole exchange—him admitting he's attracted to me, telling me in detail how he masturbates to the thought of me, the wet spot on his pants now the size of a golf ball.

But thankfully, he doesn't call me insane for such a question. He smiles and says, "Yeah. You can. Sure."

I reach for the his belt buckle, and he says, "Whoa. I thought you meant—"

I pull back as though I had been burned. "I'm so sorry!"

"No, no." He smiles. "I thought you meant you wanted to . . . touch my arm or something. Or get on top of me . . . and kiss me."

I nod. "I mean, I do. But I wanted you to show me first, how you get yourself off. I want to see."

"Ahh. Okay." He winks at me and gives me the most mischievous grin.

I unbuckle his belt slowly, and he inhales sharply when the side of my hand grazes the hair trail below his belly button. "Are my hands cold?" I ask.

He shakes his head. "When you touch me. I can't explain it. I'm so sensitive everywhere. I'm like a raw nerve around you."

I furrow my brow. "Isn't that painful?"

He shakes his head. "It's just a figure of speech. Trust me, it's not painful in the least."

I nod and keep working on his trousers, finally unzipping them to reveal cobalt blue boxer briefs. I grab his cock through his boxers, pausing when he hisses out a breath. "That feels so good," he explains before I ask if he's okay.

"Sorry I'm so inexperienced at this," I say.

"You're doing just fine." He lifts his head to watch me run my hand up and down his erection, squeezing at the tip a little bit when I make it there. "Fuck," he whispers. When I do it again, he becomes completely incoherent and I find that I love it. I've never made anyone incoherent from just touching them lightly like this before. I feel so powerful. Like an ancient goddess who wasn't just the deity of flowers, she was also the deity of trees and mountains and fortune and, yeah, making men come so hard, they forget their own names.

I really, really want to make Adam come so hard that he forgets his own name.

I slip my hand into the slit of his underwear, and when I palm him, I swallow a gasp at how hot he is. At how hard he is. This erection has got to be painful. I don't care what he says. I don't think any man can be as solid as a piece of granite for this long, leaving pre-cum all over his pants, and not at least feel the pain of not having orgasmed yet.

"Sky," he moans when I give him a light squeeze.

"How do you get yourself off?" I ask him. I'm running my hand up and down his length now, slowly. When I gather the pre-cum in my hands and do it again, this time slicker, his whole body tenses.

"Like that. That's good. Sometimes I go really fast. I pretend—" He chokes on his words when I squeeze him again, this time hard.

"Pretend what?" I ask with a tone of innocence.

"I pretend you're on top of me, riding me. I'm watching you using my cock to make yourself feel good."

I gradually increase the speed of my hand. "You like imagining me come?"

"Fuck yes." The "yes" turns into a hiss when I jerk him off even faster. He moans, and then says through choked gasps, "I just love . . . have always loved . . . making a lover come. It's the whole point to me. Her—" By now I'm going as fast as I can. The muscles in my forearms and wrist are burning (how often does he do this? Does he count this as a workout? Because he should), but I don't care. Just watching him writhe and groan on the bed is such a treat. God, he's so sexy.

His shirt has flung up a little, and I can see that the muscles in his belly are completely flexed. He's barely breathing. "Sky," he gasps out. "I'm close."

"Good." I'm probably smirking, but I don't even care. Being able to reduce a man to this with just a few passes of my hand is making me feel like I could become some significant world leader tomorrow if I wished.

He looks at me, his eyes begging me for something I don't understand until he says what he says next. "I want to kiss you. Before I—please. I don't want you to make me come before I kiss you."

With my hand still wrapped around him, I lean over and press my lips to his. It's just as intense as our first kiss, it's almost like we're kissing for the first time all over again: Adam, moaning against my mouth, as he comes and he comes all over us.

24

I GO TO MY BATHROOM TO RINSE A CLEAN WASHCLOTH IN warm water, and return to help him clean up. "I'll do that," he says, but the words almost come out slurred. He's practically catatonic.

I giggle as I wipe over him, his clothes, the comforter—he really did come hard—and when I look up, he's smiling at me, his cheeks still pink from exertion. Then something occurs to him and he frowns. "I can't believe I came before you." He pushes himself up on shaky arms. "That's not how this goes."

"What's wrong with that?" I ask.

"It's just—well. My orgasm is guaranteed and pretty straightforward. If you're like most women, then you need more time and finesse. And it's my job to prioritize your pleasure, not just because mine is a given, but because—" He looks at me up and down. "Well. Your pleasure would also be mine." He pauses, like he wants to say something else, but then he looks down and laughs. "Jesus. My dick is still out."

"I thought it might need to cool down or something," I say,

and this just makes him laugh even more as he tucks himself back into his pants and zips up. I'm glad to see he doesn't redo his belt buckle. Maybe he would let me jerk him off again in a little bit, once he got over the refractory period. I'm assuming he has one. I've done some research and most men his age do, with an average of thirty minutes.

I check the clock on my nightstand, and Adam says, "Do you have someplace to be?"

"No, I'm calculating the end of your current refractory period."

He chokes on a laugh this time. "Sky. Don't worry about me. Here." He stands and takes the washcloth from my hands and I hear him rinsing it in the sink. When he returns, his eyes are the strangest mix of mischievous and feral. There's no other way to explain the expression on his face.

"Are you thirsty?" I ask. "Shall I get us water?"

He shakes his head slowly. "The only thing I want right now is to make you come."

I freeze. "Me?"

He doesn't respond, not even to point out how stupid a question that was. "If you're okay with it. I want to do all the things to you that I said I had been imagining all week."

I swallow, a little bit nervous and excited all at once. "Are you sure?"

Adam tilts his head. "Are you not sure?"

I shake my head. "Don't answer my question with a question. That's confusing."

He nods. "I'm sorry." He walks toward me, taking my hand in his. I blink down at our interlocked fingers and realize that this is a familiar gesture by now. He's always grabbing my hand when I am nervous or anxious. "We don't have to. We could just go down to my car and I will take you wherever you want. The beach. Dessert. Even Cincinnati, if you had some inexplicable desire to visit." He swallows and looks up to meet my gaze. "But I've wanted to do this for a long time. So, yes. I am sure." His voice becomes even more raspy and deeper, which I would not have thought possible before this moment. "I've never been more sure of anything than the fact that I want to know what you sound like when you come." That . . . makes my breath catch in my throat. He squeezes my hand. "But again. We don't have to. I never want to do anything unless you're one hundred percent on board."

I nod. "I appreciate your saying that. And I want to. I'm one hundred percent on board. But . . ." I squeeze his hand back, and he wraps his arm around me to settle his other hand at my hip. "But I want to start slow. Like, really slow. I'm not ready for you to be, like, all in there yet."

He offers me a wide, reassuring smile that makes the edges of his eyes crinkle up. "Of course. Anything you want." He lets go of me and kicks off his shoes and adjusts his shirt sleeves, which had unrolled a little during the whole Coming So Hard He Forgot His Own Name situation. I watch, swallowing when the veins in his forearms catch in the light. How can a man be so beautiful?

"How do you want me?" I ask.

"On the bed. Sitting."

I nod and pull the straps of my dress down, and roll the whole thing down my hips, letting it fall to the floor. I step out of it, wearing nothing but a nude and white lace strapless bralette with a matching G-string. When I reach behind my back to unclasp the bra, he says, "Wait." I drop my arms as he explains. "Let me undress you."

I don't really see the point, but I nod and sit down on the bed. He sits right beside me. "I want to kiss you first. That kiss just now, when you and I were . . ." He huffs out a laugh. "Not my best effort."

"I enjoyed it," I tell him.

"Good. Let me show you something better, though."

He cups my face with one hand and leans in. I close my eyes and just allow the warmth of his lips over mine. We kiss like this for what feels like a whole minute, and then he nudges my lips open, sliding his tongue gently over my bottom lip. I do the same to him, almost gasping when our tongues meet. It starts soft at first, but soon I'm moaning. One of my hands is tangled in his hair. The hand he'd been cradling my face with is now over my breast. He keeps thrusting his tongue in my mouth, over and over, in a way that makes me think of shallow, hard fucking.

I pull back suddenly and say with breathless intensity, "I've changed my mind. I want you inside me."

His smile is so bright. "I'll give you whatever you want, Sky. Let me take care of you first, okay?"

I nod. "Okay."

He has me lie back on the bed, my head on the pillows. "Do you not like it when someone rides your face?" I ask.

He laughs. "You're going to make me hard again, well before the refractory period's over."

"That's a yes?"

"It's definitely a yes. But for your first time, I don't want you to worry about what you're doing. I just want you to enjoy yourself."

I nod. "Okay. That makes sense."

He begins with a light kiss on my lips, then moves down to my neck. I grab his forearms tight, as he sucks in places I didn't realize would ever have the capacity to contribute to the wet between my legs.

He kisses and sucks my left nipple through the lace of my bra. "That—" I begin, then stop. What if it's not sexy to tell him when something doesn't feel right?

He lifts his head to look up at me. "Tell me."

I shake my head. "It's nothing." He raises his eyebrow at me in a silly way, with one pointing this way and one looking that way, like a cartoon or something. I relax and laugh. "Just . . . it hurts a little bit, with the lace there. It's not the most comfortable fabric . . ."

"Got it." He lowers the straps down, exposing my breasts to the cool air. I feel my nipples pucker even more. They must look like the most insane pencil eraser nips of all time.

This time, he moves to my right breast, and he begins much slower, lapping me up with languid, hot swipes of his tongue. I can feel the electric connection between my nipples and clit, and I'm certain the comforter is soaked between my legs, right through my underwear.

He moves toward the other nipple and gives it the same treatment. By now I'm squirming and moaning with abandon. I feel as though if I reached down and barely touched myself, I'd come hard enough to break the space-time continuum. In fact, I move my hand to do exactly that, but he stops me. "Don't you want me to suck it?" he asks, wiggling himself farther down the bed, until I can feel his warm breath over my right hip. "Don't you want me to suck your clit till you come all over my face?"

I inhale shakily. "Are you enjoying this?"

He laughs and I can feel the vibrations of his voice between my legs. "I'm pretty sure I'm harder than I was twenty minutes ago."

I can barely consider what he's saying. I'm so horny, I feel like I might burst into flames. I want to squeeze my thighs together, but I can't, since my legs are spread for him. I squirm, trying to somehow get pressure where I need it the most.

"You need some friction, huh?"

"Please," I moan. And then he does something I was never expecting. He pulls my G-string up between my legs, until the fabric is pulling right against my clit.

I groan as the pleasure shoots up into my belly. He pulls my underwear this way and that, using it to grind against my slit, getting me fairly close to orgasm without touching me with his hands or mouth at all.

"Fuck, you're so fucking sexy right now," he murmurs, shifting my underwear even more. "I wish you could see yourself. God. You're so wet. You're so fucking wet." As though on cue, I hear slick sounds emanating from where the underwear is sliding against me.

"Oh my God," I whisper as he pulls the panties from my slit and then slides them right to the side and gives me one long, hot lick, from my opening all the way up to my clit. He does it again, and again, and the last time he holds his face still so I'm forced to grind myself against his tongue.

"Sorry. Sorry." He pulls back with a smile as I whimper. "I said I wasn't going to make you do any work."

I'm so far gone, the words out of his mouth have barely any meaning to me. "Make me come. Adam. Please. I need to come. I need it."

"On it." He pushes his fingers under the waistband of my

underwear and pulls the whole thing down my legs, tossing it somewhere behind him. He lifts my legs, placing a thigh on each of his shoulders, and dives in. He laps, licks, and sucks at me. I'm a quivering mess. Sounds are coming out of me that I'm not sure any human has made before, and I find that I can't bring myself to care.

And then Adam reaches up and finds my nipples, and he teases my nipples in tune with the way he tongues my clit. When he flicks at them with his fingers, he does the same lower with his tongue. When he slides his warm tongue over my clit, he does the same with his warm thumbs above.

And when he pinches and pulls my nipples as he closes his lips around my clit and sucks, I can't hold back anymore, not that I was really trying to.

I moan. My body jerks this way and that, as though this orgasm is a wrathful spirit that possesses me for one long, glorious minute. And it really does last a while. Just when I think it might be finished, a wave of pleasure crests again, and I find myself arching my back so hard, I idly wonder if I can somehow break it from having too powerful an orgasm.

By the time it's done, I feel even more spent than Adam was after I gave him a hand job. Catatonic was how he seemed, but feeling it myself, I want to say *on the glorious edge of death* is closer to the truth. I feel as though I just experienced so much pleasure, I touched the World of the Dead, the World of Ghosts, all of them, all of them, like some little piece of me exploded and made brief appearances in all the worlds and all the spaces between the worlds. It was like falling down, spending eight years in the woods, and returning, but as I am now, a woman, and all in a single, mind-blowing minute, thanks to Adam's clever fingers and tongue.

25

When he pulls back, I can tell that he is definitely satisfied with his work. He goes to the bathroom and comes back. "Clean washcloths?"

"Mirror," I say, and even though it comes out more like "Moo," as in cow, he understands. I roll up all my clean washcloths and stack them behind the mirror, because I like any prescriptions and skincare items to be where I can see them and remember that they exist—so those remain on my sink, lined up in a neat row.

He returns and the washcloth is steaming and feels so good on my inner thighs and between them. He lifts my hips to get to all the places where the, ah, moisture had gotten, and I want to blush when I remember what he said he wanted to do next. Put his tongue—his very, very talented tongue—back *there*.

As intrigued as I am at the prospect of experiencing that particular sexual act, I'm relieved when he says, "Let me get us some water," and disappears down the stairs. I'm a little too . . . exhausted? Overstimulated? One of those descriptions, or maybe some combination of the two, to rush right into the second act of . . . sex.

It hits me at once. I just had sex with Adam! Adam and I totally just gave each other orgasms.

Okay, so it wasn't intercourse—yet—but I've been researching, and everything we did could totally be considered sex. Defining intercourse as the only way to have sex is completely heteronormative and even ableist.

I run to the bathroom to pee as quick as possible, and after washing my hands, I grab my phone and text my sisters in the group chat:

Adam and I totally just did stuff!!!!!!!!!!!!!!

I look over my message and realize that could literally mean anything. Before I can add any clarification, I hear his footfalls make it up the stairs, and I quickly put my phone back on my nightstand, grab a sap green knitted throw blanket from where I'd draped it on the headboard, and cover myself just as he walks inside.

He does a double take when he sees me clutching the blanket to myself and says, "Is everything okay?"

"I—yes? I just realized how completely naked I am. And you—you're completely dressed! That's a bit odd, isn't it?"

He smiles warmly and shuts the door with his foot behind him. "Considering what we just did to each other . . . plus the fact that I'm not comfortable wandering your aunt's house in the nude . . . not that odd, I'd say." In his arms are the carafe of cold water I always keep in the fridge—hydration is important—and two tall pink plastic cups with built-in curly straws.

"Where did you find those cups?" I jump up to help him get

everything on the nightstand that doesn't have my phone charging on it. "I'm pretty sure the last time I saw those, Sage was trying to convince me and Teal to drink green smoothies when we were tweens."

"They were just in the cupboard," he says. "You want something else instead?"

"No, this is fine." I pour water for us and sit back on the bed, the blanket still wrapped around me the whole while. He joins me, and after a few sips, he takes my feet in his hands and begins to rub them, digging his thumbs into all the sore bits I never knew were so tense. "Wow. That feels so good. Thank you."

"It's my pleasure."

I lean back against the mountain of pillows I always stack at the headboard and close my eyes. "Adam?"

"Yeah?"

"Are we . . . I mean." My face begins to heat. God. The last thing I want to do is sound like a little kid in front of Adam, but I feel like that's exactly what I want to ask resembles. And yet. I need to know. "In the spirit of direct communication. We're together now, right? This isn't temporary for you, is it?"

He runs a hand through the scruff on his face. "Like I said. I'm not doing this right if you can ask me things like that." He lets go of my foot with his other hand and sits beside me on the bed. "I want you to be my girlfriend. But if you want this to be a temporary fling—"

"I don't," I cut in quickly. "I want you to be mine, too."

He grins in such an open, joyful way that I can't help smiling in return. He kisses me gently and leans back against the pillows again, placing an arm around my shoulders, nudging me to lie against his warm chest.

It's now well into the evening. The light coming in through

the windows is so long and deep ocher, making the shadows look all the darker and all the bluer. The sky through the balcony French doors is pale baby blue with the slightest hint of honey, foreshadowing the oncoming sunset.

"Why did you stop dating women?" I ask him.

"What do you mean?" His mouth is kissing my shoulder in an almost lazy manner. His words come out garbled, and I laugh.

"That tickles." He pulls back and I say, "You said you hadn't been with someone in two years . . . ? Right?"

"Right. I did say that."

I wait for more of an answer, but it doesn't come. "It's okay if you don't want to say." I turn toward him. "I'm just always curious about everything all the time. But you can tell me if you're not comfortable with a question anytime."

"It's not that. It's just a lot to put into words, I guess." He meets my gaze. "My mother died two years ago."

I inhale sharply. "Adam. I'm so sorry. I know that William had mentioned it—"

Adam laughs. "Yeah, William has always been a big blabbermouth. I mean, you should know by now."

I nod. That man is not interested in polite society or propriety or anything like that. Sometimes I wonder how he found a wife to put up with him for so long. My conclusion was he must've been a lot sweeter to her than he was to anyone else.

"She had a heart attack. She actually survived the initial cardiac arrest, but didn't make it when they did emergency surgery." Adam sighs. "She kept begging me to come down and visit her and my siblings in the whole year leading up to her death. I didn't come. Not once."

"You couldn't have known," I say gently.

"I could have been better regardless. A better son. A better sibling." He sighs. "My sisters really let me have it during the funeral."

I furrow my brow. "Why? That's the worst place to blame someone for anything, whether it's true or not. You were grieving your mother."

We've both slid down the bed so we're lying back, heads on the pillows, facing one another. Adam sighs. "Yeah, I guess there could've been a better time. But I was always running away from my problems, you know? I never forgave my mother for staying with my dad."

"William's son, right?"

"Yeah. You ever heard Gramps talk about my dad?"

I nod, widening my eyes a little bit as I remember. "Yup. He isn't . . . well. He's not impressed with him, I can say that."

"My dad is an alcoholic." Adam winces. "Like me. But unlike me, he gets mean and violent when he drinks. He started when his own mom died, when we were little. And honestly. That's when I started getting carried away with my cups. When my mom died. Apple doesn't fall far, I guess."

"Is your dad still drinking?" I ask.

Adam lets out a sad sigh. "Every damn day, far as I know."

"See," I say. "The apple isn't as close as you fear."

"Maybe." He doesn't sound convinced. "Anyway. Yeah. My sisters really got on my case, and I can't say that I didn't deserve it. I should have visited more. Answered the phone more. But like I said, my MO is to run away. I ran away from my family because I was so angry at my parents. I stayed away from my siblings because I wanted what they had—spouses and kids—but I didn't think I was good enough to have it. Seeing them was painful, so I just stopped. Got busy with work. Traveled as much as I could. Took on as many assignments as I could, and then some." He clears his throat and I'm under the impression that he wants to cry but will not. "And yeah, when my mom died, that whole game plan just crumbled to dust. I sometimes drank a little too much in college, but that was it beforehand. After the funeral, it started as a drink after work, every day. Then two. Then the whole six-pack. Then one day, I looked at the empty bottles in the recycling and had a flashback to my childhood. My dad's weekly pile of bottles. That's when I stopped completely. Six months ago."

"Six months sober?" I ask.

"Six months sober."

"You should tell your siblings about it," I say to him. "Your anger. The pain. Your journey in sobriety."

"I should, but I don't know what to say. I'm in the family group chat and I never participate. They probably have a separate group chat just to talk shit about me." He chuckles, but it's such a sad laugh that I wrap my arms around him and squeeze him tight.

"They don't text you at all? Not even a *Hey, how have you been?*"

Adam shrugs. "I mean, yeah. But I don't really know what to say back. I can feel the weight of their accusations every time they get in touch. Gramps says that's just my guilt talking, but . . ." He sighs.

I decide to try to the steer the topic into what are hopefully happier memories. "I'm so sorry your mom died, Adam," I say as softly as I can. "Can I ask, what was she like?"

Adam leans back and closes his eyes, and I can almost see the memories gliding through his brain. A half smile appears on his face, and his shoulders relax, and I instantly know that she was good. A good person and a good mother, even with her faults that caused so much anger in him. She had to have been, for his nervous system to completely relax at the thought of her.

"She liked baking and cooking for people. Like you, actually." Adam opens his eyes, staring at me and blinking a few times. "But she focused more on the baking."

"What was her specialty dish?" I ask.

"Cheesecake. She would blow her baking budget on real vanilla pods from the fancy health food store. When we were little, I used to watch her slice them open and scrape the seeds into the cheesecake batter. When I got older, she began making her own vanilla extracts. Birthday gifts were so easy for her. Get her a dried vanilla pod variety pack from all over the world. She would screech with happiness every time."

I smile. "Was it always vanilla cheesecake?"

"In a way, yes. Her cheesecakes always had vanilla. Like, that was her base. But she'd made every flavor imaginable. We used to joke that she could open the dessert portion of Cheesecake Factory from her kitchen."

"Which flavor was your favorite?" I asked, leaning into his shoulder, running my hands over the soft fabric covering his chest.

"Peanut butter chocolate. She would make the thick, homemade whipped cream and make it even better by adding chocolate flavoring to it. She'd put it in one of those bakery bags and pipe it all over the cheesecake, then shave chocolate on top."

"Mmm." I close my eyes, and I can see it: the dessert, delicious and beautiful and lovingly made. "That sounds so good. Was the cheesecake peanut butter flavored or chocolate flavored or both?"

"Peanut butter. Then she'd make this ganache and drizzle it

over the top. It's what she—" He chokes up. "Sorry." He takes one deep, slow breath. "She always made it for my birthday. Except for the year she died, since I didn't make it down."

"Do you need to cry? It sounds like you need to cry." I glance up at him.

He shakes his head. "I probably do need to cry, but I really don't want to right now."

I nod. "Okay."

I push up onto an elbow and lean down to kiss him. I don't know why, but the kiss deepens quickly, and I feel the space between my legs heat just as fast. We both moan and the throw slips off my shoulders and I lift one leg to straddle him.

He looks up at me, awe in his eyes. "Look at you." His gaze drops down to my hips, which he then grabs with his hands. "Jesus. Just look at you." He slides his hands up to my waist, tightens his grip, and flips me around until he's behind me, my face pressed against the pillow. He lifts my hips so that my ass is completely in the air. He grabs me and pulls me apart and I gasp.

"I want to make you come again," he says. "Is that okay?"

I nod, and realize he probably can't see me. I lift my face a little bit and say, "Yes. Please." And then bury my face back against the pillow mountain.

At first, it's not what I expected, feeling his mouth and tongue at what is probably the most vulnerable part of my body. It feels warm and wet, and I can't get past those neutral descriptors until he does something with his tongue that makes me moan, and when he does it again, whatever it is, I push my ass back into his face even deeper. When he moans in return, I feel it everywhere. Everywhere.

Adam slides his hand between my legs and slides his fingers into me. I'm so wet, I can feel it dripping down my inner thighs, and I think it surprises him and turns him on because he moans again and his licks become more and more sloppy.

He works his fingers into me and I reach back to adjust his hand. "There," I say with a whimper. "There." According to my research, what I'm referring to is my G-spot. I looked up how to discover it for myself and it wasn't hard at all. I'm shocked at how many men deny it exists. "I like it hard," I tell him, and he obliges, finger-fucking me hard and fast and I moan so loudly, the pillow does nothing to smother the sound.

The orgasm builds up quickly. I feel like I'm on the edge for ages, and when Adam reaches up and pinches my clit, I'm done for. I moan and moan into the pillows, and I can feel everything contracting as I come—my pussy, my ass, even my lower belly and thighs feel like they're joining in.

When I'm done, I collapse on the bed for a few minutes. "I'll get another washcloth," Adam says, laughing at me. He cleans up in the bathroom first, then brings back the washcloth, starting with my thighs, and then everywhere else.

"That felt so good," I tell him lazily.

"Good." He smiles at me, and I think we're having perhaps what might be one of the most intimate moments of just looking at each other, when my stomach betrays me by growling so loud, it sounds like there's a trapped wildebeest in there.

We both laugh at the same time. "There's plenty of leftovers," Adam says, pointing his thumb toward the stairs. "Or we can get something. Or go out. Whatever you want."

"Definitely leftovers. That was so good."

"Which part?" he asks with a wink, letting me grab his arm so he can assist me off the bed.

"The paneer." I reach into my armoire and grab a fluffy cerulean robe. "And the naan. And the pussy eating. And the ass eating.

All the eating. And watching you come. I liked that a lot, too." I pause after I've tied the robe around my waist and look up at him. He's staring at me with an expression that is uncomfortably close to *adoration*. "Did you have fun?"

He smiles slowly. "It would be an egregious understatement, but yeah. I had fun, Sky."

"Okay," I say, just as my stomach growls again, and he laughs again.

"Come on." He gently guides me toward the stairs as though I'm precious to him. "Let's eat something."

26

Adam can't stay the night because he's too worried William might have another bad night. "I'm just scared he's going to hurt himself, knocking around into furniture in the middle of the night, and tripping over shit," he says apologetically as we chat on the porch by the front door.

"Shit, Adam. Does this mean the doctor is right with his suspicions on dementia?"

Adam puts a hand over the stubble of his chin. "It definitely doesn't look good. I need to get him reassessed, given some of these new symptoms."

I shake my head. This is heartbreaking. "Don't worry about not staying. I get it. I don't want anything bad to happen to him, either."

He smiles, kisses me slowly, then moans a little bit as I grab his head and pull his hair. He ends up pushing me against the door, lowering his mouth to my neck, and then I'm the one moaning. He pulls back abruptly, laughing. "Okay. Okay. We gotta stop or I'm going to throw you over my shoulder and march you back upstairs."

"You never put it inside me," I say, lightly touching where he's hard again.

"Fuck, Sky." He laughs again. "If that's what you want, next time, okay? Next time."

"When is next time?"

He pauses. "I wanna take you out to dinner downtown. I want everyone to see you're mine. After that I want to"—he grins—"what did you just say? Put it inside you?"

I have my hand on my heart and I feel the beginnings of tears stinging my eyes. "Everyone? You want everyone to see I'm yours?"

He kisses my forehead so gently, a tear actually does make it to my cheek, despite my best efforts to hold it in. He uses his thumb to wipe it away. "If you're fine with it. Yes. I want everyone to know you're mine."

I swallow. "Okay. Um. My next evening off is Tuesday."

"I'll pick you up then."

We kiss good night again, and then again, and then we both laugh because I guess everything about this feels so good. I know it's mostly due to endorphins and oxytocin and whatever other hormones are responsible for human romantic attachment, but I don't care. I want more of this, more of him. It feels unfair now that I don't know what he would feel like, banging me hard against my bed.

I even wistfully watch him cross the street, making sure he gets inside his home safely.

I'm so full of energy—left over from my nervousness earlier, when I was scared I would probably be Adam's worst lover he's ever had, as well as my nervous system trying to deal with the intensity of post-orgasmic euphoria—that I know I need to take a walk in the woods. I go inside to grab a hoodie and slip on some sneakers, and I make my way down the street. Just beyond the cul-de-sac is a skinny trail that, as far as I know, only I and the opossums, skunks, and raccoons use. But before I can reach it, there is the low rumble of a car engine getting closer behind me. I step into the nearest yard so they can drive around me, whoever they are. But instead they go even slower. They come even closer. I don't look back. I sense this all with my ears, even as I pretend I do not hear them. Who is following me in the dark with their headlights off?

Finally, they step on the gas and reach me. When I turn, it's Janie, the cranky lady next door who always acts like I can't see her spying on me and obviously hating on me through her kitchen window. "Can I help you?" I ask.

Her face is completely expressionless. "Was that Adam Noemi I saw just leaving your grandmother's home?"

What the fuck is she asking that for? Does she need Adam for something? "Yeah?"

She shakes her head. "Haven't you done enough to the reputation of this town?" My jaw drops, because although I knew she was a nosy busybody, I didn't think she was also a nasty gossip like that. I guess I should have known, but honestly, I try not to assume the worst of people every chance I get. I probably should change that, considering all they do is prove me wrong.

She goes on, "What have you done to him? He knows well enough to stay away from the likes of you, so you must've done *something*."

I almost jump when I feel a quick bump of something furry on my hand. I don't have to glance down to know it's a coyote I've named Granola, for his beautiful toasted-oat coloring. "Oh," I say so soft it's a hum, when I sense that he's brought his whole family, eleven coyotes in all. He nudges my hand again and I know he's here, that they're all here, because he sensed my fear. They're my backup. My beloved, beautiful backup.

I turn back to Janie and decide to go with my earlier plan from what feels like ages ago now. She wants to believe I'm evil?

Okay. Let's do this, then.

I look right into her eyes—she's still got that nasty, holier-than-thou expression on her face—and then I begin to bark.

I growl and chirp and when I begin howling, the coyotes surround me and they do the exact same thing. They howl, too.

She was pretty freaked out when I began barking, but once the coyotes join me, she opens her mouth and screams. And of course, that just makes the rest of us louder.

She hits reverse and doesn't even take the time to turn her white SUV around. She reverses it all the way down the street, and I cannot help it. I chase her and keep howling, my backup adding to the chase, joyfully joining me and yipping while running in circles around me.

I know she will tell people. I know that by tomorrow, the whole town will know about Sky Flores's barking escapades. But I find, as I arch my back and howl for the final time, good and long at the blue ink sky—that for the first time in maybe ever, I simply do not care.

"SKYYYYY."

The scents of bacon and coffee awaken my stomach, but I'm still half in a dream about spending the night in a coyote den, sprawled in a big pile with them, relaxing while watching videos on my phone.

"Oh, Skyyyyyy!!!" the voice chirps again.

"What," I mumble. It's not Nadia or Amá Sonya, because they would never take it upon themselves to disturb me while I was still asleep, which means it's got to be one of my annoying sisters.

"Did you get the plate next to her nose?"

"I tried, but her face is buried in the pillow!"

Or *both* of my annoying sisters, rather.

I lift up my head and the first thing I focus on is Sage's hands, wrapped around a plate full of what looks like breakfast tacos. Both of my sisters are great cooks—we kinda all had to learn because Nadia sure as hell didn't cook for us—but these look a little bougie, which is Teal's style. The corn tortillas are fried with chili powder, making them much more golden than usual. Inside each one are scrambled eggs cooked with spinach, or maybe kale, with fried potatoes and scallions. Each is topped with a fan of sliced avocado, a drizzle of crema, and chopped cilantro. On the side are three slices of bacon that don't exactly look right, so I'm assuming they're turkey bacon or maybe made out of soy.

Motivated by hunger, I sit up and rub my eyes. Teal places the plate in my lap. "There ya go."

"Thanks." I reach for the water at my bedside first, and take in the scene. Teal's standing next to me, arms crossed, like she's some kind of boot camp leader monitoring if I'm going to eat her food properly or not. Sage is sitting at the end of the bed, legs crossed, her own plate in her lap, working on her last taco, from the looks of it. She looks around and gestures with half a taco in her hand. "When the hell did you do all this?"

I furrow my brow and say, "Oh right. The décor. A while ago."

"It looks amazing." She points at the furniture and my bed and the wallpaper. "Jesus, you need to be an interior designer, Sky."

I laugh. "I don't think so. The whole thing was a big headache, even if it was worth it in the end." I glance around myself, only I'm looking for a car seat. "Where's the baby?"

"Tenn took him to the Finger Lakes with a cooler full of pumped milk."

"Best lakes in town." I put my water bottle back, grab a taco, and just as I'm about to bite, I look up. "So . . . what are you guys doing here? You're not just feeding me from the goodness of your hearts."

"What do you mean?" Sage asks through a full mouth. "Can't we make you food just because?"

I shake my head. "You can. But you don't."

"We want to know what happened with you and Adam," Teal says, pulling out her phone so I can look at the last text I sent them. Adam and I totally just did stuff!!!!!!!!!!!!!!

I swallow my bite. "Oh. Yeah."

"We figured you meant, you know." Sage makes a gesture with her finger and hand that I think is supposed to indicate intercourse. "And we wanted to hear about it!"

"And make sure you were safe. You're not on birth control, are you?" Teal is still looking like she's either a cop or a military sergeant, and I guess now I understand why.

I suppress a sigh. I'm glad my sisters want to know about my life, but I'll be so happy when they let go of this idea that I'm some little kid who doesn't know anything about anything.

They want to know what happened? Fine. "I gave him a hand job, and he came all over my comforter, which is why it's rolled up in the corner over there, and then he ate me out, and then he ate my ass while finger-blasting me. Oh, and he brought a ton of Indian food from out of town, so if you want any, you can pack some up in Tupperware whenever you leave."

"He ate your ass!" Sage gasps. "What was that like?"

"Tenn's never eaten your ass before?" Teal asks.

"No. We don't do ass things. We've never really talked about it but he must not be into it, I figured."

"Maybe he wants to receive," Teal suggests.

Sage frowns thoughtfully. "Hmm. Anyone want to watch the baby sometime next week?"

"So you can eat your husband's ass?" I ask. "I can watch Oak. That's an important endeavor."

"Deal," Sage says, then turns to Teal. "Why do you sound surprised that we hadn't done it before? Is everyone getting their ass eaten but me and Tennessee?"

Teal shrugs. "I don't kiss and tell."

I roll my eyes. "You told us about the time Carter fingered you in the kitchen but then stopped short of getting you off, plus a great deal of other intimate moments. So you should amend your statement to *I don't eat ass and tell.*"

Teal scoffs playfully. "All I can say is, if you're going to eat a man's ass, reach around and tease his dick at the same time. He will sound like he's going to die, but don't stop till he—" She makes an explosion sound at the same time she opens her hands in front of her.

Sage raises her eyebrows. "Noted!" She turns to me. "Okay, soooo. You two didn't do penetration."

I swallow a bite of what is definitely turkey bacon. Not bad, but not exactly awesome, either, not that I would ever tell Teal that. "Why do we call it penetration, anyway? That's pretty focused on the cis male experience of intercourse, isn't it?"

Sage nods. "I see. Yes. Okay, so you didn't *receive* him yesterday." She gestures to her crotch. "Your *receptionist* didn't accept a new *appointment*."

I roll my eyes. "No. We did not. But when and if we do"—on

Tuesday most likely, but I don't include this—"I can text you guys. Do you want to know after or while he's still inside me?"

"Hey." Teal sits next to me and puts her hand on my knee. "I'm sorry if we sound patronizing."

I sigh. "I just get frustrated sometimes at how much I missed, you know? I went from sixteen to twenty-four. And now I'm twenty-six. I feel like I know nothing, and I know you all mean well, but sometimes I feel like you treat me like I'm incapable. You know?"

"I get it. I'm sorry, Sky. When I got that text yesterday, I panicked because I realized that you never really got the big-sister birds-and-the-bees talk like Sage gave me."

I breathe out slowly and nod. "I know. I didn't. But I have done it before, you know."

"With Ramón!" Sage says. "*No one* thought you two were fucking. That boy acted like he was trying to literally be Jesus with his purity. He wouldn't even laugh at the most vague dirty joke!"

I laugh because it's true. Ramón wanted to have sex with me so badly, but he also had so much shame about wanting it. It's probably one of the many reasons why the very few times we were able to were really . . . forgettable, to put it as kindly as possible.

"Do you want us to help you with anything?" Teal asks. "Birth control, condoms—"

"We could go to Lucky Treasures," Sage says. "They'll have all that. Well, not oral contraceptives, but condoms, lube, lingerie."

I brighten. "Lingerie?"

"Yeah! I need something new. My drive is coming back, now that I'm feeling less anxious and paranoid about everything."

"Okay, well, they open in thirty minutes," Teal says, checking her watch. "I gotta get back to work in about an hour and a half, so we should leave soon. Sky, get dressed while I do the dishes."

I roll my eyes. "Okay, bossy."

"Oh, you love it," Teal calls as she makes her way toward the stairs.

Sage reaches for my dirty plate and gives me a little hug in the meantime. "I'm so glad you and Adam are doing things!" She smiles. "He seems like a good man."

I can't help but grin back as I think about him, and all the ways he is good. "He really is."

"Yes. That's what you deserve." She stands. "Okay, go get ready. We have some sexy underwear to purchase."

27

LUCKY TREASURES IS WAY ON THE OPPOSITE SIDE OF DOWN-town, inland, in an old shopping plaza that, from what I remember from childhood, used to have some cute mom-and-pop restaurants and furniture stores but now is a collection of really run-down-looking electronic and dollar stores. The building itself looks just as old as the surroundings, but the people in charge obviously keep it a lot nicer with what looks to be regular pressure washing and daisies and coneflowers planted all around the parking lot.

After we walk in, it becomes clear that we are definitely the only customers, which makes me relax muscles I hadn't realized I'd been tensing. While I still mostly don't care that my shenanigans last night are possibly the talk of the town, that doesn't mean that I want people to call me names and act like I need to adhere a big red *F* on my clothing for *Freak* while I'm trying to figure out which piece of raunchy lace Adam would like the most.

We wander from display to display, giggling and chatting

about which pieces would be the most flattering for us. I end up falling in love with a shimmery lilac bodysuit that has the whole crotch, ass, and breasts cut out. "It's so absurd," I say. "But also very pretty."

"That kind of describes most lingerie," Sage agrees. "Absurd and pretty."

Sage ends up with a corset, though, and a thigh-high mix. Teal decides to grab some lube and a travel bullet vibrator. She wants to buy me condoms as a sort of "congratulations on your first real adult sexual relationship" gift, but I wave her off, telling her about the massive variety collection I already have.

After saying goodbye to them, I drive to work, saying my usual greeting to Anise before going down into my lair. As soon as I put my handbag on my desk, my phone dings. The notification is for Matchmakr.

I narrow my eyes as I open the app, and there it is. From @tryingsomethingnew: Hey girl. Wyd?

I snort. I'm at work. Wyd? Didn't William have a doctor's appointment? How was it?

Got him in the office barely on time. He had another bad night.

Oh no. I'm sorry, Adam. How is he now?

Snoozing. At least the doc could see what I was talking about and prescribed him some sleep meds. I need to pick them up from the pharmacy in a few.

I tsk. Poor William. Was he always so grumpy, or did it become a thing as he got older?

Ahhh . . . yeah, Gramps was always a hardass. Sweet on my grandma, though. It definitely is getting worse with age, though, so both.

Are you okay? Do you need anything?

Just wanted to hear from you. 😊 My salt sea girl.

My heart feels so warm on its next few beats as I read him calling me his. I'm here. If you need to chat. My . . . uh. Trying Something New Guy.

Lmao. That's not nearly as endearing a username. Ah.. I gotta run. Pharmacy's calling. Chat later?

Of course. Have a good day.

I look at my desk and see the architecture book I had been so engrossed in only a couple days ago. I shrug and push it aside. I don't know why, but finding out what was happening under St. Theresa's Catholic Church for Wanderers and Pilgrims doesn't feel so urgent right now. I guess maybe my brain can only handle so many exciting things at once. And right now, Adam is taking precedence. And I wouldn't change the Brain Priorities List even if I could. I just . . . want Adam.

All I do at work is think about how much I want him. As I categorize books, I also categorize all the sexual positions I know, and make note to research more later. As I read through some annoying paperwork, my mind drifts off to think about whether Adam would enjoy an ass-eating, like apparently Carter does. I think about the sounds Adam might make, similar to all the ways he groaned and moaned every time we touched yesterday, and yup, just like that, I'm wet. I squeeze my thighs together and shake my head.

How can I focus on anything when Adam Noemi is officially mine? And we're going on a date tomorrow? And are banging for the first time afterward?

I barely manage to make it through the workday and wonder how on earth anyone gets anything done when they have a partner as hot and as lovely as Adam Noemi.

THROUGHOUT THE BEGINNING OF MY WORKWEEK, THERE ARE many things I ignore in addition to my previous church investigation. One is the increasing number of text messages Amá Sonya sends me, each one more morbid than the last. I am your only grandmother and we all know I will not be around much longer. You need to go on a date with someone I approve of at least once. After that, she wrote: COYOTES?? And the last text is simply: I suppose I must come to you. But if it comes down to that, you might have regrets. Don't say I didn't warn you.

I send Teal a screenshot of all the texts and write, Please tell her, in the kindest way possible, to leave me the fuck alone. Teal sends a thumbs-up with an On it, and then reminds me about her art opening this coming weekend. I'd nearly forgotten, so I pencil it in my planner right away, then text Adam to invite him. I'd love to 😊 is what he writes back.

Tuesday comes a lot quicker than I expected, considering all the daydreaming and humming and smiling to myself I've been doing. I get off work at three, then look in my closet for what feels like an age, wondering what on earth to wear for my first official, real date with Adam.

I decide on a little black dress that fits me like a glove, emphasizing the curves of my hips and ass, featuring a square neckline that is high and elegant. It reaches my midthigh and has a small slit that reveals my brown, moisturized skin, so the skirt is a little bit slutty. Slutty and elegant. That's me. I contain multitudes.

I pin up my hair according to a Pinterest tutorial promising to make me look like I'm an elven princess, put on smoky eye shadow and pink lipstick, and spray on a perfume that smells like autumn to me, the most romantic season, with notes of pumpkin, nutmeg, and coffee.

I'm slipping on Mary Janes at the door when Adam knocks. I open it and give him the biggest smile as I jump on him to hug him.

"Whoa," he says, laughing as he slides his hands under my ass to hold me up against him. "Wow. What a greeting." I slide back down him and he takes a step back. "And wow. You're so fucking gorgeous. Look at you."

I turn around, giggling. "It's Calvin Klein. My grandmother got it for me, but she said I would need to get the skirt redone by a tailor to have it go to my knees."

"I'm glad you ignored the advice." He gives me a long look of approval.

"You look handsome," I say shyly. He had put on a forest green dress shirt with black slacks and shoes. "I love green on you."

"Yeah?" He gives me a half smile. "My mother told me green was our color. Because of our red hair."

"You got your red hair from her?"

He nods. "Yup. Me and all my siblings. And my dad's hair is black. You'd never think red was recessive with the way it took over our family. Only one of my sixteen nieces and nephews has dark hair. The rest, all different shades of red."

"Maybe your mom had the rare dominant redhead gene," I say as I shut and lock the door behind me.

Adam chuckles. "Wouldn't surprise me."

"So where are we going?" I ask after we settle in his car.

"That depends." He glances my way. "How do you feel about seafood?"

"Some of it is weird. I don't like the slimy sorts. But I love the other ones."

He grins at me. "What are the slimy sorts?"

I scrunch up my nose. "You know. Anything in a shell. Like oysters?"

"Ah, yeah." He nods. "Slimy definitely describes oysters. What are some dishes you love?"

I shrug. "I love blackened fish. Grilled fish. To me, crab is a little bit slimy sometimes, but crab cakes are good."

"I see. So you have strong opinions on texture." He frowns and nods. "Well, they have a steakhouse downtown called Jackson's. I don't know why it's called a steakhouse when most of the menu is seafood. You ever been?"

I shake my head. Jackson's Steakhouse is one of the most popular restaurants in Cranberry. I've certainly had many reasons to prefer the woods since my return from the oak tree.

Adam grabs my hand. "Does that sound okay? You want to go there?"

I hesitate for a moment and say, "Sure. I'm sure that will be fine."

Adam doesn't say anything for about thirty seconds. My body tenses—is he mad at me? Did I say the wrong thing? But then he says, "There's also this new place that just opened up last summer. It's inside an old house. They have candles, tablecloths. Very intimate."

"Oh!" I smile. "Intimate sounds good. What kind of food is it?"

"I'm not really sure. I was chatting with someone a few weeks ago, and he said he took his wife there for their anniversary."

"That sounds expensive, then. We can go to the steakhouse. You mentioned that one first, so that's what you'd prefer, right?"

Adam glances at me with a relaxed smile on his face. "You want something quiet, I'm guessing?"

I nod. "Yeah. I don't like crowds. Or loud music. I hate having to try so hard to focus on what the person I'm with is saying."

"Okay. Noted. Let's go to the other place."

"I'll pay for my dinner," I say quickly. "Oh! I can treat! I can get both of our dinners."

Adam laughs, but it's not unkind. "Sky. *I* asked you out on this date. It's *my* treat. Don't worry about money." For a couple of minutes, we drive in silence, the town whipping past us in a blur of a mix of older neighborhoods with enormous oak canopies alongside pockets of new developments, most identifiable by the homes that are identical with virtually no trees. I'm thinking about what the energy bills of those new homes look like when Adam says, "Correct me if I'm wrong. But about the conversation we just had."

I knew it! I did say the wrong thing! "Yes?"

"Do you always feel like you're a burden? Or try to make yourself have as few needs as possible?"

I swallow. "Probably." He's patient as I go over my thoughts. "It's . . . well. My whole life, people who didn't want me were forced to take care of me. Like, in the beginning, my father didn't want to know I existed. My mother left when I was a baby. Nadia didn't want to raise me, so she made Sage do it, and later on, Teal also helped with rearing me. And then I fell, and returned, and they still are having a hard time letting go of those roles, you know? I don't like it." I swallow and look out my window, noting the thin, bright clouds rolling across the blue sky. "And I guess one way I try to make up for being the one everyone's always worried about is by trying to not have any needs. Otherwise . . . what if they leave me, too? I don't ever want to be too much. Although that seems unavoidable most of the time, given my whole life and personality."

Adam nods and squeezes my hand. "But you know that no one's going to leave you. Your sisters do the things they do because they love you."

I shake my head. "Maybe, but when they both got super busy this spring, with their families and their lives, they both kind of . . . ignored me. I know they both had a lot going on. But it bothers me that I was dropped. It didn't help my fears."

"I understand. But . . . just speaking for myself. And us. I don't want you to try and minimize your needs around me. I want to know what it is that you need. If that means you want a quiet dinner, let me know. I want you to be comfortable."

I nod. My heart almost hurts because this might be one of the sweetest things a man has ever told me. "What about you? What do you need?"

Adam laughs. "To make you smile like you're smiling right now."

I roll my eyes. "Yeah, yeah. That's still about me, though."

"Okay. I need to make you come again by sucking on your clit while pinching your nipples."

"Holy shit." I wasn't expecting that kind of talk to come out of his mouth right now. I cross my legs and squeeze my thighs together. "Wait. That's still about me! You're trying to distract me!"

Adam laughs again, but this time it's a deep belly laugh. "Okay. Yeah." He takes a breath as he pulls into the parking lot of what I'm assuming is the restaurant. He turns the car off and looks at me. "I'm still trying to figure that out, you know? My needs. Because for a long time, I just grabbed a beer."

I nod. "I get it."

"I know you do. But I think, right now, I need to just take things easy and slow. With everything. Sobriety, figuring out my life here in Cranberry, caretaking."

I think about this for a moment. "Do you need me to do anything to help you with that?"

"Not a damn thing." He leans over and kisses me, hard and quick, and I nearly whimper when he pulls away. I can't believe how ready I am for him over nothing but a few dirty words and a brief kiss. "Just let me take you out to dinner, and if you still want to, let me make love to you after."

"I want that," I say quickly. "All of it."

He laughs again. "Okay. Let's go eat, then."

28

THE RESTAURANT IS CALLED BLACKSTONE CROSSING, WHICH sounds more like a train station to me, but the inside is exactly what Adam had promised: completely romantic and cozy. While the outside was a three-story home with an almost industrial, chipped-paint look, inside it's all small converted bedrooms with only three or four tables in each one. The windows are open to various views—trees, the ocean, the parking lot, still pretty and filled with flowering bushes—and each table is covered in a cottagecore, red gingham pattern. Wall lanterns accompany the table candles, making everything flicker in golden orange, and I feel like I've stepped into a restaurant run by a happy hobbit or something.

"This is lovely," I whisper to him as we wait for our table.

He smiles at me. "I'm glad you like it."

We're seated in a blissfully private corner. I order the pecan-crusted fried chicken with mashed potatoes and sautéed peas. Adam gets the blackened scallops with cheesy grits and collard greens. We chat so easily that it feels like the food arrives in only a minute, and it's so good that I moan with every bite. Adam's face gets pinker and pinker until I straight up ask him, "Is my eating making you hard?" And he sputters in a way that the answer can only be *yes*.

As soon as we get back in his car after eating, I climb on top of him and kiss him. We make out slowly at first. Sweetly. His hands reach my ass and grab me tight, and when I moan, our kiss becomes frantic and hurried, like we only have minutes to fuck before the world implodes.

"Your place or mine?" he asks, breaking the kiss breathlessly.

"I don't want William to hear me having an orgasm," I respond. "And Nadia is never home."

"Got it. And yeah, I don't want Gramps to hear you having an orgasm, either."

I chuckle and we kiss again, and Adam pulls back, laughing. "We gotta stop or I'm going to come right now, Sky."

I push up and look down. "Really?"

"Yes, really." He drops his head back. "I don't understand this. How out of control you make me feel."

I shrug. "It's hormones. Oxytocin and dopamine and serotonin." I climb back in my seat and glance up to see him shaking his head.

"No. Because this has never happened before, with women I've had flings with. It's something else."

"Hmm," I say, wondering what it could be—it has been a long time for him, hasn't it?—but he shakes his head and turns on the car before I can form another thought on the matter.

"I want you so badly. I'm going to have to restrain myself from breaking multiple speed limits."

I can feel how wet I am between my legs without even squeezing my thighs. I wonder what it would be like to tease Adam in a place where he can't really participate—only observe. So I lift my skirt and slide my hand up my right thigh. When I pass my fingers over my panties, I gasp. I, too, am really close to coming. Really close.

"Oh Christ. Sky. Are you touching yourself right now?" He glances at my skirt. "You are, aren't you?"

"Do you want me to stop?" I ask.

"Hell no. Fuck no. I've thought about this too much. Watching you. Fuck, this is so hot."

I slide my fingers under my panties and moan when I feel how slippery I am. "I'll come if I keep doing this."

"I want you to. Please." Adam's voice is nearly a whine.

I work myself, squirming and shifting my hips all around as I gasp and moan. A couple of times, Adam grips himself at red lights, which only makes my fingers go even faster. He pulls into the driveway and hits the brakes a little too hard. I slide forward and the pressure between my underwear and fingers makes me break apart instantly. The orgasm is fast and hard and afterward, I collapse against the seat, my hand still under the skirt of my dress.

Adam pulls my arm up and wraps his lips around my still very wet finger. "Oh my God," I whisper as he cleans me up with his tongue. The warm, wet feel of him and the noise of licking is already making another orgasm build up.

"You taste so fucking good," he murmurs, his eyes heavy-lidded and his deep voice unbearably raspy.

"Let's go inside," I say, taking my hand back to open the door.

"Good idea."

We make out against the porch door as soon as we're in. In the kitchen, he places me on the table and steps between my legs and grinds his erection at my core. He kisses me and pulls the top of my dress down so that my breasts are exposed to the cool air. My nipples tighten further under his mouth, and he reaches between my legs and does the same thing to my clit with his fingers that he's doing with his tongue on my nipples.

I love that he learned so easily what I like. That he remembered. That he listened to my reactions and responses. It's exactly how I imagined it would be, with Adam.

Then he lowers himself to his knees, and before I understand what's happening, my underwear is tossed somewhere on the green linoleum floor and his tongue is smooth and hot against my clit.

This orgasm is slow. The buildup takes so long, but when I finally come, it is syrupy and strong and lasts forever. After I'm finished convulsing all over his face, he jumps up, kisses me again, and then does what he says he was going to do earlier. He tosses me on his shoulder and takes me upstairs, one hand on the backs of my knees and the other on my ass.

"Do you like your ass fingered?" he asks on the way up.

"I—don't know?" I can barely speak. The blood is rushing to my head all at once.

Soon enough, he gently places me on my bed and we kiss again. "We can find out whenever you're ready if you like that."

"Okay," I respond as his lips reach my neck. "Um. I have condoms."

"Me too. Do you have a preference on the kind you like?"

"Um. Well, as you know, it's been a while. But I think the ones that are thin, like a second skin? And smooth. I remember hating anything ribbed."

"Got it."

We kiss more, and he pulls back to unbutton his shirt, basically ripping it off once it's open. He pulls his undershirt over his head, exposing his beautiful, freckled chest. Before he can reach for the buckle of his pants, I stand and pull him toward me, kissing him as I wrap my arms around his waist. I moan when his chest hair brushes my nipples, still bare from when he pulled my dress and bra down in the kitchen.

Breaking the kiss, I open his belt buckle and reach in, grabbing him and squeezing. He gasps against my neck and I love it. I love listening to the sounds of his pleasure, and feeling it, too, with his heavy breathing on my skin.

He pushes his pants down and kicks them off, and I do the same with my dress and underwear. He urges me to lie back against the pillows, and then he watches me as he teases my clit. I groan and then whine when he stops abruptly, looking into his face. "Are you sure you want this?" he asks. "We can do all the other things we've already done. If you would rather that."

I shake my head and take a shuddering breath. "No. I want to feel you inside me."

He smiles at me and says, "Okay. I want that, too." He slides a finger inside me, working my G-spot, and I squirm on the bed when he adds two, three fingers. He thrusts them inside me hard and fast, just as I like it. I hold my breath as the beginnings of another orgasm begin to build, and he removes his fingers. "Shit," he says. "Where are your favorite condoms? I can't even remember which sort I brought right now."

"Here, here," I say, reaching over and throwing open my nightstand drawer. I grab one. It's smooth, but also . . . "Do you care if it warms up? According to the packaging, that's what it's supposed to do."

"I can't bring myself to care about anything right now, except making you lose your mind with my cock."

I frown playfully and nod. "Good plan. Good priorities."

He laughs as he takes the condom from me, and I watch closely as he slides it on. I can't remember the last time I watched someone, well, only one someone, do that. I try to fold the event in my mind so I can pull it out for reference if I ever want to slide one on him myself.

He climbs on top of me and kisses me, gently lowering his lips to my neck, then my breasts, until I'm wiggly and so, so, so wet. I feel the head of him between my legs, and I hold my breath when he slides himself inside, one inch at a time.

"You good?" he asks.

I nod, furrowing my brow. "It feels really tight."

"Does it hurt?"

I shake my head. "No. I just wasn't expecting to feel so full."

He laughs. "I'm so glad I'm secure in my size right now."

I roll my eyes. "Come on. You're above average. I just mean, I'd forgotten this part. The particular sensations."

He pulls out the tiniest bit and thrusts back in and something pleasurable begins to bloom in me. Like the orgasm he was building me up to with his fingers hasn't left, and his dick has decided to finish the job. "Do that again. Harder."

I gasp when he pushes out and then back in roughly, just as I'd asked. "Again."

He obeys me immediately. Two, three, four times. Ten seconds of thrusting and I say, "Oh, I'm so close."

He grabs my waist and rolls us over, never breaking the connection between our legs. I blink when I find myself on top, looking down at him, a half smile on his gorgeous face, his hair already so messy, pointing this way and that.

"I've wanted to see you like this for so long. I want you to make yourself come using me like this."

"Oh!" I put my hands on his chest and move my hips around in a circle. "I'm not really sure how I'm supposed to do this." I've never been on top before.

"There's no one right way. Well, except what gets you off. Whatever makes you come is the right way for you."

I push against him to lift my hips a little, then drop back down on him. His jaw goes slack as our pelvises slap together. I find I like that. Watching his face as I ride him. I like that a lot.

So I keep doing the same movement, allowing the display of his pleasure to contribute to my own. But I don't really find my groove until I squat on my feet, with him still inside me, and begin to rock back and forth like I'm completely feral. That's when I get the exact right pressure I need, and I begin to moan.

"Fuck," he says, throwing his head back. The muscles in his neck and chest are all tense. His brow is furrowed up, his eyes are closed until he seems to remember he wants to watch me, too, and then he forces them back open, glazed and heavy-lidded.

It's only after about three or four minutes of this particular stimulation—the sounds, the view, his cock—that the orgasm comes over me in layers. I don't stop moving as I moan.

"I feel you coming," he moans. "I can feel it. Fuck."

And the amazing thing is . . . this triggers his orgasm. Just as I'm nearly finished, his whole body goes as taut as an arrow on a bow, about to be launched . . . and then he lets go. He whines and gasps and moans so loudly, and so deeply, I tuck the sound away in my mind for masturbation fodder. I will definitely be replaying that again in the near future. It might be the hottest thing I've ever heard in my life.

After I'm certain he's done spasming inside me, I slowly lift myself so he glides out, and then lie back on the bed next to him. He shifts so we are staring at one another, side by side, looking very much like two people who just fucked each other very hard.

I snort and then begin to laugh. Before I know it, I'm doubled over, laughing deeply with my belly, and Adam is laughing, too. "What are we laughing at?" he asks between breaths.

"I don't even know," I say. "It's the hormones. The serotonin—"

"And the oxytocin and the dopamine," he finishes. "But again, this has never happened with anyone else before for me."

"Everyone is different," I say primly.

Adam raises a brow with a smile. "You're pretty resistant to the idea that I feel like the connection I have with you is unlike anything I've ever felt before with anyone else."

I blink. "I am?"

"Well, I shouldn't say it like I know for sure. But you seem to be resistant to the idea. Like when you mentioned dopamine before." He shakes his head. "This isn't the dopamine, Sky. I don't understand what I'm feeling for you, but it's something more."

I frown. "Are you saying you're in love with me?"

"I—" He hesitates and my heart jumps. I wasn't expecting anything close to an affirmative when I asked the question. In fact, I was expecting a hard *Of course I'm not, it's only been a few days and three sexual encounters*. And so I'm floored when he says this next: "I've never been in love before, Sky, but I have to admit, when I imagined what it would be like . . ." He gestures a little bit, like he can't find the right words. "It was exactly like this, with you."

I put my hand on my heart and close my eyes and try to find the words for what I'm feeling myself. "Kind of like your chest is so full you're afraid it might rip open and illustrated pink hearts will come flying out and attack everyone?"

"That . . . wasn't the imagery I would have gone with, but that actually sounds about right." He chuckles and places his own hand on his fuzzy chest.

"Well, if that's love, then maybe I'm feeling it, too."

He whips his head toward me, his eyes a little wide. "Yeah? Really?"

I nod. "Yeah. That's how my chest feels right now. Like it's going to explode into a million flying hearts and murmur all around us."

He barely lets me finish speaking. He comes to me so fast, my last word is cut off short by his kiss.

This isn't a normal kiss, at least so far, for us. This kiss is full of feeling, and passion, and . . . maybe love. I don't know. It's all new to me, too, like it is for him. And before I know it, Adam has another condom on, and he's inside me again, just like this, side by side, face-to-face, my leg draped over his hip. He enters in and out slowly, kissing me. I know I'm not going to come, and when I tell him this, he says okay. He finishes, and it's a beautiful thing. And then, before I know it, I'm straddling his face, his fingers at my nipples, mimicking his tongue at my clit, and then I'm coming so hard, I wonder if someone can die from having too many powerful orgasms in a day.

"What a way to go," I murmur as I slide down to rest my head against his shoulder.

At some point, I shower, and Adam joins me, which I find I don't actually like, since his broad shoulders steal all the water. So I kick him out after he's done washing, and then we brush our teeth and he watches me, smiling, as I put on my skincare products.

And then we return to bed. And for the first time in my life, I sleep with a man. The man I've wanted for years, even before I had returned to this body to enjoy him with. If only I could have gone back and told myself when I was a ghost. I'd have never believed such a fortune could befall me.

29

I AM AWAKENED ONCE AGAIN TO THE SCENT OF BACON, AND I wonder if my sisters are back, in my room, watching me and Adam sleep like a couple of creeps. I open one eye to check, but the room is empty and beginning to fill with light. This means the scent must be wafting all the way upstairs from the kitchen, and I can only assume that indicates that Nadia is home. She must know Adam spent the night. I can't think of any other reason why she'd be cooking breakfast. Certainly she wouldn't think it was worth her while if it were just me alone.

I perform what feels like sneaky ninja moves to get out of bed without waking Adam, and in the bathroom I decide my hair definitely needs washing. Copious amounts of sex turned it into one big tangle.

When I get out, wearing my fuzzy robe, Adam's sitting up in bed, furiously typing on his phone. He looks up at me with a big, lazy smile. "Good morning."

"Morning." I sit on the bed. "Sorry if this is weird, but I'm pretty sure Nadia is cooking us breakfast downstairs. She's probably going to do some gloating and take credit for setting us up and all that."

He laughs. "No worries. Trust me, I deal with my fair share of weirdness from a grandparent."

He grabs a bag he had brought in from the night before. I was nosy and peeked in it. He'd packed a change of clothes, shaving stuff, things like that. He was prepared, which I appreciate.

After we're dressed, and after we've made out enough that we have to take some time to readjust our hair, and for Adam, readjust elsewhere as well, we make our way downstairs. We are chatting, joking, and giggling the two floors down, and when we get into the kitchen, we're looking for all the world like . . . what did William say? Lovebirds. Lovebirds who are maybe in love, in addition to all of the bonding hormones coursing through our veins.

And the first person to witness it isn't Nadia.

It's Amá Sonya.

I stop so fast, Adam nearly collides with my back. He wraps an arm around me instead, keeping us both upright, and Amá stares at the point of contact with the most unimpressed expression on her face. "Sky. You kept refusing my offer of brunch. So I had to bring brunch to you." She opens her arms at the table, which is set as though we are fine dining at a fancy restaurant uptown. After glaring at me some more, she glances at Adam. "Mr. Noemi, I take it?"

"Uh—" Adam furrows his brow, clearly trying to figure out what the hell is going on. Which. Same.

"Adam," I say quickly. "This is Sonya. My grandmother. Nadia's sister."

She stands and holds her hand out to him as though she's a

queen and he's supposed to kiss it. He takes it slowly, wrapping his other hand around it, and turns on the charm. He gives her his most disarming smile and says, "It's great to meet you. I've heard a lot about you."

"No you haven't," Sonya says primly, pulling her hand away. "I need to speak with my granddaughter now. In private, if that wasn't clear."

My eyes about pop out of my head. What the fuck did I just hear? "Amá Sonya. Adam and I had plans—"

She raises her eyebrow at me, completely nonplussed. "Plans? Like the plans you and I had last week?"

I narrow my eyes. "Those weren't plans for *us*! That was a blind date you lied to me about!"

"We all want what's best for our children and grandchildren." She makes a very discreet gesture toward Adam that I'm pretty sure only I see. I hope only I see, because she clearly means she doesn't think Adam is what's best for me.

"Sky." Adam turns to me. "It's okay. I've gotta check on Gramps, anyway. Make sure his night was okay, and that he gets his morning meds."

I breathe out a sigh and finally nod. "Sure. I know. Tell William good morning for me."

Adam kisses my forehead as he slings his bag over his shoulder. He turns to Amá Sonya and dips his head. "It was a pleasure to meet you, ma'am." She raises her eyebrow at him in response and doesn't speak again until he's out the door.

"Well?" She gestures to the table. "Shall we?"

I pull out the chair opposite her. "Did Nadia know you and I had brunch plans today?" I have to fully restrain myself from making air quotes around "brunch plans."

"No. But I have an extra key she gave me about thirty years ago."

I've seen Sonya here so infrequently that I wonder if this is her first time using her spare key ever. Another thought occurs to me, though. She's so in my business, so intrusive, that what if she comes in the house and tries to find out our secrets or something? I smother a snort when I imagine her coming across my four enormous packs of condoms in my room.

"Is something funny?"

Oops. I guess I didn't smother that laugh hard enough. I shake my head. "Of course not, Amá."

She hmphs and opens up the lids of the serving bowls. Inside is what looks like a breakfast pasta, with eggs, bacon, vegetables, and cheese. It sounds like it could be a mess in theory, but it looks incredible, right down to the most perfect sprig of parsley on top for garnish. There's another bowl of sweet potato fries and one more of fresh fruit surrounding a porcelain bowl of thick whipped cream.

"Thank you for bringing brunch," I say, because I am absolutely starving, and even though from the way she's treating me, it's possible she's poisoned the food, that's not going to stop me from digging in.

"You're welcome."

We both serve ourselves and eat in silence for a few moments. Finally, she says, "That man is no good for you."

I swallow my bite. "You've said this, yes."

"Do not give me sass, Sky Temple."

I nod without speaking and focus on eating instead. I don't know how to not give her sass right now. She's been asking for far worse than sass for a long time, as far as I'm concerned.

She takes her cloth napkin from her lap and dabs at the corners of her mouth, even though she eats in such small bites, there's no way for food to get anywhere but where it's supposed to go. Finally, she gets to the point. "Adam Noemi has been questioning many people in this town about you."

I blink and swallow. Has Adam been talking to more people than my sisters? I can't hide my immediate feelings. She notes this and her eyes flare as though she's won the battle. Anger rises in me but I take a page from her book and stay very calm on the outside. "Yes. He told me he would. Because of the piece he's writing about me."

"Right." She cuts her pasta into tiny pieces and continues to take bite sizes suited for a mouse. "The *piece*." She puts down her fork and her knife with a clatter. "Based on what these individuals said he'd asked, Sky, I regret to inform you that this piece does not paint you in the best of light."

My stomach sinks. Adam asked people about me? People who are not my sisters? People who he had said I deserved better treatment from?

I refuse to allow my face to show my doubt. "And what is your evidence for this claim?"

"The questions he asked them." She throws up a hand. "Had Ms. Flores disappeared before going missing? Did Ms. Flores have a boyfriend outside of town? Did Ms. Flores show signs of . . ." She shakes her head. "Psy . . . Psy . . . I cannot say this word."

I furrow my brow. "Psycho? Psychopath? Psychic powers?"

She points. "Psychosis." It comes out as a hiss. "The man thinks you're not sane. And he's trying to use your affections to get access to our family secrets."

I laugh. "That is not . . . No." I almost say *He loves me*, but then I realize that I will sound like a child, trying to convince her parental figure that her good-for-nothing boyfriend isn't good-for-nothing. Which will play right into the narrative she's trying to create right now. "Adam isn't asking people if I've experienced psychosis." . . . Is he?

"It's not a matter of is or isn't. It's already done, Sky. He's asked the questions. They've been answered." She raises her eyebrow and looks me up and down. "Do not tell me he got you to tell him about our . . ." She looks around, as though anyone else could possibly have snuck into the kitchen. "*Gifts.*"

I say nothing.

She sighs and puts her hand on her head. "I think I'm getting a migraine, Sky; do not tell me that you told this man about these things!"

"He doesn't know everything," I tell her. Which is accurate.

"The last thing this family needs is another scandal!" She raises her voice. "First, your mother, and now you? No wonder my hair went gray in my thirties!"

"I wasn't even alive when you were in your thirties," I shout back, because yes, I guess we're shouting now. "And why the hell would you care if I was involved in a scandal, besides the way it would make *you* look?" I take a breath and look down. "You don't even want to be seen with me now. Some new scandal wouldn't change anything between us."

She crosses her arms. "What are you talking about, I don't want to be seen with you?"

I shake my head. "You think I haven't noticed that you never take me to the same brunch place you take Teal? That whenever you want to catch up, it's always somewhere on the edge of town, or outside of town?"

Amá Sonya sighs. "People talk, mija."

"People talk. They call me names. They play cruel pranks on me. And you know what would've been great? To have my powerful, rich grandmother do something about it, instead of cowering in fear in her four-point-eight-million-dollar beachside mansion, only coming here because you think your reputation is at stake. Not because you actually care about me." I toss my own napkin on the table. "I'm going to the woods."

I don't stop to hear what she has to say to that. I just run out the door.

30

It's incredibly stupid, but after wandering around the trees for a bit, with a blue jay on my shoulder (I call him Blueberry. Predictable, I know, but I think he loves the name), I make my way to Nadia's backyard, toeing to the cliff until I'm one footfall away from falling, and I sit and dangle my legs on the edge.

It's not a sharp drop-off. If I slipped, I would roll, but the risk wouldn't be like before, where the force of hitting the ground is what would get me. More likely, it would be hitting my head on a rock, or maybe getting impaled by a tree branch along the way.

Blueberry flaps his wings and walks all around on my legs. I sigh and lean against the tree trunk to my right—a young pine tree with long, sap green needles. "Blueberry," I murmur. "This fucking sucks."

I actually don't care right now that I yelled things at Amá that she probably won't forgive me for. What would change in our relationship? The grandmother who's ashamed of me won't speak to me anymore? Oh no, not that!

It's what she said about Adam that's messing up my head.

I think about everything that transpired between us for a long while. I try to remember every conversation. Every expression. Was there something I missed?

I want to say the way he's been treating me . . . the way he acts around me. Bashful and haunted and . . . well, if not love, he acts like he likes me a lot. I want to believe that.

But I also know men trick women all the time. So I can't use that as evidence that he doesn't have some horrible plan to discredit me for all eternity in Cranberry.

I shake my head. It's not what Amá says. It can't be. Because everything I told him about me, about our family, was freely given. He never pressured me. He barely even had to ask. I told him because I wanted people to know the truth.

The whole thing was my idea from the start. Not his.

I breathe out a sigh of relief. Amá is out of her mind. She spends half her time looking for people airing her "dirty laundry." She just focused on Adam this time. Probably because she doesn't approve of his lack of what she would consider a "high-quality" job. Which is classist and gross, but that's Amá for you.

"Okay," I tell Blueberry. "Thank you. I'm better now." When I stand, he flaps around me a few times and then flies away, doing this wild, cheerful squawk.

When I open the door to the kitchen, everything is gone. I kinda had figured, since there's no sign of Amá's car out there, but it's still surprising that there is literally no sign that she had ever been here. The tablecloth, the napkins, the food—it's disappeared. Not a single crumb is left. It's like she was never here at all.

My phone buzzes, and I half expect it to be Amá, informing me of her taking me off her will or something, but it's Teal in the group chat.

Don't forget! Grand opening! Saturday at 6pm.

"Shit," I mutter. All I want to do for the rest of this week through the weekend is mope in bed with fried food and *Gilmore Girls*. But there's no way I'm missing Teal's fashion debut. Plus, Adam's coming, and he always helps me feel better, even about cranky grandmothers conspiring against us.

FOR TEAL'S EVENT, I PUT ON A GOLD, SPARKLY SHEATH DRESS with a tiny black bag, rose-embroidered stockings, and black Mary Janes. I apply heavy black eyeliner, pulling it out from the corners of my eyes to make a cat-eye look, something yet again taught to me by the internet. I had to do the right one twice, but in the end, I think I look how I wanted to: like a gold goddess who communes with all cat-eyed cats. And maybe all animals for that matter, too.

Adam had to take William to another doctor's appointment, to a specialist out of town, so he said he'd have to meet me at the boutique. Which is fine. I'm guessing Amá Sonya will be there, and I can tell her to leave me and Adam alone before he gets there, so she doesn't make it as awkward as things got yesterday.

The boutique is called Crème de la Crème. The lay of the store is sort of horseshoe shaped, and every single wall is filled with art from local artists. I pass by rows of handmade books and paper; watercolor paints made with local blackberry honey all poured into a beautiful display of palettes; colorful, geometric-patterned quilts; and jars of homemade jams before I find Teal's space.

I spot her first, before anything else, and she sees me at the same exact time. Squealing, we run to each other, laughing and hugging. "You're early!" she says.

"And I'm glad for it. This place is busy!" I say, looking around.

"Hey, Sky," Carter says, walking up. He leans in for a kiss on the cheek, the Latine way of greeting relatives. "How are you?" He looks around. "Did you bring that guy you're seeing, or . . ."

"He's coming," I say.

Carter puffs up his chest. "Good. I gotta let him know not to fuck with you. That's what big brothers do."

Teal rolls her eyes and smacks his arm. "My God, you're so corny." She turns to me. "But seriously, we do need to tell Adam that he better not fuck with you."

I force the smile to stay on my face. They're just joking. But in light of what Amá accused Adam of yesterday . . . it doesn't feel like a joke. I shake it off and instead focus on Teal's work. Which is . . . oh my gods, stunning.

On her wall in the shop are all kinds of leatherwork, in all shades of brown, from whole grain mustard to the deepest black bear fur, with red holly flowers and green leaves curling in the browns to become what appears to be her signature style. There are mostly handbags, with a few belts, wallets, and even a pair of boots! "I had to collab with a cobbler for that one," she says, laughing as I touch the tooled leather.

"These are amazing, Teal. Holy cow. No wonder you were working so hard." I touch and marvel at all the details of the handbags, which are far better quality than many of the luxe bags Amá Sonya is always carrying around.

I choose a belt bag with intricate stitching, a few sewn-in ruby leather flowers, and a magnet clasp. This will be great for when I'm wandering the woods and need my hands to be free for digging for stones and petting bears.

"Family discount," Teal says when I try to pay her. She blocks all my attempts to give her my money.

I'm not happy about this. "Teal. You made this. You deserve to be paid no matter who I am."

Teal shakes her head and pretends to karate chop me away. Finally Carter whispers in my ear, "Go to the lady up front; she'll ring you up." I smile and thank him. I love that both of my sisters have people who support them. And, I guess, I have that, too. I think. No, I do. I have that, too.

Speaking of which, I glance at my phone. Adam should've been here by now, right? I try to remember our last conversation about logistics, but that's when Sage walks in with Oak and Tenn, and all of a sudden, I am swept away again, into familia, hugs, kisses, and holding the cutest little chunk in the world until he wants to nurse again.

It's about a half hour later when I get a call from Adam. I make sure to purchase the belt bag before stepping out of the store to call him back.

Downtown at this time of night is so peaceful and beautiful. Everything looks like it was painted in all kinds of blue, from cornflower to midnight, contrasting the yellow ocher street lanterns and warmly lit storefronts. I take a breath of the humid seaside air before hitting the callback button.

"Hey, Sky," Adam says. "I'm so sorry. I'm still outside of town right now."

"Is everything okay?" I ask, furrowing my brow.

"Yes. Everyone's good. There was a four-car pileup on the way home. We were stop and go—mostly stop—for an hour and a half. Gramps is starving so we just stopped to pick up food. I checked the time and realized I'm probably going to miss your sister's opening. I'm so sorry. I should've texted sooner."

I shake my head, even though he can't see me. "Don't worry about it. I'm glad you guys got through that safely."

"Yeah. It was rough-looking. I hope everyone is doing okay." He clears his throat. "I've got a favor to ask you, though. Gramps—" Adam lowers his voice. "He just told me now, of course, that he's not certain if he turned off the toaster oven. Since it's going to be another hour before we're home, I was wondering if you could check that for us?"

In the background, I hear William grumping it up with phrases like "If it burns, it burns! That's what insurance is for!" and I stifle a laugh.

"Sure. I'll be glad to. I've already spent time with my family, so I can go now."

Adam breathes a sigh of relief. "Thank you so much." He lowers his voice even more. "I'll have to make it up to you later. You know. With my tongue."

I swallow and nearly stumble on my next step. "Well, I expect no less for my being such an upstanding neighbor."

Adam laughs and we chat for about another minute, until William begins to groan about not getting the French fries he'd ordered with his burger, and Adam has to go figure that out. After we hang up, I say goodbye to my sisters, their hubbies, and my baby nephew, and make my way to my car.

The sky is dark ocean blue above me, and gray whale blue in front of me, the clouds all glowing purple and yellow on their undersides from the just-about-set sun. In my mind, I make plans for what I need to do before Adam comes over. Wash my comforter—again. Consider whether I need to purchase a special comforter just for sex, because we both get so slippery for one another. I want to shower and make sure I smell awesome with this new lotion I got from another artist at Crème de la Crème tonight. It smells like pumpkin vanilla cupcakes with chai spices.

When I tried the sample on, I about fainted from how amazing it was. I should find a corresponding recipe for my fall baking. Or see if Nadia would like to make an inspired new flavored flan. Also, I should put on the new lingerie I got yesterday for Adam. My stomach flip-flops at the thought of his expression as he sees me in it.

My mind rolls into itself, going back and forth between the gorgeous, ever-changing skyline to my ideas, to my anticipating having Adam again tonight, as I pull into the Noemi driveway. I find the spare key just where Adam said it would be—slid under the loose frame of a front window—and make my way inside, gently shutting the door behind me.

I'm relieved there is no smoke, no smell of anything burning. When I make my way to the kitchen, the toaster oven is definitely off. I breathe out a sigh. Either one of the men had turned it off and forgotten, or maybe William's ghost wife, Emmie, helped them out.

Thinking about ghosts has me glancing around the dark house. I don't know why. I wasn't expecting to see Emmie standing there, see-through and wispy-white, asking me what my intentions are with her grandson or something.

But something about standing in this home alone . . . It reminds me of my own ghost days. A feeling comes over my stomach—not a bad one. But kind of like I've been given a strange gift to briefly experience what it was like once more. And what did I do the most as a ghost?

I snooped.

I'm not saying I decide to go through William's bank records or see how many pairs of underwear Adam owns. I just decide to go to the cherrywood china display in the living room and pull open the tiny drawer on the uppermost right side. Inside should be a pair of scissors, a few rubber bands, and some rolled-up fast-food napkins.

They're still there.

I don't want them to be here. I want them to appear different, to have a random highlighter or hand lotion tube thrown in so I know firmly that I didn't spontaneously leave the Land of the Living and become a ghost once more. I hate that I have to do this regularly, always when I'm faced with a scene or sensation of something that reminds me of my experience of ghosthood—but I can't stop till I prove to myself that I'm alive.

I reach for the next drawer under that. The last time I looked—when I was split from my own body, warm and asleep in an old tree—it'd had a collection of bottle caps and marbles inside it.

They're still here.

At this point, I'm overcome with fear that I've turned back into a ghost. Or maybe that I had never returned to start with. That this whole life, since my awakening in the woods, has simply been a dream, and I'm actually still back there, snoring away like Sleeping Beauty or Rip Van Winkle.

I place my hands on the walls and breathe out a sigh of relief when I'm met with firm, cold solidity. I do the same to the chairs in the dining room, and to the table, reveling in the wood beneath my palms.

This is real. I'm still real.

I pull back my hands quickly and accidentally hit one of the chairs with my wrist. I rub the sore spot, blinking when the laptop on the tabletop bumps awake, the screen suddenly bright and blue in the dark.

"Oh," I say, startled. I blink some more, my eyes adjusting to the light. And the whole thing just reminds me of where I am. What I'm actually doing.

I've probably been here too long. Adam's going to pull up with William and they're going to find me in the dark, touching all textures of matter in here, and then Adam really is going to wonder if I've experienced psychosis before.

I swallow and freeze then. Because that word. *Psychosis.* It didn't just pop into my head just now from my conversation with Amá yesterday.

It's on the stack of papers that are on the table, now brightly lit by the computer screen.

As though the word has stretched out newly formed arms and gripped me with its claws, I am sucked back toward the paper pile. I pull out a chair and have a seat. I do not know why I'm doing these things. It is as though decisions are being made for me, and for my body, and the only say I have in the matter is how quickly it happens. I take a deep breath and begin to read.

> Psychosis is clinically defined as . . . when I asked if they'd ever heard of Sky Flores experiencing a break from reality . . . told about the family's reputation for witchcraft . . . believes that wild animals come to her on command . . . the myths surrounding the Flores women are difficult to believe as they are.

My chest is undulating in a manner it's never done before. I guess what I'm experiencing right now could be described as severe hyperventilation. I want to cry, but I'm too shocked and . . . freaking *angry* to cry.

How dare he?

How dare he throw my family under the bus like this?

How dare he make me believe he was falling in love with me?

Doesn't he know what kind of a nightmare he will unleash after this article is published, not just for me but my entire family? For all he's been going on about how much I deserve better from this town?

It's almost like he's been lying this whole time.

I don't know how long I sit there, reading the article draft over and over again. It's not like the words are going to change if I somehow take them in long enough, but I can't seem to tear myself away.

Adam's writing an article about a woman—me—who seems out of her mind, and her whole family enables her ill mental health. Her alleged "psychosis." He's only included interviews with townspeople who really, really don't like me. The ones with my sisters didn't even make it in here.

I don't snap out of my fixation until the front door's knob shakes.

They're back.

31

I JUMP UP AND PUSH THE CHAIR IN, RUNNING TO TURN ON THE dining room light. I shouldn't try to make this situation more palatable for him, really. But I don't want to contribute to Adam's idea that I'm not in my right mind. Now that I know he really does think I'm unwell mentally—and damn him because I'm going to have to go to Amá Sonya now and tell her she was right!—I don't want to contribute to it.

William walks in first. He spots me and pauses. "What's up? Did you have to call the fire brigade?"

I shake my head. "It was off."

Adam follows behind, holding a couple of bags in his arms. "Sky. We saw your car . . . is everything okay? The toaster oven—" He glances in the kitchen.

I repeat my words tonelessly. "It was off." My arms are folded to try and stop my body from trembling with my anger.

Adam looks back at me and double-takes. "What's—" His eyes land on the stack of papers in my trembling hands. I can see the pieces being put together in his brain as his face falls. "No.

That isn't—whatever you've seen there. It's not what it looks like."

"You mean you're not writing an article about how fucking out of my mind I am?" I ask. "That's not why you included the *clinical definition* of psychosis?"

"Psychosis?" William grunts, taking a seat in his armchair. "Who's got psychosis?"

"According to Adam, I do." I lift up my arm. "According to Adam, I'm *beyond* bananas. The only plausible theory for my disappearance is I ran away. Maybe I caught amnesia, but that's pretty doubtful!" I shake the papers so forcefully, one or two drift right to the floor.

Adam runs a hand through his hair. "Sky. That was . . . it's such an old draft . . ."

"I don't care that it's old! Actually, no. The fact that it's old is worse, because you courted me while thinking I was missing half my brain!"

Adam closes his eyes. "I can't, Sky. I can't write the article you want me to write. That right there is my old draft, and it's going to change. Immensely." He sighs and looks at me. His eyes can only be described as pleading. "But I can't keep out everything that you don't approve of. I have to include citations, research, for all the possibilities. I can't just write that . . . old deities kept you alive back then. That would never get published." He takes a step toward me, but I take one back like I'm a mirror to him. "I don't think you're missing half your brain. Or any of it. This is just . . . a complicated subject."

I square my jaw. "I'm a human. I'm a *person*. I'm not a *subject*!"

Adam shakes his head and clenches his jaw. "This . . . this is why I knew it might not be wise to do this. You know, become . . . more than our professional roles—"

I barely hold back a gasp. "So you regret us now? Is that what you're saying?"

"No! Of course not!"

William grunts in disapproval. "Could've fooled me, son. You're going to push away another person who loves you? Just like you did with your siblings? Just like your father did when—"

"Don't you dare tell me I'm like my father!" Adam bellows, and I startle enough to jump back farther away from him.

William lifts his hands. "Look at the way you're behaving. It speaks for itself, son."

"Gramps. I'm saying this nicely. Mind your business." Adam turns back to where I was, but I'm now by the front door.

"Sky. Wait. Don't leave."

I huff. "I don't like angry, yelling men. I didn't know you were an angry, yelling man."

Adam's shoulders drop. "I'm sorry. I'm sorry, Gramps. I lost my temper. But this—this conversation is so unnecessary. It's absurd. Just come read my new draft. You'll see. I don't mean these things the way they read in the one you've seen."

I shake my head. "That doesn't make sense. Why is the old one still available, printed nice and tidily on the table?"

"Because I have to reference older drafts when I rewrite them. That's all." He walks toward the dining room, gesturing for me to follow him.

He looks so sure of himself. That I would just run toward him, like a naïve puppy. It hits me then. That's how he sees me now. Like a puppy. Like a *child*. Just like when he first saw me at the wedding, little animals in my arms, and he lectured me as though I were eleven years old.

Even if he's written something new. Something truthful. He

went into this agreement in bad faith. He *knew* he had planned on making me look insane. Even if he'd changed his mind because he slept with me. Does this mean we are one bad argument—this one bad argument, even—away from him thinking I'm insane again? Is that the kind of man he is?

I look down and take a deep, shuddering breath, willing myself to not burst into tears. "You cried the night William had the flu and you thought it was pneumonia."

Adam glances up at me. "I'm sorry?"

"Right there. You sat in his chair and wept. Your face turns pink when you cry. Did you know that?" I point toward where William is. He's still watching. Still listening. "And you use your wrists to wipe away your tears. It made me wonder if that's how you cried since you were a little boy."

Adam shakes his head and peers at me. "How did you—"

"And in the mornings, when you wake up, you always, always stretch everything. Even your toes. And then you drink a whole glass of water before breakfast. That's your routine. I don't even know if you know it, but that's what you do." I swallow. My voice is somehow steady still, even as tears run down my face. "And you have several books on love letters."

Adam shakes his head. "I—they—those books have been in storage for a long, long time."

"I know. I was there when you put them in there."

"No you weren't. You were—" Adam pauses. "When I moved my stuff here into storage, when Gramps was sick. That was around three years ago. You were . . . you were missing then."

"I was a ghost, Adam. I saw all manner of things." I close my eyes. "I had the biggest crush on you. When I was a spirit. And that one day, you had that girl over . . . the one with the black hair and the nose ring. You came here to check on William and make sure he was still breathing. You looked at me. You looked at me twice that night and I thought that meant that somehow we were connected. That if I had lived, you would be mine." Okay, well. My steady voice is now obliterated. I try to take shaky breaths between my sentences, but it's difficult with all the sobbing. "The things you doubt . . . the things that have happened to me that make you want to call me crazy . . . are the very things that brought us together. It's what you made a goddamn list about, remember? Those eyes you saw, watching you. They were my eyes." I push the tears from my face furiously. "Isn't that something? Isn't that some shit?"

Adam shakes his head firmly. "Sky, you just need to see what I'm working on now. Then you'll know—"

"No. Because that won't stop me from knowing how a part of you will always see me."

We all turn our heads when scratching and banging begins at the door. It's loud. Whatever it is, it's *big*.

"What in the hell is that?" William stands up. "Don't open it till I get my gun."

I close my eyes and hold up my hand. "Don't. It's just Lily."

"Who the hell is Lily?"

I open the door and even through my tears, I smile. "Lily's a bear."

She's sitting on her hind legs. She must've felt my distress. The animals always do. I don't know how, but they always have.

"Jesus! Shut the door, girl! I'll get my gun!" William begins to dart away again.

"William! No. She's—" It's not accurate but I can't think of a quicker way to make him understand. "She's a friend. A really large, furry, kind friend." I open the door wider and scratch her head. "See?"

William stares and then announces, “I’m going to bed. I’ve seen enough for today.”

As he walks toward his bedroom, Adam approaches. “Sky—”

“Don’t you dare come closer,” I say to him, and the tone of my voice makes Lily growl. Adam freezes. “I’ve said all I need to say to you.”

If Lily were a horse, I’d have gotten on her back and ridden into the dark woods as my smooth, cool exit. But she’s not. So when I make my way out the door, I tell her I’m okay. I give her a big hug and encourage her to stay away from humans for a while, especially these humans. I’m not convinced about William and his gun. In fact, I think, given his health, Adam needs to confiscate it. But I don’t want to see Adam right now. Everything hurts so much, I think if he offers to let me read the newest version of his article, I might break and do it. And I can’t let myself forget that this man will always be half-convinced that I’m not quite right, that I’m downright insane. And that is unacceptable.

After Lily has disappeared into the brush, I get in my car and park at Nadia’s, pretending Adam hasn’t been watching me the whole time from the window like a creeper. I pretend like I don’t have plans to do exactly that once I’m inside. The best view of the Noemis’ is from my old room. I thought it was synchronistic, considering my huge crush on Adam, and then later, my concern for William’s well-being. But now it just feels kind of pathetic. How much time I wasted, watching from my room once I returned. Including right now.

I guess I expect that the lights would go out in the house, one by one, like they normally do at bedtime. But instead they stay on. I see their figures by the window here and there, either directly or their dark gray silhouettes. It looks like they’re fighting and I hate that I’m so worried about them. I’m scared I’m going to see William wielding a big gun soon, so I can't tear away until it seems like all is calm.

But things just . . . escalate, I guess, though thankfully sans gun. The front door opens and Adam rushes out. My heart drops when I see a big duffel bag slung over his shoulder. William marches out, yelling things I can't make out from all the way over here. Adam shouts things back, waving his arms about. William keeps talking to him, lifting a fist in the air as Adam packs the bag into his Jeep. There's one more yelling match before Adam gets in the car and . . . drives away.

William stares down the dark, dimly lit street until maybe he can't see the lights of Adam's car anymore. And then he goes inside and slams the door shut.

I fall back on my old bed and remember what Adam had told me. Running away is his MO. When things get difficult . . . that's what he does. He runs.

Where is he running to? I pray to the old gods it's not a bar or a liquor store. Even though he's no longer mine, I also pray it's not to another woman. I'm too selfish to leave that out of my prayers.

I drag my feet up the stairs and once I'm in my room, I pull off my beautiful, sparkling gold dress and throw on a T-shirt that reaches my knees. I wash my face and brush my teeth. And when I reenter my room, I freeze.

Because it's filled with *owls*.

Tiny, brown screech owls line my bed. Barn owls sit at the window slats by the sloped roof. One enormous great horned owl sits at the threshold of the open balcony door. "Hello?" I say. "Nice to see you."

I don't know what the owls are doing here, but I'm going to assume it's similar to when I'm upset and bears or foxes or coyotes come. They are here for comfort. "Thank you for coming. But I'm okay."

They all just stare at me with their enormous, dark eyes. I sit back on the bed and say, "Okay. I guess you can stay if you want. Just shut the door behind you when you leave, okay? I don't want ghosts to get in here."

I'm not making any sense. Ghosts don't need an open door to get in anywhere. I should know that more than anyone. But I'm too emotional right now to be logical, even in my own thoughts. Everything aches. I close my eyes and will sleep to rescue me from my pain.

Thankfully it doesn't take long for this prayer to be answered.

32

ADAM ISN'T BACK BY THE NEXT MORNING. HE'S NOT THERE when I get home from work, either. Neither is Nadia, of course.

I text my sisters. Hey, what are you up to? Does anyone want to grab dinner tonight?

Teal: I'm so sorry but I can't. I got dehydrated last night at the opening and woke up with a gnarly migraine.

Sage: Oak is cutting his first tooth. He was up more than half the night. I'm going to collapse as soon as Tenn gets home from work. How about tomorrow?

We make tentative plans and then I sit down at the kitchen table, wondering what the hell I'm supposed to do with myself tonight. I'm aware I'm experiencing my first heartbreak ever. According to the series I like to watch, that means I should go to the store and get a bunch of chips and ice cream and veg out while eating my feelings. But the thing is . . . I woke up feeling kind of numb. I don't have access to the feelings I should be eating. So food right now, beyond what I need to get my stomach to stop growling, it just doesn't seem appealing.

I bury my face in my hands and wonder if a Tylenol PM would be a good plan, just to go to sleep far earlier than normal so I won't have to deal with this restlessness, when I lift my head and blink at the first thing that I see.

It's the key holder mounted on the side of the cabinet, right next to the entrance into the living room. It's old as hell, been there since I could remember, which means it might've been there when Nadia bought this house decades ago. I stand up to examine it, because something about this is bothering me. And I can't figure out why.

It comes to me when I see a sticky note next to a collection of keys on a ring hanging on the rightmost hook. *Return to Mother Michelle ASAP.*

I nod. These are the keys Nadia borrowed from the church for the summer festival. Clearly she's pretty delayed in returning them to the nun who wanted her to have them for the event, in case someone got locked out somewhere.

Which means I know how to properly distract myself now.

IT DOESN'T TAKE ME LONG TO FIND THE DIRECTOR OF EDUCAtion's office. Almost all the buildings around St. Theresa's are open, even this late in the evening. There's choir practice happening in the sanctuary. Bible study in some of the classrooms Nadia used to force me to teach Sunday school to little kids in as a teenager. The director's office is hidden behind two large rooms. One was where we used to eat Thanksgiving dinner with other churchy kids while Nadia did churchy things with their churchy parents. The other was where youth group used to meet up and eat pizza after evening Mass every Sunday. I glance in the big trash can on my way through the room, and yup, it's got some empty Papa John's boxes stuffed into the bottom. Very little has changed around here.

The director's office is locked. I go through the keys on the key ring, and it only takes three to pop the door open. I close and lock the door behind me, and then I am alone in the quiet room. There are two desks wedged in here, between a number of bookshelves filled with Bibles and other religious books. Sage said this was where the strange room was. The one that might answer all my burning questions about the cult that may or may not have met up here for literal decades.

I feel a curl of glee around my belly. Whatever is going on, this is working. I'm barely thinking about the way Adam ripped my heart out and stomped on it last night. It only took committing several crimes, is all.

It takes me a minute to find the door. The room being dark doesn't help, but I skim my hands on the wall until I find a small, silver knob. From there I make out the door edges. They're very tight, and both the door and the wall are covered in busy wallpaper featuring piles of books, cups of coffee, and apples in a pattern over a deep green background. Makes me think it was chosen intentionally, to draw the eye away from secret cult entrances. Actually, who am I kidding? That's exactly what happened. Everything here is intentional, from the removing of key architectural plans in the old book still on my work desk to the wallpaper choice in here.

I slide the keys in, one by one, and it is the smallest, most ornate one—decorated in carved swirls—that fits.

As soon as I turn the key, the door eases open without a

sound. I have to bend down to peek inside. A smell of earth and moss comes up my way, along with thick humidity. I use my cell phone flashlight and face down into the dark. Well. It's a good thing I didn't just march through. Because it's nothing but stairs as far as the light can reach, made of stone and covered in Hooker's green lichen. I'd have fallen right onto my face and smashed a cheekbone open, or worse.

Someone grabs the office doorknob behind me and I gasp, leap onto one of the stair steps, and shut the secret door behind me just as the office door swings open. My door locks. It seems to echo all around me, and down into the staircase, with a final sort of dread. I hold my breath, waiting for someone to throw this door open and demand to know what the hell I'm doing. But I hear next to nothing. Footfalls, maybe. Whoever's in the office isn't paying much attention to their surroundings. Which, good. Means I can make my way down the stairs now without worrying about being chased.

And that's exactly what I do.

THERE IS NO RAIL TO HOLD, SO I HAVE MY LEFT HAND CLUTCHing my phone, holding the light up, and my right one using the wall for leverage. Because these stairs are not flat, or even stable. One of them has a crack and wobbles under my feet. I shudder when I imagine what on earth could be beneath that I might fall toward if this whole thing broke apart on my next step. An underground river? A den of lions? It's only now that I begin to get a sense that what I'm doing might not exactly be the fun sort of distraction, after all. I might well encounter something straight from a horror film.

Finally, I reach the end of the steps and look around. I'm in a room. I think. My iPhone light isn't exactly going too far in the pitch black. I look along the stone walls with my lamp and my hands, and finally I find a switch. I hesitate for a moment, my hand hovering above it. What if clicking it on means some alert goes off somewhere? What if it sets off a trap?

Then I remember my heartbreak. Adam's gone. My entire body remembers the pain of everything, and it resounds deeply, as though the hurt were a bell someone rang through my cells, and so I flip the switch as quickly as I can.

An enormous light fixture set in the middle of the low ceiling goes on. It's huge and long with frosted glass set into windowlike panes around the lamps inside. And I can see everything.

It's not much. The room is empty. The walls and the ground are made of the same stones, large and curvy. The beach walk downtown is cobblestone, and these remind me of that, except they're discolored and porous. From age, maybe. I get the feeling that this place is really old, older than the church above me, even.

Behind me are the stairs, and in front of me is what appears to be a dark hallway. I slowly make my way to its entrance, my footfalls oddly soundless against the stone. I glance down at the threshold.

I guess the light switch worked here, too, because lightly glowing fixtures illuminate the way. The hallway is narrow, much tighter than I'd like. Since returning from the woods, I am much more claustrophobic than before. But the only alternative is feeling what it's like to have a heart that's just been ripped to shreds and then lit on fire. So I keep going.

It's only about thirty or forty feet when I find the end of the hallway. There's a weird setup here, and I glance around, looking for a door or anything like an entryway elsewhere. But there isn't any.

So I focus on the . . . thing in front of me. The light here is so dim, I can't really see the details. But I can hear it. Whatever it is, it involves water.

I angle my phone torch at it and blink. It's . . . it's a fountain. A wide, cement bowl comes right out of the wall, and water is bubbling up into it, creating constant, gentle waves. I look underneath, expecting to see some piping, but there isn't anything like that. It's just the continuation of the stone wall meeting the stone floor, all the same type of stones that were in the one circular room behind me.

Something glimmers at the edge of the fountain's bowl and I bend closer, bringing the light with me. It's . . . well. Piles of coins. Some American currency, but lots not. And tiny little pieces of paper, folded up into impossibly small squares. And . . . beads. Some made of wood, some of what might be semiprecious stones. There are also what look like seeds. Tiny black round seeds and enormous purple beans. Sage would know what these are.

I grab my phone to send a text, but curse when I realize that, unsurprisingly, I have absolutely no service down here. Considering it wasn't exactly early when I broke into the director of education's office, I realize I need to head back as soon as I get some photos of this fountain—which is also an altar, I'm realizing—as well as the round room.

I sit down to get a detail of the bottom of the bowl when I accidentally angle my phone too high and freeze.

There's something etched into the wall, high above the fountain. I jump up to stand on my tiptoes and hold my phone above my head, high.

THERE IS NO SUCH THING AS SIN.

That's what's carved right into the rock in loopy all-caps.

Goose bumps prickle over my skin. Despite the message being pretty peaceful and nonthreatening, I get the feeling that I don't actually belong here. Not just the breaking-and-entering feeling. But there's a primal *knowing* that comes over me, about my intrusion. Something primordial. I don't belong. This is a cult and I haven't been initiated. Everything I am seeing, I haven't earned the right to see it. And what's going to happen to me if they—whoever they are, whoever keeps up this place and leaves coins and seeds on the altar here—find out? I don't want to know, actually.

I turn around and go back the way I came, through the narrow hallway, through the big, round stone room, and I click the lights off as I reach the staircase. I take a big sigh as I think about how far I've come and how far that means the incline is. I'm not Teal. I don't spend my free time running up and down hills. Nevertheless, I begin the climb.

It takes longer, not just because it's a much more difficult workout, but because I keep banging my toes against stone. And they hurt, even through the leather of my shoes.

When I finally reach the top, I sit down, catch my breath, and reach for the keys in my bag.

Only they're not there.

I try to open the door, wincing because I'm pretty sure it locked behind me earlier. And yup, it's definitely sealed as all hell. I try and shake it, and even give it a good kick, but it's not going anywhere.

I look closely at the knob of the door and realize there isn't even a keyhole. Even if I'd had the keys, I wouldn't be going anywhere.

And now I want to kick myself for not thinking this through at all.

It's Adam's fault. It's definitely Adam's fault for breaking my heart and forcing me to break into an ancient cult gathering space under the big Catholic church.

I hold my phone against the door, hoping it picks up service, but it remains completely disconnected from the outside world. No matter where I move it, the little bars at the top right corner refuse to light up.

I sigh and lean back against the cold stone wall of the step I'm sitting on. It being Adam's fault doesn't change the fact that I'm locked in and not a single soul knows where I am.

Instead of running from my heartache, I have found myself stuck in the dark with no choice but to feel it.

Finally, I begin to cry.

33

I'M LUCKY BECAUSE I ALWAYS PACK ESSENTIALS IN MY HANDbag, and I'm also lucky that I thought to bring my handbag. I have water and snacks. I have a little travel first aid kit. I have plenty of tissues, which are definitely the most important supply I have on hand. I blow my nose into another one and curse myself out once again for not telling anyone what I was up to. To be fair, anyone I can think of would've tried to talk me out of it. Which really goes to show I shouldn't have done it to begin with.

I don't want to be alone with these thoughts, or worse, thoughts of Adam, but there is little else to do. If I have to spend the night here, I'm staying where it's most near where someone will hear my banging on the door first thing in the morning. I wince as I imagine what the town will have to say about that. Sky Flores, town freak, locked herself in a secret room overnight in the church after breaking and entering.

Honestly? That wouldn't matter, either, considering what Adam's going to publish about me. There's really no use in trying to belong anymore.

I place my handbag on a step above me and use it as a pillow. I've cried all the tears I can. I've worried all the worries I can. Now I am beyond exhausted and it would be great if I could just sleep instead of remembering my current circumstances.

Except, just as I close my eyes, the door handle jangles loudly. I sit straight up so fast, I get dizzy. The door swings open right in front of me and there stands a familiar silhouette.

"Sky?"

I rub my eyes. I've got to be hallucinating. "Adam?"

"Hurry. Hurry. I'm pretty sure one of the priests is calling the cops on me literally right now."

What he says doesn't sink in, but the tone of his voice does. I'm on my feet in an instant, allowing him to pull me through. Nadia's key ring is in his hands, meaning I definitely dropped it before I got inside the underworld back there, when I was trying to move too quickly without being caught.

Adam pulls me out of the office of education, and I see a man in the distance, on his cell phone. It might be Father Phillip, the nasty know-it-all who didn't believe I hadn't anything to confess during my first confession. I really didn't. I was a good kid. What was I going to do, make up some lie about my sins? Which would literally be a sin, if you think about it. That's what he wanted, I guess, because he told me I was sinning right then and there by lying to a father of the church. I'm glad his sleep is disturbed right now. It's what he deserves.

Adam pulls me to run with him across the courtyard of the tiny K–12 school behind the office's building, and we cross through a thicket of trees into the parking lot of the neighboring Denny's. "Inside," he says. I obey without words. I don't feel like I really have words right now, anyway. I'm barely able to process what's happening as it's happening.

Adam nods to the waitress and we take a booth as far away from the entrance of the restaurant as possible. He stares at me in a way that makes me think my exhaustion isn't anything compared to his.

My phone begins to buzz uncontrollably, and I pull it from my bag, frowning. "What is—"

"That would be me. And your sisters. And your aunt. And your grandmother. They're all at your aunt's house right now."

"Because of me?" I ask incredulously.

"Yes. Because of you. Nadia noticed you weren't home when you usually are."

I shake my head. "Nadia never notices when I'm not home."

"She checks on you at a quarter till midnight every night. She called me up—I don't know how she got my number—"

"Meddling Latine elders," I mutter.

"But she wanted to know if you were with me."

I glare at him. "Obviously, I wasn't."

He sighs and looks down. "Obviously. But then she called your sisters. She called everyone in your circle . . . no outsiders, she said. No cops."

"Every cop is a bastard," I say. As if on cue, police cars rush past on the main road through the window, their sirens and lights on. "You think they'll, you know. Find me? Or you, rather, since Father Phillip probably gave them your description?"

Adam shakes his head. "Nah. Beatrice—" He nods toward the server. "As far as Beatrice knows, you and I have been sitting here drinking coffee and chatting for hours."

"You're making her commit a crime?" I whisper.

He shakes his head. "Beatrice and William go way back. She's trustworthy. And none of these places—not this Denny's, not the church—none of them have any kind of surveillance. There's nothing the police will know except that the priest saw a guy go in and come out with another person. Nothing damaged. Nothing stolen." Adam shrugs. "Don't worry, Sky." He has his phone out. "I'm texting your people. They're going to want to see you as soon as possible." He swallows. "You gave them quite a scare." His next breath is shuddery. "You gave us all quite a scare."

I roll my eyes. "What would you have lost if I'd disappeared, Adam?" I wave my arms around. "Oh no. The lying, crazy woman won't bother me anymore." I shrug. "It's not fair for you to pretend like you actually care."

Adam nods and reaches into his sling bag he'd slid into the seat beside him. "I deserve that. I know I keep saying things like 'I'm doing it all wrong if you think that about me.' But I really am doing it all wrong. All so fucking wrong."

He hands me a pad of loose papers, held together with a paper clip.

"What's this?" I ask.

He stares at me and swallows. "It's— Sky. I know I don't have any right to ask you anything. But please, I am begging you to read it."

His voice makes my chest ache. It almost sounds like his heart is broken, too, but that certainly doesn't make any sense. Does it?

"Do y'all want anything besides coffee?" Beatrice asks us as I clutch the papers.

Adam looks at me and I nod. "Some pancakes, please, with lots of strawberry jam and butter and whipped cream." All of a sudden, I'm starving. Not eating all day is hitting me hard now.

When she leaves, I begin to read.

At first, my heart drops further than where it's been since last night.

Because it's the article. Adam wants me to read the article, and haven't I already read enough of this damn article?

But then I realize . . . it's not. I mean, it is the article, but it's something entirely new.

> When I set out to find out what happened to Sky Flores, I thought that I'd meet someone whose narrative could easily be explained by someone with mental health struggles or a troubled history of running away for long periods of time.
>
> Instead, I fell in love.

Adam goes on to explain that he's never met someone who was more honest than me. More grounded. More aware.

> Hawks land on her shoulders. She can coax chipmunks and pigeons into her arms for cuddles. Clearly, there is more to this woman than I ever could have known. There's more to Sky Flores than all of Cranberry deserves to know.

It's not a piece, or an article. It's a love letter. Adam wrote a love letter to me.

"When did you write this?" I ask. My voice is little more than a whisper.

Adam takes in a sharp breath. "Last week. I was trying to get the details right. That's why I had the first draft up. But after last night . . . when I saw how much I had hurt you. I rented a hotel . . . just to get away from William, who would not leave me alone about how bad I'd fucked up with you. And I wrote the story I really, really wanted to, since I began to get to know you. Since I began falling in love with you." He swallows. "I wrote the story you deserve. Not because I want you back, even though I'd be lying if I said I didn't. But this . . ." He gestures to the papers in my hands. "This is the truth, Sky." He holds my gaze. "I believe you. I believe your family. And I hope—" His eyes water and he rubs them with his wrists. "I hope you can believe that I love you, too."

I think of all the ways his love has come. Making sure I'm taken care of. Always apologizing and making things right. Punching a man in the face who had tried to hurt me. And now this: a love letter, written for me.

"What if this is too sappy? What if your career is ruined because you're writing about falling in love with your subject?"

Adam shrugs. "I don't care, Sky. I've been enjoying learning carpentry lately, flipping that house. I can always be a woodworker." He smiles. "But these things—" He gestures to the papers. "The ones told from the heart have a way of becoming more successful than anything else. If you even wanted it published, that is. It's up to you."

Just then, Beatrice brings my pancakes. They're huge, stacked up like a little tower. "You want to share?" I ask Adam, who laughs.

"Even when I've broken your heart, you want to share your pancakes with me."

I shrug. "You did just break and enter the church and bribe our server to keep me safe."

He nods. "That I did."

"And you still owe me an orgasm with your tongue."

Adam's eyes widen. "I . . . I do, don't I?"

"And once you publish this, everyone's gonna know about how much you love me, so. Why not share some pancakes?"

Adam laughs and stands fast, coming to my side of the booth. "Jesus. Sky. Does this really mean?" A tear escapes his eye as he holds my hand. "You want me back?"

I nod slowly, my own tears coming. "Of course I want you back. But please don't run away again. I would rather we work things out in person, you know? That way I won't be forced to uncover a secret lair in the church."

Adam laughs and kisses me then. And it takes both of our wills to stop and finish the pancakes while they're warm. And then, of course, we kiss again, and again, and again.

EPILOGUE

One month later, I am in bed, slowly awakening to the scent of coffee. My favorite flavored coffee of all time, one that brings memories that are happy—me and Nadia dancing in the kitchen after we figured out how to replicate it for a fraction of the price—and sad: me, a ghost, conjuring this coffee like a spell alongside prayers of desperation. A coffee I haven't had in a *long* time—raspberry chocolate.

I push up, fully expecting Sage to be there, cup in hand. After all, this was the exact kind of coffee I used to bring her as a ghost, especially when she forced herself to stop crying for years. *Please don't forget me* was my prayer with this gift. And she didn't. Even though it seemed like both she and Teal had forgotten me because of their anger with one another, they never did, not really.

Instead, though, it's Nadia, the big white mug in her hand.

"Here, mija," she says, and I hold back a wince from her calling me that. *My daughter.* Most times, I hardly feel like some cousin she's never met.

Even after that night when I returned from St. Theresa's with

Adam, and my sisters all greeted me crying and shrieking, so much so that we accidentally scared poor Oak, and then Tenn had to go take him on a little walk down Catalina Street to get him to calm down . . . even after that, things with Nadia returned very quickly to how it had been. Her being gone all the time.

And while it's better now, with Adam keeping me company, and I'm seeing my sisters more and more . . . I still don't like her calling me that. I'm no one's daughter. That's how it's always been.

Even Amá Sonya has been kinder to me. She took me out to brunch at her favorite spot, the spot where she always takes Teal, right in the middle of town. She told the server I was her granddaughter. And sure, she looked around to see who was listening to this scandalous reveal, but it shows me that she wants to be better.

So I take the mug from Nadia, but I don't say anything. She pulls a sheet of paper around from seemingly nowhere and gives it to me.

"Uh—" I say, rubbing my eyes to read. I nearly drop the paper when the words on it register. I take a big sip of coffee, because maybe I'm reading it all wrong and surely caffeine will help. But nope. Even after that enormous glug, the words have remained unchanged.

"This is the deed to the house," I say.

She nods. "It is."

"And it says it's mine."

Nadia nods again. "It is. All yours."

I choke up. My eyes fill with tears. I can't help it. "Why? But why? You're not dying, are you?"

Nadia laughs and shakes her head. "No. I'm in good health. But I'm also closer to eighty than seventy, Sky. And I think this house belongs to you." She pauses. "Can't you feel it? Of all your sisters, you've been firmly rooted with this place. Even when you were a spirit, asleep in the woods." She looks me over, at my jaw still dropped. "Drink your coffee before it gets cold."

I obey her, taking another long sip. The coffee is perfect—the perfect balance of the raspberry and chocolate flavors, with the bitterness of the dark brew all marrying together. She even put a little bit of whipped cream on top.

After my next sip, I place the mug at my side table. "I—I don't know what to say, Nadia."

"Say nothing. Because I'm not done yet." She nods toward me. "I'm sure you have questions about what you discovered under the church."

I frown. "Questions? Church? There's something under the church? What?" Adam and I both agreed that we'd say I found exactly nothing under the church. The story was, I had just gotten locked in the director's office while looking for Nadia that night. Naturally, I told my sisters the truth, but I didn't want the cult—whoever they were, wherever they were—to figure out I'd been snooping around.

From the look on Nadia's face, I'm not doing the best job convincing her I don't know what she means. "The old gods have told me that one day, you'll join us."

I gasp. "Join you?" I lower my voice to a whisper. "So the cult is real?"

Nadia smiles. "It's not a cult. Not the way you're thinking."

"But it's something. Where you get together with other women and dance naked in the woods? Right? And you have been, for decades and decades? Right?"

Nadia laughs this time, placing a hand on her belly. "You'll find out. You will."

I shake my head. "I—hold on. I don't understand how you've been in a cult . . . or whatever you want to call it . . . basically our whole lives and somehow we never found out?" Even as a ghost, I only remember Nadia's grief, and how she started going to the church even more than usual. Granted, I didn't feel compelled to follow her and watch her pray and whatnot, but surely something . . . culty . . . would've stood out?

Nadia raises an eyebrow. "You really think a community of brujas wouldn't have protections in place? Secrecy? Logistical as well as magical ways to keep anyone from finding out?"

I slump back in bed. I mean, I should've guessed. I straighten my back once more, though, when a thought occurs to me. "But *I* got into the top-secret underground chamber. That means it wasn't *that* protected, was it?"

Nadia scoffs. "That's because you're destined to join us, and it was time for you to learn. If it had been anyone else, they couldn't have gotten through."

I know that's all she's going to tell me, so I push down all the questions bubbling up inside me. She gestures behind me, beyond the walls and out there. "Your sisters and their husbands have arrived." She raises an eyebrow. "Adam's here, too. Your soon-to-be husband, no?"

Nadia and her *knowing*. Adam and I aren't engaged, but . . . it feels like it will happen sooner or later. And I'm so okay with that, I can't help but grin, even as I say, "Shit. I'm not dressed yet. What time is the baptism, again?" Sage wasn't keen on getting Oak baptized at the church, but she decided she wanted to welcome Oak earthside in a better kind of way. We're going to the Finger Lakes to bless his head with lake water, and then we're having a cookout and celebrating his beautiful new life. Me, Adam, Teal, Carter, and Sage and Tenn. Nadia declined, naturally, blaming her knees. Amá Sonya thinks beach cookouts are for plebeians. But that's okay. With the seven of us, it will still be awesome.

"They're early. Don't stress out." She stands. "You know, once I'm gone, there is plenty of room for them and all their families here at your home." She nods toward the deed in my hand. "I always thought you sisters were at your happiest when you were together."

With that, Nadia leaves. And I think, maybe in this way—I clutch the deed tighter in my hands—I do have a mother figure. Not someone who would make sure to have meals with me and just hang out while watching *Gilmore Girls* surrounded by bowls of junk food. But someone who checks that I'm safe at a quarter till midnight every night. Someone who gives me a whole flipping house because she senses this house loves me as much as I love it. And someone who makes room for the maybe of one day, my sisters rejoining me here with their families.

I stand up, stretching, and that's when Teal and Sage come in, followed by Adam. "You're not ready yet?" Sage asks.

"It's early!" I echo Nadia, even though I've no idea what time it is.

Adam's eyes crinkle up in a smile and I can't stop smiling back at him. "I just came up to see if you needed anything," he says.

"I'm fine," I tell him. "And by the way. Good morning."

"Good morning." His husky voice makes me grin even more, and Teal rolls her eyes and huffs.

"Come on," she tells him, pointing toward the stairs. "You're gonna slow her down even more, and I'm starving."

"Starving?" I ask. "It's going to be at least a couple of hours before the cookout's ready, Teal."

"Exactly," she says. "We decided we needed breakfast beforehand. No one felt like cooking."

Adam winks at me as he descends the stairs, which makes Sage mouth *Aww* while clutching at her chest.

"Bye!" I call to him. "See you in five minutes!" I grab my swimsuit and stuff it in a bag.

"Wear your necklace," Teal tells me, lifting up hers from her chest.

Sage made these for us three years ago. They are crafted of the same slice of agate, one that looks like a wide, wild landscape. When we were little, Sage used to show us the view outside this attic's very balcony, and tell us that we were out there, as well as in here, all along the horizon—the green of the woods was Sage. The ocean in the distance was Teal. And the sky, of course, was me.

I clasp the necklace on immediately. Before they leave my room, I shout, "Wait!"

"What's the matter?" Sage asks right as Teal says, "What the hell, Sky?"

I don't answer. I grab both of their hands and go toward the balcony.

"Oh man. Not this again," Teal mutters.

"Not too close to the edge, Sky. Remember my nerves," Sage adds. "Things have only gotten worse since I had Oak."

Sometimes I like my sisters and me to stand here, just like when we were little, and watch us out there—the green, the sea, the sky. They both act like they hate it, but the truth is, they secretly love it. I know they do, because after we spend time here, holding hands and staring out, they both have glassy eyes. Just like right now.

"Okay, enough of this sappy crap," Teal says. "Let's go eat. And then grill food and eat some more."

"Sounds like a plan," Sage says with a smile.

I close the doors of the attic balcony and click the lock shut, noting the sage and teal and sky of the landscape once more.

Nadia was right about us sisters. Our happily-ever-afters have *always* included each other.

ACKNOWLEDGMENTS

Learning you're autistic in your thirties is kind of like awakening from a yearslong supernatural slumber in the woods. As I shaped Sky, and as she began to form and shape herself, it became clear to me why I related to her the most of all the sisters—even as everyone tells me I'm Sage!

In my mind, it will be a few years before Sky receives her autism diagnosis, but I wanted to write this book from the perspective I know so well—feeling like all you do is stumble, be misunderstood, and be left out, without having the faintest idea why. The answers are forthcoming, but for now, Sky realizes she *is* accepted and unconditionally loved. I hope this is a healing read for these reasons.

Thank you to Ansel, who helped me see so clearly what we deserve in our wild and precious lives. I love you, mijo.

Thank you to my readers. You're the reason why Sky got to get her happy ever after.

Thank you to Elizabeth Bewley. For seven years, you have been the best champion I could have ever asked for.

Thank you to everyone at Berkley who made this series possible: Kristine Swartz, Mary Baker, Stephanie Felty, Jessica Plummer, Kristin Cipolla, Hillary Tacuri, Chelsea Pascoe, Carrie May, Sarah Oberrender, Amy J. Schneider, and so many more.

So much gratitude to my Appalachian and Indigenous communities. One day I will write a proper thanks, but for now, you all know who you are, and I hope you can feel how thankful I am to know you, and how much you mean to me.

Thank you to Land, and her Spirits and Inhabitants, to the Ancestors, Guides, and Deities who have surrounded me with protection, support, and guidance. In roots and in dreams, in ceremony and brujería, I honor You and Creation.

The Magic of Untamed Hearts

Raquel Vasquez Gilliland

READERS GUIDE

DISCUSSION QUESTIONS

1. For much of Sky's story, she feels like everyone around her is surpassing her, like she just can't keep up when it comes to "adulting." Have you ever felt like you were left behind like this by your friends and family? What do you think of the way Sky resolves this?

2. Sky says of Adam's need for "proof" of her gift with animals that the mindset he encompasses believes "a thing must be seen in order to be known." Do you agree or disagree with this belief? How can a thing be known without "seeing" it or otherwise proving it in a Western scientific way?

3. How do you think communicating with each other virtually and anonymously helped Adam and Sky become closer offline?

4. At what point do you think Adam fell in love with Sky—or was it more of a longer process than a moment? When did Sky fall for Adam?

5. The first we hear of a cult in Cranberry is in the first book of the series, *Witch of Wild Things*. We finally learn more about it in Sky's story through her investigation. If you've been following from the beginning, did you have any predictions on the cult and Nadia's role in it? Or did these developments surprise you, and if so, how?

6. Sky has spent eight years in a supernatural sleep in the woods. Missing out on life for that long took its toll, especially on her social interactions and self-esteem. How different do you think it would be eight years from the current year? If you missed those years like Sky did, how do you think you'd catch up and cope?

7. Sky's ability to communicate with animals means she can call for their help when needed and sense them anytime she tunes in. What would you do with these abilities? Which animal would you call upon the most?

8. Nadia gives Sky the deed to the house in one of the last scenes of the book. She suggests that all the sisters and their families live there in the near future. Do you think Sage and Teal would move back in? How do you imagine that household would be?

Keep reading for a preview of Sage and Tenn's story in

Witch of Wild Things

Available now!

1

MY GREAT-AUNT NADIA SAYS IT'S A BAD IDEA TO REJECT a gift from a ghost.

It's 'cause ghosts like to slide inside all kinds of worlds. They don't just roam the land of the living or the dead. They can show up in our dream worlds to meddle. They can touch the world of shadows and eat the light from your own home, just sucking up the long, thick gold of nightlights and fixtures like dead black holes. "Just ask your prima Cleotilde," Nadia always says, her wine-red acrylic nail in my face as she points. "She once offended the ghost of her abuelo, and boom. Lamps didn't work around her for *years*."

The scariest world that ghosts can touch is the world of gods. The old gods. The ancient gods. The gods we've heard of and the even more numerous gods we haven't. Nadia pours one cup of espresso to these gods every single morning. This woman would rather light St. Theresa's on fire than skip this daily offering.

And if you've got a ghost haunting you, there's no way to tell if one of *these* gods favors *that* ghost. So you offend a ghost? You reject her gift?

You might be offending a god.

Apparently, it's a *really* bad idea to offend gods. That's how you end up with the women in our family and our *gifts*.

This means that when I climb in my janky-ass minivan and see the cup of coffee in the console? Yes, *that* cup of coffee—the mug, a gift from one of my former students, hand thrown and glazed the color of lilacs against a lightning storm. The one steaming with notes of raspberry and a hint of chocolate. The one that I most certainly did *not* place there. The second I smell it—because yeah, I smell it first—I throw myself into my seat and press my face into the steering wheel. "Shit," I say in a long exhale.

I hate gifts from ghosts.

In order to distract myself from the sweet steam swirling around me, I grab my phone, hitting buttons as fast as my fingers can go.

Laurel picks up even before the first ring ends. "Hey! You on your way yet?"

I glance at the back of my van. Every seat is pushed down to make way for half a dozen boxes, triple that in plants, and an antique reading chair. Most of the boxes contain books—I can see a sliver of Joy Harjo's *She Had Some Horses* peeking through cardboard I hadn't bothered to tape shut. It's my favorite of her collections, because it reminds me of the stories Nadia used to tell us when Teal, Sky, and I were tiny enough to squeeze onto one twin bed. I can still hear Nadia's smoky voice filling our room. "In the beginning, there were only gods. Gods and this earth . . ."

Now Teal, Sky, and I will *never* be all together again. I take a shuddering breath as this reality sweeps over me for the millionth time in eight years, like the garnet-sharp winds of a tornado.

There and gone in a moment, but leaving behind painful, devastating destruction. That's how grief works.

"Sage Flores, are you ignoring me?"

I blink and jerk my face toward the console. The coffee is still there. Jerk. "No, of course not. I'm just about on my way. I'm in the van and everything."

"Okay, well, that's a good start. Next step, take your key, you know, the shiny silver thing in your hand right now, and push it through that teeny hole on the side of—"

"Literally giving you my middle finger right now," I say, but I'm laughing.

"Seriously, Sage. You've got this."

I glance up at my apartment—well, I guess it's not mine anymore. It's the third floor up, and the balcony still has dirt on the rails from when I watered my basil plants a little too violently. I take a deep breath, hoping the scent of that basil can calm me.

All I smell is ghost coffee.

"Want me to distract you?"

I put the phone on speaker and place it in the cup holder next to the mug. "Go for it."

"You'll never guess who I saw last night. At Piggly Wiggly of all places."

I sit back in my seat. I get the key in the ignition as I say, "Piggly Wiggly?" I think of who wouldn't be caught dead there. "Amá Sonya?"

Laurel draws out the response long and slow. "Tennessee. Reyes."

It may well be the absolute last name I'd expected her to utter. I think I would've been less shocked if she'd announced it *were* Amá Sonya at Piggly Wiggly, naked as birth, juggling plums in the middle of produce.

My breath's gone way too shallow, my hand gripping the key so tight it's cutting into my fingers. I turn the ignition, hard, but stay in park while clearing my throat. "Tennessee Reyes?" As though there were any other on the planet. "You're certain?"

"It was him, Sage. Trust me."

I close my eyes. "But . . . he moved to Denver and then got off social media and, like—"

"Disappeared off the face of the earth? Yeah. But I guess he's deigned to walk the earth's face once more, because he is in Piggly Wiggly, in Cranberry, Virginia. Or was, as of yesterday."

My heart's finally gone back to a normal rhythm and so I slowly begin reversing the van, angling my head back. "How does he look?" The question's out before I can stop it.

"Oh, gosh. Somehow *better*."

"Better?" It comes out like a squeak. *Better* doesn't seem possible.

"He's . . . I dunno. He's grown into those legs. And he's got this yummy almost-beard thing happening . . . hold on." Her voice gets distant. "No, hon, of course I'm talking about you! Well, I mean *if* you grew a beard thing!" Laurel sighs. "I think my husband just heard me verbally ogling another man."

Normally I'd laugh and keep up with their teasing each other, but my stomach keeps making stupid, roller-coaster-y loops somehow in my rib cage. Because Tennessee Reyes is back in Cranberry.

Tenn is back in Cranberry.

"Well, that's something." I've made it to the edge of the lot now without hitting any parked vehicles in my emotional state. That's also something.

"Guess that distracted you good, huh? You sound like you've morphed into some kind of zombie." When I give a flat chuckle in response, Laurel adds, "You okay, Sage?" in a soft voice. I hate that voice. It only comes out when I'm near tears. And to me? The consequences of crying are worse than those of offending gods.

I blink and blink and then respond. "Oh, yeah." I try to make my voice smooth, but it's as useless as ironing linen. "I'm just not looking forward to—you know. Moving back with Nadia." With Teal.

Laurel hears what I don't say. "Maybe she won't be as bad as you remember."

The last time I saw my sister, she cracked my lip open so wide, I needed four stitches. Later she said she didn't mean it—that she'd forgotten she'd worn such a sharp ring that day—but that just tells me that she did mean everything else. As in, the whole situation of her fist in my face.

"Oh, yeah." I finally make a right onto the main road as someone starts honking behind me. "It won't be that bad."

"I'll make you pollo a la plancha the second you get here."

I manage a smile. "Now you're talking."

"Nothing like Cuban comfort food to get settled in." There's a muffled noise in the background. "Ah, I gotta go."

"Tell Jorge I said hi."

"Drive safe and text me the second you get to Nadia's, yeah?"

"Of course. Love you."

"Love you more."

When I merge onto the highway, I do a double take at my reflection in the rearview mirror. My eyes are wide, the brown almost citrine in the sunlight, and my mascara is already smudged even though I applied it less than an hour ago. My hair—a mass of curls I'd braided and pinned up—looks like it's trying to break the hair tie keeping it from reaching down and steering this car without any of my help. I look like a twenty-nine-year-old who is freaking the fuck out.

I *am* a twenty-nine-year-old who is freaking the fuck out.

Why on earth is Tenn back in Cranberry?

I take a deep breath as I veer toward my first exit. It doesn't matter. What happened between us, it was over a decade ago, which feels like a dozen lifetimes by now. And that's exactly where anything between Tenn and me will stay—buried in the memories of seventeen-year-old me, back when I thought heartbreak was the worst thing that could happen to a person.

I have better things to worry about now. I take a long sip of my now lukewarm coffee.

Like ghosts.

2

MARCH 2, 2001
14 YEARS AGO

silvergurl0917: what haven't you noticed today?

RainOnATennRoof: Wow

RainOnATennRoof: What didn't you say?

silvergurl0917: what didn't you laugh at

RainOnATennRoof: What didn't you do?

silvergurl0917: what didn't you think about

silvergurl0917: . . . you there?

RainOnATennRoof: You

RainOnATennRoof: I didn't think about you. Until now. :)

RainOnATennRoof: Who is this?

silvergurl0917 has logged off Messenger.

PRESENT

It takes exactly four hours and seventeen minutes to reach Catalina Street in Cranberry. Without even thinking about it, I slow the car down well before Nadia's house, eventually pulling over in front of Old Man Noemi's in-street parking. From here I can see enough. There's the emerald ivy curling over Nadia's place like a clawed, leafy hand. When I crane my neck a little, I make out the glow from her kitchen, through the daisy-patterned curtains she sewed herself when we were little kids.

From here I can look at my new life and think about all the senseless mistakes that led me to this moment.

Sleeping with the department head.

Deciding to never again sleep with the department head.

All that stupidity leading to a very convenient firing under the evergreen excuse of budget cuts.

In my mind's eye, I'm back in Gregory's office, tucked in the basement of the art department at Temple University. It is one big square with no windows, and there are piles of random objects everywhere. I had found the mess charming once, but this day, all I see is trash. A constellation of Skittles peeks out from under his desk. At the very bottom of a pile of abstract expressionists' biographies is a first edition of *For Whom the Bell Tolls*, covered in a thin layer of mold after a coffee spill.

My classroom is right above us—the jewelry studio. It's my favorite place on campus, maybe even in the whole city. It's got a dozen jewelry benches, each one made of rustic, knobbed wood. A wall of windows faces northwest, which means my classes get the most luscious gold afternoon light—the perfect setting for photographing finished pieces. A raw turquoise, blue as photos of the deep sea, bezel set in brass. A silver locket that opens to a faceted Montana sapphire that glows like a lantern made of cornflowers.

Every day, my students amaze me, but my favorite part of teaching is witnessing the ways they amaze themselves. How they go from *I can't do this* to *Holy shit, I did that.*

And now Greg is taking it all away.

Greg's arms are crossed as he gives me a big, fake sigh. "I tried everything, Sage. It's just . . ." He waves his hands. "You know how it is."

And that's how he dismissed me from the life I'd pulled together from nothing. The one I'd slept in my van for. The one I'd sold basil starts at farmer's markets for. The one I'd stitched and scraped and carved up from the thinnest air, all to get away from the one place I never, ever wanted to live in again.

And now I'm looking right at it.

Cranberry.

My eyes well with tears before I can stop them. "No," I whisper. "No, no, *stop*—"

A single tear makes it to an eyelash, and I violently swipe it away.

But it's too late.

Next to me, in the passenger seat, a figure materializes like the pale curls of coffee steam. It's only one tear, so her edges stay as blurry as a dream. It's only one tear, so the ghost is gone before either of us can say a damn thing.

And what would I say, anyway? *Sorry for killing you? Thanks for the coffee? Leave me alone now, please?*

I take a breath, as deep and long as I can make it, and turn the car back on.

Photo courtesy of the author

RAQUEL VASQUEZ GILLILAND is a Pura Belpré Award–winning Mexican American poet, novelist, and painter. She received her BA in cultural anthropology from the University of West Florida and her MFA in poetry from the University of Alaska Anchorage. Raquel is most inspired by folklore and seeds and the lineages of all things. When not writing, Raquel tells stories to her plants, and they tell her stories back. *The Magic of Untamed Hearts* is her fifth novel.

VISIT RAQUEL VASQUEZ GILLILAND ONLINE

RaquelVasquezGilliland_Poet